A DOUBLE LIFE

CHARLOTTE PHILBY

THE BOROUGH PRESS

The Borough Press
An imprint of HarperCollins*Publishers* Ltd
1 London Bridge Street
London SE1 9GF

www.harpercollins.co.uk

HarperCollins*Publishers*
1st Floor, Watermarque Building, Ringsend Road
Dublin 4, Ireland

This paperback edition 2021
1

First published by HarperCollins*Publishers* 2020

A catalogue record for this book is available from the British Library

ISBN: 978-0-00-836521-9

Set in Adobe Garamond by Palimpsest Book Production Limited, Falkirk, Stirlingshire

Printed and bound in the UK by CPI Group (UK) Ltd, Croydon CR0 4YY

MIX
Paper from
responsible sources

FSC
www.fsc.org

FSC™ C007454

This book is produced from independently certified FSC™ paper to ensure
responsible forest management.

For more information visit: www.harpercollins.co.uk/green

For Jesse

Also by Charlotte Philby

Part of the Family

'The path of least resistance leads to crooked rivers and crooked men'
Henry David Thoreau

Mirror

In my mother's house
is the friendly mirror,
the only glass in which I look
and think I see myself,
think, yes, that's what
I think I'm like,
that's who I am. The only
glass in which I look and smile.

Just as this baby smiles
at the baby who always
smiles at her, the one in
her mother's arms, the mother
who looks like me, who
smiles at herself in her
mother's mirror, the friendly
mirror in her mother's house.

But if I move to one side
we vanish, the woman I thought
was me, the baby making friends
with herself, we move to one side
and the mirror holds no future, no past,
in its liquid frame, only the corner
of an open window, a bee visiting
the ready flowers of summer.

Maura Dooley

Prologue

The woman's lips were blue, the same shade as the evening sky that shone in through the window, calm and unbroken.

The knot around her neck had been pulled tight. The note, propped against the hallway table, was short.

'I'm sorry, I couldn't do it. I love you both, please forgive me.'

Chapter 1

Gabriela

It is hardly warm enough to warrant an evening in the garden, but something about the house is pushing her out. After all these years, and all the memories she made here in her teens and early twenties before Tom had so much as set foot inside its four walls, their home is already taking his side. So when he goes out for a smoke, savouring the single roll-up he still allows himself each day now that he is staring down the barrel of forty, she follows him into the starless night.

Pulling on a jacket, she brings with her the slightly too warm bottle of Sauvignon she picked up at the off-licence near Dartmouth Park Hill on her way home, partly to calm her nerves, partly for the excuse to partition off this section of her life, to annex it safely away from the day she has just left behind. The beginning of the end.

'Ten ninety-nine?' Tom takes a swig of his beer, incredulity written in the lines above the bridge of his nose. She follows his gaze to the bottle she is clutching by the neck and for a moment she feels herself on the cusp of laughter that will mutate into sobs if she is not careful. Screams that will reverberate through the house where their children sleep.

How the hell are they talking about the price of a bottle of wine? But he has no reason to suspect this is anything but an ordinary evening, the end of a day just like any other.

'How was work?' he asks as she takes a seat beside him on one of the worn garden chairs. It shifts precariously on cracked paving, the

1

same shoddy stones that have been there since her father first bought the place, more than two decades ago. The memory of those days, however complicated they might have seemed at the time, soothes her briefly.

'Work?' she repeats, buying herself time, wondering if Tom notices her bristle as she pictures her desk; the job she fought tooth and nail to get and then to keep.

Before she can answer, he continues, uncharacteristically forthright. 'I'm worried about you, Gabs. This case. Ever since you came back from Moscow . . .'

'Jesus, Tom, it's not supposed to be easy,' she snaps, immediately holding out her hands by way of apology. 'I'm sorry, I'm just tired.'

It is true, she thinks: *I am so tired.* It is not the whole truth but what more can she tell him? She is bound to secrecy, her lips have been sewn shut. As he watches her from across the lopsided plastic table, she registers the sound of a car moving too fast on the street outside. She imagines the needle pushing through the skin at the edges of her mouth. Instantly, she is transported to the bedroom upstairs, just a few weeks after she and her father had moved in. She and her best friend Saoirse in matching crop-tops, kneeling on the floor, her head level with the mattress, her earlobe flat against the CD case, which Saoirse has placed on the bed.

'You've burnt the needle properly, right?'

'Obviously,' Saoirse says as she clamps Gabriela's shoulder with one hand and with the other removes the ice cube she has been holding against her skin. Cold water trickles down Gabriela's neck. As her friend breathes in sharply, Gabriela feels the remaining ice slide to the floor, Saoirse holding her shoulder a little too tight as she pushes the pin through the soft nub of flesh.

More than twenty years later, she touches her earlobe. The memory of her own cries of pain, tinged with defiant euphoria, ricochets around her head as she looks up to the window of that same room, where now stands the goose-shaped lamp that keeps guard on Callum's windowsill. The lamp which, now that he is five years old, her son claims to have outgrown, though he never pushes the point. Secretly, she knows he is no more keen to grow up than she is to lose him to the girls and then the women or the men who will inevitably step in to claim him. The hands that would have taken him from her even if she hadn't already made it possible for them to be torn apart.

Sadie is in the kitchen, already dressed in school uniform, fastening the clips on the violin she chose for her most recent birthday, when Gabriela heads downstairs the following morning. Seven years old: how the hell did that happen? Briefly, she wonders what the fall-out will be for Sadie, after all this. Will it send her over the edge? But there is no point trying to second-guess her daughter, whose emotions are always more nuanced, less discernible than her own at the same age. There is an air of pointedness about Sadie's refusal to cause trouble for them in the way that Gabriela is prepared for that she finds unsettling. No, she reprimands herself, her fists tightening – it is not Sadie whose behaviour she needs fear.

'Mum, have you seen my sheet music?'

As her daughter speaks, Gabriela's eye catches the wine glasses from the night before, which stand marooned on the table where she is packing her school bag.

'This what you're looking for?' Tom squeezes past cradling a cup and drops the pristinely kept wad of paper onto her school bag, winking at her as he settles on one of the chairs squeezed up against the kitchen table.

'Made you a tea,' he says and Gabriela fixes her jaw into a smile, moving forward to clear away the cereal bowls that will otherwise languish until she comes home, and then she stops. *I will not be coming home.* She hears the words as a whisper between her temples. There is a brief moment when she is struck by the enormity of it, but then she sees her son walking into the room and instantly everything is as it was. Once again she is Sadie and Callum's mother and she is preparing for a normal day at the office, for a job that Tom watches her forfeit so much of their life together, without ever making her explain why. The job in which he has watched her rise through the ranks while he takes bit parts as a freelance architect, picking up the pieces without so much as a suppressed sigh.

'Want me to walk you in?' he asks Sadie, leaning back in his chair, rustling open yesterday's copy of the *Guardian*. Sadie throws him the same look she has been giving him since she was a toddler – something between despair and total adoration. For the past few weeks, Tom has let her make the short journey alone and Gabriela can't tell him why it makes her so uncomfortable, their child being so far out of their reach.

Enjoying the familiarity of the rapport between himself and Sadie, the reversal of the traditional parent/child roles, he shrugs, widening his eyes as if to say, *What? We don't have to leave for five minutes.*

'Leave the girl alone,' Gabriela plays along, batting his feet off the table as she passes, sweeping up the trail of cups and bowls and opening the dishwasher.

'I'll do that,' he calls over from his seat, without moving.

Ignoring him, she stacks the crockery in a neat row.

'Are you out tonight or in?'

'Jesus, Tom . . .'

'I know, I know, I'm messing with you! I hadn't forgotten. It's on the calendar, right there, where it always is. So you'll be back on Thursday?'

'That's right.' She swallows, keeping her eyes trained on the dirty cutlery she is placing in the stand.

'You're going away again?' It is Callum's voice this time, and her heart strains so that it feels like it might tear.

'Oi, what's so bad about hanging out with your old dad? Come on, love, Mum's got to work, you know that.'

It's always Tom's instinct to dive in to protect her from the decisions she has made, and his refusal to let her defend herself grates on her.

'I'll make it up to you,' she says, the lie lingering in her throat. 'I promise.'

* * *

As she opens the front door, she watches Sadie disappear around the corner of their street. Part of her wants to run after her daughter, to throw her to the ground and to hold them both there – to stop time, her face buried in Sadie's neck, and somehow to go back and unravel the knot. Not back, she scolds herself as she loses sight of her daughter, for the last time on this street. How could she think that?

The walk to Tufnell Park tube station helps clear her head, gently easing her mindset from the domestic world to her other life. The trees lining Dartmouth Park Hill radiate new energy, their shoots a reminder that whatever happens, the world will go on.

Preparing to cross at the traffic lights, she starts to think through everything she has to do, and only now does it strike her that she has failed to buy credit ahead of time for the second SIM card she keeps tucked in the lining of her handbag. She swears under her breath as the green man fades to red, cursing herself for allowing such a pivotal element to fall through the net. But it's pointless berating herself for it now – it is not an option, at this stage, to let things fall apart.

Heading into the newsagent's diagonally opposite the station, she skims the headlines of the newspapers to distract herself from the fear that pummels at her stomach as she makes her way through the aisles, making sure there is no one here she recognises, no one to pull her up on why she is using a burner, probing her with their hilarious quips about her being not a civil servant after all but a spy, or maybe a drug dealer.

It was the kind of joke Tom had made when she was seconded to Russia, her first posting after joining the FCO. And her last.

'What are you, some sort of double agent? Working for the FSB now, Gabs?'

But the jokes had stopped by the time she returned. In the days leading up to her most recent stint in Moscow, Tom had long since ceased laughing. By the time she got back he looked at her as though he didn't know her at all – and he was completely right.

'Seven months?' His look had been disbelieving at first, as if he had been waiting for her to remind him it was April Fool's Day.

'I know, it seems like a long time.' She felt sick but she couldn't let him understand how wrong this was. The situation had to be presented as non-negotiable – a necessary but surmountable task.

'What about the kids?' His face changed then. 'We could come with you. It could be an adventure. You always said you wanted one of those.'

Her cheeks burn as she remembers how quickly she had snapped her reply.

No.

It must have been impossible for him not to notice the change in her since she came back, but he has worked so hard not to push her on it. He does not comment on the physical shifts, which she can't avoid when she looks at her reflection. Nothing about her body is unscarred, though it is her mind that will truly never be the same.

Leaving the newsagent with her phone topped up, she crosses towards the tube station. The carriage is unusually empty as she settles onto a seat, taking out the Burberry trench coat she bought to match the boots she denied to Tom when he asked if they were new.

Holding her bag tightly on her lap as if holding on for her life, she feels the outline of the car keys press reassuringly against her fingers, through the leather. Distracting herself, she looks up at the map of the Northern Line. For a moment, she pictures herself walking through the arch at King Charles Street, greeting the security guards who know her name and those of her children by now. She imagines familiar faces as she makes her way towards the main entrance, collecting her bag as it emerges from the scanner, nodding to the receptionists before heading through the turnstiles, the sound of metal grating closed behind her.

Except today this is not her route. Now, as the train stops at Embankment, she stands back to let an older lady off the train first, before stepping out onto the platform, walking past the exit sign, following the arrows indicating the District Line. There is a chance she will see someone she knows from the FCO but they will not question it; the sight of her heading away from the office in the direction of the Westbound District Line will not cause them any concern.

Taking a seat a few metres along the platform, she listens to the wind whistling through the tunnel. It is both warm and cold, and as the train approaches she stands, registering the air brushing against her face. Breathing deeply, taking a moment to gather herself, she steps forward towards the yellow line, looking to her right, watching the carriages tearing towards the crowd. For a moment, she meets the driver's eye and sees a hint of dread, and then he is gone and the train has stopped and her legs shake as the doors open and she steps inside.

It is fifteen stops until it's her turn to get off. There is too much time to think and so she closes her eyes, concentrating instead on the gentle rhythm until she hears the announcement: *Kew Gardens*. Opening them again, she is met by daylight as the train pulls into the outdoor station.

On the platform, she follows the familiar path towards the exit. The sun presses against her cheeks as she steps out onto the pavement, holding her head down, her hair falling in front of her face, reaching into her bag and pulling out a pair of sunglasses.

Putting the glasses on, she turns slightly and catches a glimpse of herself in the reflection of the boulangerie, and she is struck for a moment by the image of a woman she no longer recognises. Standing straighter, hardening herself against any doubts, she follows the familiar route, down Lichfield Road, past the perfectly manicured privet hedges, the pristine gravel and obligatory plantation blinds, turning right into an unsigned side street. A moment later she reaches into her bag, pulling out the keys and pressing the button to unlock the door. With a flash of the headlights, the Range Rover clicks open and she steps into it, breathing in the smell of fresh leather.

As she turns the key in the ignition, the radio blares a song she knows and the shock of the unexpected noise makes her cry out. It takes a moment to compose herself, palms pressed against the steering wheel, before she looks over her shoulder and reverses, taking her usual route along the wide open streets of South-West London, towards Richmond. It's a different world here and she feels not so much safe as anonymous. These are not her people, and in this car with its tinted windows and hyper-clean paintwork she is almost certainly unrecognisable.

On Richmond Road, she turns into the Waitrose car park and pulls into a space. There is silence as the engine cuts out, apart from the sound of her breath rising and falling in shallow bursts in her chest. Stepping out onto the pavement, she helps herself to a trolley, working her way through the aisles, selecting the sort of basics you might buy for a picnic. As she turns into the baby and toddler aisle, she gives a cursory glance over her shoulder. Once she is sure she is alone, she continues walking, picking out a selection of organic purees she would never have dreamt of buying for Sadie and Callum.

It takes several minutes to gather all that she needs, making her way to the till as she pulls out the phone and dials. When Polina answers, she speaks more quietly than usual, unable to keep the relief of this contact out of her voice.

'How are you?' Gabriela asks, affecting her brightest intonation, giving a polite wave of recognition to the cashier and an apologetic smile at the rudeness of talking into the phone while the woman begins to scan the items on the belt.

'How are you?' Polina's voice asks on the end of the line and she replies, 'I'm good. I've had a change of plan with work so I'm on my way back now – I'm just at the supermarket picking up some supplies. Is there anything we need?'

Before Polina can answer, Gabriela adds quickly, 'How's Layla?'

'I'll put the phone to her ear,' Polina says.

Reaching into her bag for her purse, Gabriela stops as she hears the child's breath. The lump that has been rising in her throat softens into something thick and expansive, so that she can only stand stock-still, drinking in the broken inflections of her daughter's voice.

Gabriela's voice breaks. 'Oh baby . . . My baby, I've missed you. Mummy will be home in a minute, OK?'

Chapter 2

Gabriela

The sky was full of movement the night she and Tom met, or maybe it had just been so long since she'd last looked up.

The queue outside the Jazz Cafe ran behind a shabby blue velvet rope so that she was pressed against the building on Parkway while Saoirse tucked the laces into the side of her trainers. It was Saoirse who had bought the tickets, turning up at Gabriela's house and making her dad let her in even though she'd told him she wasn't in the mood for visitors. But what could she expect? He was always so bloody weak.

She had just returned from her year abroad, in Paris, as part of her degree, and was back for good this time – or until she could find a way out. The last time she'd been home was an overnight return to London for her mother's funeral, earlier in the year. In Paris, she could almost forget that she was gone, but here in London the memory followed her so that it felt safer to keep still.

'Please, Saoirse, I just don't fancy it. Take someone else, yeah?' she had protested but Saoirse wouldn't back down.

'It's been four months – you have to come out sometime.'

Gabriela had wanted to scream at her, to take her face in her hands and tell her that her mother was dead and that she had hated her and she didn't know how to live without her and that she was terrified.

But instead, she said, 'Lee Scratch Perry? Never heard of him.'

'He's a complete nutter,' Saoirse grinned. 'If you're lucky he'll be wearing a disco ball on his head . . .'

Inside the club, the room was dark and thick with cigarette smoke and dry ice as they moved through the crowd towards the bar.

'What you drinking?' Saoirse asked.

'I don't know,' Gabriela shrugged, as if what she wanted no longer counted for anything.

As Saoirse leaned in to order, Gabriela turned away and that's when she saw him, across the bar, watching her.

'Here you go . . .' Saoirse handed her a shot of tequila and Gabriela winced, licking the line of salt from her hand, the granules rough against her tongue, feeling the burn of the alcohol in her throat as she tossed back her head, sinking her teeth into the flesh of the lemon, her eyes squeezing together, pushing against the pain.

'Shit!'

'Right, another one!' Saoirse lined up two more shots. This time when Gabriela looked up she felt someone next to her and as she turned she saw him there, an inch or so away. Saoirse raised her eyebrows and grinned as if she were about to say something, but then she turned and started speaking to someone standing next to her, and then she was dancing on the other side of the room.

'Same again?' Gabriela lip-read his words through the smoke machine, his voice straining above the clash of the keyboards.

She shook her head, shuddering, and a moment later he passed her a beer.

Pausing briefly, she took the drink and clinked the base of her bottle against his.

'Thanks.'

He nodded and smiled, as if he was considering something.

'What?' She couldn't help but smile back at him.

He shook his head, still holding her eyes. 'Nothing.'

* * *

The walk from the Jazz Cafe to his flat, in the basement of one of the tall smog-stained terraces that clung to one another on a short stretch of Prince of Wales Road, was surprisingly warm even at this time of night. The fact of the onset of summer, when she thought of it, knocked her sideways. If there had been a spring to speak of that year, it had completely passed her by.

In her mind, winter still enveloped London, her brain hovering over the funeral back in March, the scene flickering like a paused film: a small group of friends and family wrapped in black coats and colourful scarves lining the edges of the plot in Paddington Old Cemetery, their heads bowed against the wind; her dad's face ashen amongst them.

The immediacy of the memory stung at the corners of her eyes, but then she felt Tom's hand brush against hers as he worked the key in the front door, and the image fell away.

'It's a bit damp, hence the smell,' he said without a hint of apology. Away from the noise of the bar, she noticed the trace of a Scottish accent.

He moved ahead of her, making no attempt to kick away the coats that lay strewn on the floor, as if he'd left in a rush, cups scattered across every surface of the studio flat. Beneath the clutter, there was a certain order to the space: the guitar propped up on a stand in the corner, music stacked beside a small Yamaha keyboard. The table was rounded at the corners with A-line legs.

It occurred to her then that she had no idea what he did, this man whose flat she was suddenly inside. She had no idea how she had even come to be here.

'I'm a student,' he said as if reading her mind, and she squinted in disbelief.

'Really? How old are you?'

'Forty-two,' he shrugged and noting the faint look of alarm on her face, tilted his head. 'Oh, come on. Really? I'm twenty-four. But I'm studying architecture which takes about ninety-seven years, so . . . How about you?'

She yawned. 'Younger than that . . . just.'

It can't have been much later than midnight but any energy she'd felt in the bar had faded so that all she wanted was to lie down and close her eyes.

'Would you like a drink?'

She shook her head.

He moved towards her slowly, so sure of himself and yet unimposing.

'You look knackered.'

She nodded.

'You can have my bed.' He pointed towards a single mattress in the corner.

'Come with me,' she held out her hand to him. They passed out sometime later, his arm pulling her towards the warmth of his body, pinning her there in a way that was both suffocating and yet so comforting that she had to wait until he was asleep before pushing him away.

Chapter 3

Isobel

I look up through squinted eyelids, German techno beats sliding around my head. From here, above the outline of people's limbs, I can see it is dark outside. Around me, the party is still heaving so that I can only just make out a vague impression of Jess a few feet away on the sofa talking to a man, her lips moving in slow motion.

As if pushing through a brick wall, I manage to draw the strength to sit up, willing my eyelids to follow suit. My cheeks, the inside of which I've chewed raw, feel like they are sinking away from my face towards the floor.

'Jess?' My voice is unexpectedly loud, though no one else seems to hear it. I try again but the effect is a slosh of vowels.

Across the room, the man Jess is talking to inches forward and they both laugh, she stretching her head back as he nuzzles her neck.

Jess?

This time my voice sticks in my throat and I give up, succumbing to the weight of the exhaustion that has taken hold from the inside out, the chemicals prowling through my bloodstream, squeezing the life out of me. Letting my eyes drift shut, I feel the leather sofa swallow me whole. As my brain shuts down, I picture myself standing, taking my friend's hand and running down the stairs, out of the front door; the two of us tearing down the street at Chalk Farm, screaming at the top of our lungs.

* * *

By the time I open my eyes again the music has descended into a low ambient throb; bodies, half-dressed, are scattered across a wooden floor; a man in jeans and a cowboy hat leans precariously against a yucca plant. The sky through the window has started to lighten, signalling it is time to leave. Slowly, as if bound in clingfilm, I turn to where Jess had been but now there is no one there.

Letting my eyes open and shut several times, I feel for my bag and fumble for my phone before realising the battery is dead.

Shit.

Taking a minute to unpeel my legs from my seat, I step across a sea of semi-comatose bodies into the hall.

In each room, different beats fall over one another, the same stale smell of smoke and spilt beer following me through the house. Finally I find Jess's boss slumped at a table, a black Amex card in his hand.

'Hugh,' I say, but he ignores me, a smirk impressed across his features.

'Oi!' I say, louder this time, and his head twists to look up at me.

'Is-o-bel,' he rolls each syllable of my name on his tongue, and I feel my stomach turn. 'The roving reporter returns . . . Listen, when are you going to give up that local paper shite and come work for me? Tell you what: wash your hair every so often and you'd have a face for TV.'

'Have you seen Jess?' I ask, focusing on the smudge of dye that has leaked from his newly chestnut locks into the peak of his receding hairline. Christ, if I'm still rolling around in shit-holes like this when I'm his age I only hope someone slits my throat. With that fleeting image, I remember the spate of stabbings in Somers Town I'm planning to dig into next week, focusing on the circulation of weapons across our part of the city. If I can pitch it around the ongoing tensions in Camden, I'm pretty sure I can spin a legitimate local interest angle.

'Yeah but what's the *angle?*' I picture my news editor, Ben, pre-empting the words of the editor, tucked away in his cheap glass box at the back of the room. 'We're a local paper, Isobel, not the New York fucking Times.'

Hugh's face contorts, as if he is trying to place Jess's name - the name of the woman who has been his assistant for the past six years . . . *Assistant Producer, actually,* I can hear her voice correcting me in my head.

'Sit down,' he slurs. 'Want a line?'

He returns his attention to the table, haphazardly scraping and crushing white powder with his card.

'Have you seen her?' I repeat and he looks up again.

'Who?'

'I'm all right for shit K, thanks, Hugh,' I say, not bothering to answer, and he puckers his face into a grin, attempting a South American drawl.

'Issy, darling, this is pure cocaine straight from the streets of Ecuador!'

Is it fuck. 'Can I use your phone?' I ask and he slides it across to me before returning his attention to the pile of powder.

Jess's number goes straight to voicemail.

'Where are you?' I whisper into the handset before tossing the receiver back at him.

'Go on then,' I say, snatching the rolled £20 from his fingers, hoovering up both lines, wincing as the chemical hits the back of my throat.

Grateful for the instant burst of energy, I stand.

'Wait, where are you going?' I hear his voice fade into the distance as I move across the kitchen, through the doorway and towards the stairs, without looking back.

Walking out onto the street, my whole body seems to move as if by remote control. Sunglasses on, though autumn has long set in, I drift along Chalk Farm Road. Ordinarily I'd have walked through Camden Lock, past the tube station and onto the high street where my shoebox of a flat awaits me above the newsagent's. But this morning, the coke rushing through my veins, I need a horizon – the prospect of main roads, of roaring traffic, of crackheads and knowing shopkeepers making my chest tighten.

Moving towards the estate, I weave instinctively through a warren of concrete alleys, the streets I have walked so many times that I no longer see the dog-ends or the piss stains on the walls.

I have no idea how long it takes, moving on autopilot down Prince of Wales Road towards South End Green, where the air has a certain clarity. Flinching, I step back as an ambulance swings past the curry house; the steel shutters clamped to the floor, the body of a man slumped in front of it.

My feet keep moving and soon I pass the old cinema which has been transformed into a chain food hall, towards Hampstead Heath overground, past the Magdala pub, and up past the terrace of big stucco-fronted houses. A woman leans out of the front door of the most beautiful building on this stretch, with tiled steps and wisteria hanging precariously over the top. She is stooped over as if shielding herself from the outside world, collecting the morning papers from the step, her pale blonde hair falling in front of her face. When she looks up and sees me, there is a flash of fear and for a moment I see myself through her eyes.

The image haunts me as I move, more quickly now, drawn onto the Heathland I know so well. Instinctively, I drift away from the path. It must be sometime around 6.15 a.m. and yet I cannot face the prospect of bed, knowing there will be hours of tossing from one side to another before sleep finally comes. For now, the Heath is calm and familiar: safe until the hordes descend with their flat whites and Bugaboos.

Steering across the hill towards the pond, I reach down and slip off my trainers, enjoying the sensation of the dewy grass against my toes; above me, the sky lingers somewhere between night and day. When I reach the bench overlooking Kite Hill, I sit, pulling my knees up under my chin, aware of the smell of mould and earth seeping up through the slats of wood. As a wave of cognisance strikes, I push it away, trying not to think about the press conference with the local council I am due to cover on Monday. It's the kind of painfully provincial story that makes me remember that I was approached by one of the nationals, just before everything fell apart. Would I even have taken it? Either way, there is no point thinking about that now.

My mouth is dry, my eyelids heavy and at the same time bolted open as if held in place with a match. Fumbling in my bag, I pull out a tiny block of hash and a lighter, enjoying the burning sensation at the tip of my thumb as I crumble it into a Rizla. The first drag burns the back of my throat.

Some time later, I feel a welcome wave of exhaustion float in from behind. The new day is sneaking in and soon London will be ablaze with sirens and the clinking of coffee cups. The park bench has started to embed itself into my bare thighs; suddenly drawn by the prospect of a pillow and fresh sheets, I stand, feeling in the pocket of my denim shorts for my front-door key and my phone, my trainers protruding from the top of my bag as I start the final walk home.

As the path splits, I veer slowly towards a forested patch of parkland. Pulling out a bottle of water from beneath my shoes, I take a sip. The pressure against my bladder is almost instant.

Above, I hear the distant calling of a crow as I lower myself beneath a thick canopy of trees. Pulling my hoodie closer around me, I shiver, the air cold and dank as I weave beneath the branches; by now my head is throbbing, the silence no longer comforting.

Finding a spot, I squat down in the shade of the tree, trying not to pee on my bare feet. Just as the relief comes, a warm trickle forming a pool beneath me, I feel my skin scratch against something sharp, a twig or a piece of glass.

The unexpected sharpness of it makes me jump and I glance down, a sliver of dark red blood trickling down my ankle.

'Shit,' I mutter, unsteady as I balance my weight on just one foot, lowering myself into a dark patch of moss and rummaging through my bag for anything that vaguely resembles a tissue. As my fingers comb the contents of my bag, I forget about the tissue, distracted by a more pressing realisation. Patting with increasing desperation amidst the crumbs and the loose tobacco lining the bottom of my bag, waiting for the tell-tale brushing of my skin against the small plastic baggy containing the hash. I can't have lost it, but I have. My fingernails dig into the palms of my hand at the memory of how much I had paid Tariq for that quarter.

Briefly I consider turning back, retracing my steps to the bench, but the thought fills me with fear, imagining the morning runners and the early-bird mothers with their toddlers who by now could well be roaming the pathway.

What I need is to get home, back to a safe space in which to let my mind melt into perfect nothingness. Slowly I stretch my legs back to standing position, ready to retreat to the safety of my flat with its four solid walls to fester behind. One moment I am standing, feeling my shorts brushing against my thighs; the next I hear a scream, which at first it might be another crow circling in the distance. And then I hear voices, unmistakably human, like a wall clattering down around me, fixing me to the ground.

For a moment in my disorientated state, I wonder if I have imagined it. It wouldn't be the first time, after all. But then they are there again, close enough that I can almost smell their breath. Taking a slow step forward, a twig quietly crunching beneath my foot, I hear a man's voice again, this time followed by a name: *Eva*. Amidst a distorted mush of syllables, a language I cannot understand, I hear the girl speak; I don't know the words but the meaning is clear. Stop, she is saying. *Please stop!*

The man's presence hangs in the air like an omen. Willing my body not to move, I feel my weight shift involuntarily below me as the air struggles for space in my chest. Any second now one of the twigs beneath my feet will crack under the pressure.

I am like an animal under attack, each of my senses amplified so that every smell, every sound, every taste rushes through my body all at once. And then I hear it, the snap as a tiny shard of wood gives way beneath the heel of my bare foot.

I feel the girl's face before I see it, turning slowly towards me. Time seems to slow down as the image is scored onto my memory:

the dark unblinking brown eyes, pupils frozen in horror. For just a second our gazes lock, a bolt running down my spine, and then, without another thought, I feel my body rise.

No longer aware of the blood gathered in clots at my toes, I lunge towards my escape route, a tunnel of light spilling through the clearing; I manage two giant steps, my feet guiding me through a rotten knot of roots and bark. And then it comes, the scream, chasing me down the hill. I know it instantly: the sound of a life being torn out by the roots.

Chapter 4

Gabriela

That first summer with Tom passed by in a haze of picnics on the Heath, and evenings spent with her dad at the house watching TV in easy silence while Tom attended rehearsals with his band – an anachronistic jazz four-piece that at least explained the terrible dress sense. The nights he was around, and she wasn't working at the pub on Arlington Road where she did four shifts a week behind the bar, they spent at his place, her skimming through textbooks for the final year of her degree. He cooked and washed up, helping her sort through the endless paperwork relating to her mother's estate, finding ways to care for her when she was incapable of caring for herself.

Unable to deal with it personally, Gabriela had handed the task of clearing her mother's house to a company in the West Country which Tom had found – recommended through a friend of a friend. She had visited just once, refusing his offer to accompany her, and collected a single box of photo albums and books before renting the place out through a local estate agent. She had always hated that house – or rather what it represented: the choice her mother had made to move out of London; her decision to abandon her only child wrapped up in the guise of selflessness, a refusal to uproot her at such a pivotal time in her life. *I couldn't do that to her*, she would overhear her mother tell her friends. Not that she'd ever asked Gabriela if she'd wanted to stay.

'So you were abroad when your mum . . .' Tom mustered the courage to ask one night as they sat at his table, poring over papers.

'How do you know that?' Gabriela asked.

'Saoirse mentioned it. Sorry, if you don't want to talk about it—'

'It's fine,' she cut in. 'I was in Paris, finishing off my placement.' She swallowed as she formed the words, her gaze held steadfast to the page.

Paris had pulled her in like the warm embrace she longed for, that year at the Sorbonne. Arriving in the July and staying until the following summer, with intermittent trips back to London, wafting between her tiny apartment above the bric-a-brac store on the Rue Galande and the university. With every step, she felt herself becoming someone new: the sort of person who sat in the grounds of the Greek church overlooking Notre Dame, sketching the spires that rose above the scaffolding; the sort of person who would go to the cinema at the end of her street, alone, to watch art-house films; the sort of person she and Saoirse would have called a cunt. But Saoirse wasn't there and she was, and for as long as her sojourn lasted, London, and everything that it entailed, simply didn't exist. And for that, she could not have been more grateful.

Within a couple of weeks in the city, Gabriela found a job at one of the cafés on the Place de la Sorbonne, serving overpriced coffee and stale croissants to tourists and overworked professors; the convenience of the location made up for the pitiful wage and the wandering hands of the maître d'. It was here that she met Pierre, as genuinely pretentious as the version of herself she had created, but so good-looking and so *French*, his opinion of himself so robust that it was difficult not to believe he was the god his body language told you he was.

He was sitting on one of the chairs in the square at the end of summer, smoking a cigarette, the first time she noticed him watching her as she moved between tables so that her skin tingled with the unnerving thrill of it. When she went over to ask him what he wanted, he dipped his eyebrows and pulled on his Gauloise in a way that told her exactly what, or who, he wanted. And she was in the mood to give it to him. Intermittently, from then on, she spent nights at Pierre's flat overlooking the Seine, one of a number of properties his father owned along this stretch, not far from the Hôtel de Ville. They were in the bar next door, eating breakfast, his leather jacket slung over the back of her chair, his helmet held on his lap like a baby, the day death came.

To her credit, Valentina had never pushed for Gabriela to stay in England; she never so much as attempted to make her feel guilty for wanting to go even once it was confirmed that the cancer had returned. If anything, it might have been a relief, not to have to make room to deal with her daughter's feelings alongside her own.

Since going home for Christmas, spending two weeks by her mother's bedside at the house in Somerset, unwilling or unable to believe that she was as ill as the doctors said she was, Gabriela's attitude towards Pierre had cooled, and the less she wanted him, the more he hounded her.

'Come back to the apartment,' he'd said as he scooped up his change, and she shook her head, leaning in to accept his kiss.

'I have work. I'll see you tomorrow.'

He made an expression that suggested she was the one who was missing out, and she watched his bike disappear over the bridge before making her way towards the canal.

During her time in Paris, her French had come on so well that she was close to fluent, but there were still things she didn't know, cultural references she had little reason to encounter in everyday conversation. In a bid to widen her vocabulary, she took to browsing the titles of the books stacked on market stalls along the banks of the river, reading voraciously: historical texts, biographies of French footballers, devouring whatever she could get her hands on. This particular morning a bright sky had opened up, luring her into a false sense of security as she took a few moments to stop and peruse the selection, choosing almost at random a battered old book on the economy from the Seventies, and another on the evolution of insects, her eyes skimming over the words *dimorphisme sexuel* as she flicked through the illustrations, ignoring the sounds of the traffic on the intersection behind.

Even though it was nearly spring, a cold wind sliced the top of the river as she made her way down the walkway at the Port de la Tournelle, looking up at the statue of St Genevieve, her arms resting protectively over her child. For a moment she thought it was someone else's phone ringing, but when she felt in her pocket she saw her father's name flashing on the screen. He rarely called her mobile, suspicious of the concept of a phone that could be taken out of the house, not least in a foreign country, and instinctively she stopped walking.

'Hello?'

'Gabriela, it's your father.'

'Hi Dad, how are you?'

There was a pause and she heard him stifling a cry. 'Gabriela, your mother died.'

She stayed very still, preserving that moment before stepping forward into the abyss.

'Are you there?'

'Yes, Dad, I'm here.'

She breathed in as deeply as she could, her hand feeling for a wall, the coldness of the stone, the tangibility of it, soothing. It was relief, she realised later, that stung her eyes. Relief that this was the worst thing that could happen and it had already happened, and she was still here. Relief, too, that Valentina was gone, and Gabriela would no longer be plagued by her expectations. Though in hindsight, any expectations had been self-imposed; her mother had always been far too busy thinking about herself.

Tom coughed self-consciously, and Gabriela looked up, blinking. 'I was away and she died, so I came back. There's not much else to say. Listen, I have to get to the pub, my shift starts at six.'

* * *

Her father's house stood on the corner of one of the streets that ladder behind Highgate Road, a Sixties new-build a stone's throw from the Heath. It still baffled her how he had been able to afford a place in this prohibitively desirable enclave of Dartmouth Park, however poky it might have been, with his share of the sale of the ramshackle Victorian terrace off Camden Road that had been their family home. Sometimes she wondered if her parents had made a secret pact when they divorced, whether her mother had agreed to take a lesser share of the proceeds on the condition that she didn't have to take her daughter with her.

The day Tom came over for the first time, Michael combed his hair neatly to the side and pulled on his best clothes, a chequered M&S shirt he'd worn every other day after being taken on as maths professor at a nearby college, neatening the display of tins and condiments he had started to stockpile the day he bought the house, and had barely made a dent in since. Moving through the hallway that morning with Tom, past the mismatching table and chairs, the brown flocked sofa that once belonged to her grandparents, she noticed Michael had placed a small bunch of yellow flowers on the table for the occasion.

It was the following January when her phone rang. They were having a drink at the Pineapple with Saoirse and Jim, winding down after a day sending out ever more CVs in the hunt for a proper job, or at least an internship, that would pull Gabriela out of her own head, now that her degree was finally coming to an end. There was something about the letters flashing on the screen, their shape solid and unyielding against the garish light of her phone at this time of night, *No Caller ID*, that made her hold onto the edge of her seat by her fingernails.

'Ms Shaw?'

She flattened her hand against the cracked leather seat of her stool and stood, the microphone warm against her ear as she pushed her way through the crowded bar and out onto the street.

'Speaking.'

'I'm calling from the Whittington Hospital, we have your number from a past calls list of Mr Michael Shaw, of . . .'

Before the woman on the end of the phone could finish saying her address, she felt the pavement rush up to meet her. By the time she turned to see Tom moving through the heavy velvet curtain and out into the street after her, a few moments later, she was sitting on the kerb, her vision blurred through the tears.

Chapter 5

Gabriela

One Year Later

She arrived early at Westminster tube station that first morning at the FCO, taking exit five onto Parliament Street as per the instructions she'd been sent, letting her eyes take it all in as she looked back towards the Houses of Parliament – the tourists gathering for photographs in front of soldiers on horseback, men in suits bustling with their briefcases into the backs of taxis, their phones pressed to their ears. As she approached the stone arch at the foot of King Charles Street, a security guard directed her towards the open brown metal gates where another official passed her bag through a scanner before she was pointed towards a reception area and handed a lanyard with her name on it.

'You're here as an intern, yes? I'm Lauren,' said the young woman who arrived to escort her across into the main building, not waiting for an answer before leading the way through the metal turnstiles which opened like a mouth, its teeth clamping shut behind them.

Gabriela thought of the night before, turning away from the mirror towards Tom, who was on the other side of the bedroom they had shared since making the decision that rather than sell her father's house, they would move in together.

'Stop worrying, you're not going to mess it up.' Tom's face had been serious. 'You're brilliant, everyone knows you're brilliant. You have a degree in languages, you work hard. I promise you, there is nothing to worry about.'

'I just want it so badly,' she said, noticing a tiny crack in the top corner of the mirror.

'I know you do.'

'But what if . . .'

'Just enjoy it, for God's sake. Why do you always have to catastrophise? Everything's going to be *fine*.'

'This way.' Lauren turned sharply left, holding open the first door they came to and leading the way up a flight of stone steps, past a couple of offices and a tiny Costa concession, where the queue stretched out the door.

Inside, the offices were more old-fashioned than Gabriela had imagined, semi open-plan, little more than a bunch of desks, suit jackets discarded on the backs of chairs. Placing her bag on the desk Lauren had pointed her towards, she removed her camel-coloured cashmere coat, one of the few items of her mother's clothing that she had kept.

A while later, a woman a couple of years older than her approached to give the grand tour, introducing herself as Madeleine.

'Is it what you had imagined?' she asked as they weaved back through the hallway. 'My own theory is that this whole structure is built for people who know nothing other than quads. Went to public school (quad), Oxbridge (quads), and now the FCO – guess what? Architecture to comfort public schoolboys.'

Madeleine had grown up in the service, she explained as they walked. Her father, a diplomat in countries across the Middle East and Asia, had been tipped to become Permanent Under-Secretary before dropping dead in the shower on the morning of his fifty-second birthday. On paper, at least, it seemed to Gabriela that Madeleine was born for this world; the gilded corridors of King Charles Street seemed to widen a little for her as they passed through.

Outside, corridors snaked around the quad, with lettered entry points and numbered offices. Noticing Gabriela looking, Madeleine said, 'The whole thing is apparently designed with the intention of confusing as many people as possible at once. In that respect, at least, it's a highly effective system. You all right for lunch?'

'I brought sandwiches with me.'

'Good, and you know where the coffee is?'

Gabriela nodded again. 'What do you do here?'

'Me?' Madeleine scoffed. 'Oh, you know, make up numbers. Here's a fun fact: did you know until the late Sixties a woman had to leave when she got married? I shit you not. We all move around rather a lot, often completely arbitrarily, which I can talk you through in a bit more detail once you've been through clearance. As for you, the thing with the FCO, as you will learn, is that it equates Young People – that's you, and even me, would you believe – with "the internet".' She made fingers around the words. 'So as far as what you will be expected to do, it will mainly be monitoring online forums for now. I'm afraid there is a risk that you will die of boredom before you manage to finish your placement . . .'

When they arrived at the foot of a gilded sweeping staircase, quite a way inside the building, Madeleine pointed upwards. 'This is probably more what you were imagining, no?'

Gabriela took in the portraits that lined the walls with watchful eyes.

'Perhaps we can take a proper look another day . . . That's the Foreign Secretary's office at the top of those stairs.'

Madeleine paused for a moment and then fixed her seriously with her gaze, as if considering something before deciding to go ahead, lowering her voice. 'The only other thing you need to know at this stage is that the Director, Guy Emsworth . . .' Her words drifted off. 'Just, if you have any questions, any *concerns*, you come to me. OK?'

Gabriela felt a sudden chill run down her back and Madeleine, noticing her shiver, started to walk back into the bowels of the building.

'I know,' she said. 'Just you wait. It gets colder in here than you'd ever expect.'

* * *

She spent most of her first week, as per Madeleine's prediction, scouring online message-boards for 'suspicious activity', whatever that was supposed to mean. It was a few days before Guy Emsworth appeared beside her chair. She wasn't sure whether to stand up, but when he stooped over the corner of her desk, it was as if he was fixing her to her seat.

'Guy Emsworth.' He held out a hand, his palm clammy against hers. 'You're our new recruit, am I right?'

From the hours she'd spent poring over the FCO website in preparation for this moment, she knew Emsworth was a director of the Joint International Counter-Terrorism Unit, the department to which she was to be attached – singled out, according to the feedback from her application, as a result of speaking Arabic, French, Spanish and Russian.

She smiled. 'Well, I'm here for the next month, hopefully longer – I'm Gabriela.'

He considered her for a moment, his eyes moving briskly over her body before he stood straight. 'Gabriela . . . Very good. Well, you seem like the sort who could stick around.'

Three weeks later and she was one of the last in the office, finishing off the report she'd been compiling for Lauren, when she spotted Emsworth in his office with his back to the door. She was on a high, having noticed what she believed to be a series of potentially significant codewords being used on a forum linked to a magazine which sold itself as an aspirational lifestyle publication but was in fact funded by an Islamist terror cell that was part of a growing concern in the wake of the invasion of Iraq. She had been preparing to leave a print-out of her findings on Lauren's desk for her to pass on to her boss the following day, but at the last minute she'd paused, deciding instead to hand the document to him herself in the morning. After all, it was her work: why risk someone else getting the credit?

As she walked past his office on her way back to her desk, she glanced through the semi-open door, hardly expecting him to still be there. Even with his back to her, she could sense there was something important about the conversation he was having on the phone, something in his stature giving it away.

He cut off the call a couple of seconds later and stepped out of the office, signalling across to her as she gathered her coat.

'I didn't know anyone was still here,' he said and she was pleased he'd noticed her putting in the hours. 'Listen, Gabriela. What are you doing now? A few of us were going to have a quick drink, if you fancied joining? They've gone ahead.'

She stood for a moment in the empty room, momentarily wondering why the head of the department would invite the intern along for after-work drinks, before smiling back at him, blotting out the warning voice in her head.

'Oh bugger, it looks like the others have already left,' he sighed, slipping his phone back into his pocket as they crossed Parliament Street towards the Red Lion, its colourful hanging baskets a counterpoint to the endless grey, and she felt another scratch of disbelief. But she could hardly turn back now.

Inside, the bar was heaving.

'Grab us that seat, and I'll come and join you.'

He didn't ask what she wanted to drink, returning a few minutes later with two glasses of gin and tonic, the sweat from his palm leaving a handprint like a slap mark in the condensation. Settling beside her, too close, he said, 'So, tell me, where did you go to university, Gabriela?'

She took a sip of her drink before answering, 'UCL. I graduated last summer.'

'Excellent,' he replied, his eyes moving briefly to her chest. 'And you live in London?'

She nodded. 'At my father's house.'

She didn't mention Tom, whose idea it had been to give up his damp rented studio flat and pay to live at hers instead. For him, the new arrangement had meant the chance to live in a house that represented a slice of the modernist dream that defined so much of his degree, which would soon, finally, be coming to an end. For her, it was a practical solution that afforded her the option of holding onto the house. Besides, Tom was good company, he was a good man, and it was easier to go along with it than to push back in a way that was bound to have hurt him.

She would wonder later about the things she had and had not told Emsworth that night. The things that might have given him the wrong impression, that might have made what followed – at least this particular segment of events – partly her own fault.

She took a sip of her drink as Emsworth's phone pinged. Reading the words on the screen, his face dropped. He cursed under his breath, placing the handset back in his pocket, the gold ring flashing on his third finger.

'Gabriela, I'm so sorry, there's been a bit of an emergency and I'm afraid I'm going to have to dash back to the office. You stay and finish off your drink and I'll catch up with you tomorrow, all right?'

He leaned over and squeezed her knee and she had to curb a reflexive desire to kick him.

Watching through the window as he left the pub, rather than heading back to King Charles Street as he said he was going to, she saw him hail a taxi, moving into it, pulling out his phone and placing it to his ear. Glancing over his shoulder, he paused for a moment before talking into the receiver, his face suddenly unrecognisable from the one seated opposite her just moments before. As she necked the last of her drink, the bubbles caught in her throat, causing a tear to form in the corner of her eye.

Lauren was characteristically blasé as she made the offer the following day.

'The guy who was supposed to be coming in for a month after you has cancelled. So if you wanted to stay on a bit longer . . .'

'Wow, I'd love to,' Gabriela replied.

She paused before emailing Emsworth, unsure of the protocol, then decided that since he would have had to have signed off her extended stay, it would be rude not to acknowledge it.

Opening a new message, she typed: *Thank you for offering me an extended placement. I look forward to working with you and the team. Best wishes, Gabriela.*

His reply was almost instantaneous. *No need to thank me. Good to have you on board. GE.*

It was another six months before she was taken on properly, in her first official role – *fast-streamed* – enabling her to do a year in two different departments, one policy-based, one most likely corporate, before taking her first foreign posting.

'Bugger me, Gabs, you're in the Foreign Office!' Tom had enthused, lifting her off her feet when she got home that night, having rung on her way to share the news, too excited to wait.

'I'd rather not, if you don't mind,' she pulled a face before continuing. 'I mean, it's not official yet. There's some security clearance checks that have to be made first, which will take a couple of weeks. But if that's all good, and bloody hell it should be, then . . .'

'This deserves champagne,' he said, popping open a bottle of Cava. 'I mean obviously we don't have any, but if we did . . .' He handed her a glass. 'Seriously, though, I'm so bloody proud of you. This is massive.'

'I know,' she said, taking a sip of her drink, ignoring the whispers telling her, even then, that it was too good to be true; voices that grew louder in her mind as she fell asleep that night, so that in her dreams they were shouting, begging her to run and not look back.

Her first year proper at King Charles Street was spent working under Emsworth in Counter-Terrorism, still mostly trawling the internet for signs of suspicious activity, which she would deliver to him along with an analysis of how she believed the information she'd found fitted in with what they already knew of existing organisations – analysis she was desperate for him to give more credence to than appeared to be the case. Nevertheless, she was there, and she was on course to making herself indispensable, of that much she was sure.

Emsworth had stationed her at a desk near his on the basis that he could delegate when necessary – really help *lift her up* through the organisation.

'To give him a better vantage point from which to ogle your tits, more like.' Madeleine kissed her teeth when she saw her friend there, and Gabriela was pissed off that she didn't believe she'd earned his interest by virtue of her obvious talents.

She felt her cheeks pinken when Emsworth's email came through the following day.

Let's go for lunch, talk through any ideas you have for strategy? GE.

'I know it's a bit of a walk away,' Emsworth said as they reached the Italian bistro on Crown Passage that he referred to as his unofficial office. 'But wait until you try the lasagne – you'll understand why it's worth the stroll.'

The bistro was tucked at the end of the alleyway so that you could almost miss it if you didn't know what you were looking for. Inside, it was furnished in the sort of deep reds and wood veneers that reminded Gabriela of the Italian cafés that were all over Camden when she was growing up. The kind of place her mother would offer to meet her on their weekends together as a teenager, as if the warmth of the pizza would make up for the coolness she couldn't help but exude towards her only child.

'What will you drink?' Emsworth asked, once they were settled at a table.

'Oh, I'll just have a Coke.'

'Nonsense,' he said, without looking up from the wine menu. 'You can't leave me to drink alone. White or red?'

'I don't mind,' she replied as the waitress came to take their order, greeting him in a way that confirmed he was a regular.

'I was interested in what you mentioned in the briefing about, what was it, terrorism and *branding*? Very intriguing.'

She sat straighter in her chair. 'Oh, OK. Well, I was just saying that from the data that's beginning to be collected in other countries, it seems that terrorist groups are manipulating emerging social media platforms to create an identity which helps to propagate their own narrative, rather than that foisted on them by traditional media.' She sounded like an automaton, churning out lines verbatim from what she had read, but he didn't seem to notice.

'The fear is that with the recent emergence of platforms like Myspace and Facebook, these groups will be able to access potential recruits in ways that we can't see and therefore can't monitor . . .'

As the waitress settled the bottle on the table, she felt Emsworth's eyes on hers in a way that she found both thrilling and unnerving.

Pausing to take a sip of cold wine, he said, 'Gosh, you really are more than a pretty face. Do carry on.'

As per another of the organisation's peculiar, and frustrating, habits, just as she was catching her stride in Counter-Terrorism, she was pulled into Digital Diplomacy, an 'emerging department' pivoting around the sort of PR work that made a mockery of the whole place. Madeleine, meanwhile, was hoisted kicking and screaming, almost literally, into Communications.

'I swear to God, they're trying to kill us off.' She gesticulated with her cigarette as they stood outside the Red Lion one evening after work, clots of traffic leaking out fumes on the street in front of them.

It was that autumn when Gabriela was offered her first foreign posting, in Russia, Emsworth delivering the news personally as she made her way back into the office from lunch.

'What do you say? Two years in Moscow back working under me, from a distance. It's a pretty good option for your first posting. Could do a hell of a lot worse. I've worked hard to wangle you this – don't mess it up.'

He wagged his finger in her face as he uttered the final words, like a teacher doling out the star part in the school play. She felt her heartbeat rise, her chest seeming to vibrate with it. As if something inside her knew what was coming and was beating at her ribcage in order to escape.

Madeleine nearly dropped her sandwich when Gabriela told her the news about Moscow. They were sitting on a bench eating their lunch on the stretch of riverside overlooking the Thames.

'What about you?' she asked, knowing that Madeleine, too, had been offered another placement, and having already refused her first one would be expected to take it.

'Fucking Dubai. *Bastards*,' she hissed.

'What's wrong with Dubai?' Gabriela asked, stifling a laugh, trying not to sound smug but unable to suppress her pride at being sent on the more serious posting. 'Loads of people would kill for Dubai; you should hear Johnny banging on about the bottomless brunches in the compound . . .'

Madeleine gave Gabriela a look of hateful despair at the thought of it and Gabriela smiled back sympathetically, taking a drag. 'Sorry . . .'

It wasn't that she relished Madeleine's self-perceived failing – on the contrary, she would have loved for her, too, to get the posting she craved, the one that she deserved. But did she feel guilty about her tenure, knowing as she did that Moscow was high on Madeleine's list of preferred destinations? How could she? It was out of her hands. Besides, dog-loyal as she was, there was no way Madeleine would have spared her a moment's guilt, had the tables been turned.

'You're not going to take it?'

'Am I fuck,' she said, grabbing her lighter from the bench and inhaling sharply. 'I'm telling you now, it's that bastard Emsworth, he's had it in for me since the moment I arrived. I should have lied about my geographical preferences, there's no way he is not doing this to spite me.'

'He's not even involved in Communications,' Gabriela reasoned and Madeleine scoffed, taking another drag of her cigarette and kissing her teeth. 'Not involved? Oh fucking please. Like he doesn't have his hands in everything that is going on around here.'

Chapter 6

Isobel

Inside my flat, I collapse against the door, my back pressed against the wood veneer, my breath filling my throat so that it is a struggle to breathe. Too terrified to sit with the thoughts tumbling around my head, scared that they will bury me, I haul myself up.

Looking down at my feet, I notice, as if for the first time, that I'm not wearing shoes.

Automatically reaching inside my bag for a cigarette to steady my nerves, my hands brush against the packet. As I pull it out, even in my confused state, I know something isn't right. Where are my trainers? Rummaging inside the bag, as if something might suddenly appear from the emptiness, I feel my heartbeat strain in my chest. The shoes aren't there, and neither is my purse.

Holding the bridge of my nose between two fingers, I move towards the kitchen table in the centre of the room that was already small but whose walls now seem to press at me from both sides, and I make myself sit.

Desperately attempting to slow down my mind, to impose some sort of order on the images that move in and out of focus, I have a flash of memory: me on my knees in the undergrowth, scrambling around for the hash, rummaging through my bag. In my panic, I must have knocked the shoes and the purse out of the bag, and not even have noticed before the sound of the woman's screams sent me hurtling down the hill. The memory hits me like a wave and I stand, desperate to escape it.

Picking up a lighter from the table and inhaling deeply, I move around the bedsit, through the makeshift door into the bedroom area, where clothes and old books are strewn across the floor.

Looking up, I catch my gaunt reflection in the mirror. As if studying something new and confusing, I pull at the knot of hair on top of my head, which has slumped to one side, pinching the skin under my eyes as a car alarm starts to wail in the distance. For a moment I stand there, my senses still heightened, the sound of Camden stirring on the street below.

It is that time when the drugs have nothing left to offer; instead, what is left circulating in my system starts to feed off my body, slowly sucking all the goodness out. I can almost feel myself withering, my vital organs shrivelling.

Come on, I tell myself, willing my mind to come back to me.

Oscar.

His name comes to me like an epiphany and I reach for my phone in the pocket of my shorts before remembering it is dead. A wave of adrenaline kicks in then, as if from nowhere, my mind's final lunge for survival, and I scrabble together a handful of coins from the counter before grabbing my keys and shuffling down the stairs to the phone box two metres to the right of my front door.

It is the only payphone that still works on this stretch of Camden High Street and as I pull open the door with the full weight of my body, I am met by the overwhelming stench of urine. Dialling Oscar's number by heart, the same number I dialled night after night for so long, my eyes flit over the usual collage of calling cards layered one over another in a surreal tapestry of swollen nipples and painted talons. Holding one hand over my mouth, I suppress the urge to vomit.

There are three rings before the answer machine kicks in, and I hear my money being swallowed by the machine. Out of habit, my mind stumbles as it pictures him asleep in someone else's bed, and then the image is gone.

The voice at the end of the line is mechanical and unusually polite.

'This is Sergeant Morley, I'm away from my desk. Please leave a message after the tone and I'll call you back. If your call is urgent, please try the Kentish Town police main office . . .'

At those words, I throw the handset back onto the cold metal receiver. For a moment my fingers hover over the nine button but there is no way I can talk to the real police, not now. Despite his artificially elevated position in the force, in my mind Oscar Morley will never be that. Admittedly, a number of the officers around here have dubious social lives of their own, as I've inferred from conversations overheard in the hours I've spent shadowing PCs for various pieces on community policing, or waiting in the station for press office-approved updates on a case, but that doesn't make it acceptable for me to turn up with pupils like the inside of a well to report something I'd seen happen in a bush on the Heath on my way back from a squat party.

In any case, what would I say? What had I actually seen?

Go home. The voice in my head is adamant, any doubt confirmed when I catch a glimpse of my reflection in the glass door, my jaw swinging as though only partially hinged.

Before turning back towards the flat, I insert two more coins and dial Jess's number. When her answer machine kicks in, I clench my fist, kicking the base of the booth with my sore foot, and letting out a cry.

Back home, just before I collapse on my bed, I reach into the drawer, pulling out a box of fluoxetine and popping one of the capsules in my mouth. Reaching in further for a bag of Xanax, I crack one in half and swallow it without water before letting my body sink back, a smudge of glow-in-the-dark stars staring back at me from the ceiling.

In my dream I find myself in a field with Jess and we are walking in silence. At some point, I notice the rain, the sky melting to a dappled grey behind us. As the drops fall against my face, I lift my chin, feeling renewed by every splash. It is a while before I notice the party behind us, the roar of it having faded the further away we walked into the field; the clatter of cans and pulsing techno stretch out into a low hum. When the rain stops I hear her breathe in deeply beside me.

My heart is beating heavily against my chest and the air is cold in my throat as the wind gets up, whipping against the bare flesh of my calves.

'What time do you think it is?' I ask. We have come to a halt by a cluster of cows who continue to gnaw at the ground, oblivious to the rain lashing against their coats. It is so cold, I think, the rain making my bones ache as it drives against my skin. I can no longer remember whose idea it was to come up here and all I want is to be somewhere else.

Opening my eyes and turning back to face the way I'd come, I see she has already gone.

Chapter 7

Gabriela

The chill of the night air clawed at her the moment she stepped onto the runway in Moscow. It was nearly 9p.m., five hours since she had made her way up the stairs to the jet at Heathrow, holding the handrail to steady herself against the wind. Once she'd stowed her rucksack in the overhead locker, she pulled out the eye-mask Tom had given her as they'd said goodbye at the doorway to her house, which he would continue to rent from her for the two years that she would be away.

It had begun to rain as the plane took off, the wind causing it to judder as they pushed into the unremarkable afternoon sky. Looking down, she thought briefly of her mother, of how she would always insist they sit at the front of the plane, and then pop a couple of pills from the box in her bag and spend the flight ignoring Gabriela as she flicked through the radio channels, struggling to adjust her headphones.

She had been prepared for the weather in Russia in November, and had packed accordingly back in London, her *Teach Yourself Russian* CD whirring in the background, refreshing her memory as she stuffed her suitcase with as many base layers as she could feasibly fit in. It would be seven o'clock at home now, she thought as she stepped down the metal staircase onto the tarmac, imagining Tom settling in front of the news with a microwave meal before heading out to his weekly rehearsal, his guitar slung over his shoulder. Closing her eyes, she breathed in the fumes of the plane and smiled.

Her driver, Oleg, was waiting at the Arrivals desk, ready to usher her through the crowds.

'Have you been to Russia before?' he asked.

She shook her head. 'Never. I hear it's a beautiful country.'

He said nothing as he pulled open the passenger door for her, remaining silent as the car sped along a single road that cut through endless pine forests. With no streetlamps to light the pitch-black night, the motion of the vehicle lulled her to sleep, and when she woke up to the sound of Oleg slamming the driver's door closed, she saw that they had arrived, the city lights casting an eerie glow across the sky as she stepped out.

'You've done well,' he said as he led her towards a luxurious block lining Patriarshiye Ponds. 'All this used to be communal apartments. You've read *The Master and Margarita*?'

She nodded.

'Mikhail Bulgakov lived around here in the Thirties and this was where the tram scene at the beginning of the book was set. As you can see, it's a very different place now.'

Looking up, she took in the tiers of grand windows set within a sand-yellow façade, and felt a shudder that she put down to the cold.

'Surely, this isn't . . .'

Oleg made a face to show that he was as surprised as she was by the scale and grandeur of her sleeping arrangements.

Unlocking the door, he shrugged. 'Apparently your apartment hasn't been sorted out yet, so you're staying here for a few nights. Your boss, Guy Emsworth, it's his place when he's in town . . .'

Noting her expression, Oleg said, 'Oh, he's not here now. I'm sorry, I assumed you knew. But I don't think there's any hurry for you to leave. He won't be here for a couple of weeks . . .'

Gabriela nodded, trying to keep the excitement from her voice. 'Sure, that's fine.'

'You have everything you need?' he asked, leaving her alone in the flat, her single suitcase in the middle of the room looking pitifully small below the high gilded ceilings.

'I have,' she said under her breath, throwing open the windows the moment he left, closing her eyes, focusing on the night air stinging her skin, the distant car horns blaring, the sounds of millions of other lives across the city crushing against one another. In that moment she felt so alive that it was as though, if she jumped right now, she would fly.

It was part of her role with the embassy to help foster good relations at ground level, to befriend local officials with a view not so much to working together as to keeping an eye on who was doing what. The ramifications of the South Ossetia war with Georgia, the closure of two British Council buildings in Moscow, all in the context of the fallout of the poisoning of Alexander Litvinenko and the UK's refusal to extradite the wanted businessman Boris Berezovsky, were contributing factors to a climate of relations between Russia and Britain that was, at the least, cool. To be here now, for her first ever placement, was both terrifying and fortifying and seemed to offer definitive proof that she was trusted in a way that she could barely have dreamed of – a way that perhaps might have made her ask more questions than she did.

When her accommodation was finally sorted a few days later, Oleg returned to move her across town to a more befitting flat above a neon-lit bar a few streets behind Red Square. It was hardly the Art-Nouveau glamour to which she was fast becoming accustomed, but she didn't care.

People said that everywhere you stepped in New York was like being in the movies, but for her, Moscow, with its austere grandiosity, and its buildings and the sky both steeped in a sense of sorrow-tinged romance, was the perfect backdrop for the film onto which she projected her own life.

It wasn't easy assimilating herself into a diplomatic sphere still tainted by the suspicion of the Soviet era, and now freshly challenged by Putin, who had come to power a decade earlier. It was a world where strangers avoided eye contact in the street and you learned not to bother asking for directions. A world where you had to treat everyone as an enemy until they were proved to be a friend. And once they had, be warier still . . .

It was daunting at first, but after a few months she loved it. Day to day, she was notionally based at the embassy, but in reality she spent most of her time attending events on its behalf, shaking hands and smiling until her cheeks ached.

She had just returned from a week in St Petersburg with local business representatives, her legs aching from the walking tours of the palace, the endless meetings and the nightcaps. Walking through the door, she noticed the red light blinking on the answer machine. *Six new messages*.

It would be Tom, she thought happily, looking forward to catching up with him. Their regular chats provided the perfect foil for the guarded diplomacy that shrouded her every other interaction. When she pressed play, with each recording Tom's voice escalated in pitch and intensity so that by the last one he was practically screaming down the phone for her to call him back. The strength of emotion was so at odds with his usual character that she was terrified of what she would learn when she called him a moment later, the foreign dialling tone reminding her of the distance between them.

'Gaby?'

'Yes, hi, what's going on?'

She had barely finished her sentence when she heard a sigh of relief followed by his voice, riled this time.

'What the hell, are you OK?'

'Of course, I'm fine.'

'What do you mean, of course you're fine? I've been out of my fucking mind – why didn't you call?'

'What are you talking about? I was on a work trip, I told you I'd be away for a few days—'

'No, you didn't.'

'I did—'

'No, you fucking didn't, Gaby. A *week* I've been trying to reach you. After everything you've told me about how fraught things are there . . . You didn't think it would be courteous to call me, when you're on the other side of the world?'

'Oh Tom, for God's sake, calm down, would you? I'm tired.'

It was unfair to be so dismissive of his feelings, but she resented the implication that she was under some kind of obligation to him.

There was a silence as they settled into their stalemate. She was the one to break first. 'Look, I've just got in, I have to unpack and—'

'Whatever, fine. I'll speak to you sometime.'

'Tom, I—'

But he had already hung up.

When she tried to call back a moment later, he didn't answer.

Opening the fridge and then the cupboards in search of a bottle, she found nothing. Pulling her coat off the rack and slipping her feet into a pair of heeled boots which would barely withstand the snow that still lined the streets in March, she slammed the front door of her apartment. Several sets of bloodshot eyes looked up at her as she passed the bar below her flat. Pulling her coat around herself as she kept walking, her hood pulled high above her head, she set a brisk pace through the unsettling quiet of the back roads lit with the artificial tinge of occasional streetlamps. Moving on autopilot, she made a beeline towards Red Square and Tverskoi Ryad beyond, where she looked forward to the wide open streets and the reassuring movement of people.

Already her nose was beginning to tingle from the cold, and as she turned to check her reflection in the window of an unassuming bar, she saw him, seated opposite a white woman with long dark hair and porcelain skin, and beside her, a black man in a cream linen suit. Illuminated under the dingy lighting of the bar, Emsworth's eyes caught Gabriela's and his look was as though he had been shot.

Stepping forward through the doorway, she watched the woman stand as if sensing her enter, then turning away from where Gabriela hovered and moving towards the bathroom. The man opposite him noticed the young woman enter and looked sideways at Emsworth, who took a long slug of his drink.

'Gabriela . . .'

'I didn't know you were in town,' she said and when he smiled, his eyes were cold.

'I didn't expect to see you here either.'

It was the first time she had seen him since her arrival in Moscow. Their communication had been surprisingly sparse, just the odd work-related email, and the note she'd sent him thanking him for the loan of his apartment.

'You're settling in OK?' he asked, his voice uncharacteristically brusque. 'I'm sorry,' he added, turning to the man in the suit. 'This is Gabriela, she's a colleague of mine.'

'A pleasure to meet you,' he said in an accent that might have been French African, and Gabriela smiled coolly at him before turning back to Emsworth, an uneasy feeling shunting through her veins, wrong-footed as she was by everything about this interaction.

'Very much so,' she said, in response to Emsworth's question.

Subconsciously, his eyes moved again towards the door where his second companion had disappeared a few moments earlier.

'So will I be seeing you at the office next week?' she added, as keen by now as he clearly was to bring the conversation to a close. He shook his head.

'As I say, this isn't an official visit. Probably best if you don't mention it to anyone else. I don't want the others to feel peeved that I didn't drop by.'

'Sure. Well, nice to meet you,' she replied, turning to the man at the table as she heard the lavatory flush in the direction of where the woman had disappeared.

'Good,' Emsworth said with an unconvincing smile. 'Let's be in touch.'

As she left the bar, she saw the woman returning to the table, her long dark hair swishing against a poker-straight back. Emsworth leaned in again and the conversation resumed. When she looked back, she couldn't say exactly what made her do it; she didn't think it through consciously as she pulled the phone from her pocket and aimed it discreetly at the three of them. The single shot revealing a picture she could not yet understand.

Chapter 8

Gabriela

Tom met her at Arrivals when she returned for Christmas, clearly regretting the homemade *Welcome Home* sign he held weakly at his chest.

When he saw her face, he let it drop a bit further, gritting his teeth, and she smiled, shaking her head.

'Hi,' she said as she kissed him, feeling her cheeks redden as she handed him one of the bags that hung from her arm.

He paused, taking her in, his eyes soft with love. 'Look at you, you look even better than I remember.'

She nudged him self-consciously. 'Ah, shut up, I've always looked this good.'

'A lot can change in a year,' he replied, taking her suitcase and pulling her arm as she moved instinctively towards the signs for the train.

'For instance. . .' He made a drumming sound as they made their way towards the short-stay car park.

'Ta-da!'

It might have been the first Renault 5 ever to have fallen off the production line and the door almost took her out as she opened it to step into the passenger seat, but there was something about it that was so perfectly Tom that she couldn't help but grin.

'Yeah, sorry about that, I might have been a little over-zealous with the WD40,' he said as she nursed her elbow.

'Oh my God, it has an actual tape deck. This is amazing, I feel like it's 1984,' she said. 'I'm glad you went for red. Boy-racer style. So you.'

'I'm thinking of getting it lowered, maybe some strip-lights under the bumper,' he said and she laughed.

'Missed you, Gabs.'

'I missed you, too. But I'm back for two weeks, so let's make the most of it, OK?'

She watched his face focused on the road ahead as the motorway shuttled them towards the grey cityscape. Making their way back through familiar streets, the relative sluggishness of the London air straining in her lungs, she felt such fondness towards him that she pushed away the sensation that her internal organs were being compressed so intensely that she could barely breathe.

Tom had been in the midst of a freelance project when she moved to Moscow, working on a commercial development that conveniently would last about as long as her trip abroad. This was to be his first big job since he graduated; he couldn't just disappear, he'd said, as if she'd invited him to go with her.

They were equals, of sorts, in that moment: him immersed in a new job, playing landlord in her house while she tried out life in foreign service with the same uncertainty with which one tries on a new coat, slipping her hands in and out of the pockets, taking discreet glances at the back and sides, checking if it fits.

The conclusion, for her, was that it fitted perfectly. There was a lot to be desired about some aspects of the trip, but the possibility of what this life represented: the potential for travel, for learning, the opportunity her role at the FCO afforded her to try out different lives under the guise of someone who knew what they were doing, of someone who was supposed to be there . . . Once she had a taste of that, she knew she could never give it up.

Tom recognised the change in her, the new-found grown-up self-assuredness, as she immersed herself in London life for the brief time that she was there. And he wasn't the only one. On Christmas Eve Saoirse and her partner Jim came over for drinks and a blissfully unfestive kebab. They had recently exchanged Kentish Town for a battered two-bed on Wilton Way near London Fields, since rents were still relatively affordable in Hackney.

Like most of Gabriela's friends who'd grown up in this now boujie pocket of North London – those whose parents hadn't conveniently died when they were in their twenties – Saoirse had left the area not long after coming back from university, in her case in Leeds.

'You seem different,' Saoirse said as the four of them sat around the kitchen table, necking cheap wine. Jim was an old university friend of Tom's and Gabriela had known within minutes of meeting him that he and Saoirse would either hate each other or fall head over heels in love. As she predicted, when they met there was an energy between them that was so alive she would find herself just watching them and feeling her jaw tense with envy.

'Different how?' she asked.

'I don't know,' Saoirse smiled, as if trying to work something out. 'Different in a good way. Grown up.'

Gabriela raised her eyebrows. 'Fancy . . .'

'Very fancy,' Saoirse said and then she paused. 'Speaking of which. . .' She turned to Jim. 'We're getting married . . .'

Gabriela squealed with genuine delight, falling across the table to hug them both. 'That's amazing, and really weird, 'cause surely you're still only twelve, so how could you be getting married?'

'Great news, guys,' Tom said, lifting his glass. He tried to meet Gabriela's eye and she looked away.

When he tried to talk to her in bed later that night, she pretended to be asleep.

It was strange being back in London, for those couple of weeks.

Aside from occasional after-work drinks with colleagues from the embassy, in Moscow she had taken to spending weekends alone, relishing the visits to the market outside the city, flicking through old Soviet memorabilia, or trips to one of several new galleries which were opening across town. There, even just a walk around the old hotels or shopping malls felt like an exotic experience. Though the work itself, in Moscow, was less obviously rewarding.

For a while Tom seemed confused by her focus on the job, unsure how to deal with it. But, to his credit, he always encouraged her; his belief in his girlfriend was absolute. Other women complained that their male partners felt threatened by their successes, as if a woman's progress outside of the home was an inherent form of emasculation, but Tom was nothing like that. Once he understood it was the job, not another man, that had piqued her interest, he basked unquestioningly in her rise through the ranks. Fundamentally, she thought, Tom understood that the more space he gave her, the less likely she was to bolt.

Chapter 9

Gabriela

One Year Later

'Where are you taking me? I'm cold.'

It was 6.30p.m. and the streetlights cast reflections like puddles of liquid amber over the pavements leading across the bridge to Primrose Hill. The last time she had been here was five months earlier, a fleeting London visit for Saoirse and Jim's wedding: a quick exchange of vows followed by pub-hopping through Camden, past the Princess of Wales, ending up at a lock-in at the Steeles in Belsize Park.

If it was anyone else, he might have felt hurt by her sulky tone as they made their way into the gates of the park, but Tom was built with an extra layer of resilience. Clearly, he had a plan in mind, a sweeping gesture, and already, as he guided her up the hill towards the bench looking out across London, she could hazard a guess as to what it was.

'Cold? You came back from Moscow twenty-four hours ago, you're supposed to be able to handle a British attempt at winter in a bikini by now,' he goaded.

It was true, the weather had reached minus 26 degrees the day she'd left. On the drive to the airport, the snow stretched on for miles, an abandoned blanket, impossibly white, suffocating the endless pine forests which seemed would never end until, without warning, they disappeared and in their place sprawling industrial sites suddenly blighted the horizon, buildings like metal insects lying dead amidst the snow.

Moscow had grabbed her with a force she could never have expected, given the relentless cold and the mistrust that permeated every exchange: there were so many reasons why she should have found it inhospitable – but, like the most unlikely of lovers, the city had her gripped. The harder it pushed her away, the tighter she had held on. Now she was back in London with Tom, she didn't know which aspect of her two lives felt more foreign, or which place less like home.

But there was a sense of relief too, at the prospect of returning to the office, of being back in the thick of it. Emsworth's visits had been scarce in Russia, though he was in constant contact from London, checking in on any progress with an avid interest. Gabriela knew that for him to have chosen her to go out there at a time when tensions were so high, she must be regarded as a valuable member of the team. And yet, she had started to feel as if she was being wheeled out as a sort of PR representative rather than anything more meaningful. She had only seen Emsworth a couple of times since the episode in the bar – a meeting neither of them had mentioned since – and she couldn't shake the feeling that she was being kept at arm's length.

She shivered as she went to sit on the bench at the top of Primrose Hill, the city lights stretching out before them, punctuated by the tips of the cages at London Zoo. Tom stopped her from sitting, reaching into his backpack and pulling out a blanket, which he laid over the bench before directing her to sit.

Refraining from questioning the wisdom of laying a pale blue wool throw over a damp park bench, she watched him lean into the bag again and lift out a hot water bottle, giving it a squeeze. Satisfied, he placed it on her lap.

'It's still warm,' he said triumphantly as he reached into the bag for the final time and retrieved a flask and a wedge of tin foil.

'Ham or cheese?' he asked, a look of self-satisfaction spreading across his face, and she smiled, hoping he wasn't going to do what she already knew he would.

'Either,' she said, accepting a soggy triangle, taking a swig of coffee and brandy and appreciating the warmth of it moving through her body.

'You're not going to propose, are you?' she asked, unable to stop herself, taking a bite and feeling immediately guilty as she watched his expression drop. So she had found his pain threshold, after all.

'Oh Tom.' She leaned forward and kissed him, before shifting closer.

'Bloody hell, Gaby, talk about pissing on my bonfire.'

'Babe, I'm sorry. You know I love you, I just . . . I don't see the point.'

It was true, or maybe it wasn't. She had seen the point as she watched Saoirse staring into Jim's eyes at the registry office off Euston Road, the pair of them disappearing from the pub afterwards and returning with her hand locked in his, the top of Saoirse's skirt tucked into her knickers. But for them?

'It's fine.' He took the Thermos from her and drank, turning so that she couldn't see his eyes shining with disappointment.

'Look, one day I might feel differently, but right now I'm just not . . . It's not that I'm not committed to you,' she added, stumbling on her words, for a moment remembering the exhilarating freedom of Moscow, of being fully immersed in life as an autonomous unit.

It wasn't as though she'd done anything to betray his confidence. Even when the thought crossed her mind, she had never been unfaithful.

'Besides, I have to go back to work in a couple of weeks. It's not practicable.'

'*Practicable*? Sure,' his voice was dismissive and she longed for his usual carefree tone.

'Ask again, in a couple of years, I might feel differently.'

He didn't tell her to go fuck herself, as she would have done if the tables had been turned. Instead, they sat there in silence and finished their sandwiches and then walked back to the house, had sex and fell asleep on opposite sides of the bed.

* * *

They didn't speak of it again. Perhaps he couldn't bear the possibility of another rejection, or the conversation such a setback might lead to in terms of where this was all going. Tom was never one to rock the boat.

The day she had returned to London for good, Gabriela felt like she had left a part of herself behind, that a piece of her soul was still roaming the streets of Moscow. Soon enough, though, they settled back into their usual routine, evenings lounging at the house with a book, Tom standing occasionally to select another record from the vinyl collection that took up half the living room.

'It's good to have you back,' he said one night a few weeks after her return as they lay in easy silence, head-to-toe on the sofa. When she looked up and saw him there, splayed across a cushion in his characteristic state of repose, she smiled. In that moment she didn't want to be anywhere else.

At King Charles Street, the pace of life provided the perfect contrast to time with Tom. In her absence, new faces had emerged as old ones moved on and out into different departments, pursuing other careers or scattering themselves in bureaus across the world.

Emsworth, on the rare occasions when he was actually in the office, seemed more distracted than usual, troubled by something, though she could hardly imagine who or what, given that he seemed to come and go as he pleased, apparently answerable to no one.

Still, it seemed that, as far as he was concerned, she could do no wrong. Finally, her earlier idea of gathering intelligence from social media surveillance was being implemented across various departments, and was fast becoming a technique instrumental in infiltrating terrorist cells as well as organised criminal gangs. Emsworth had not directly credited her for the idea yet, but he had made it plain that there would be something substantial coming her way as a reward for her commitment, a more permanent place-ment, he implied – maybe even Washington or Paris – something that would give her the option to start a new life, a life full of the excitement and adventure she craved.

Although perhaps she would be offered a role she'd never even considered, and she would be open to that too. After some of the cases she had seen evolving in Moscow, even if only from a distance, she had her sights set on Human Rights, which would mean making her way into the department of Multilateral Policy. But things might change and that wasn't necessarily a bad thing either. So long as there was enough progress that she could feel the movement towards where she needed to be, then she would be happy to work her way up. She was willing to do whatever it took. And he knew it as well as she did.

'I'm expecting big things from you,' Emsworth said one day. 'Just as soon as the right opening comes up, I think you're ready for the next step.'

She had blushed at that, and yet the praise felt deserved. If her role at the embassy in Moscow was a delicate balance of innovation, deference and being able to hold her drink (and her tongue) through an endless roll-call of dinner parties designed to test and ingratiate, on both sides, then in every sense she had excelled. The reports from her seniors at the embassy had been nothing but glowing. The Russians liked her was the overall feedback. They trusted her – and eliciting trust was the name of the game.

In response, over the coming weeks Emsworth amped up her responsibilities, at least unofficially. One afternoon when everyone but she and Johnny, the sharp-elbowed policy support officer who had come up on the same fast-streaming round as she had, were out at lunch, Emsworth came to her desk. She was in the middle of several tasks and struggling to keep pace but nevertheless she stopped what she was doing as he approached.

'Are you busy?' he asked, without waiting for an answer. 'I need a couple of files pulled out. It's a bit of a sensitive one, I need someone I can trust to do a good job.'

Subconsciously, she flashed a look towards Johnny who she knew was at a loose end, envisaging all that she had to do before she could get home and put her feet up. She was suddenly so tired, it was as though her body was surrendering already, and this made her want to push back harder against it. Besides, if she didn't do it, Johnny would.

'If you're busy I can do it myself,' he said, clocking her expression and making as if to walk away.

'No,' she said quickly. 'Of course I can do it. What do you need?'

'Just a couple of files pulling out, like I said. Some wonderfully tedious stuff about trade deals in Equatorial Guinea.'

She didn't pause to ask her boss what he might need with such documents, given that they had no obvious link to any work being done in their department. In hindsight, she would justify it by telling herself she hadn't believed it was her place to question him.

'Sure,' she said, 'I could probably clear some time this afternoon and email it across to you.'

He cleared his throat. 'Well, the thing is, I really need a physical copy to look over on my flight to Moscow next week; it's a time-saving exercise more than anything. I wondered whether you might download something and print it out for me? You know what a Luddite I am.'

'I don't think we're supposed to . . .'

In Counter-Terrorism, middle-weight employees like Gabriela had access to three different levels of email service – open, confidential and top secret. But each of these, she knew as well as he did, was trackable. For anyone other than the digital bods with their access to a 'dirty network', there was only one option if you wanted to take a document out of the building: the printer.

He smiled. 'As I say, I could do it myself, only I have so much to sort before I leave and you know how cack-handed I am with all that technical mumbo-jumbo.' He made a self-deprecating hand gesture, tossing her a knowing smile. 'Or I could ask someone else.'

She thought again of Johnny, of his constant attempts to upstage her in front of their boss, how he would revel in this opportunity to do Emsworth's special bidding.

'No,' she said quickly, telling herself she was just being a jobsworth for her doubts; this was her boss after all. Besides, no one would ever know. Bags were only frisked coming into the building – never on the way out . . .

'I can do it,' Gabriela said. 'Just tell me what you need.'

When he came to her a while later and asked that she probe Madeleine for details of work she was doing in Krakow, where she had unfathomably managed to bag herself a placement instead of Dubai within weeks of Gabriela leaving for Moscow, alarm bells finally started to ring with an urgency she couldn't ignore. She knew from their intermittent emails while they were both away that Madeleine was immersed in a pre-existing operation there, working to infiltrate a human trafficking ring, which had little reason to concern Emsworth, removed as it was from his jurisdiction.

And yet that was no longer entirely true, was it? During Gabriela's time in Moscow, the Counter-Terrorism department to which she was assigned had started to work with other units in the organisation on a case involving a highly complex and far-reaching network of criminals with links to human trafficking, VAT fraud and arms trading. Departments could not work wholly distinctly from one another, and the overlap in this case, which straddled various parts of the organisation, would go some way to explaining the files Emsworth had asked her to pull up, which concerned the movement of goods between the UK and parts of Central Africa. Although what it didn't account for was his reticence to pull the files himself.

Gabriela and Emsworth were seated at his favourite table at the Italian bistro on Crown Passage, and she felt the pasta stick in her throat when he raised the Madeleine question.

'Could you not ask her?' Gabriela replied.

The look he gave her made her skin burn.

'It's just that I know we're being encouraged to work together, but I didn't think it was protocol for someone of my level to monitor another department's work . . .'

He paused, lowering his voice, leaning in so that she could smell the red wine on his breath.

'Be that as it may, it's also in our interests to make sure we're not being kept out of the loop with things that might serve our own investigations. You and I both know that we're very willing to share our findings with other departments, but sometimes others aren't so forthcoming. Egos get in the way, you know what it's like. I just want to make sure we have all the information available to us, and I know you and Madeleine are close.' He stopped, considering me before deciding to carry on. 'Look, this is completely between us, but we have to be a bit careful about who we speak to. It would seem there's a leak somewhere; information relating to this case has been flowing into the wrong hands.'

'What do you mean?' She sat straighter and he shrugged, as if in defeat.

'I mean just that. We have a mole. And I'm not for a moment suggesting that your friend is tied up in it . . . All I know is that we have to be careful about who we say what to. Besides, if there is information available that could be useful to our work, I want to be sure we have access to it, without jeopardising anything else. You understand?'

She nodded.

He refilled their glasses. 'I'm glad you challenged me on it, though. It's admirable. I know you young ones like to follow the rules, but take it from me: that isn't always the best way to get things done. You know? Sometimes you have to use your initiative. I mean, this is national security we're talking about, not a school exam. You don't get prefect points in the real world, not when lives are at stake.'

He was full of shit, but she knew she needed to help him – or rather, she needed him to believe she would. Rumours had started flying by that point about an opening for a long-term tenure in New York attached to the UN, and despite only having been on one posting, she reckoned she could feasibly apply, if she put in the hours, reminding her superiors of how keen and able she was.

She had no way of knowing how far in over her head she was being dragged.

When the exhaustion kicked in a few weeks later, she brushed it off as a natural reaction to an intense period of readjustment. It was a shock coming back to London from a culture so wildly different to her own. Going from that life to this, it was enough to explain away the sudden mid-morning slumps at her desk, the evenings she found herself passing out on the sofa before dinner, Tom reading a book or strumming endless bloody chords beside her when all she longed for was silence. And then the sickness started, the gassy, bloated sensation that made her both ravenous and unable to nibble more than a mouthful of anything with a more complex flavour than toasted cheese.

She had watched women at work, brilliant women, slide down the ladder after they had children; you could almost see it, the drive they once had draining out of them, like blood seeping from an open wound until there was no life left in them.

'I take it this wasn't planned?' the doctor asked gently as she stared back, tears welling defiantly in her eyes, the words ringing in her ears: *You're pregnant.*

'No.'

'So you'll need some time to think through the options . . .'

'I don't want it,' she said, her voice absolute.

The doctor nodded thoughtfully. 'I understand. But you might feel differently, given time . . . It's a big decision and there is no harm in taking a couple of days to think it through . . .'

'I don't want it,' she repeated.

The doctor paused, and then turned to her computer.

'OK, well if you want to make an appointment with the sexual health clinic, they'll explain everything that's involved and then you can make an informed decision.'

Gabriela nodded curtly. 'Thank you. I will.'

* * *

She didn't tell Tom. She didn't need to make an excuse to slip away to the women's centre one morning before work. After all, she was barely showing, certainly no more than the sort of post-pizza distension which caused her to protrude with what Tom had endearingly labelled her recurring food baby (*'We could name her Margherita'*), and certainly not significantly enough to provoke any sort of unwanted questioning, either at work or at home.

The nurse at the clinic shrugged this point away when she raised it at her appointment a few days after checking in with the GP, presenting her relatively unchanged body as possible evidence that they had got it wrong about how far gone she was. 'Different women respond differently to pregnancy, physically and emotionally. Though to be honest not all women do show this early on – it's mainly wind that makes the belly pop out at this stage . . . We can get a more accurate reading on dates once we've done the scan,' the nurse said, making her quiet assessment with a glance that said she had seen women like her a thousand times before.

She led Gabriela back through the waiting room, past the faces pressed firmly into phones and magazines, avoiding eye contact.

'Have you had a scan like this before?'

Gabriela shook her head.

'OK, so I'll need you to lie back on the bed there for me . . .'

She pulled the curtain around them so that the world they inhabited was suddenly very small.

Rubbing the cold gel against Gabriela's abdomen, she pointed to the monitor with her other hand. 'That's where we'll see the foetus, which I'll measure in various points, to give us a better indication of where we're at.'

Gabriela swallowed and instinctively turned away from the screen, averting her gaze as the shape took form. In hindsight, she couldn't say what changed. She didn't know what happened between pulling up her trousers, jolting at the sensation of the cold gel rubbing against her shirt and the short walk back to the consulting room, but less than ten minutes later, she knew in her bones that she couldn't get rid of it.

'So, the GP wasn't far off with her calculations. It looks like you're almost twelve weeks,' the nurse said, consulting her notes. 'That's still well within the time when you can safely have a termination. If that's what you want.'

Her mind was distracted, doing the maths. If she had become pregnant in January, not long after she got back from Russia, then she would be due in October.

'Which date?'

The question caught the nurse off-guard. 'Sorry?'

'Which date in October would it be due?'

'The twenty-sixth.'

Her mother's birthday.

She never told Tom about her trip to the doctor. When she presented it to him a couple of days after the appointment, once she'd confirmed in her own mind there was no way she could get rid of the baby, the news of their imminent shift into parenthood was met with unadulterated joy.

His parents back in Edinburgh were also thrilled, they said, but quick to point out that what with their age and Elsie's knees, they could not promise to be as hands-on as they might wish.

'Well, that's a relief.' Tom had whistled as he got off the phone from sharing their news.

'Stop it, I like your mum,' Gabriela retorted dutifully. Though she couldn't say she really felt much beyond a sort of anthropological curiosity towards her and Graham, with their outdated views on the world, their days structured around mealtimes and whether it would be appropriate to use the formal or informal cutlery sets. It was a wonder that Tom had turned out as well-adjusted as he was.

'Are you OK?' he asked a couple of days after the revelation, noting her muted smiles as he swelled with excitement at the prospect of a child, clucking around the living room, fetching her pillows she didn't need and googling vitamins, like her pregnancy was a school science project for which he was determined to win first prize.

'Course,' she said.

He sat beside her, taking her wrist in his hand and squeezing it gently. 'You seem worried.'

She shrugged. 'It's just a bit of a shock.'

'You don't need to worry, you know that. This doesn't have to change anything, except for the better.'

She wanted so badly to share his enthusiasm, but already she felt herself depleted.

'What if I can't do it?'

'Do what?'

'Be a mother,' she said before she could think it through, adding quickly, 'you know, with my job . . . things are already so full on.'

'You'll be an amazing mum,' he replied, unfazed. 'Why wouldn't you be? Once the baby's here, you'll see. Besides, you have me. You'll never be alone.'

The words, even then, felt like both a promise and a threat.

Chapter 10

Isobel

At 8p.m. I am awoken by the sound of a door slamming. For a moment I lie uneasily in the dark, imagining a figure slipping through the hallway. I hold my breath, straining to hear a noise. The flat is unusually still and I pull the sheet more tightly around me, hardly daring to breathe.

Hauling myself out of bed, I take the other half of the Xanax and down a glass of water from the counter before moving quickly back to bed, vaguely aware of the sound of water dripping from the tap as I finally pass out again. When my eyes peel open once more it is 2.56a.m. I see the numbers glowing red from the clock resting on the chair. The chemicals from the night before are still moving through my bloodstream like a virus, but within seconds I am alert, something pulling me into consciousness, drawing me back out of bed into the main living space.

It is cold as I move through the darkness, registering the sensations of the crackled silence, the putrid glare of the streetlights jutting in through the blinds.

'Hello?'

Nothing looks out of place, at least no more so than usual; there is the same scattering of clothes and books, the overflowing ashtrays and empty bottles. The unopened bills piled on the kitchen table alongside several used mugs. Yet, despite the exquisite silence – the shrieks of the outside world temporarily muted – the room rattles with the feeling that I am not alone.

'Hello?' I say again. Grabbing an empty whisky bottle from the floor, I hold it outstretched, working hard to focus my vision as I walk slowly towards the door. The blood pounding through my body now, I lift the bottle a little above my head with one hand and wrench open the front door with the other . . .

As I step onto the landing, I see it at once, at the bottom of the stairs amidst a pool of shattered glass.

Holding onto the wall for support, I reach the bottom of the stairs and lean over to pick up the brick. The words on the note, as I peel off the elastic band, are a childish scrawl: *KEEP YOUR MOUTH SHUT.*

Chapter 11

Gabriela

It was a perfect spring morning, the sunlight reflecting along the tops of the buildings that stretched up King Charles Street as she approached the office, early enough that the tourists who flocked to this part of Westminster had not yet clogged the streets. The sky glistened, as if in anticipation, and she felt a rush of pride as she moved in synch with the conveyor belt of civil servants and politicians, their shoes clipping the pavement as they made their way purposefully towards their respective offices.

Looking up, she could almost feel the power bouncing off the buildings: the decisions being made, deals thrashed out, the phone lines fizzing with the dynamics of cause and effect, reaching from one continent to another.

At four months pregnant, the sickness had finally subsided and with it the fatigue that had taken hold in those early weeks. The pallid colour of her cheeks, which colleagues had joked was the result of her time spent in Russia, gorging on dumplings and vodka in a serotonin-deprived purgatory, had lifted in the second trimester so that she felt brighter than she had in a long time as she sashayed through the doors at KCS.

Tom had been brought on to a project in Shoreditch a couple of weeks earlier, which could last until just before Gabriela was due to give birth. They had spent the previous evenings ironing out the details: she would stay at work until a week before her due date, and then take a few months off before returning to her job full-time, when Tom would step in as the primary carer.

She had felt a rush of confidence about her plan to inform the office of her pregnancy that morning as she headed off towards the tube station, Tom squeezing her arm lightly as he saw her off with the words, 'You've got nothing to worry about.'

'Morning, Lauren,' she greeted Emsworth's secretary as she approached her desk, her eyes surreptitiously casting around for signs of her boss in his office.

'Good morning.' Lauren smiled, looking up from her computer screen.

'Is he in?'

'Not yet. He's in meetings all morning, let me check . . . OK, he has a lunch later but it looks like he'll be back by three . . .'

She managed a smile, pushing down her disappointment at being made to wait. Already the buoyancy she'd felt on her way in, her belief that everything would turn out well, that all she needed to do was to be upfront and give plenty of notice as to her situation, had started to wane. As if attuned to impending disaster, the minute hand crept ever more slowly around the clock over the course of the morning, towards the end of days.

'Gabriela, Lauren tells me you wanted to see me?'

It was quarter to four by the time Emsworth arrived at her desk, his eyes shining with drink.

Glancing around the open-plan room, noticing the heads pretending not to be listening, she stood. 'Do you mind if we speak somewhere more private?'

Emsworth paused before holding out a hand in the direction of his office.

'I've just been having lunch with a few colleagues, one of whom you met in Moscow – Peter Bradford, you remember him? He was very impressed, speaks highly of you . . . Do take a seat,' he said, holding the door open for her.

'Yes, of course,' she said, picturing Bradford's face at one of the long dinners held by the embassy, his hand holding onto hers a moment too long as they were introduced. He and Emsworth were clearly cut from the same cloth.

'It sounds like you settled in extremely well over there . . .'

'I loved it,' she nodded, feeling a tug of emotion.

'Good. Excellent. Well, we're delighted with your work. Now, what did you want to tell me? Does this have anything to do with Madeleine?'

Gabriela paused, confused for a moment before remembering Emsworth's request, which had not so much slipped her mind as been shoved aside. Of course she wouldn't spy on Madeleine, she didn't need to. Whomever the source of the leak was, Madeleine had nothing to do with it.

'No, I've been struggling to get hold of her,' Gabriela lied.

There was no easy way to deliver her real news, and so with a sharp inhalation of breath, she said it, keeping her face as bright as she could: 'I'm pregnant.'

There was a moment's hesitation as Emsworth kept his gaze steady, the carefully arranged smile at his mouth barely flickering, and then he replied, 'Gosh, congratulations.'

'It's due in October,' she added, trying her best to keep the conversation businesslike, to keep control of negotiations, as if this was nothing but another event in the timeline of her career.

'So I'll be off for six months and then back in April next year. I was thinking I could start to take on a bit more responsibility over the next few months, in preparation for—'

He cut her off. 'Oh, there's no need to be worrying about that. Not now.' His tone had shifted, in a way that would be barely perceptible if she hadn't worked with him for so long.

'OK, I just want to make sure that you know that my commitment to this job hasn't changed. If anything, it's stronger. I still very much want to move up the ranks, and—'

Once again, he silenced her, this time with a slightly raised hand.

'Gabriela, think no more of it.' He stood, indicating that it was time for her to do the same.

The day she went on maternity leave, Emsworth was not in the office.

'He went on annual leave yesterday,' Lauren confirmed when Gabriela asked, having already packed up a pathetically small box of possessions from her desk, a 'good luck' card awkwardly signed by a few of her colleagues (*All the best with it!*) balanced precariously on the top.

'Really? But he didn't say—' Her cheeks reddened as Lauren looked back at her impassively, her expression a simple shrug conveying the words Gabriela knew she was thinking: *And?*

Emsworth had hardly spoken to her since that meeting in his office. He had certainly never asked about Madeleine again, even after her return from Krakow a few weeks later. At this point, Gabriela simply assumed he had forgotten that he'd ever suggested she probe her colleague for information, or that perhaps he had found an alternative explanation. Whatever his reasons were, if he could forget the incident then so could she.

She had almost blurted it out in a moment of heightened emotion at the farewell drinks Madeleine had arranged in Gabriela's honour the week before she went on leave, dragging her along to a pub on Derby Place. But as soon as she opened her mouth to speak, she felt herself pull back.

There would be no point warning Madeleine; it wasn't like she had anything to hide. And Gabriela knew that if she did tell, Madeleine's temper would mean she would be unable to resist confronting Emsworth, and that would backfire on both of them. Especially with Gabriela about to bugger off on maternity leave, she couldn't afford to give him a single reason not to support her.

Pushing the words back in before they could form on her tongue, Gabriela had winced as she took a sip of red wine which tasted like paint stripper, lifting her glass to toast impending motherhood.

No. The easiest thing would be to forget he ever asked.

'How was your day?' Tom said when she got home, having walked along the river before boarding the train at Embankment, making the most of her last weeks of freedom as she instinctively saw them, before the baby arrived.

'Good,' she managed a smile as he swung his legs onto the sofa next to her.

'Glad to hear it. And the best thing is, now you're on leave you won't have to think about that place for months. And when you go back, you've got the promotion to look forward to. It's all happening, babe.'

She leaned back, nodding along, not willing to tell him that the prospect of the job Emsworth had as good as told her was hers had been snatched away so violently that the palm of her hands stung. Because to tell him would mean to face it, to think about something that was easier to ignore than confront. So she didn't, telling herself that everything would be fine, imagining away the feeling of the unspoken lie swelling in her throat.

Chapter 12

Isobel

After a short deliberation, trembling in the pitch-black hallway of my flat, the air drifting in through the shards of broken glass, I decide against dialling 999. Even if I felt capable of having a rational conversation at three o'clock in the morning while dosed up on barbiturates, the idea of inviting the police into my home is not an option. For all I know, any one of the officers I work with on a day-to-day basis might turn up.

Somehow, after taping up the hole in the door with newspaper and Sellotape, I manage to fall back to sleep, and only wake again twelve hours later.

It is Sunday, I figure as I lie under the covers with my eyes closed, my mind blissfully devoid of thoughts beyond this moment; but then I see the patches of blood on the sheets, the cut on my hand from where I'd reached through the glass to pick up the brick, and the rest of the world comes hurtling back into view.

The note, scrawled on an otherwise innocuous piece of white paper in childish handwriting, still lies on the table as I move into the kitchen. After taking a shower to clear my head, washing the blood from my hand and my chin, I pick out an outfit at random from the pile of clothes strewn around my bed, feeling in my coat pocket for my keys, and only then remember the missing purse and shoes. I make a mental note to call the bank as soon as I get to the newspaper offices tomorrow to order a new card. It can wait that long – it isn't like there is any money in my account to steal between now and then.

Sweeping a handful of pound coins from the counter into my palm, I pour a whisky to take the edge off the headache that has taken hold and close my eyes at the soothing, burning sensation against the back of my throat.

Kentish Town police station is just a short stroll from the flat, and I take the back route to get there, cutting through the Stables market, breathing in the familiar scent of burnt falafel and cheap incense.

The brisk afternoon sun has already receded behind the buildings as I settle on the steps of the station, fifteen minutes later, to finish my cigarette before heading inside.

The officer behind the glass counter pronounces her words pointedly, looking at her watch as she draws her conclusion.

'So you saw something happen, when was it – *Saturday morning*? Although why you didn't report the matter at the time . . .' I clench my jaw, my fingers pushing against the counter, out of her view. *I'm sorry,* I imagine telling her. *I desperately wanted to say something but I was off my face on a variety of Class A drugs, and I knew that not only would you not believe a word I said but that thanks to the completely lopsided and ineffectual drug laws you have chosen a career to uphold, you might also have foreseeably had me arrested, thus risking my job, my livelihood and my home.* I say nothing, and she continues.

'All I am saying to you now is that I can't quite see the connection between this . . . *incident* . . . and the brick that you say was thrown through your door some twenty-four hours later . . .' the woman continues and I hold her eye for a moment before pulling away, nodding as I walk out of the station, pulling out another cigarette and feeling a shiver as I light up.

Despite the officer's implication that the attack I'd witnessed on the Heath and the brick through my window hours later were most likely unrelated – if indeed she had believed me that either event had actually happened at all – I can't ignore the tightening in my chest as I walk – every car horn, every bustling body a threat as I move along Kentish Town High Street.

Unable to shake the unbidden soundtrack in my head, I toss the half-smoked fag in the gutter and enter the loudest pub I can find and order a large whisky, allowing my thoughts to be drowned out by the churning of the crowds. It's the same pub where Maureen and I had first met, just a couple of streets away from the refuge she runs, but today as I scan the bar she is nowhere to be seen.

Once the drink starts to take the edge off, helped along by the half of Xanax I slipped into my mouth as I left the police station, the anxiety clinging to my chest loosens its grip.

Regardless of what the police officer had suggested, what I had seen was more than a lovers' tiff. Still conscious of the breath drawing in and out of my lungs, I work through the facts in palatable fractions. What had I really seen?

Wrestling with myself, with the other memories that threaten to overshadow this one, I allow a picture of the girl's face to form; concentrating my mind on the area around her head, her face moving more clearly into focus as I do so, like a magic eye picture taking shape. Swallowing a mouthful of whisky, I see her eyes blink open and shut, her face white and glazed over. As the image gains clarity, it shifts so that suddenly the eyes in front of me are someone else's, and now it is all too much.

Unable to differentiate between the two events in my memory, I feel a pair of hands grabbing my shoulders and pulling me away.

No, get off me!

I don't know I've spoken aloud, but when I look up the barman is standing in front of me, proffering the bottle, a concerned look on his face.

'No, you're all right, Ted,' I say after a moment, pushing my stool back. 'I'm going to head off.'

'OK,' he says, every eye in the pub turning to watch me leave. 'You take care of yourself.'

* * *

By the time I arrive back in Camden, a police cordon is stretched across two bus stops opposite my flat. I recognise the officers guarding the area from a glorified puff piece I was forced to work on a while back about community policing initiatives, as part of management's attempt to ingratiate itself with the local force.

'PC Allan?' I say, fixing him with my best smile as I approach. 'What's going on?'

'Another stabbing. Couple of Somers Town kids, usual shit. Obviously don't quote me on that . . .'

'Fuck,' I reply, shaking my head. 'You're all right, it's Sunday, I'm not working. That's my flat.' I point to a dark window above the newsagent's, a boarded-up shop on one side, a kebab shop on the other.

'Actually, don't go anywhere. I'll be back in a minute. I'm just going to get a pad . . .'

As I walk past the phone box, I flinch at the outline of a ghost-like figure through the glass, but when I look again I see it is my own reflection.

Chapter 13

Gabriela

It is a cliché to say that having a baby changes a person, but the day Sadie was born, Gabriela and Tom became different people.

'You should rest,' the midwife said, once the baby had taken her first feed. Gabriela was weak and grateful for the nurse's capable hands as they stretched towards her, taking Sadie and placing her tiny body in the tiny plastic cot next to the bed, then pushing it towards the pillow end, within easy reach.

'Are you sure you don't want to sleep with her next to you?' Tom asked, and Gabriela was grateful when the midwife interfered.

'We prefer if the baby stays in the cot. It's safer that way.'

Gabriela could see that he wanted to argue with her on that point, according to the parenting books on attachment he'd started to read and to cite in the weeks before their daughter arrived, as if it was his body, not hers, she would be attached to.

When Tom disappeared behind the curtain in search of a cup of tea, leaving Gabriela alone with her daughter, she felt like she'd been placed in the middle of the ocean and her life-raft was drifting away from her, the force of the love for her baby and the helplessness she felt in this moment threatening to drown them both, to dice her into pieces of herself that could never be put back together. She felt the severing as a series of sharp stabbing pains in the taxi home from the hospital the day they were discharged, Sadie asleep in the car-seat behind her, the pain slicing at her insides every time they went over a speed bump, serving as a reminder that her body – and her life – were no longer her own.

Whatever scene she had painted in her head of what maternity leave would look like, the image was obscured by Tom's constant shadow. He didn't hover over Sadie the way she did, anxiously checking her daughter's breath on a hand mirror in the middle of the night to make sure she was still alive, but rather he simply couldn't leave Sadie – or her – alone.

'Where are you going?' he asked for the tenth time, the day they were discharged.

'Just to the loo, going to try doing a piss without pulling out a stitch, if that's all right with you?' she snapped and he winced.

'Sorry,' he said, looking hurt.

'It's fine. I know you're just trying to help.' She brushed his head with her fingertips as she passed. And he was, but the more he tried to do for her the more she wished he would back the hell off.

It wasn't fair, to find herself aggrieved by his constant offers of help, to feel a swell of resentment for the disproportionate impact of their daughter's birth on her life compared to his, for how liberated he was to enjoy their new circumstances free from the physical and hormonal shifts of becoming a mother. Yet some days the rage she felt towards him was so great she would fathom excuses to leave the house: an imagined errand she'd announce before heading out to sit on a bench on the Heath, smoking a cigarette. And then she'd come home and find Tom and Sadie asleep on the sofa, his body curled protectively around hers, and she would find herself suddenly overwhelmed by a surge of love. Hating herself, she would sit and watch her daughter's tiny fingers clutching Tom's thumb as if she sensed that something was coming for them in this world she had suddenly been propelled into, and she had to hold on for dear life. The urge Gabriela felt to protect her child, to protect all of them, in those moments, was so strong, so all-consuming, that she couldn't imagine that anything would ever tear them apart. She couldn't have foreseen the force of the wave that would sweep them all up, and then spit them out again so far from home.

'What's wrong?'

'I can't get the breast pump to work,' she said, pushing at the valve that was failing to connect to the tube, the evening before she was due to go back to work.

'What's wrong with it?' Tom asked, taking it from her gently.

'I don't know what's wrong with it, that's the problem,' she snapped, and Tom held up his hands.

'Just trying to help.'

'Massive help,' she muttered under her breath as he moved out of the line of fire, putting on the kettle, because all any of them ever needed was a cup of fucking tea.

'I just don't know how I'm supposed to work properly when I can't think straight, when my tits explode every time she makes a bloody noise,' she cried later, once Sadie was down for the night and it was just him and her on the sofa making their way through the remains of the previous night's takeaway.

'Are you sure you want to go back so soon?'

'Seriously, Tom, is that supposed to be helpful?'

He lifted up his hands in an act of surrender. 'I'm just responding to what you're saying. There is no pressure from me for you to go back to work so soon. That's all.'

'Right, and you'll pay the mortgage?'

'I can get a job, Gabriela, you're not the only person in this house with a brain. Jesus, you're the one who said you wanted me to stay home with the baby and for you to w—'

She exhaled loudly. 'Please, can we not argue? I'm just worried. I'm allowed to be worried, aren't I?

* * *

83

There was someone else at her desk when she arrived at the office the following morning, dressed in the newly expansive suit trousers and blouse she'd bought to mark her return to work.

'Hi,' she said to the girl in her seat, who was wearing trainers and jeans and made Gabriela feel about 300 years old.

'Hi,' the young woman said, looking up as she continued to type, as if waiting for Gabriela to ask her a question. Her hair was pulled into a long dark ponytail and her fine fingers danced over the keyboard even as she maintained eye contact.

'I'm Serena.'

'Gabriela.'

Again there was an uncomfortable silence, so Gabriela said, 'I've just come back from maternity leave, this is – this *was* – my desk . . .'

Blushing, Serena stood. 'Oh God, sorry. I started a couple of months ago and this has been my desk ever since. Nobody mentioned . . .' Her voice petered out and she waited there awkwardly, as if unsure whether to clear a space on the desk beside her.

Gabriela held out a hand, trying to keep the unreasonable level of contempt she felt off her face. 'It's fine, I'll wait until Lauren gets here. I'll just pop to the café . . .'

'I'm really sorry,' Serena called after her and Gabriela shook her head, reassuring her not to worry, telling herself it was just a misunderstanding.

'You'll be sitting here now,' Lauren explained an hour later, pointing to a smaller desk at the far end of the office, not mentioning that this put her as far away from Emsworth as was conceivable without hanging her from the window by a noose.

'Sure,' Gabriela said, trying to smile.

If she had been under any illusion as to whether or not Emsworth still intended to put her forward for the promotion once she'd had the baby, that illusion was instantly shattered, scattering shards as sharp as glass which lodged themselves in her skin.

'Welcome back, Gabriela,' he managed a few days later, sweeping past her desk and patting her shoulder briskly as he continued moving through the office towards Serena.

'You should go home,' Madeleine insisted on her way out, later that day. Glancing at the desks which were largely empty aside from Johnny who was still beavering away, she placed a hand on Gabriela's shoulder.

'Come on. Presenteeism is horribly passé, Gabs. Besides, none of these guys will give you any credit for being the last person here – I don't think your daughter will thank you for it either . . .'

'All right,' she snapped. It was easy for Madeleine to say, having made a niche for herself working government-to-government under the Multilateral Policy Directorate, between London and Krakow, while Gabriela was at home grappling with the benefits of reusable vs disposable nappies.

Madeleine might have been able to bypass Emsworth and his whims and grab the role that she was due with both arms, but Gabriela was stuck, and the only way to prove she was equally serious about her job, now that she had the baby, was to push herself into the sightline of superiors from other departments.

'I'm just saying, there are more important things in life. Go home to your family,' Madeleine said, leaning down to kiss her friend on the cheek as she made to leave, her skin electrifying as their cheeks touched.

Chapter 14

Gabriela

'So what's new?' Gabriela asked Madeleine a few weeks later as she lit her cigarette at the bottom of the stairs that led from KCS to the park.

Madeleine shrugged. 'You know, this and that.'

There was something about her tone, the way she exhaled without looking at her that made Gabriela study her face more intently. 'What does that mean?'

Madeleine was a terrible liar. 'We've been told we have to be careful about how much we share with other departments.'

Gabriela paused. 'OK. But it's just me.'

'I know,' Madeleine said, facing her briefly and then looking away again.

'What aren't you supposed to talk about?'

'Gabs, please don't ask me to talk about stuff that I've just told you I can't talk about.'

Gabriela's mind spun back to the conversation with Emsworth, his mention of information finding its way into 'the wrong hands'.

She paused, compelled to press Madeleine further, but one look at her face told her not to bother. Yet how could she feel hurt by her friend's refusal to confide? It wasn't like Madeleine was the only one who had chosen to keep secrets.

* * *

It was a few days later and everyone else seemed to have cleared off when Gabriela went to the printer to collect some documents she needed before finishing up for the day. As she approached, she heard the whirring of the machine and suddenly felt Emsworth push ahead of her.

'I think that's mine,' he said firmly, and instinctively she took a step back.

'Sorry.'

'No problem.' He smiled tightly before heading back to his office and filing the papers into his bag.

She waited where she was, collecting her own documents and then lingering until she saw him head out towards the loo.

Before she could second-guess what she was doing, she felt herself move towards his office, making her way straight towards his bag and pulling out the papers, her heart pounding in her throat. Flicking through, she had barely scanned the first page when she heard a flushing from down the hall. Pulling her phone from her pocket, she took a photo of the first page then stuffed the papers back into the bag and ran back out into the office, making it to Lauren's desk just as Emsworth moved back into the room.

'Still here?' he said.

'Just finishing up,' she replied, not daring to meet his eye, hoping he did not notice her quickened breath.

Walking to the tube station twenty minutes later, she couldn't shake the feeling she was being watched. With a quick glance behind her shoulder, she faced forward again and pushed the idea out of her mind, putting it down to the sense of guilt for what she'd snuck a look at, distracting herself from the lingering sense of unease by committing to memory the name she had just seen on the paper: *Francisco Nguema.*

Chapter 15

Gabriela

'You're coming to this Christmas lunch?'

The first thing Gabriela saw of Madeleine was her perfectly painted fingernails tapping rhythmically against the corner of her desk. When she finally looked up from her notes, she smiled and pushed her chair back so as to get a proper look at her, the sequin pencil skirt and low-cut leotard.

Giving a wolf whistle, Gabriela raised her eyebrows. 'Wowzers, glad to see you're getting into the spirit of it. To be honest, I didn't see you as a natural enthusiast for this sort of thing.'

'Bof.' Madeleine raised her eyebrows. 'Let's just say I have my mind set on a certain present this year.'

Without turning, she indicated Serena, who was laughing effusively with one of the guys from Operations.

'Oh God, not you too—'

Madeleine kissed her teeth. 'So, you coming or what? You can be my wing-woman.'

Gabriela groaned, leaning into her desk drawer, pulling out the Christmas bauble earrings that Tom had presented her with the night before. Afterwards, he'd shown her the miniature reindeer outfit he had picked out for Sadie, his face creasing with laughter as their daughter teetered like a reckless drunk at a stag party across the living room which already felt ten times smaller than when it was just the two of them, incapable of holding her in.

For all its faults, not least the way her once buoyant career was toppling towards a dizzying freefall, the system Tom and Gabriela had created had started to work. After months spent finding their feet, feeling out the balance of power, they had in many ways adjusted to the new rhythm of their lives.

Of course it wasn't perfect, but what arrangement was? Their familial set-up was a work-in-progress, she reasoned to herself in moments of doubt – a temporary solution until Sadie went to nursery, at which point Tom would return to freelance work. The firm he had been working for ad hoc on the project in Shoreditch was rolling out its operations and would be keen to have him back, they said, just as soon as he was ready. And by then, she would have worked her way back up the ladder, having regained the trust of her superiors. At that point she would be free to give Emsworth the two fingers he so royally deserved.

'Too-wit too-woo,' Tom had wolf-whistled when she walked into the kitchen that morning, where he was doling out slices of buttery toast to Sadie, Chet Baker flooding out from the stereo.

'Look at how hot your mum is,' he said, nudging Sadie with his elbow. 'You can see why I put up with her, can't you? Even if she's going out on the razz again.'

She laughed, rolling her eyes. 'I'm sorry. To be honest, I'd actually rather not go. I'm bloody knackered.'

'It's fine,' he said. 'You have to be there. Anyway, there's an episode of *In The Night Garden* we haven't watched yet and I for one am extremely excited about it. You just never know what Igglepiggle will do next . . . Isn't that right, Sadie?'

Sadie looked up at him, her expression wide with love, her chin shiny and smeared with crumbs, and when she and Tom caught each other's eye, for a moment Gabriela didn't want to leave.

'I'll call you later,' she called out as the milk in the pan ran over, making a hissing noise as it hit the flame of the hob. Tom ran to the cooker, swearing under his breath as she leaned in to kiss their daughter on her head, dodging her greasy fingers as Sadie reached out to touch her, scared she would ruin the only dress she seemed to fit into these days.

An hour later, she pulled at the hemline, which felt shorter than usual as she made her way up the stairs towards the allotted room in the suitably archaic pub in town someone in the office had booked for the annual Christmas lunch. As she and Madeleine walked in, Gabriela spotted Emsworth engaged in conversation with a couple of senior faces she recognised from other departments.

Feeling Madeleine's hand on her arm, she followed her beeline for the table, decked with garish tinsel and essential-range crackers.

Madeleine placed her hand on the chair next to the one with Serena's coat hung over it. 'You're sitting there.' She tugged Gabriela's arm towards the chair on the other side of hers as their colleagues, already sloppy with drink, gathered around like scavengers in search of food.

'What are you having?' Madeleine asked as she grabbed a bottle of Chardonnay from the table, eyeing the label disapprovingly before pouring liberally.

'Whatever,' Gabriela replied, holding up her glass. The truth was, she didn't fancy an alcoholic drink at all. What she really wanted was a cup of tea and a bed to lie down in. By some cruel twist of fate, now that Sadie had finally decided to sleep through the night, Gabriela felt worse than ever. Every morning recently she seemed to wake up feeling more worn out than the night before, despite having a full eight hours' sleep. Some evenings, she found herself bypassing dinner altogether, passing out with her daughter tucked into her chest on the sofa, her body so weak that she thought she might never wake up.

But there was no way she was going to let these guys see that.

'Gabriela! Would you mind?'

It was Peter Bradford, pulling out the chair next to hers a while later as she took a gulp of her second glass of wine.

'Not at all! Peter, how lovely to see you again! I thought you were still in Moscow?' she said with a rush of exhilaration, tinged with discomfort.

'Oh, you know, taking a little break – thought I'd come and see what's going on in Blighty. I'll be back there in a few weeks. Between us, I'm moving into a new role in Human Rights and Democracy. I'll still be based in Moscow, so I'm just pulling some things together for the department this end before I head back . . . But enough about me – how are you? I hear there have been some changes since we last met?'

'Good,' she said, too quickly, her head still ringing with his words: *Human Rights and Democracy*. This was exactly where she wanted to be. A department reshuffle meant the possibility of a new opening . . .

'So what's the plan, with the new department?'

She knew it wasn't the subtle approach preferred by Bradford and his sort, who still favoured clandestine winks and backslaps over brandies in quiet members' clubs. But he would be going back to Moscow soon, and this might be the only chance she got to impress on him how keen she would be to apply. To remind him how useful she could be.

The sound of Madeleine laughing at something Serena had said drowned out her words and, reaching for the bread basket, Bradford continued, 'You've started a family, haven't you?'

'Yes, I have a little girl, Sadie. My partner looks after her . . .' she added quickly, desperate to move the conversation back to where it had been, to remind him how capable she was. How deserving of this chance.

'Wonderful stuff. We have three,' Bradford replied breezily, taking a mouthful. 'My advice to you would be quit while you're ahead. Ha!'

There was a sudden twinge in her stomach and a shuffle of chairs as she attempted to process his meaning – was he saying she should quit before having more children, or that she should quit the job?

'St John, old boy!' Suddenly Bradford was standing, before she could stop him, leaning in to shake the hands of a man in a tweed three-piece suit.

'Gabriela?' Madeleine's arm jabbed hers, and she turned, dismayed by how abruptly the previous interaction had ended.

'You guys know each other, right?' Madeleine asked, indicating towards Serena.

'Yes, I mean we haven't really . . . Hi,' Gabriela said, aware of her cheeks growing hot as she looked back over her shoulder, only to find Bradford had already gone.

When she looked back around Serena was smiling at her. 'Nice to meet you properly.'

Moving her attention back to Madeleine, she added, 'I'll meet you down there.'

'We're going for a smoke,' Madeleine said, and not knowing what else to do, Gabriela followed her. Pushing her way through the crowd, her eyes scanned the room for signs of Bradford, but by now it seemed all the upper echelons had left.

'Who are you looking for?' Madeleine asked once the two of them had settled in the pub garden.

'No one. What do you think of Emsworth?' Gabriela asked, suddenly unable to contain her thoughts, the wine having loosened her lips.

Madeleine snorted. 'I think you know very clearly what I think of him. The man's a complete —'

'Yeah but, more than that. I think he's . . .'

The moment she started talking, Madeleine looked up, her expression changing. 'What?'

'I don't know, there's just something . . .' Gabriela reached for the cigarettes, her fingers trembling with the cold. The sight of Johnny heading out with a couple of the lads stopped her in her tracks. As she inhaled the smoke from the cigarette, she coughed, feeling suddenly light-headed, holding onto the table with her free hand.

Madeleine turned to follow her gaze towards Johnny and the boys before turning back and considering Gabriela for a moment.

'Are you OK, Gabs? You look a bit—'

'I'm fine, just knackered as per fucking always,' she replied, glad for the conversation to be moving away from what she had just raised. This was not the time or place for such confidences; she was drunk. But she was only just starting her third glass, it wasn't like her to be so affected by wine.

'What happened to your girlfriend?' Gabriela asked, changing the subject.

'She's gone to the loo, and then she's getting her coat, ready to come back to mine.'

Gabriela couldn't be sure if she was being serious or not, and she couldn't summon the energy to pretend to give a shit, the headache that had begun to sneak up an hour or so earlier now reaching fever pitch.

'Seriously though, are you all right?'

'I feel terrible, actually.' She spoke quietly, subconsciously rubbing the base of her back with the tips of her fingers. 'I just— I don't know. End of the year, probably.'

There was a moment's pause and then Madeleine made a sound of acknowledgement. 'Oh my God, you're pregnant.'

'Piss off,' she said, taking a drag of her cigarette.

When she looked up, Madeleine was staring at her, an indecipherable expression moving across her face. 'You're pregnant.' She said it again, this time without inflection, and instantly the pain in Gabriela's head spread to her stomach.

'Of course I'm not pregnant,' she said, the words settling over her with a chill. Except, on the odd occasion when they had had sex recently, they hadn't exactly been careful.

'Hey, mind if I join you?' It was Serena, her face crooked with a smile as she wove her legs under the table next to Madeleine, stifling a hiccup.

'Oh my God, sorry, I've got hiccups! What are we talking about?' Serena said, too drunk to notice the loaded silence that had settled as Gabriela processed the dawning realisation she'd been suppressing over the past days, holding its head under water, ignoring the bubbles floating to the surface.

'Is she telling you about Hanoi? Urgh, I'm so fucking jealous. When are you leaving?'

Serena stopped then, finally aware of her own babbling, her eyes widening with an awkward recognition as the silence stretched out between us, even louder now.

'Hanoi?' Gabriela said, her voice quiet. 'You're going to Vietnam?'

Madeleine sniffed, taking a drag of her cigarette, and spoke more brightly than her expression suggested. 'I was about to tell you. The human trafficking work I started in Krakow . . . There's a sort of link-up with a new agency in Hanoi, part of an effort against modern slavery; they wanted someone to head up a team and – I go in January.'

'Shit,' Gabriela replied, her face breaking into a smile, tears forming at the corners of her eyes for reasons she couldn't fully fathom. 'That's amazing, Mads.'

Madeleine smiled back at her.

'It's what I wanted. I'll miss you.'

'I know,' Gabriela said, trying to keep her expression bright, suppressing the scream rising through her body. 'I'll miss you, too.'

'Hey, Gabs,' Madeleine asked a couple of days later, as Gabriela gathered her things at the end of the day, her mind distracted by the result of the pregnancy test she'd taken the previous day. 'You know what you started saying at the pub . . . About you know who.'

Madeleine glanced quickly around the office. Satisfied no one else could hear, she continued, 'What were you going to say?'

'Oh, you know,' Gabriela replied guardedly, wishing she'd never said anything – though she hadn't, not really. 'Just that he's a creep. Anyway, why should we give a shit? You'll be in Hanoi soon, and I'll be off popping out a baby.'

'Shit, I was right!' Madeleine said, laughing, and Gabriela tried to smile back at her, ignoring the clawing in the base of her belly.

Chapter 16

Isobel

I stop at my usual café on the three-minute walk to work the following morning and order a large coffee and croissant, which I pick at, once settled at my desk in the offices of *Camden News*.

The office spreads over two floors of a dilapidated Victorian terrace on the main road, wedged between an off-licence and a 99p shop. As usual I am the first one through the door. Ordinarily, it's the time of day I like best, cracks of light straining through horizontal plastic blinds, illuminating a space that once would have been the living room of an elegant town house, but is now characterised by cracked ceilings and floors, semi-carpeted with brown and green florals, and a series of messy desks.

I've worked in the office ever since joining the paper three years ago, months after dropping out of my second year of college. As usual, Jess was the one to pull me into shape, getting me a shoo-in onto the paper via a friend who did music reviews. Even after everything that has happened, they've made no effort to get rid of me.

Si's desk stands somewhere between mine and Ben's, a battered copy of *McNae's Essential Law for Journalists* and notes scrawled in shorthand strewn across it as testimony to the NCTJ training I never managed. He and Ben will be in soon, and at once the peace will be shattered. On another day I might have taken this moment to drink up the silence, to register the endless piles of papers and the smell of unloved carpet, grateful not to be working in a proper media office, like Jess's glass carbuncle a few streets away, with its upright leather sofas, mood boards and a coffee machine with individual colour-coded capsules.

Today, however, the space around my desk feels bare, like a carcass picked raw. Despite the October sunshine outside, there is a damp chill in the air which crawls over me, forcing me to pull my hooded jumper tightly around my waist.

Knowing it will be at least another hour until anyone else gets in, I light a cigarette before heading across the room to push open the large sash window. Hesitating, I spot a tiny gap where the window hasn't been properly shut. It explains the cold air seeping into the office from the dilapidated garden beyond. It also confirms that no one has done anything to fix the lock, which looks like it was fitted with the original window more than a hundred years ago.

It is just a matter of time before someone breaks in and helps themselves to the prehistoric computers, in the process destroying the order of the mountain of used reporters' pads dating back years – 'going digital' in this office means not replacing the broken fax machine.

I am preoccupied by my thoughts as I reach my desk, flicking for the number for Missing Persons in the Rolodex that contains the name of every official contact I've made in my three years as a reporter.

After two rings, the voice on the other end of the line answers.

'Hi,' I say. 'This is PC Taylor from Kentish Town. We've got a body and I need to check whether it matches anyone on your register . . . That would be great, thank you. Of course, my badge number is . . .'

Reaching into my back pocket, I retrieve the identification card I swiped from the PC on the front desk when her back was turned the day before. It is absurd that the Missing Persons register is only accessible to the police when surely it should be a matter of public record, I muse as I finger the badge, wondering how long it will have taken her to notice it is missing.

'No, we don't have an ID on her, but we do have a first name,' I reply. 'Eva. Looks like a female aged between sixteen and twenty-five, brown hair, brown eyes . . . That's no problem, I can hold.'

I feel my heart quicken as the woman at the end of the phone makes her search.

'Hi, thank you . . . Oh, I see,' I say a few moments later, trying not to let my disappointment show.

'I understand. Yes, please do hold onto the information and if anything crops up . . . I tell you what, I'll give you my direct line. PC Taylor, that's right . . .'

It is unlikely the call will come through – things are rarely so swift or straightforward – but if it does, I am not worried that my answer machine will give away my true identity. My voicemail greeting simply informs callers that I am away from my desk.

Hanging up, I light a cigarette and pick up the phone again. This time I try Maureen, out of the need for a companionable voice, if nothing else. In the years since we first met, at the pub next to the women's refuge Maureen runs just off Kentish Town High Street, she has proved one of my closest confidantes.

As Maureen's number goes to voicemail, I hang up and immediately the phone rings.

'Hello?' I say.

'Isobel, it's me.'

'Oscar, hi . . .'. There is something about his voice that still has an infantilising effect on me, though I am a month older than him, and I hate him for that above anything else.

'I've been trying to get hold of you,' I say.

'So I hear. I got your message from the station.'

'And?' I continue, waiting for the conversation to descend into the usual dressing down.

'And we're looking into it.'

'Really?'

'Sure, I'll call you in a bit.'

'OK,' I say, holding out the phone receiver in front of me as it goes dead.

At that moment the door opens and Ben, the News Editor, walks into the room.

'Isobel,' he says, throwing down a battered briefcase. 'Why the fuck aren't you at the council briefing?'

My ability to compartmentalise is one of the things that makes me so good at my job, Ben will occasionally concede after the several pints it takes for him to say anything vaguely complimentary to anyone. But apparently this time I've divided the many tasks in my mind so efficiently that I've completely forgotten the meeting that had nearly brought me out in hives to think of it on my way back from the party. Though, in my defence, there have been a couple of things to distract my attention since then.

'I've got something else I think you'll be interested in,' I say without stumbling. 'There was a stabbing on the high street at the weekend. The nationals haven't got a whiff of it yet, and off the record police confirmed that they're treating it as connected to the ongoing tensions between two rival gangs in Mornington Crescent I've been looking into . . .'

'That's my girl,' Ben says.

As I talk him through the details, I feel the events of Saturday morning begin to fade, the woman's face sweeping in and out of focus in my mind like a figure stepping in and out of the shadows, until, for the moment, she vanishes altogether.

Chapter 17

Gabriela

Madeleine was still in Vietnam by the time Callum was born, the following July, in a labour that lasted less than six hours from her first contraction to the moment Gabriela held him in her arms for the first time – on the same ward at the Whittington Hospital in which she'd been born three decades earlier.

'I was sure it would be another girl,' Gabriela whispered to Tom as their son blinked up at the world, their eyes meeting for the first time. He reminded her of an exotic bird fallen from its nest, a creature to which she had no more immediate connection than that of an anthropologist exploring new and treacherous lands.

She agreed to take the full year's leave after Callum was born, on Tom's request. He had been offered a job working on a residential project in Islington, with Jim. He had been so desperate to do it, and she had been keen to let him. She didn't want to always be the one calling the shots, and it was Tom's turn. Besides, she reasoned, she might enjoy it, the extra time with the kids, long walks on the Heath, building up a bond with Callum before heading back to work for good.

But within days of agreeing to it, the resentment started to build like a wall in her chest. Storming the streets of Dartmouth Park and Gospel Oak in those early weeks, desperate to get Callum to sleep, his relentless wailing rising from the double-buggy, for a moment she considered pushing the whole thing into the road. She didn't, but the fact that in that moment she had wanted to was enough to scare her, to prove that she had that in her, just below the surface. How easy, she thought, it would be to cross the line from which there was no return.

'He can smell your milk, that's all,' the health visitor said by way of comfort when she confided that she felt constantly hounded by him.

'Is it true that boys tend to be more needy?' she asked, desperate for confirmation that it wasn't a reflection of something she was doing wrong.

'I mean, they're babies. They *are* needy, because you're their mother – they need you to survive.' She said it as if it was the most simple thing in the world. It was ironic, she thought, that with the birth of her children, Gabriela should be granted the most powerful role in the world, and yet it was a role that made her feel completely and utterly impotent.

When Madeleine called to say she was in town and would Gabriela like to meet for lunch, it was like being offered a reprieve. She practically counted down the minutes to their meeting, which took place at Daphne's, an old family-run restaurant in an unassuming spot in the backstreets of Camden Town, roughly equidistant between her house and Madeleine's flat in Marylebone.

Leaving Callum with Tom, she couldn't shift the sense as she walked down Royal College Street that she was not alone. Putting it down to the anomalous feeling of going out for a grown-up lunch without the baby after so long, she refused to turn around. The moment she saw Madeleine at their usual table in the window, her red lips wrestling with a piece of bread, any concerns she had melted away.

'Look at you!' Madeleine beamed up at her, taking a moment to inspect Gabriela's features before kissing her warmly on both cheeks. 'I've missed this face.'

She smiled. 'Bloody hell, don't look too closely . . . I've slept about three minutes this week. Anyway, that is almost literally the most boring sentence I have ever uttered – sorry. Please can we get a drink before I start talking about hand, foot and mouth disease?'

Madeleine grimaced and Gabriela gave her a look that told her not to ask, though part of her wished she would.

'That's the attitude, and I'm one step ahead . . .' Madeleine passed her a glass of white wine from behind the menu propped on the table between them, and poured another for herself.

'The children, oh my God, how are they?'

'Well, Sadie is two and very sweet, and Callum is exhausting and gorgeous and has destroyed what was left of my tits, and that is the last word I'm going to say on the subject because I actually can't be trusted not to turn into a tedious wretch if I start chatting about my kids . . . Cheers.' she breathed in as she lifted her glass. 'God, I've missed you.'

Madeleine shrugged. 'You're only human . . . So you're looking forward to going back to work?'

Gabriela exhaled. 'I suppose so. I mean yes, desperately, just to get out of the house, to be doing something with my brain . . . But the office is actually intolerable without you. Emsworth, he's—' She took a gulp of her drink before leaning back, making a groaning noise. 'I just hate him.'

'Tell me something I don't know,' Madeleine said.

Gabrielle held her eye for a moment. 'OK then,' she said, a rush of excitement taking hold as she reached down into her bag and pulled out the envelope she had been carrying around for so long, as if challenging herself to say something, hardly believing she had finally found the nerve.

'So,' she said, bolstered by seeing Madeleine again, by this brief window into her other life, but still aware she was making an insinuation that she could never retract. 'Look, I don't know if it's anything, but when I was in Moscow, I saw Emsworth having a meeting. I don't know who with, but it was fucking weird. He made me swear not to tell anyone in the department that I'd seen him. It could be nothing but it didn't sit right . . . The way he was acting was . . . the whole thing was odd.'

Gabriela paused before sliding a photo across the table, looking away and carrying on before she could lose her nerve.

'I took this picture. And it's not just that. He's been printing off information. Papers relating to an African businessman called Francisco Nguema. When I looked him up in the files, it seems he is tied up in corrupt business dealings with a number of British businessmen, as well as internationally. There wasn't a photo but when I googled him. . . I think it's this guy.'

She pointed to the man in the suit.

When she looked up, Madeleine's eyes were shining. 'Bloody hell. You've been sitting on this since Moscow?'

Gabriela blushed. 'I'm sorry, Mads. Really, I wanted to tell you. I tried. I just. . .'

Madeleine shook her head. 'I get it. I mean I don't get it at all, you moron, but it's good that you told me. I'm sure as hell going to look into it.'

She breathed in. 'In the meantime, Miss bloody Marple, I've been wanting to ask you something too. . . How about, when you finish maternity leave, coming to work for me instead?'

Gabriela's whole body was vibrating with excitement as she left the restaurant.

Keen to escape the crowds that battled it out come rain or shine across the bars and pubs and the same market stalls selling the same tatty T-shirts and bongs, she headed past the doorway she and Saoirse would duck into as schoolgirls, having snuck out of school early to smoke bidis on the canal. Saoirse. When she thought of her now, she felt a pang of guilt. Jesus, how long had it been since they had last spoken? Had Gabriela even called to say thank you since their last trip to visit Saoirse and Jim at their new home near Teignmouth, having traded in hipster Hackney for the Devon coast?

She would ring her later, she told herself as she crossed the bridge before Chalk Farm Road and headed on to the canal. Walking west towards the zoo, she lifted her mind away from the towpath and the couples vying for space with cyclists, away from the weeping willow and the lawns extending down to the water where colourful boats pushed out plumes of smoke. Slowly, she allowed herself to think through Madeleine's offer of a new role on her return from maternity leave.

'I'm working on an ongoing project, coordinating efforts between different departments who work with victims of human trafficking from Vietnam, tackling the networks that facilitate the trafficking . . .' she had explained. 'The victims tend to end up in in nail bars, fruit-picking, sex work . . . I'm looking to bring someone in from the existing team in London to help tee up efforts here that at the moment are being made almost in isolation, with the objective that if we work unilaterally we can get the best results. A theory that one might have assumed would be par for the course in an organisation such as ours, unless, like us, you work for it . . .'

Tom was running a bath by the time Gabriela arrived home, just after six, a couple of parcels in her bag filled with gifts for the kids, and a compendium of modernist design for Tom which she suddenly panicked she might have bought for him the year before. It was only a fortnight until Christmas and she'd barely had a moment to think about presents, let alone putting up a tree, operating on the premise that anything that could present a physical hazard if tugged at would be instantly destroyed by Callum, the Human Detonator as Tom had affectionately renamed him.

'How was lunch?' Tom called out from the bathroom when he heard her feet on the stairs.

'It was good,' she said joining him, her eyes shining. 'And guess what?' She felt an energy rush when she considered it, unlike anything she had felt in years.

'I've been headhunted for a new role— Hello, my darlings . . .'
She leaned in to kiss her children on their heads.

'No way?' Tom looked as happy as she felt, his whole face lighting up to reflect hers. 'That's brilliant!'

The sincerity of his expression was touching, and she stopped to look at him for a moment, wondering how much she should tell him, before turning to pick up Callum from where he was propped in a bath-chair next to his sister, wrapping him in a towel and pulling him onto her knee as she perched at the edge of the toilet seat, for want of anywhere else to sit.

'So, what is it? Actually, look, I'll get Sadie out of the bath . . . Come on, Princess. And then I'm going to make us a drink and you can tell me all about it.'

'Thank you,' she said after a moment and Tom laughed.

'What for? I didn't do anything. If you're happy, I'm happy. You know that.'

She swallowed, aware of how true his words were.

Chapter 18

Isobel

I have to work fast; there's only so long I can hope to have a story like this to myself. With knife crime all the rage in the national press at the moment, it's just a matter of time before the bigger papers come sniffing around, wanting the number of a hard-won contact in return for a pitifully small *finder's fee* and absolutely no acknowledgement in their subsequent piece that the legwork wasn't theirs.

Hesitating for a moment, I reach below my desk and pull out a hardback black book, filled with names not kept in my Rolodex. The pages inside are floppy and worn, brimming with scraps of paper: names of old school friends and neighbours who've turned their hand to one line of work or another and proved useful contacts in the process, people who certainly wouldn't be willing to stand up in a court of law.

There are so few leads to go on, but there is one person I can rely on to talk. Standing, I pull my coat over my shoulders and head for the door.

I am on the 253 bus moving east down Camden Road when Oscar calls back. It is the same bus route I would take to sixth form college back in the days before my parents upped sticks to a shiny new house in the South of France the year after I left school, leaving me to move in with my long-term boyfriend.

'I've just been up to the Heath to have a look,' Oscar says, and I don't mention that I had just been thinking about him, that I am currently on the same bus we'd taken together so many times that I could almost feel him next to me, sharing a pair of earphones. Except now when I think of him, all I hear is the memory of my own screams.

Feeling my body lurch forward as the driver suddenly brakes at the junction with Holloway Road, I hold tightly to the handrail.

'Really?'

'There's nothing there, Is.'

I pause, trying to slow the conversation down. 'So you've been to the Heath already? I'd have come with you . . .'

My eyes flick to my phone screen: 10.57a.m. 'I mean, Jesus, it's not even eleven o'clock yet, you can't have been there long. Did you know exactly where to look? Maybe you missed something. I—'

'Issy, seriously, it's OK – there's nothing to worry about.' Oscar clears his throat, trying to sound upbeat. 'It looks like whatever you saw, it was nothing. Probably a couple of crackheads fighting over the last toot. You know what they're like . . .'

Of course I know. I want to shout down the phone, *Of course I fucking know.*

I keep my voice as level as I can. 'But what about the brick through my door?'

'Issy, what about the bloody brick? You can hardly say you're surprised. Frankly, I'm shocked it hasn't happened before. You're a journalist, for God's sake – and a pretty fucking relentless one at that – of course people want to shut you up. Christ, if I was a criminal I'd want you . . .'

His voice is running out of patience, hissing down the line. I imagine his colleagues have finally cleared the room and he can now speak freely.

'I mean, what the *hell* were you even doing in a bush on the Heath at six a.m., Issy? Seriously. Actually, please don't answer that.'

Stop calling me *Issy,* I want to shout at him.

I hear him cover the mouthpiece with his hand and mutter a greeting to someone before clearing his throat and resuming his lecture, his tone altered again.

'Sounds like you've had a bit of a mental weekend. Why don't you take a couple of hours, yeah? Go home and have a rest. I'm sure the paper will survive without you for one day . . .'

Holding the phone away from my ear, I find myself unable to speak, not that he notices.

'It would be good to see you soon anyway. Give me a shout if you're—' Before he can finish his sentence, I have ended the call and shoved my phone back in my pocket, pressing the button to stop the bus.

The warehouse stands on a secluded backstreet just off Holloway Road, a makeshift mixture of concrete and corrugated iron. Determinedly ignoring the gazes of a throng of builders nearby, I buzz the intercom and when a man's voice answers, I reply.

'I'm here to see Tariq.'

'Tariq ain't here.'

'Tell him it's Isobel,' I insist. 'Tell him it's important.'

I look up at the camera above my head. The voice goes briefly quiet and then a moment later the door clicks open, and I take a breath as the smell of skunk hits me inside the hallway.

By the time I reach the next internal door, the final bolt is pulled open by one of Tariq's minions. He looks me up and down with disapproval as I step into the room, and I hold his gaze before taking in the familiar scene: a makeshift bar on one side of the room, a pool table with men scattered around it casually smoking spliffs and talking in muted voices.

It's the same set-up every time, ever since I started coming along to these pop-up drugstores with Oscar when we were both still in sixth form college. Back then, it had taken more persuasion on his part to get me through the doors. Thankfully, Oscar had proved such a good customer in those days – the days before his dad found out what he was up to and forced him to sign up to the police station where he was top dog, and where he could push his son through the ranks – that he'd convinced them to let him bring in his girlfriend; it helped that

I had been in the year above Tariq's younger brother at school, meaning the kind of trust and connection that money couldn't buy.

Since then I've become a regular customer, and over the years have been increasingly impressed by the efficiency with which the operation is run. As a trusted client, you know that every few months or so the venue will change, and if you aren't there at the right time to get the new address, it's tough luck. The next time you try to ring, the phone line will be dead and the shop shut up, any trace of its existence gone for ever.

But it was more than weed that I'd managed to pick up over the ten years or so since my first visit. It was to this place, and so many others like it, that I had come for information which had led to a series of scoops involving rival drug dealers whom Tariq and his men had been only too happy to see wiped out.

I bite my lip, pushing away the memory, concentrating instead on the story ahead of me.

For fear of reprisals, I had written those past articles under a pseudonym; I didn't need to find out what happened to journalists who were found to be helping police uncover dealers, in return for exclusive tip-offs. Though anyone who watched the doors of the office at the newspaper would notice I was the only woman who walked in and out with any regularity, other than the receptionist, Elaine. It wouldn't take much of a dig to work out who was writing the stories. It isn't like there's a budget for freelancers these days.

The false name is helpful to sources like Tariq, though, who feel less exposed when talking to me, less concerned that a link will be made between him and his most unlikely customer.

What makes Tariq so appealing to me this morning, other than the lost hash that needs replacing, is that he grew up on the same estate that is now riddled with tensions assumed to be the root cause of the stabbing on the high street last night.

Even in the middle of the day, it's dark inside the warehouse as I walk towards the doorway at the back of the space where I see Tariq waiting, amidst a couple of old rolled-up carpets.

'Safe, Isobel,' he greets me once I am within greeting distance.

'Tariq,' I smile.

'Come in.' He indicates towards his office – a windowless room furnished with a desk, a chair and nothing else but a single calendar lining the wall.

'Business or pleasure?' he asks, pouring me a glass of water.

'Both,' I say and he raises his eyebrows.

'There was a stabbing at the 29 bus stop opposite my flat—'

'I heard.'

I pause. 'OK, that's a good start. I need a bit more about the gangs involved.' I raise my hand before he can object. 'Nothing on record, obviously. Just a bit of background. There's no way anyone could ever trace it back to you. You know how it goes.'

After his usual insistence that he has nothing to offer, Tariq won't shut up. As far as he is concerned, it's inevitable that as one group starts to take precedence, challenging the existing power, then there will be war.

By the time he's told me everything he knows about ongoing tensions in the estates around Somers Town, nearly an hour has passed.

'That's all I'm saying. If it's not this beef, it's some next beef. That's what it is on them estates. It never ends. Same thing round these ends, except here it ain't the Asians, it's some next level beef. You know me, I'm no racist, but seriously, it's too much. Now you look round, it's all Albanians, Romanians. I'm telling you, you don't even know about that. These Eastern Europe mans are aggy.'

He looks up, as if suddenly aware of how much he's said. 'Anyway, the other thing. How much?'

'A half,' I say and he nods. 'Isobel, man. You smoke too much.'

Chapter 19

Gabriela

They spent Easter before she was due to return to work at Tom's parents' house in Edinburgh, in their two-up two-down, which had clearly not been touched since 1973.

'We're only staying two nights,' Tom reminded her under his breath as they piled out of the estate car Tom had finally upgraded to, and made their way up the path, her carrying Callum, Sadie holding Tom's hand as if for dear life.

Though she had been dreading this trip and the prospect of playing happy families with Graham and Elsie – envisaging the rations of overcooked lamb before After Eights on the sofa with a highlighted copy of the *Radio Times* – in the end she rather enjoyed the change of scene. Knowing, as she did, that she would be starting a new role the week they got back, working under Madeleine's leadership, Gabriela felt a tension lift.

Watching her children play in the garden the morning after they arrived, hunting for the stash of colourful chocolate eggs Tom had smuggled in in spite of his mother's distaste for such commercialisation of a sacred holiday, she savoured the brisk air rubbing against her cheeks, making them tingle.

It was the closest to contentment she had felt in a long time.

'So when is Callum starting nursery?' Elsie addressed them over breakfast the next morning, and Gabriela felt Tom's muscles tense beside her.

'He's going to be with me for a while, like Sadie was,' he replied with a forthrightness that made the corners of Gabriela's mouth lift in appreciation.

Elsie raised her eyebrows, and Graham cleared his throat.

'That's right, with me,' Tom answered the unspoken question, smiling intently at his father. 'We think it's important that he's at home for as long as possible.'

'I agree, I always thought it was so important that a child stays with its mother,' Elsie replied without missing a beat, chewing her single slice of toast with such slight movements of the mouth that it was a wonder she ever made it through more than a single mouthful in one sitting.

Before Gabriela could say anything, she felt Tom's foot pressing against hers under the table. When she looked at him, he was fixing her with a gaze that pleaded with her not to bother, and so she didn't.

Working with Madeleine as the senior lead in London felt like a new lease of life. Madeleine was so straightforward, so gloriously capable and trusting of those to whom she delegated, and the sense of growth Gabriela felt under her reign was liberating.

While Madeleine coordinated with government agencies in Vietnam, it was Gabriela's job – with the help of a small team – to garner interest and negotiate ways of working not just to prevent trafficking to the UK but to support victims, liaising with relevant departmental leads whilst bringing these services together on the ground.

Eventually, Madeleine said, there would be the chance of another secondment, to one of the countries involved in the trafficking chain, anywhere from Pakistan to Belarus. But for now it was about forging relationships, setting up teams who could coordinate efforts from the UK.

Any concerns Gabriela might have had about potential tensions arising at home from her escalated role at work were immediately put at ease. If she'd worried Tom would feel resentful of the increasing time and resources she was ploughing into the job, there was no need. Almost the opposite was true; the harder she worked, the more satisfied she was when she came home. And the more delineated the roles between them were, the better they worked together as a team, even if inevitably compromises had to be made.

'A place has come up for two days a week at the children's centre. There's an open day, I thought we could have a look around,' Tom said one afternoon, calling her as she was heading into a meeting.

'When is it?' she asked.

'Thursday.'

'Shit, I can't make it,' Gabriela said. 'You go, tell me what it's like.'

There was a pause. 'But I think it's important we both see it.'

Another member of the team walked past into the meeting room and Gabriela smiled at her, indicating she'd only be a moment more. 'Tom, what am I supposed to do, ask for a day off at this short notice? Come on, it's nursery. Anyway, I'll have a look at the Ofsted – and you have a look around. I trust you to make the right choice.'

'Sure,' he said, a hint of resignation in his voice. 'I just thought you might want to be part of it.'

Despite the inevitable blips that were surely part and parcel of family life, soon things fell into a satisfying rhythm, that first year working with Madeleine. With Sadie part-time in the children's centre, Tom was freed up to take on a small residential project, working on weekends and while Callum napped. As the months passed, Callum began to sleep through the night. The following year, as September drew nearer, so too approached the moment when Sadie, who was turning four, would move into the school nursery, freeing up even more time. At last, Gabriela conceded, it was impossible not to believe the stars were aligning.

Then, just after Madeleine had come back from Hanoi, and they were starting to make proper progress in the office, the summons came from the Permanent Under-Secretary's office.

Not one to shy away from a public showdown, the big boss chose mid-morning on the Monday before the Commons broke up for summer recess to hold the one-on-one meeting, ensuring the maximum audience in front of whom to wield his axe. Gabriela was waiting at the bottom of the staircase while he and Madeleine talked, their voices rising from the room like balls being thwacked across a tennis court.

'But you can't do this . . . *He* can't do this!' Madeleine's voice rang from behind the closed door. When it swung open twenty minutes later and she ran down the stairs, her fury left a trail beneath the portraits of countless men with all the power of empire at their disposal.

Gabriela followed her out of the building. 'Madeleine, stop, talk to me – what's going on, what did he say?' They were halfway down the street before she finally slowed down, her body trembling as she reached into her bag for a cigarette.

'He's pulling the plug,' she said simply, flicking repeatedly at the flint until the flame appeared and she inhaled deeply, as if gasping for life. 'Fucking *bastard*,' her teeth were gritted and her eyes shone with astonished rage.

'What? Who?'

'Emsworth,' she said, spitting his name. 'Who do you think? Apparently there are funding issues across the whole organisation, cuts need to be made and we are deemed dispensable. He claims he can absorb our roles into his department.'

'But he can't— What do you mean?'

'Oh, don't be so bloody naive, Gabriela. Of course he can. He already has.'

Gabriela was so dumbstruck that she didn't go after Madeleine, her feet cemented to the pavement as she moved away, and with her the prospect of any meaningful future disappearing into the distance; the tsunami drawing back, preparing to strike.

As she settled back at her desk a while later, ignoring the concerned looks of her colleagues trying to catch her eye from their desks, the adrenaline only now beginning to pulse through her body, she found an email from Serena.

What's going on?

Inhaling, she deleted the message.

If she had given it more thought, she might have prevented at least some of what was to follow. But maybe, she would wonder later on, she didn't want to think too deeply about what was really happening. Maybe she was too busy thinking about herself.

'Everything OK?' Tom asked that evening as she stormed into the kitchen, throwing down her bag and filling the closest glass with wine.

'Mama!' Sadie ran to her and, without thinking, Gabriela pushed her away. 'Not now, please, I just need a minute.'

Sadie whirled round and raced out of the room, tears brimming. Gabriela lifted her hands to her face.

'Mummy just needs to decompress,' she heard Tom say as he closed the door behind her and Gabriela instantly regretted her briskness. And yet, as Tom walked back into the room, her mind went back to her day at work. How could she tell him? If the department was being torn apart and she was about to be made redundant or shifted across somewhere she didn't want to be, in order to survive her focus now had to be on making herself indispensable, to cling on with both hands.

However she presented it to him, she knew that he would support and cajole, as needed. Most likely, he would conclude that this break in the trajectory of her career provided an excuse for them to hang out together more, to go on the long-haul family holiday they had been planning but never managed. They didn't need the money so badly that she would have to find another full-time job straight away. She could retrain, in something more flexible. Tom could take on more projects, which would enable her to take a step back for a while, spend more time with the kids, with him. She'd envied them briefly, hadn't she? The women she'd met at the stay-and-play on the Heath she'd taken Sadie to when Callum was born. But it wasn't their life she wanted, it was their complacency. How she wished she too could be content with a life at home, the endless hours spent milling between playground and library and various playgroups, singing rotations of the same songs, out of tune.

She tried to picture it again: chatting with the other mothers at the school gate, signing up to the PTA, perhaps to stand as a governor. Mentally, she drew the image: filling the days between drop-off and pick-up, running errands, doing household chores; she might feel compelled to take up a hobby, join the local choir.

'Gaby?'

She looked up at Tom and after a moment's pause, she swallowed. 'Everything's fine.'

Chapter 20

Gabriela

Everything was exactly as it had been, and yet completely changed, as she made the journey from the tube station to KCS the following day.

Having failed to reach Madeleine on the phone, she wasn't sure whether to expect her at the office. But when she arrived, Madeleine was already there, her demeanour undented, her lips perfectly accentuated in her signature red lipstick.

'What the hell? I couldn't reach you,' Gabriela said, moving over to her desk, looking around for confirmation that they were alone.

Madeleine paused before standing, leading the way outside, away from the eyes and ears that she seemed to believe might follow them despite the absence of bodies in the room.

'There's nothing we can do about it,' she said flatly. 'They don't need two senior leads in London, they can't *justify* it, and they don't want me back in Hanoi. So this is where we are.'

Gabriela looked at her, awaiting further explanation. For a moment, Madeleine looked like she might say something more, or as if she thought Gabriela might, but then she took a drag of her cigarette and shifted her gaze away again.

'What the fuck, they're firing us?' Gabriela probed.

'No,' Madeleine inhaled sharply. 'They're smarter than that. They'll be planning to push us out, one way or another, but I'm not hanging around for that.'

'What do you mean?'

'Last night I went to see a friend who works at the NCA. They've been trying to tap me up for a while. And, you know, you should be happy; if I leave they'll have no excuse not to keep you on.'

'You're leaving? Jesus, Mads. The National Crime Agency? I thought you laughed at those bastards.'

'No more than they laugh at us.' She shrugged. 'What does it matter? You know I hate it here, but I love the work, when I'm allowed to do it properly, and I'll essentially be working on the same things but from another side.'

'What am I going to do without you?'

'Well, for a start you could look into why the fuck Emsworth was so keen to get rid of us.'

Gabriela felt her chest lift at the words and she narrowed her eyes. 'You think he's . . .'

'Oh come on, we can both stop dancing around it now. You know as well as I do that there is something going on in this place, and that man has something to do with it. With my new contacts and resources at the NCA, I can do a bit of digging from my end. You'll be here, in the thick of it. It's perfect. Perhaps it's for the best, what's happened.'

Madeleine looked at Gabriela and she grinned.

'OK.'

Madeleine crushed the rest of her cigarette against the wall.

'OK. Let's get that fucker and stick his head on a spike.'

Chapter 21

Isobel

Tariq's words are still rolling through my thoughts when I arrive back at my desk. The light is flashing on the answerphone machine and I press play, but the crackling white noise at the end of the line is almost deafening, and after a moment I press delete.

There is a back catalogue of emails to catch up on as I settle back at my desk and I stay there, with my eyes fixed to the screen, for a couple of hours before standing up to have a cigarette.

I've barely taken a drag, finally allowing myself to return in my mind to the spate of stabbings, when my thoughts are interrupted by Ben, calling out from the office. 'Answer your phone, would you? I'm about to throw it out the fucking window.'

Moving inside, I get to my desk just as the ringer stops. Looking over at Ben, I shrug and he rolls his eyes.

'Have you written up that piece on the new parking proposals yet?'

I make a face. 'But I'm working on the stabbing . . .'

'Isobel,' he says. 'This is a local paper, you can't ignore the bread-and-butter stories at the expense of the steak.'

'Right,' I mutter under my breath. 'I really must get my priorities straight.'

At 4 p.m., Si arrives in the office, straight from court. I notice my pulse quicken when I see him, looking away before he can catch my eye.

For a moment, I consider going over to him, talking him through what happened on the Heath. If this was a story I needed to work through, he would be one of my first ports of call. But what would be the point? I've reported it both officially and to Oscar, and there was no sign of anything having happened. Maybe the truth is I have fabricated the whole thing in my mind. In the circumstances, it's not an unreasonable conclusion that I might have misconstrued the situation. I was, after all, what would be officially classified as off my fucking tits at the time.

Two hours later, I file my last piece, Si watching me as I shut down my computer.

'You're off early. You all right? You look like shit.'

'Apparently so, thanks for reminding me,' I say.

He grins, 'Oh don't worry, I'd still shag you.'

Reluctantly, my face cracks into a smile as I swing my bag over my shoulder.

'Night, Si,' I say as I move towards the door.

'Fancy a drink?'

I shake my head without looking back. 'Not tonight. Apparently I need some beauty sleep.'

'Fair enough. Oh yeah, a package came for you earlier,' he adds flippantly, and I stop, turning slowly on my heels.

'For me? What was it?'

'I don't know, I thought it might be considered bad manners to open someone else's post.' His eyes remain fixed on his screen. 'It's down there.'

Following his gesture towards the corner of the room, I pick up the box. Something about it makes me hold it slightly away from my body.

'When did this arrive?'

'Hmm? Oh, I don't know, this afternoon. You were out front having a fag.'

Using a pair of scissors I slice along the packing tape, the blade pressing beneath my fingers until the cardboard bursts open. My fingers move uncertainly over the tissue paper as I peel it away.

Si looks up as I step backwards, the parcel in my hands falling towards the floor like a dead bird dropping from the sky. His eyes follow mine to the carpet, towards a pair of red suede trainers.

'What's wrong?' he says, standing and walking towards me.

'What the fuck?' My voice is little more than a whisper as I look from one shoe to the other.

'Si, where did they come from?' Still, I don't look at him, my eyes unable to tear themselves away from the floor, from the trainers I had left in my bag on the Heath.

'I told you, someone dropped them off. What's the matter?'

When I fail to respond he holds out a hand to me. 'Issy, what's going on?'

Looking up suddenly, I pull my arm away, my eyes darting across the room.

'Where did they come from?'

He raises his arms. 'Isobel, seriously, I have no idea. Someone left them with Elaine at reception. I just picked them up on my way in—'

Before he can finish his sentence I've pushed through the door to reception. Elaine's empty desk and a well-worn doormat are the only thing between the office and the world beyond.

'What . . .?' My hands fly to my cheeks, and my whole body shakes as I run to the front door, flinging it open and looking out at the flood of people moving back and forth across the street, my eyes searching for something they cannot find.

Si has to roar to make himself heard above the din of the World's End pub. He speaks slowly, picking up one of the glasses of whisky on the table between us. You have to drink quickly in this place to forget the stench of stale sick and rancid beer.

'So let me get this straight . . . You're saying that this guy, whoever he is, *murdered* a woman in the middle of Hampstead Heath, then saw you watching them, somehow found your shoes, discovered where you work and then brought them to your office.'

'I didn't say murdered.' My eyes are fixed over Si's shoulder, scanning the figures passing back and forth, I'm vaguely aware of my feet tapping at hyper-speed against the sticky surface of the floorboards. Si looks at me, taking another slug of his drink.

'OK, *attacked* . . . I mean, fucking hell, Is, this is nuts. Have you been to the police?'

I nod; the motion of my foot tapping against the floor causes the table between us to vibrate.

'What did they say?'

'Fuck all.' My jaw is tense, I need a cigarette.

He looks like he wants to probe further, but thinks better of it. 'OK, look. I'm not saying you're exaggerating at all, but for a moment – just bear with me – ask yourself: why would he do that? If someone attacked a woman on the Heath and he saw you and for whatever reason he knows where you work, and he found your shoes . . . Why would he return them to the office?'

There is a pause.

'You think I'm making it up?'

'No, Issy, of course I don't. I'm not saying that – I just said I'm not saying that . . . I'm just asking *why*. Why would he do that? We need to think.' His voice softens as he leans in, trying to catch my eye. 'You're a reporter, surely you've already asked yourself that question?'

'Of course I have, you patronising prick. I don't know, Si, maybe because he's a psychopath?' I hiss, looking up at him and shaking my head. 'Maybe it was a warning, his way of telling me that he knows where I am?'

When Si's considered silence becomes too much, I say, 'Maybe he is freaking out because he attacked someone and he knows I saw him and he is shitting it that I'm going to tell someone?'

I take out a cigarette and starting rolling it between my fingers, breathing out through my nose, trying to block out Si's concerned eyes, the eyes of the doctors and the nurses and all those bloody counsellors. The eyes that say clearly what the voice doesn't dare: *I don't believe you.*

I want to stand up and throw my chair at him, to storm out of the pub and run down the high street and scream in the faces of strangers who pass me until I find the man I am looking for, but instead I look up at Si and take a moment to compose myself. It's not like I have a million other people left on my side to turn to.

'You're right,' I say, forcing a smile. 'I probably just imagined it.'

'Issy, I'm not saying that you imagined it, for God's sake, will you listen to me? Jesus, you are so bloody frustrating. What I am trying to say is that if this happened – or rather *as* this *has* happened – then we need to go back to the police . . .'

'I have,' I say, quietly, looking down at the unlit cigarette.

'And?'

I don't want to tell him about my delay in going to the station, about the reason I held off, about the party and the drugs. I don't want to tell him any of it, so that he can take it back to Ben and the two of them can roll their eyes in pity, or divine some sort of intervention. I've already had more pity in the past year than I can stomach.

'They're looking into it,' I say.

He stops. 'Isobel, you know you can talk to me, yeah? I know you've been having a really hard time, with your friend and . . . everything.'

I push my chair back. 'I'm knackered, I need to go home.'

Si reaches out his hand. 'Don't go.'

'No, seriously, I'm tired,' I say, picking up my bag as he stands.

'I'll come with you.'

'No, Si, not tonight. I need to sleep.'

There is a flash of hurt and then he sits back down and takes a swig of his drink.

Looking away, he says, 'Fine then, see you tomorrow.'

The walk from the pub to my front door takes less than five minutes. Camden Town has descended into its usual haze of stumbling drunks and anxious crackheads lurking in phone boxes. Briefly I find myself comforted by the familiar tinkle of bottles smashing somewhere in the distance, car horns and swells of sound drifting onto the street as pub doors crash open and shut.

But as I reach my front door, the atmosphere changes. The prospect of a night alone is suddenly terrifying and for a moment I wish I'd let Si come back after all. Then again, I know that I need to be alone, and besides, I can't afford to give him the wrong idea, for him to think that a night out will automatically end up back at mine.

The broken pane in the front door has been sealed with a piece of cardboard and gaffer tape. I stumble upstairs to the flat, the steps creaking beneath my feet, my heartbeat racing as I fumble with my bag. The windowless hallway is in darkness and I bash my key unsuccessfully against the lock, patting my fingers along the wall for a light switch. As they find it, the sharpness of its features is a relief, but when I flick the button, nothing happens.

'*Shit,*' I mutter under my breath, making a mental note to remind the landlord to sort out the light in the hall.

It is the same feeling I used to get as a child when I got up in the night needing the toilet; that dread at having to wander through the house alone in pitch-black, imagining something I couldn't see moving closer and closer. The same rising terror circles me now as it had running back towards my childhood bed at full speed and jumping the final distance, convinced someone would reach out from under the bed and drag me down by the ankles. Except this time, as I lift my key, I remember that the bogeyman is real.

When the lock finally gives way with a crack, I fall into the room, slamming my hand against the wall, feeling for the switch and flicking it on so that the room suddenly fills with light.

It is exactly as I left it, the same cups discarded by the sink.

The previous owner of this flat, which I have rented for the past year, since everything happened, had divided it in two with a cheap stud wall, to transform it from a studio into a one-bed. Checking behind the internal door to my bedroom to confirm that I am alone,

I go to the bathroom, turning on the bath taps before moving into the kitchen, popping out a Xanax, splitting it in half and pouring myself a small glass of whisky.

As I lower myself into the bath a few minutes later, at last I allow my mind to grapple with what I've been keeping at bay all day, the memory I had begun to believe I might have distorted. This time, when the picture starts to blur and contort, the discomfort lodging itself in my chest, I push through so that certain pieces of the puzzle flash into focus: the depth of the man's voice; the name: *Eva*.

Then what? Placing myself back in the moment, I imagine tearing through brambles, emerging into the daylight and pounding barefoot across Parliament Hill, past the tennis courts, straight across the zebra crossing at Swain's Lane, narrowly avoiding a white van which blasted its horn as I darted between the sparse early morning traffic; Highgate Road rushes past in a blur; I was moving as though running for my life. My legs had not stopped until I reached Camden Town, met by a sea of strangled faces, their features blurred. Finally, I picture my hands, trembling as I reach into my pocket and pull out my key.

But what about him: what had *he* done? How does he know where I work?

The thought causes me to shiver.

He can't have followed me, not least because I would have noticed a man pursuing me through the streets at such breakneck speed, but also because I went straight home. If he knew where I lived, then why wouldn't he have sent the shoes to the flat? And yet, the brick: that had happened the very same night. Perhaps Oscar was right, perhaps the two things were unconnected. But fuck Oscar and his patronising assumptions. Besides, everyone knows there's no such thing as coincidence.

And then it hits me. The purse. Amongst all the crap – the bar receipts, the outdated loyalty cards – was my business card. Five of them, each a little creased, with my name on the front: job title and work address.

For a moment, the voice of reason raises its head. Perhaps then it was a dog walker who returned my shoes to the office, or a jogger? Someone simply found my purse and shoes and had the courtesy to send them back to me. *Silly girl*, the voice says. The voice of the nurses and doctors, the voice of someone whose mouth was pursed in a knowing smile, one leg pressed over the other.

Except, where was the purse? The only thing that could have given away my identity was nowhere to be seen. If more evidence were needed, there was no note. Encountering local heroes is a hazard of the job when you're a reporter, and I've learnt a bit about the kind of people who get off on this kind of community spirit. Nine times out of ten, they want their picture taken and paraded in the local rag. It isn't so much about doing good things as about being seen to be doing them.

And yet whoever sent me the shoes didn't leave a note. There was only one thing the parcel could represent, and that was a message. As I dunk my head beneath the water, holding the air in my lungs until my chest feels as if it will burst, I know it – regardless of what Si or Oscar or anyone else has said. I feel it, and sometimes that is as much as one can hope for.

As for finding out my home address, the truth is that it would have been pitifully easy. I'm not on social media, not anymore; I haven't unwittingly given away pieces of my life online for any stranger to map together. This is more straightforward than that. Anyone who had got into my office – and hadn't someone left the window open over the weekend? – would only need a couple of minutes of looking through papers to find my address. For God's sake, I keep my payslips in the drawer. Easier still, he could have followed me.

Despite the fact that there are no windows in this room, I find myself crouching over to protect my body from prying eyes as I step out of the bath. The room is bitterly cold. Aside from the muted sounds of the outside world seeping through the cracks in the kitchen window, the flat is silent.

Moving across to the kitchen counter, a towel wrapped around me, my chest rises and falls in heaving movements. Turning, I grab a chair and then another and lodge them against the door, jamming the handle.

Every inch of my body is hyper-alert so that I am like a wolf stalking through a forest as I move through the bedsit towards my bedroom – except wolves move in packs, and I am alone.

It is extraordinary how quickly people disappeared after it all kicked off. Some were happy, at first, to send a text or occasionally a card telling me how much they cared and wanted to meet up, but it was rarely followed through. Those who did visit were clearly there to absorb the details first-hand, and then fell away again once their thirst for gossip had been satiated.

Besides, there is only one person I want to speak to now, and she isn't here.

Chapter 22

Gabriela

With Madeleine gone, her role was unofficially absorbed into Gabriela's, so that she was now reporting again directly to Emsworth with their once ten-strong team culled to just four. Not only did this give Gabriela the chance to prove herself as a leader, but it provided the perfect vantage point from which to watch his every move.

It was the sweetest of feelings, him believing he was using her to keep an eye on everything that happened in the department, insisting on rubber-stamping every decision that was made, being kept abreast of every action taken, every morsel of information uncovered, and all along knowing that she was watching him, keeping tabs on exactly what piqued his interest – and handing everything she discovered straight back to Madeleine at the NCA.

'Do you think we should speak to someone here about our suspicions?' Gabriela asked one day.

'Absolutely not. We can't trust anyone there. Not even Serena or Johnny,' Madeleine replied without hesitation.

'But when you said, months ago, that there were suspicions in your department about confidential stuff being leaked, surely whoever it was that alerted you might have more information, and we could work together?'

'Gabs, leave this to me, OK? No one can know what we're doing. Not yet. Not until we know more about what's going on. Oh, and do me a favour,' Madeleine added thoughtfully. 'Let me know when he's next off to Moscow . . .'

'Why?' Gabriela asked, and she could almost hear her friend smiling at the end of the phone.

'Just do it, would you? Don't worry, I'll let you know if we get something.'

'I know you will,' Gabriela said, and as she hung up she felt a buzz like electricity charging through her veins.

Despite the satisfaction of these calls, and of knowing the work that was going on to catch Emsworth out in whatever it was he was involved in, it had become a tic of Gabriela's to refresh the internal jobs board, imagining herself in another department, rising up through the ranks.

And finally she saw it, the following year: an opening for a senior lead in Human Rights and Democracy. Not only was it precisely the role she had been aspiring to for so long, but there was enough overlap with what they had been doing of late to ensure, in anyone's mind, that she was as qualified as one might hope to be. She shivered at the possibility as she made her application, knowing in her bones this role was meant for her.

'I'm thinking of applying for the job in Human Rights,' she said to Emsworth at the end of their next briefing. After all, she could hardly keep it from him, and it would be necessary to have his support.

He looked thoughtful for a moment and then he nodded. 'Very good. Well, I'm sure you're an excellent candidate.'

The positivity of his response briefly silenced her. 'Thank you very much. I'm very excited about applying. Does that mean you'd back me, to Bradford, in my application?'

'Why wouldn't I?' he asked and she stood, relieved, a brief stir of guilt before reminding herself of all he'd already put them through. Besides, it would hardly be an act of generosity on his part to lend support for her application: she had earned this.

In characteristically convoluted FCO style, it was February by the time applications were considered and the new recruit announced.

It was a particularly mild morning and the remnants of the rain overnight left a light sheen on the pavement outside as she gathered her things in preparation for dropping Sadie at nursery. Tom was staying at home with Callum, who was unwell and had been up most of the night so that none of them had slept properly.

Retrieving items of clothing from across the house and grabbing Sadie's scooter on their way out of the door, Gabriela feared she was already running late. She'd need to drop Sadie off early if she was to make the 9.30 a.m. briefing. Whatever bug Callum was carrying, Gabriela was about to be struck with it too: her head was pounding and her nose feeling as though it had been filled with rags. But she couldn't afford to get sick, not now; not with the decision about to be made about the new HRD job – though, given Bradford's indiscretion in the final interview, she already knew it was as good as hers.

'Sadie, please, hurry up!' she snapped, though the voice in her head reminded her this was not her daughter's fault.

Sadie was making her way along the pavement without allowing herself to touch the lines between the slabs, hopping between each with an intense focus that should have been endearing, or, if she'd been paying better attention, a sign that something was off. It was a behaviour Gabriela herself had adopted at times in childhood when life felt particularly beyond her control; one of those incongruous ways, along with the counting and the systematic blinking, that helped her feel like she had some sort of hold over her universe, which seemed already to spin either too fast or too slow.

Pulling her gloves off with her teeth, Gabriela typed an email on her phone to Madeleine, whom she was supposed to be meeting for lunch. Gabriela had had to cancel their last get-together and, though today was already looking rammed, she couldn't cancel again – even if she had embarrassingly little to share. Recently, Emsworth had gone remarkably quiet, indicating no particular interest in any of the work he signed off. It was almost as if a shutter had been pulled down.

She typed with her index finger, the wind causing her eyes to stream.

1.30 at the restaurant is perfect – see you then x

She pressed Send and felt a rush of panic at the prospect of everything she had to do. How was it possible to be this tired and still be standing upright? And it wasn't just the rough night's sleep that had done her in. Recently, with her amped-up workload and preparation for the interviews she'd been undertaking, things had started to spiral so that some days she felt so overwhelmed she had to hide in a cubicle in the bathroom and remind herself to breathe. To complicate matters, she couldn't tell Tom about her recent job application. As far as he was concerned, she was still working under Madeleine as she had been when she was in Hanoi. To tell him about the change in circumstances would have been to give him a voice in the conversation around her career that she simply didn't want him to have.

Perhaps she was thinking about the satisfaction she'd seen on his face those mornings while she was on leave when he went out on the job with Jim, the look that belied his insistence that he was happy to stay at home while she went out to work. Perhaps she wasn't willing to start a dialogue that might lead somewhere she didn't want it to go – and maybe that was perfectly reasonable, given her history.

She was able to draw a line between her desperate need for control and the experience of being abandoned as a child. She understood that a therapist might have rationalised the increasingly secretive behaviour as another manifestation of her need to manage aspects of her life, triggered by the inevitable chaos of becoming a mother – and the shift in identity that comes with that.

There was also another, more simple possibility: that she was just selfish.

By the time she got to the tube station at 8.35, having dropped Sadie at the nursery, she felt like she had been put through a blender. As she reached the platform, rats scuttled through the arch of the tunnel, heralding the arrival of the train.

Exiting the tube half an hour later, she had to push against the wind that blew through the station, ducking into a coffee shop where she ordered a double espresso before making her way to the bathroom. The tap spat out hot water, scalding her hands as she rinsed off the soap.

Removing the grey beret Tom had bought her the previous Christmas, she reached into her bag and pulled out a brush. It had belonged to her mother, and her mother before that; the soft tufts of horsehair had rubbed away in parts over time, and the smooth curve of the handle urged her to hold it tight. By the time her mum had died in her early fifties, struck by the same cancer that had taken her own mother around the same age, Valentina had barely a grey hair on her head. Gabriela's own wavy locks were still the same colour they had always been, though the texture had coarsened since she'd had the children, as if bolstering itself against the implications of motherhood.

For a moment she considered her reflection. Despite having recently hit her thirties, a smattering of freckles over the bridge of her nose gave her a child-like quality. Her relative youth was something that both served and blighted her, not least in the diplomatic quarter where disarmament could be one's greatest asset. What at first drew in men like Emsworth, attracted by the vivacity and apparent malle-ability of inexperience, emboldened them to belittle and reject in that distinct way that men had with young women, without thinking twice. Without believing there would be any consequences at all.

Serena was already in the office, fresh-faced and straight from the gym, when Gabriela arrived. She smiled across at her as she settled at her desk. 'Bad journey?'

Gabriela bristled, annoyed at how easily Serena read her mood, but she managed a smile.

'No, just cold. I'm going to get another coffee, want one?'

'Not for me,' Serena waved her hand. 'I've got a meeting at nine-thirty.'

'You're not coming to the briefing?'

Serena frowned. 'That was cancelled, didn't you get the email?'

Gabriela paused. 'What? No, when?'

'On Friday evening – I'm sure you must have been . . .'

She scrolled through her emails and then clicked open the message, hovering over the recipients before pulling a confused expression. 'You're not in CC, you must have slipped off.'

Gabriela nodded, working hard to seem unconcerned, despite the feeling of unease working its way up her back, like an unseen hand.

'Yes, that must be it.'

It was midday when Emsworth finally surfaced. Feeling emboldened, Gabriela gave him a minute to settle at his desk before she made a beeline for his office, striding straight past Lauren who raised her hand.

'Sorry, do you need something?'

'I just need to see Emsworth,' she replied, her fingers already rapping against the wood.

Walking in as soon as she heard his voice, she noted the annoyance in his face. For someone with a hypothetical open-door policy he appeared remarkably surprised to see someone walk through it.

'Gabriela. How can I help?'

Moving into the room and settling on the seat opposite his desk, Gabriela said, 'Hi, I was expecting to see you earlier but the meeting was cancelled, apparently.'

His face barely moved. 'That's right.'

Brushing over the fact that he hadn't bothered to tell her about it, she continued, 'So I just wanted to make sure everything was teed up. We haven't had a meeting for a while and I think it's important we're all up to date.'

'Actually, I was going to drop you a line later, about the job.' Emsworth's expression changed and she watched him, slowing down, lining up his words for the perfect delivery.

Noting the blankness of her expression, he said, 'They haven't told you? They've made a decision – that's where I was this morning. And it looks like good news for you . . .'

Her whole body vibrated with excitement. 'Oh wow!'

'Wow, indeed,' he said, delivering the news with a smile. 'You see, you're just doing so well here, it would be a shame – a *real* shame – to lose you. And they understood that, when I explained it to them. They understood why I needed to keep you, what with Madeleine walking out on us like that. Anyway, like I said, it's good news for you! Without Serena in the department, we can apply for an extra pair of hands, so you're not struggling to keep on top of things quite so much . . . You do seem to be struggling. And like I said, I'm always here, to watch over things.'

'Serena?'

It was as if someone had turned down the volume on the world. For the next few seconds, she watched Emsworth's features moving – the too-soft shine of his cheeks, his lips puckering as he enunciated her defeat, but the meaning remained unclear.

'What the fuck?' The words slipped out before she could control them.

Emsworth visibly recoiled. 'I beg your pardon?'

'That job was mine. You said so; Bradford, in the final interview, he told me it was as good as sealed . . .'

'Oh Gabriela, come now, don't be ridiculous. Firstly, there's no way anyone would make a promise like that without due process. And frankly, I thought we were doing you a favour. This role, it's loaded with responsibility, you'd be taking on infinitely more . . .'

'I know, that is precisely why I applied! I don't know if you've noticed, but ever since Madeleine left I've effectively been doing several roles at once, without any additional pay or recognition, and you told me— This job, please, it means everything to me . . . *Please* . . .' There was a desperation to her voice that repulsed them both.

'Well, that's quite an admission.' He was quiet for a few seconds and then he shrugged. 'The problem is, it's all about trust. We need someone we can rely on 100 per cent.'

'You can rely on me,' she said, and he sneered.

'Can I?' As he leaned forward, she felt a chill move across the room.

'You know you can.'

Without saying anything, he reached into his bag and pulled out a camera. Zooming into the screen he dropped it on the desk, the image of Gabriela and Madeleine in the window of Daphne's staring back at her. She looked up at him and he arched an eyebrow before picking the camera up again and zooming in further so that she could see, pixelated but clear enough, the image she was holding in her hand: the photo of Emsworth's meeting at the bar in Moscow.

'Did you really think I wouldn't be watching you? That I wouldn't find out?' His words were perfectly enunciated, as if he was savouring every one of them.

For a moment Gabriela felt as though her voice box had been cut out, and then she spoke, as though controlled by an outside force.

'You think you can blackmail me? I know all about you, about *Francisco Nguema* . . .' She enunciated every syllable with precision. 'I'll tell everyone.'

His face shifted then. 'Oh, Gabriela.' He paused, as though genuinely regretful about what he was about to do, and then he reached again into his bag. This time the photographs he pulled from the envelope made her gag: dismembered body parts, a woman with her teeth and eyes pulled out, lying next to the corpse of a child.

'Jesus . . .' Gabriela bent double and when she sat back up, Emsworth was holding another wad of images. The first was of her house, the ordinariness of the building peculiar to her, in this context. As he pulled out the next picture, she thought she would be sick. Tom, Callum and Sadie on the walk to school, Tom's head at an angle as if turning to say something to Sadie who was lingering behind in that way of hers.

'You . . .' She couldn't think of the word. Her mind was spinning, all the blood in her head throbbing at her temples, blotting out Emsworth's voice as he spoke again.

'What kind of people do you think we're dealing with here?' he asked, his words quiet and measured.

She stood, taking a step back, away from the images of bloody limbs juxtaposed against those of her children's faces.

There was a ringing sound in her ears as she stood, her legs threatening to buckle.

'You . . .' Her whole body was shaking; her voice when she spoke again was little more than a whisper, as though she'd been kicked in the windpipe.

He spoke as if he hadn't heard. 'Gabriela, if you mention a word of this to anyone – Madeleine, your husband – sorry, boyfriend – any friends – and here I would name specific ones, but to be honest you don't seem to have many . . . If you mention a word to *anyone*, they will find you and they will kill you. Do you understand what I am saying? If you ever so much as mention my name, or that of anyone you think you know anything about, your children will die.'

With that, he reached forward and picked up the photos, shuffling them neatly into a pile as if preparing to create a family album.

'Oh, and with regard to handing in your notice, I'll explain to HR. Just send an email explaining that you've had a family emergency, you had to leave without working your notice. Keep it brief. Don't worry, I'll vouch for you, smooth things over here. And you can leave your work phone on your desk. You won't be needing that anymore.'

Gabriela said nothing, moving backwards towards the door as though she had been shot.

Chapter 23

Isobel

At six-thirty the next morning I pull myself out of bed. Casting my eyes across a sea of ashtrays, papers and dirty glasses, I walk to the bathroom, slapping the boiler to life, the water starting up with a heaving growl.

By the time I step out of the shower, the whole room is a fog. Wiping the mirror with my hand, I see my own face staring back at me through the steam. My reflection comes as a shock: the fine, clear skin I remember has been replaced by dark rings circling bloodshot eyes.

Pulling on the same skinny black trousers and jumper I wore the day before, I walk into the kitchen, switch on the kettle and scrabble around for a mug.

Once I've removed the barricade of chairs from in front of the door, I walk downstairs and onto the street. Whatever sun there might have been has disappeared behind a thick cloud which threatens to smother London.

The day is fuzzy, pigeons gathering on the cables running across the street. Lighting a cigarette, I cross the road and feel an arm brush against mine as I reach the other side, followed by a tiny shock of electricity. When I turn, it is just a young woman moving in the opposite direction, a hood pulled above her head.

Inside the café, stodgy air billows out of the heaters. I have just finished ordering my coffee when I hear my name. Turning, I find Hugh about half a foot behind me, his hair gelled into a limp fifties-style quiff clearly left over from the night before, his skin grey, pores secreting the stale smell of vodka.

'Isobel,' he says.

'Hugh. What are you doing here?'

He gives me a confused smile. 'Going to work. Some of us do have proper jobs.'

'Right,' I say, turning to the counter and collecting my drink.

'It was good to see you the other night.'

'Yeah, it was,' I lie.

Something about Hugh's face is making me feel anxious. 'I'm running really late, but good to see you.'

Just as I reach the exit, he pulls at my arm. 'Is everything OK? The other night, you were acting . . .' His eyes are manic, and I sense other customers looking up from their paper cups.

'Everything's fine,' I say quietly, desperate to get away from him with his rancid breath and desperate stare.

'Listen,' he says. 'I wanted to talk to you, about Jess . . .'

I pull my arm back. 'No.'

My voice is louder than I'd intended and Hugh takes a step back, composing himself.

When he speaks again, his voice is quieter. 'I think it would be good to talk—'

'I said no. Now leave me alone.'

'OK,' he says, raising his hands. 'OK. Well, I'll see you then.'

Once he has left the café, I stand there watching him move down the street, my whole body shaking.

Waiting until I know he will have gone, when I finally go back outside I feel a chill rush through me. Before I have time to acknowledge where I am going, I feel myself turning left. At the fork in Camden Road, I go forwards, my body moving as though a magnet is dragging me back through Kentish Town, pulling me by the chest towards the Heath.

As I enter by the tennis courts, with each blink I see the girl's face, fuzzy and out of focus, the details just out of reach.

The sky above me is thick and oppressive. Wiping a thin line of perspiration from the top of my lip, I move towards the clusters of trees. Someone else might struggle to differentiate one copse of trees from another, but I know this place better than I know myself.

The hill feels steeper than usual, the distance between each stride elongated as my eyes sweep over the skyline, the contours of my childhood spreading out before me. For a moment I imagine all the millions of lives hidden from view behind all those tiny glass windows, on the other side of the city.

It has rained overnight. The ground is unsteady beneath me and I feel my feet slosh and slide, and the same dank, earthy smell pounds through my nostrils, filling my chest.

All I need is a clue, some tiny detail that will lead me to the next step. That is what it is about, little steps, sequences, following one path until you get to another.

It doesn't take long. Combing every centimetre of ground, waiting for something to click, I scour the surface with an almost euphoric strain in my chest. My feet move carefully, slowly treading one in front of the other, retracing my steps from that night, until I stop.

Knocking at the edge of the rock with my foot, I feel a thud in my chest and I stand. My body shaking with expectation, I pull out my phone and dial Oscar's number.

He answers after two rings.

My voice is laced with fear and excitement. 'It's me. I need you to meet me at Parliament Hill. Now.'

Arriving at the café a few minutes later, I take a seat under one of the umbrellas in the courtyard overlooking the road.

The last time I was here was at the beginning of summer two years ago. Jess and I sat in pretty much the same spot, nursing a hangover, picking on pizza and Diet Coke, straight from the Camden Crawl. It couldn't have been more than a few months since I'd got the job on the paper, thanks to a friend of hers who'd known the music reviewer, before he – along with half the paper's better-paid, more experienced staff – was made redundant.

Scanning the roundabout, the endless stream of Volvo estates and Land Rovers cruising towards Highgate Village, I finally spot a police car, parking on the double yellow line opposite. *Sergeant Morley*, I remind myself as Oscar steps out, an overcoat partially obscuring his uniform. He's had a haircut, I think before I can stop myself, and self-consciously I run my hands over my own hair which I realise I haven't brushed in days.

Looking up, he catches my eye and then looks away again, pretending to survey the street so as to limit the awkwardness of eye contact as he makes his way towards me. I wonder, briefly, if he'll try to hug me, or offer a kiss on the cheek. It's more than a year since he last touched me. Thankfully, he pulls up a chair and nods his hello, the sound of metal scraping against concrete.

'Thanks for meeting me,' I say, businesslike, suddenly nervous in his company.

'It's good to see you. I can't be long . . . Give me one of those then,' he reaches across and pulls out a cigarette, using my lighter.

When did he start smoking again?

As he looks up at me, his voice shifts uncomfortably. 'So how have you been? After yesterday I wasn't sure I'd hear from you . . .'

'I'm fine. Look, Oscar,' I say, cutting to the chase, uneasy about where this conversation might otherwise lead.

'It's about what I saw . . . on Saturday . . . I've found something.'

He doesn't reply at first, so I continue, 'I went back to the scene. There's something I need to show you.'

I stand, pushing back my chair as if to leave as the waitress comes over.

As if he hasn't heard, Oscar looks up at her. 'Yeah, I'll get a bacon sandwich and an orange juice. The same for her.'

'Oscar, there's no time,' I say but he smiles at the waitress and she moves away, ignoring me.

For a moment he fiddles with his napkin, and it is all I can do not to reach over the table and shake him.

'Oscar?'

When he finally speaks his voice is strained, 'You went back?'

'Yes, I went back. I just told you—'

'But I told you we searched the place, Issy, there was nothing there.'

'Yes, I know you did. But you were wrong. Like I told you. I just went back there and there's something you need to see . . .'

For a moment, I see the colour rising in his cheeks.

'He's cleared the ground,' I say, not waiting for a reply. 'The spot where they were arguing, it's been cleared. The rest of the area, the ground was moist and dark, but the part where I saw the fighting, it's dry. The earth is a completely different texture. You know, the top of it, like someone's brushed away the top layer.'

Oscar continues to smoke his cigarette.

'The spot where he attacked her, Oscar! Can you hear me? There's a perfect line – one side the earth is damp, the other is dry. He must have been trying to get rid of something . . .'

At that moment the waitress arrives, setting down our drinks. Oscar nods, taking a sip and glancing indiscreetly at her chest while she fiddles around with the condiments.

Once she leaves, I lean forward. 'Please. Did you hear me?' There is a hint of desperation in my voice now.

'Yeah, I did,' he says finally. 'We'll check it out.'

His tone is nonchalant and my expression pleads with him to carry on, for him to say something, anything, that suggests for a minute he has been taking me seriously.

When he remains silent, I stand. 'Come with me. I'll show you right now. You can see it with your own eyes.'

'Is, sit down.'

There is a kindness in his expression that makes me want to punch him.

'Come on. Your hands are shaking.'

'I need you to listen to what I'm saying.'

The waitress returns and hands us two plates.

After a moment, I pick up the sandwich. 'Fine, I'll eat the sandwich.' I take one mouthful and then another, huge, tearing bites which swell in my throat. Through the chewing I speak again, 'Is this better? Now will you listen to me?'

There is a stinging silence and finally I swallow, letting my face drop into my hands.

'OK,' I say, trying a new tack. 'You're right. I'm tired. Really tired.' I bite my lip. 'I appreciate you looking out for me. I do, and yes, I need some sleep. A spa maybe, I'll have a spa . . .'

I try to smile, to look normal. To show him how reasonable I am capable of being.

'Listen, Osc, how long have you known me?' I try to fix his gaze, but he keeps his attention on his sandwich.

'Hey? Come on.' I give him my best smile, one hand tracing a finger through my hair.

'You know me, the reason I'm tired is because I'm worried. I'm really worried, because I know something bad has happened to that girl.' I move my head to catch his eye, his face struggling to resist mine. 'You know I wouldn't be like this if I wasn't sure something happened, right?'

He looks up, his eyes flinching as our gaze meets. 'It's not that I doubt your certainty, Issy . . .'

'Please, Oscar.' Without thinking, I reach out and touch his hand. My fingers rest there for a moment, and then I pull them back, the memory of the contact too much to bear.

'Seriously. I don't understand why you're being like this, it's like you don't want to find out what happened to her.'

'Don't you dare,' he spits, the people at the table next to us falling quiet.

Lowering his voice, he continues, 'You don't understand why I'm being like this?' His eyes scan my face.

'Listen to yourself! Take a look in a mirror every now and again! You look like shit. You look ill. You're supposed to be taking things easy . . .'

'Oh, come on, Oscar . . .'

'No. You come on. You *listen* to me. Whatever is with this crusade you're on, whatever this is, it has to stop. Now.'

I stare back at him, the heat rising in my cheeks.

'What?' A brief silence falls between us. It is Oscar who speaks next. 'I'm sorry.'

He looks away, sniffing hard. My cheeks feel as though they've been slapped, my skin pricking with rage and hurt and confusion and disbelief, all wrapped up in one chaotic bundle.

Oscar's face is flushed, his lips locked into line. I can almost hear him grinding his teeth.

'You know what?' I say, standing and picking up my bag. 'Fuck you.'

Chapter 24

Gabriela

The sky was an ominous grey as she stepped out onto the pavement, walking along Parliament Street and turning left onto Victoria Embankment. Even the London Eye, which hovered above the Thames, seemed different somehow, each carriage rocking precariously as if at any moment it might fall, the contents smashing onto the ground, sending glass and body-parts skidding in every direction.

The reality of what was happening was like a river splashing at her heels as she walked out of King Charles Street for the last time, the water rising steadily as she passed New Scotland Yard, her mind playing back what had just happened, on a loop, searching for a way to press pause and rewind.

The adrenaline that had kept her going this far suddenly drained from her body so that by the time she reached Westminster Bridge, she was ready to lie back and be drawn in by the current. It would be a relief, in this moment, to be pulled down into the darkness.

As if understanding the momentousness of what was taking place, the clouds burst and it started to rain, acidic water merging with tears that she made no effort to wipe away, moving without the slightest attention to where she was going. When her phone rang some time later, she was seated at one of the outside tables of a bar overlooking the river, working her way through a tumbler of gin, her fingers numb.

Madeleine's number flashed on the screen of her phone on the table and she let it go through to voicemail.

'What the fuck is going on? I just got a call from Johnny, he told me you had a fight with Emsworth, that you walked out—'

Fleetingly, Gabriela panicked that she had to warn her friend. After all, they knew about her as well. But Madeleine was big enough, and connected enough, to look after herself. Besides, she had no significant others to worry about. Gabriela's children were her weakness; with a stab of jealousy, she realised Madeleine had nothing comparable to be threatened with. Her life, and any threats against it, were wholly her own.

Pressing 'delete' on the voicemail, Gabriela looked out over the skyline, soaking in the calm that suddenly enveloped her. It was as if she had been purged and was now light as air, safely drifting in this anomalous space, completely separate from the past or any future, whatever it might bring.

When her phone rang again an hour or so later, the sight of Tom's name took her by surprise. Tom. He would be calling to ask if she would be home in time for dinner. It was nearly 5 p.m., according to the numbers on the screen as she let his call fade out, unanswered. He would be anticipating another evening of bathtime and stories; the potential for a drink on the sofa with his wife, an early night perhaps. Everything just as it always was.

As she stood to leave some time later, the buildings ahead appeared like a parade of faces, lined in judgement, watching each step that she took, their eyes never leaving her back as she disappeared into the tube.

Chapter 25

Isobel

Si is already at his desk by the time I reach the office. From the way I drop my bag by my desk, he and Ben can already sense my mood. Neither attempts to make conversation as I turn on my monitor, the machine groaning back to life. Swigging aggressively at a takeaway coffee cup while I wait for the screen to light up, I try Maureen's number again but there is no answer.

Since my conversation with Oscar, my mood has shifted between rage and bouts of self-doubt.

As soon as I am seated at my desk, an email appears on-screen from Si. Pausing for a second, I click on it.

Is everything OK?

When I glance sidelong towards where his head pokes up above his monitor, his eyes stay fixed to the screen, as if I am not sitting just a few feet away from him.

Ignoring the message, I carry on opening the document I'd been about to start work on and less than a minute later another message appears, this time accompanied by a pointed sigh from his side of the room.

Don't ignore me. Fancy lunch?

I type without looking away from my screen.

I can't.

Moments later I hear him thumping the keys with his fingers.

I just thought you might . . .

Christ, can he not leave it alone? Bloody hell, Si, take a hint. I should never have started sleeping with him. Now was not the time to become entwined with anyone, let alone a colleague.

Distraction comes in the form of the front door to the office slamming. From the nervous cough that followed from the other room, it is clear Elaine has returned from her break. Standing and walking quickly towards the internal door, I step into reception.

'Hi, Isobel,' she says without looking up.

'Hi. I was just wondering, do you remember yesterday afternoon, someone delivered something for me?'

Elaine adopts the look of someone thinking hard, eyes pointing to the right, lips pursed at an angle.

'Oh yes,' she says, after a moment.

I feel my chest lift. 'Brilliant. Can you tell me who sent it?'

She flicks through a notebook.

'Here it is. It was a courier . . .'

'Can I see?'

When I look at the paper, there is a signature, illegible. Next to it, where the company name should be, the box is left blank.

'Oh sorry,' she says, tutting to herself. 'I asked him to fill it in but he was in a terrible rush – you know what they're like – and I didn't check that he had.'

'What did he look like?'

She raises her eyebrows. 'I don't know . . . Young, wearing a tracksuit, maybe. He had a motorbike helmet. I wasn't paying much attention, to be honest, love. A courier's a courier. He wasn't one of our usual ones, though, now that I think about him. I didn't recognise him.'

'Is there CCTV in here?'

'CCTV? No, love. Why would—'

'Shit,' I say, slapping my hand against the desk, and Elaine looks up.

'What's the matter? Did you want it sending back?'

I stare at her for a moment, the urge to scream almost overwhelming. But instead I turn and return to my desk.

* * *

For the rest of the day Si and I avoid eye contact. At just after 5 p.m., he gets up and shuffles some papers before swinging on his coat.

Addressing Ben, though it is clearly for my benefit, he says, 'I'm off now. Won't be in tomorrow, I'm in court all day. I'll let you know how it goes.'

Ben grunts without looking up, 'Don't let us keep you.'

I watch him cross the room from the corner of my eye.

'Lovers' tiff?' Ben asks as the door slams shut.

My fingers tense over the keyboard. 'Fuck off.'

Scraping back my chair, I pick up the packet of cigarettes.

At the other end of the office from where we sit is a cheap latex boxroom within which is the Editor's office, his desk crammed in with a wood-effect table and a filing cabinet. Just past his office is an external door leading onto a metal fire escape covered in black peeling paint.

Outside, I smoke two cigarettes in a row at the top of the stairs, looking out over the garden, which consists of a few bald flower beds and a series of badly laid slabs of stone shaded by ancient oak and cedar trees.

In the basement Giovanni, the Art Director, is shouting at the work experience girl. For a moment I remember how, when I first started working here, I'd been quietly impressed by the 'art department' with its dark room and photo studio. Now it just looks like a dank cellar with strip lighting and a few rusting Bisleys.

Breathing deeply through my nose, the cigarette smoke pirouetting up my arm, I lean back against the wall, listening to the music drift across the gardens from an open window somewhere in the distance.

By 7 p.m., all but Elaine, who is sorting through paperwork at her desk in reception, have headed home or more likely to the pub. Minutes later, she pokes her head around the door. 'I'm going home now. Don't forget to lock up, will you?'

Once alone, I sit back at my desk. Through the slats in the blinds I see the light outside is fading, Camden Town enveloped in a haze of pinks and pale blues as dusk settles.

Working in silence, I stay another couple of hours until the room grows cold, finishing off a piece I've been working on, trying to put a positive spin on a knife amnesty which has produced a total of about three weapons over the course of a month.

Swigging at a warm can of gin and tonic, I type my final words. Just as I am pressing Shut down on my computer, the phone on my desk rings.

My fingers hesitate as they reach the receiver, before snatching it and drawing it to my ear.

'Isobel? Thank God.' The voice is Giovanni's, behind him the telltale roar of the pub.

'Bloody hell, what you doing calling my work phone at this time, you nutter?' I ask and he carries on as if I haven't spoken.

'Listen, babe, I can't find my wallet. Could you pop down for me and see if I've left it on my desk?'

I groan at the prospect of navigating my way down the fire escape into the garden and then back through the door into the basement, unlocking and re-locking doors as I go.

Giovanni makes a kissing noise down the line, 'I know, I know. Pleeeeease, Issy babe . . .'

'You're fucking lucky I'm still here,' I say.

He tuts. 'Oh come on. You're always there.'

Rolling my eyes, I stand up. 'Wait there, I'll call you back in two minutes. You owe me . . .'

It is pitch-black outside as I make my way past the back door towards the stairs to the basement. The steps make a hollow ringing sound as my feet strike the metal. On the last step, I hear a rustling and a scratching sound at the end of the garden; for a moment my whole body seizes. But then the noise comes again, followed by a lurching and a scuffle, and I see the outline of a fox, mangy with a stump for a tail, disappearing into the undergrowth.

Moving more quickly towards the back door, I unlock the basement, the rusted handle resisting for a moment against my efforts.

Inside, I feel around for a light. As I press the button, the room lights up and I see Giovanni's wallet on his desk as he had described.

I am making my way back up the staircase with the wallet in my hand a moment later when the phone rings again.

Bloody Giovanni. I curse him silently as I move back into the main office.

'Have some patience!' I say as I pick up the phone, and for a moment the line is silent.

'Giovanni?' As I speak, my eyes peel instinctively back across the brightly lit room towards the darkness of the garden. Again, there is silence. But then, with the sound of my own quickening pulse throbbing in my ears, I hear something else, a low breathing down the line, and somewhere in the distance, the faint rumble of voices.

The chill that skims across the surface of my skin is like a shard of ice. Before I can think, my fingers slowly trace the surface of my desk towards my Dictaphone, which is in its usual position, plugged into the phone. My palms damp with a cold film of sweat, I press the 'record' button, and wait.

The line remains silent for another few seconds.

'Giovanni, this isn't funny,' I say and then he speaks. His voice is muffled, deep with an intonation that is a world away from my colleague's lilting sing-song.

'Isobel,' the muffled voice says. 'I am watching you. No police, or I will kill you too.'

Chapter 26

Gabriela

Tom was at band practice when she got home that evening, a note on the table saying that Harriet, one of the mothers of Sadie's new nursery friends, had agreed to take the kids given that she'd failed to get back in time, and that Tom would pick them up on his way home as he couldn't reach her to confirm that she'd be able to.

She had drunk so much by then that she had to read the words twice before moving to the counter and pulling down a half-finished bottle of wine and filling a glass. It was still sitting on her bedside table when she woke the following morning, as if from a strange dream.

Tom and she hardly spoke, he giving her the silent treatment and she too distracted to notice as she pulled on work clothes and left the house, wondering where the hell she was going to go, the hangover compressing her head from all sides. For want of a more inspired plan, she took the tube to Oxford Circus and sat on a bench on one of the squares until her body told her she needed to eat.

Walking to the nearest Pret, she picked a sandwich at random from the shelf and paid without waiting for her change. She pulled out a chair at the nearest table, drew her phone from her bag and composed an email to Emsworth, copying in HR as instructed.

Dear Guy, As mentioned, due to circumstances beyond my control, I have to tend to a family emergency with immediate effect and

will not be able to return to the office. I hope you will understand.
I've left my phone in the drawer of my desk. Gabriela

For another month or so, her days followed variations of the same theme, waking at the crack of dawn and leaving before her family got up, avoiding the possibility of a conversation she couldn't trust herself to have with Tom, which was to say any conversation at all. How could she trust herself not to slip up; not to say something that would give her away? Because no matter how she racked her brain she couldn't think of a way to tell him that she had left the FCO without telling the truth about why. One slip-up would be all it would take. As far as she knew the house could be bugged; there could be men following her at this very moment. The children were at risk, that much she could not afford to doubt . . . But at risk from whom?

At home on the sofa one evening, she worked through in her mind what she knew of Francisco Nguema from the files Emsworth had pulled out. Even inside, she didn't dare look at the page she had photographed – and she didn't need to. The image was there, like a scan, when she imagined it. She knew from her subsequent Google searches that he was a businessman based in Equatorial Guinea. From what she could gather, the FCO's interest in him derived from his connection to a British businessman she'd never heard named, however for all her internet trawling, there was nothing to hint at the root cause of the danger that lurked behind Emsworth's threats. Whatever it was, though it was deemed worth killing for.

When she blinked, once again the image flashed in her mind of the woman, her eyes scooped from their sockets, beside her the body of the child. When she opened them, Sadie and Callum were sitting in their pyjamas side by side on the carpet, and she had to walk out of the room.

'Are you OK?' Tom asked, knocking on the door as she rinsed her mouth in the sink.

'I don't feel well,' she said, moving through the hallway towards their bedroom. 'If it's OK I think I'll get an early night.'

In the weeks that followed she feigned exhaustion in the evenings after getting in from what Tom believed was just another day in the office, before heading to bed as soon as the children were asleep, leaving little space for proper conversation. She avoided the length of time in which Tom could look at her and see the lies lurking behind her eyes. In the bedroom, she found herself covering her body as she undressed, aware that the house could be under constant surveillance. There was a sense of betrayal she felt on Tom's behalf at being unable to warn him, but she had no choice. When she pictured Emsworth's eyes that day in his office, she was in no doubt of the sincerity of his threats.

She had taken to packing a basic lunch from home along with a piece of fruit to see her through the day, topped up by occasional stops for coffee, languishing in the same café for as long as possible before the looks of the waiting staff became too pointed to ignore. Financially, she could afford to go without work for a few months, eating into what remained of her father's inheritance, but still she had to be careful.

This particular morning, however, she had heard Tom stirring in the bedroom as she placed her bag on the counter and had run out before having to confront him. She had tossed and turned for most of the previous night, her mind bending with possible solutions, and the same thoughts churned over in her mind as she roamed the streets later that day. She could tell him she'd quit, that she had changed her mind and decided to do something else, but unless she had a clear idea of what that might be, he wouldn't buy it, surely, however naturally unprobing he might be; besides, even if she did decide to retrain or apply for another role, that would involve going to the FCO for a reference. HR was hardly likely to offer her one when, as far as they were concerned, she had simply buggered off without working out her notice period. She would rely on the support of Emsworth in any such application, but how could she go begging to the man who had threatened to have her family slaughtered, the man who had ruined her life? Besides, he would never help. This was personal, for him. She had humiliated him and he wanted her to pay.

The other option, she conceded, was to claim she'd decided she didn't want to work anymore, that she wanted to be a stay-at-home mum. But she would go mad, she was sure of it, if she had to take on the duties of primary carer. Besides, could she convincingly persuade Tom of such a change of heart, particularly as Callum was about to start school? What little faith she had then in her own powers of deception.

The only remaining choice was to say she had been sacked, in order to get Tom on side. But sacked for what? What could she have done that would get her kicked out so spectacularly, and without any warning? That brought her back to the only possible explanation: the truth. And the truth just wasn't an option.

By the time lunchtime arrived she was famished. When she pulled herself out of the thoughts looping in her brain and realised where she was, she felt a tingle of excitement.

The bell tinkled above the door as she stepped down into the bistro, the familiar counter on the left, tended to by the same chef she'd seen on numerous trips here with Emsworth. There was something so gratifying about being here in his favourite spot, reclaiming a snippet of her old life, walking the line of danger, knowing that he could walk in at any moment and could do nothing about her being here – it involved just the right amount of risk, not enough to warrant any kind of revenge, after all her mere presence was no real provocation after all, but just enough to make her feel alive.

As she stepped down into the room, the waitress shooed her into a red leather chair in front of a table by the window, smiling briskly.

'Anything to drink?'

'A Coke, please . . . and I'll have the mozzarella and aubergine bake,' she added, sitting back in her chair and tuning in to the buzz of her fellow diners.

She had just taken the first bite of her lunch when the bell tinkled.

When she looked up, quietly relishing the prospect that it could be him, she noticed a man duck into the restaurant, the tight, greying curls on his head brushing against the top of the low doorframe.

Scanning the room in that way people do, instinctively, when they sense they're being watched, she felt his gaze land on her for a moment before moving to the line of foods in plastic tubs.

'Luca,' he said to the man behind the counter before speaking amiably for a moment to the chef in Italian. So he was a regular here, too.

'I'll sit in today,' she heard him add in English to the waitress. 'I'm meeting someone here later.'

She had just taken a mouthful of her lunch, a string of mozzarella hanging between her mouth and the fork, when she felt him in front of her.

'Do you mind if I—' He paused, smiling amusedly. 'Sorry, terrible timing . . .' he added, acknowledging her full mouth, and then, 'There are no free tables . . . I'll move when one comes up . . .'

She blushed and dabbed at her mouth with the linen napkin, her smile tinged with apology.

Pointing to the chair in front of her, she said, 'Of course not.'

He was the sort of man she could see in the street and feel completely unmoved by: good-looking in that self-assured manner of the very rich, his coat and buffed fingernails putting hers to shame. And yet there was something about him that made her cheeks flush as he sat in front of her, while she attempted to make delicate the act of stuffing her face with mouthfuls of oily cheese.

It was a relief when a moment later his phone vibrated on the table and he picked it up, tentatively. 'I'm sorry, do you mind if I take this?'

'Of course not,' she batted her hands at him.

'*Allyo?*'

The moment he spoke, she felt the colour in her cheeks rise again.

When he hung up, a moment later, he looked at her and smiled. 'Sorry about that'.

'You're Russian?' The moment she said it, she felt stupid.

'*Ty govorish' po-russki?*'

'*Da*,' she shrugged, before reverting to English. 'I mean, not perfectly, but I worked there for a while.'

'Really, in Moscow?'

She nodded.

'What do you do?'

The question took her by surprise. The lie formed on her lips so easily. Besides, what did it matter? It wasn't like she would ever see this man again.

'I was working for a charity.'

'Really? I run a charity, what a coincidence! Which one were you with?' He widened his eyes, laughing. 'I swear – I'm not just saying that as a dodgy chat-up line.'

'Amnesty International,' she smiled. 'What about you?'

'Nothing quite so impressive, I'm afraid. We're a small environmental non-profit. GEF – Global Environmental Federation. That's my main business, anyway.' He shrugged, acknowledging her expression. 'I know, but believe me, I'm not so painfully earnest as that makes me sound. So whereabouts were you living?' he asked, turning the conversation back to her.

'Just off Tverskaya,' she replied, picturing the wide central street alive with cars, weaving erratically between lanes of traffic, the road flanked on each side with imposing shops and hotels; impossibly glamorous couples stepping out of chauffeur-driven cars.

The man nodded approvingly, as the waitress arrived with his lunch, turning to take her empty plate. 'Anything else?'

After a moment's hesitation, she shook her head. 'Just the bill, please.'

Standing, she felt self-conscious of her bare legs.

'It was good talking to you,' he said, looking up at her with an intensity she could not have fabricated when she thought back on it, later. 'My name's Ivan, by the way.'

She smiled. 'You too. *Do svidaniya.*'

'*Nadeyus, eshche raz uvidimsya,*' he replied: *I hope to see you again.*

His words brushed over her skin as she left the building, her whole body alive with anticipation, though for what she could hardly have imagined.

Chapter 27

Gabriela

Madeleine called again as Gabriela entered the tube station, and she pressed Reject, expecting to receive another frustrated voicemail. Madeleine had been due to travel abroad for work a couple of days after Gabriela walked out of the FCO for the final time, and so there was little risk of her showing up at the house demanding an explanation. But she'd be back soon, and there was only so long she could be fobbed off without a proper explanation as to why Gabriela had left so abruptly, not least given their pact, however ineffectual it had been.

When Gabriela got home that evening, Tom was waiting for her in the living room, Sadie and Callum already asleep upstairs.

'I was thinking we could take the kids to see my parents this weekend,' he said before Gabriela had a chance to make her excuses to have a bath and head to bed. For a moment her heart leapt at the chance to get away, the change of scene, time with the kids, but instantly her anticipation turned to dread. The prospect of the drive to Edinburgh, Tom and her side by side, free to catch up in a way that just couldn't end well. Not yet. Not while she was still undecided as to what she should do.

'I can't do this weekend,' she said, pausing. 'I'm sorry. Look, I know I've been really distracted recently, there's just been so much going on at work and I—'

'It's fine,' he said, picking up his coat and walking towards the door. 'I'm going for a drink. I'll see you later.'

Over the next few days with Tom and the kids away, a stillness settled through the house. Without the constant jangle of family life, of slammed doors, suffocating silences, the constant demands for attention that were never met, the house rang with questions Gabriela struggled to answer. The main one was devastatingly simple: how long did she think she could carry on with this?

While she could hardly believe the house was really under watch from within, still she found herself rushing from one room to the next, haunted by the sense that she was being chased. As though running from a future that was inevitable as the grave.

By the time Tom and the kids returned on the Sunday, she was desperate to see them.

'Gabriela?'

She heard the shaking of keys and then Tom's voice through the front door as she lay upstairs on the bed with a book, trying to escape her own head. Leaping up, she walked quickly to the hall and down the stairs to where Tom was standing, a suitcase still in his right hand, the other hand propping open the front door.

'Hey, love.' He kissed her on the cheek and pulled her into a hug before turning to indicate their children, comatose in the back of the car.

'When was the last time that happened?' he said, and she struggled to remember. They would be six and four this year – so far from being babies, and yet where had that time gone? The thought struck her briefly as heartbreaking.

'How was the journey?'

'Oh, you know, deeply glamorous. *Matilda* and *The BFG* on loop, outbreaks of war from the back seat, occasional retching.'

'I missed you,' she said.

'If you hold the front door, I'll bring them in one at a time,' he replied before stopping and turning to her, kissing her on the mouth. 'I've missed you too.'

* * *

Lying awake one night, a few days later, she decided to tell him everything – to clear the air of all the lies swelling between them, the duplicity as destructive to her family as any threat Emsworth had mustered. Even if she couldn't expect that Tom would know what to do, just the fact that he *knew* would infinitely lighten the burden.

She placed the memory of the photos firmly out of mind, telling herself that Emsworth was all talk. He could have pulled those images from anywhere; he could have found them online and printed them off to scare her with.

She would tell Madeleine, too. Madeleine would be livid that it had taken her so long to come clean, but now was better than never. Besides, the only way in which he could definitively ruin her life was by destroying her mind, and by backing her into this corner that was exactly what he was doing, crushing her from the inside out. The one thing he hadn't anticipated was that she would call his bluff.

She chose a Friday evening to do it, building herself up to it as she made her way back from her pacing along the Thames. She'd called Madeleine earlier that morning, leaving a message to say she had something important to tell her and asking her to ring back when she could. Collecting a takeaway on her way home from her and Tom's favourite curry house in Kentish Town, she texted him en route, asking him to stick the kids in front of a movie so that they could eat in peace. *I have something I need to tell you.*

Gabriela knew something was wrong even as she reached the front door.

'What's going on?' she asked as she moved into the hall and Tom gave her a look that told her to back off.

Sadie was sitting at the kitchen table, her eyes red and swollen.

'Something happened at the park, after school.' Tom's face warned her to tread carefully.

'What happened?'

'Sadie . . . she went off with someone.'

'I didn't,' Sadie said, her voice on the verge of hysterics. 'I told you, he said he was a friend of Mummy's . . .'

A fist hit her stomach.

'What happened, baby?' she asked and Sadie looked away, ashamed.

Tom beckoned Gabriela towards the back door, stroking his daughter's hair reassuringly as he passed.

'A man . . . I don't quite understand what happened, but we were at the playground on the Heath after school and I was helping Callum on the bridge, and when I turned around, Sadie wasn't there.'

'What do you mean she wasn't there?' Gabriela said, her voice accusing.

'I mean she wasn't fucking there . . . I looked for her for about five minutes and when I found her she was outside on the path, with an ice cream. She said some man had told her he was a friend of yours and to come with him to the café, that it was a surprise that you were waiting there . . . And then he bought her an ice cream and sent her back.'

Gabriela felt a scratching down the back of her throat and she turned, lunging towards Sadie so that she jumped.

'Sadie, who was the man?'

'I don't know,' she said, obviously scared. 'He was just a man.'

'What did he look like?' Gabriela asked and her daughter started to cry.

'I don't know . . .'

'What colour was his hair, his skin, his eyes? You must remember something, this is important. Think!'

Tom stepped between them, his eyes warning her to stop.

'Sadie, it's OK,' he said, still facing Gabriela, shaking his head almost imperceptibly. 'Don't worry. It's not your fault, OK? We're not angry. We're just happy that you're OK.'

'I already called the police,' he added under his breath. 'She gave them a description. He was a white guy, brown hair, she didn't remember anything else.'

'Why didn't you call me?' Gabriela asked, and Tom shrugged.

'I didn't want to worry you – and what would be the point? Sadie was safe, and what could you have done from the office apart from panic? I know how busy you've been, I didn't want you to rush home for no reason.'

'No reason?'

'For God's sake, Gabs, please calm down. It was a shock, but it's happened and she's OK. All right?'

He held her face in his hands before pulling her into a hug. 'She's OK.' He waited a moment and then he said, 'So, your text: what was it you wanted to tell me?'

'Nothing,' she said, pressing her nails into his back. 'Nothing. It doesn't matter. Let's just all go to bed. I don't feel hungry anymore.'

Once Tom was asleep, Gabriela got up. She could not quieten her mind, the memory of the message she'd left for Madeleine replaying in her head. The message she'd left telling Madeleine to call back, that she had something important to share, something Madeleine would really want to hear . . .

Someone had been listening. Someone was listening to her messages, and they had responded with their very own, delivered to her via her daughter. For hours her mind circled the reality of what had happened, and then she faced it head on, staring it in the face so that she could see it for what it was: Emsworth had had her daughter abducted. Sadie. A man she didn't know had held Sadie's hand and led her through the Heath, a place where Gabriela believed they were all safe, and bought her an ice cream. She imagined the invisible imprint of his hands wrapped around the cone that touched her daughter's mouth.

She wanted to scream. No, she wanted to storm out of the door and run to Emsworth's house and pull one of his sons from their bed and hold a knife to his neck. She wanted to watch Emsworth's face as he saw the blood.

Calm down, she told herself, knowing such thoughts would get her nowhere. Besides, where did he live? Without her work phone, she didn't even have his mobile number.

She pulled out her phone, opening Gmail, pressing New Message. Her fingers hovered above the keys.

She knew his work email by heart, but what would she say? Any correspondence to the FCO was monitored, and how would he react to her contacting him there?

The truth was, she didn't need to contact him. She didn't need to email him or write a letter, corner him in a dark alley to tell him that she had changed her mind, that she was not going to tell. Because whatever she did or did not do, he already knew.

For a moment, she imagined running out into the street and screaming a very different message to him, into the wind. Daubing her home with the words she dared not type. Instead, she moved to the cupboard and pulled out a wine glass and sat at the table with a drink before moving to the sofa sometime around two, considering her next steps.

She was sitting at the kitchen table drinking coffee when Tom came down the next morning.

'Did you not sleep?' he asked and Gabriela shook her head.

'Me neither. I'm going to call the police this morning, follow it up.'

'What's the point?' she snapped, desperate to stop thinking about it, or at least for Tom to. Terrified that he would put two and two together, ridiculous as that seemed. Of all the conclusions he might jump to . . .

'What's the point? Really? Well, maybe that they catch the guy so he doesn't try to abduct another little girl, Gabs. That could be a reasonable point.'

'Don't say that,' she said, looking away. 'I mean, fuck's sake, Tom, why weren't you watching her?'

'Excuse me?' He turned to her so that she wished the words back in her mouth, but she couldn't stand down.

'You heard me.'

'Fuck you.' He practically spat the words. 'What a fucking thing to say. Do you have any idea how full on it is trying to watch two of them with the playground that packed? No, of course you don't, because when was the last time you took them out on your own?'

'I beg your pardon?' She pulled herself upright, her cheeks burning with combined fury and the knowledge that he was right. But she'd been working, up until a few weeks ago. She was earning money to pay for the roof over their heads. His architectural wet dream.

'Oh look, just leave it, yeah?'

'No,' she said, standing up, knowing it was a bad idea to pursue this, but unable to stop herself. 'Say what you think, Tom – you think I'm . . .'

They were in the doorway to the hall and when she looked up, Sadie and Callum were standing on the stairs watching them.

'Hey darlings. Mummy and Daddy were just talking about something. Did we wake you?'

'Come on guys,' Tom said, ushering them back upstairs without looking at her. 'We'd better get you ready for school. Your mum had better hurry, too, or she'll be late for her precious job.'

As soon as Tom had left with the children, Gabriela dressed and headed to the phone shop on Holloway Road, buying a new SIM to fit her phone.

Outside, she took her old SIM from her pocket and dropped it into the nearest bin.

They barely spoke for two days after that. When Tom did finally address her, he said, 'I'm thinking of going away for a few days. Jim and I . . . There's a gig up in Glasgow . . .'

'Right,' she said.

'It's next weekend . . .'

'OK. Fine with me.'

'Really?' He sounded surprised. 'But won't it interfere with work? The kids will need dropping off and picking up on the Friday from tennis camp.'

'That's OK.'

She moved towards the fridge to pull out a drink, and when she turned around he was watching her.

'So you're fine with it?'

'Sure,' she said.

'OK.' There was a hint of disbelief in his voice. 'I'll go and call Jim then, tell him that we're on.'

'By the way, I've got a new number,' Gabriela added before Tom disappeared out the door.

'How come?'

'They've upgraded our phones. Everyone has a new one.'

She waited for him to call her out, but he barely shrugged. 'Fine. Text it to me and I'll replace the old one.'

Tom left first thing on Friday morning. The kids' tennis club that ran for the duration of half-term didn't start until ten. Sadie had packed her things in a bag and was waiting at the foot of the stairs when Gabriela came down, just after seven.

'Is Callum still asleep?' she asked and Sadie nodded.

'Hey, listen,' Gabriela said, settling herself next to her daughter on the narrow tread and kissing her on the forehead, drawing her towards her and relishing the feeling of the child in her arms. Closing her eyes, from nowhere she pictured the image of St Genevieve and immediately her mind moved to her own mother. Gabriela winced.

Sitting up, she lifted Sadie's face to look at hers. 'That man, on the Heath . . . he didn't do anything to you?'

Sadie held her eye and shook her head. 'He just took me to the café and bought me an ice cream.'

'How old was he?' She was racking her mind for meaningful questions, hoping to elicit an answer – what kind, she couldn't be sure: one, she supposed, that would suggest it was unconnected to Emsworth, a fluke event that would free her of the guilt that ran up her back like fingers, threatening to choke her.

'Don't know,' Sadie said. 'He said he was your friend . . .' She started to cry and Gabriela wrapped her arms around her again.

'It's OK,' she said. 'It's not your fault. I promise it's not your fault. Everything's going to be OK.'

*   *   *

There was a soft breeze as she opened the front door a while later, Callum taking her hand and tottering along next to her as they made their way from the house, along Crofton Road. Sadie walked a few steps ahead, her hair swishing against the top of her rucksack.

As they approached the tennis courts Gabriela looked sidelong at Sadie to check if the venue threw up any associations from the incident in the playground a little further along the path, but her daughter looked undaunted. Briefly, Gabriela bristled at the thought of leaving them there, but then she remembered, with a further chill, that it really could have happened anywhere.

'They're supervised all day, right?' she probed the coaches before leaving.

'Of course,' they smiled back at her, just another diligent mother making sure her babies were safe. 'They won't be out of our sight.'

'I'll pick you up at four, OK?' She kissed each of them on the forehead and watched them run towards the other children, falling into easy conversation with faces she didn't recognise.

Turning reluctantly from the courts, she moved automatically towards the café, reluctant to head straight home, back to the incarceration of those four walls. Besides, she wasn't ready to leave the children just yet, not entirely.

Walking in the direction of South End Green, her feet moving of their own accord along the path they knew so well, she reached the top of Kite Hill, the view of London spilling across the skyline like the chaotic signature of a life support monitor; she considered stopping for a moment to take in the skyline. But when she reached the bench, she saw it was already taken by a couple of women lost in conversation, side by side. The younger one was seated on the bench, her hand resting on a double pushchair; the older woman in a trench coat. How she envied them. When was the last time she had been out for a walk with a friend? The very prospect of it felt odd, and yet so much of her youth had been spent here on the Heath, roaming every inch of it with Saoirse on long hot summers and dark wet winters that seemed they would never end.

Looking back through a nostalgic lens, the light bleeding through the leaves at the tops of the trees, she pictured them sprawling on the long grass at the end of Fitzroy Park, where a secret world opened out at the end of the lane. Their very own Narnia.

It was the same lane her mother and father and she would amble down years earlier, her mother regaling them with the lyrics of Keats who also used to walk here.

Where are the songs of spring? Ay, Where are they?
Think not of them, thou hast thy music too,
While barred clouds bloom the soft-dying day,
And touch the stubble plains with rosy hue

They had been sitting at the table in the garden one evening when Saoirse told her she couldn't have children. She hadn't known then that Gabriela was already pregnant with Sadie. It had made it awkward, telling her about the pregnancy mere months later, though she said all the right things, squealing when they asked her and Jim to be, in the loosest sense of the words, Sadie's godparents. But beneath the expression of excitement, Gabriela could see the pain in her friend's eyes. She could see it every time she whinged about Sadie's lack of sleep or yet another kids' party or the countless ways in which she found herself demonstrating her reluctance to be a parent.

And though it had been easy to tell herself they had simply lost touch, that they drifted apart in the way that old friends do, when she thought of it, when she really looked into the past without blinking, making herself study it in a way that was both painful and momentarily blinding, she knew this was not the whole truth.

Saoirse disapproved. Of the mother Gabriela was, or rather the mother that she had failed to be. The mother Saoirse had never had the chance to become.

It was the unspoken line between them, the force that quietly pushed them away from one another.

The morning of Sadie's fourth birthday, Gabriela had taken the train to Bath to meet the estate agents who were supposedly overseeing the rental of her mother's house. Burglars had got in while the current tenants were away on holiday and there was a dispute over liability relating to certain items which the insurance company was refusing to cover.

It was another glitch she could not afford to deal with. The previous tenants had left the place in a state and the costs of the repairs when they left had hardly been touched by the deposit the agency had taken, and the only course of action, as she saw it, was to go there and put a rocket up their arses.

Saoirse and Jim had been staying the night. By the time she got home at around three that afternoon, emotionally frazzled, only to find Tom had yet to pick up the cake she had ordered two weeks earlier in order to ensure it would be ready for the big day, she was ready to kill.

'Jesus Christ, Gabriela, it's just a cake, calm down.'

'Calm down? Tom, it's a cake I ordered for our daughter's birthday, not for the day *after* our daughter's birthday . . .'

'I'll go and get it now! People aren't coming for another hour.'

'Great, so you get to go off and do that while I sort out the birthday tea. I assume you haven't started getting that ready?' She opened the fridge and started pulling out a loaf of bread and cheese to make sandwiches.

'It's four little kids, Gabriela, I hardly think they're expecting cordon bleu. I've bought crisps and cartons of juice, the sandwiches will take five minutes, if that, and Saoirse and Jim have the balloons already blown up in their car. They'll be back with the kids at half past. Chill out, OK? It's going to be fine.'

She bit her lip so hard that she felt it might bleed.

He was right, though. The party had gone well, without so much as an outburst of tears over who won pass-the-parcel. Tom had spent most of the time topping up parents' glasses while Gabriela doled out the birthday tea, cleaning up as she went along, keeping herself busy so as to avoid any opportunity to become embroiled in unwanted small-talk.

Once the kids had all gone, Jim and Tom headed out for a pint, and Saoirse and Gabriela settled in the garden with a bottle of wine and some roll-ups Tom had left in the drawer.

'Jesus, I thought they'd never leave,' Gabriela said, pouring Saoirse a glass and lighting up.

'Who?'

'The *mothers*,' she said, turning the 's' into a hiss.

'They weren't that bad,' Saoirse said, and Gabriela raised her eyebrows.

'Yeah, well, you don't know what it's like.'

'What what's like?'

They had both had a few glasses over the duration of the party, and in the sunlight she could see the danger dancing at the side of Saoirse's eyes in that way she knew so well.

'Don't worry about it,' Gabriela said ungracefully, trying to side-shuffle away from whatever it was that was making her tetchy.

'No, Gabriela. I don't know what what's like?'

'You know, having to hang out with your kids' friends' parents.'

Saoirse snorted. 'Like you'd know either?'

'Excuse me?'

Saoirse was lighting one of Tom's roll-ups and when she looked up, she shot Gabriela a look she recognised as one her friend reserved, growing up, for other people. Never her.

'When was the last time you hung out with Sadie and her friends' mums?'

The question was very clear and yet she stumbled.

'Are you serious?'

Saoirse looked at her without replying.

'Saoirse, is there something you want to say to me?'

Saoirse didn't rush to answer, but when she spoke it was as though she had been mulling the words over in her mind for years. 'I just wonder if you should have a think about what you're doing.'

'What I'm doing?'

'About your choices. The kids, they never see you. They're growing up so quickly . . . If I had kids, I—'

'Yeah, but you don't have kids, do you, Saoirse? So what the fuck do you know?' The words shot out of her mouth with a savagery that she instantly regretted.

'Hey, love.' Saoirse's face changed suddenly and when Gabriela turned she saw Callum standing in the doorway, his eyes wide with worry. 'Your mum and I were just telling each other a story. How're you doing, is your programme finished? Do you want me to put something else on?'

'I'll do it,' Gabriela said, standing and walking across the garden to pick up Callum.

Saoirse must have slipped out while she was busy putting on *Tom and Jerry*, for when she turned back to where she had been sitting, Saoirse was gone.

'Darling, have you seen Aunty Saoirse?' Gabriela asked Sadie, who was sitting on her bed flicking through a picture book. When she looked up, there was a sadness in her eyes and Gabriela wondered if her daughter had heard them talking.

'She went to see Uncle Jim and Daddy at the pub,' Sadie said.

'Oh yes,' Gabriela said brightly. 'I think she said, I must have forgotten.'

After a pause, she asked, 'Are you OK?'

Sadie nodded.

'You had a good birthday?'

'Yep.'

'Do you want to come downstairs, watch cartoons with Callum and me?'

She shook her head.

Gabriela inhaled. 'OK. Well, we're downstairs if you change your mind.'

Callum fell asleep on the sofa, less than an hour later. As she carried him up to his room, she peeked through Sadie's door and saw the light was off.

Tucking Callum in, she headed straight to bed, worn out by the afternoon's wine and the argument with Saoirse. She was already asleep by the time the three of them returned from the pub that night. When she woke up the next morning, Saoirse and Jim had gone.

Gabriela's mind was dragged back into the present by the sound of her phone. For a moment, she imagined Madeleine's number flashing on the screen, returning her call, the one in which she had asked her to ring back, that she had something she needed to tell her . . . *Shit.* What would she say? Madeleine would be back in London soon and she wouldn't be easily fobbed off. As far as she was concerned the two of them were still committed to investigating Emsworth with their two-pronged approach. Now that she wasn't there in the office, Gabriela could legitimately bow out – except for the problem of what to tell Madeleine in terms of why she had left, and to explain away the voicemail she had left.

Though perhaps she was overthinking it. People left jobs all the time; not least women with young families. She could tell Madeleine she was disheartened having not got the promotion and had decided to take some time out to spend with the kids before they were both in school. It would be a believable enough lie, from anyone else.

But as she pulled the phone from her pocket, seeing Tom's name on the screen, she remembered that no one apart from Tom had this number. Not Emsworth. Not whomever it was he had paid to listen into her calls. And not Madeleine.

She might have felt invincible. She might have felt she could disappear off her friend's radar, avoiding the awkward questions Madeleine was yet to ask, had it not been for the fact that Madeleine worked for the NCA, meaning she could find Gabriela's home address in a matter of minutes, once she started looking. And given that Madeleine still had not been given an answer as to why Gabriela left the FCO, it would only be a matter of time before she found a spare moment to call, from wherever far-flung place she was now, to grill her on the details. If she rang and found Gabriela's old number disconnected, there was no telling how dramatically she would react, what questions she would start to ask, and to whom.

Letting Tom's call ring out, Gabriela logged onto her emails and retrieved Madeleine's number from the signature of one of her more recent emails.

Keeping her words light, her explanations fudged, she typed: 'Hey, it's Gabriela . . . Got a new phone, and a new job! Kind of. Family stuff. . . I'll explain when you're back. FYI, last message was a false alarm. Sorry. . . Know you're busy, don't bother calling before you're in London, just text me when you're back. Gx.'

Pushing her phone into her pocket, Gabriela felt briefly jubilant. That was one potential minefield kept at bay, but it didn't resolve the more pressing problem of her diminishing funds. Now that she was out of work, the money she had left from her final pay cheque and the remaining inheritance from her father could only last so long. If bills, addressed to her – because this was her house, after all, and Tom was still officially her tenant – went unpaid, and red-stamped letters started piling through the door, then surely even Tom would have to sit up and take notice. If the classes their children were enrolled into each week, the new sports kits they needed, the lunches they'd grown accustomed to at the pizza restaurant down the road, had to be phased out – *then* surely he would start asking questions. Wouldn't he?

She walked for more than an hour, with half a mind on the children, looping back towards the direction of home before she reached Kenwood, sneaking past the tennis courts and looking in, reassured to see Sadie and Callum in the throes of a game.

By the time she got home it was nearly eleven thirty. Filling the kettle, she sat for several minutes at the kitchen table with nothing but the familiar white noise of Radio 4 wrestling with the sound of the boiling water.

Standing briefly to make coffee, she pulled out the laptop from her bag and settled at the kitchen table, before logging onto a job site. After a few clicks, she reached the words 'Past employment', and instantly slammed the screen shut. Standing, she walked to the counter, held onto the worktop and screamed. The sound of her own voice soothed her and when she turned, for a moment she could see her father seated on his reclining chair facing the garden.

Quite clearly, she could recall him sitting for hours on end after they had moved in without saying a word. The thought squeezed at her chest, constricting her breath, and she realised how much she missed those days, however painful they might have felt back then. The simplicity of that contact, the complicity of the silences, the lack of expectation on either side.

The sound of knuckles rapping against the square of frosted glass at the end of the hall cut through the silence, and she took a sharp intake of breath. Applying the chain, she opened the door a fraction and saw the postman's face looking expectantly back at her.

'Oh, thank you,' she said hastily, opening the door properly and taking the pile of post from his outstretched hands.

Feeling her breath return to normal, she leaned back against the glass. Marching back to the table, she picked up her keys and headed out into the sun, surprised by the overwhelming brightness as it hit her.

She walked and walked until it was time to collect the children. As she approached, Sadie and Callum were immersed in a cool-down activity and for a few minutes she stood and watched them from a distance, a twinge in her heart at seeing them in a way that a parent rarely does; that brief insight into the person they are, without the family unit to prop them up. Callum smiled coyly, shrugging his shoulders as he returned the ball to one of the older boys. Sadie suddenly looked so much older, so self-contained, as she absent-mindedly plucked the strings of her racket between shots.

'Where did you go?' Sadie asked as they walked home, stopping for an ice lolly in the newsagent's on Swain's Lane.

'Work,' her mother said, her voice fracturing, but only for a split second.

Sadie was quiet and when Gabriela turned to her she was looking at her already, her expression unreadable.

'Why?' she asked, smiling quizzically.

Sadie shrugged. 'You haven't got your bag.'

'Well, eagle eye, if you must know, I was working from home.' They were holding hands and Gabriela hoped her daughter hadn't felt her grip momentarily tighten.

As she watched Sadie run ahead to catch up with Callum, she thought perhaps she could do this, and then she felt the doubt drifting in again, without warning, creeping up on her like a fog, barely visible from a distance, but once it hit, so blinding that it enveloped everything.

Without Tom, the weekend passed quickly; a trip to the supermarket bleeding into hours loafing around the house, Callum kicking a ball against the wall of their tiny garden while Sadie drew, her legs tucked under her, curled on the sun lounger.

That Monday, she couldn't be bothered to cook and so the three of them went for a quick pizza at the old Italian café on the round-about by Parliament Hill Fields after tennis, the kids heading straight for the sofa when they got home, not noticing their father was already back as they grappled over the remote.

Gabriela spotted Tom through the kitchen doors pacing the bottom of the garden. It took a moment to register that he was on the phone. Even from this distance, she could sense the intensity with which he was speaking.

When he came back in, his eyes widened as he saw her standing there.

'Hi,' she said.

'Hi,' he replied, attempting a smile. 'I didn't hear you come in.'

'Everything OK?'

'Course. You?'

He brushed his hand over her back as he moved past.

'Who were you talking to?'

He paused for a moment in the hallway and then replied, 'Harriet, Millie's mum. She was asking if Sadie could have a play date on Friday.'

When he turned to face her, Gabriela looked back at him in silence, acknowledging for the first time in their relationship that Tom was lying.

Chapter 28

Gabriela

It would be misleading to say that she hadn't stopped thinking about Ivan since that first meeting in the Italian restaurant on Crown Passage – the man who would peel the skin from her body and reveal the rot. Aside from the occasional jolt of recollection in the weeks that followed, she had barely thought of him at all.

There had been so much else going on. Summer was fast approaching and with it a roster of school-related events, now that Sadie was finishing her first year, which Tom and she would split between them, the bulk of the daytime duties falling to him because otherwise how could she explain her sudden availability for Sports Day after being inescapably chained to the office for so long?

And what could she tell him, without putting their children's lives at stake?

It was four months to the day since she'd walked out of the office, though the specific date only occurred to her later on. She had been distracted by the fight she and Tom had had that morning, though it wasn't so much a fight, when she thought back on it, as a stalemate: a lingering cloud of resentment that hung over every room of their home. She couldn't even remember what the argument was about, only the feeling; the same dull ache that for so long had stretched in front of them, like an elastic band waiting to snap.

Unfair as it was, she felt a growing bitterness towards him that she knew was illogical. She had jeopardised everything she held dear in order to protect them, to protect their children, to protect Tom, and yet she couldn't even tell him. Irrational though it was, she couldn't help but resent him for the burden she had to carry alone.

She had been so deep in thought that morning, browsing in Waterstones on Charing Cross for as long as she could, trying to transport herself elsewhere, before continuing to wander the streets of London, that when she looked up and saw him there again, the two of them walking towards one another on Crown Passage, for a moment she felt as if she had been tugged from one world into the next.

'Hi,' he said first.

'Ivan?'

Their eyes caught and for a moment neither of them spoke, but then they slowed down, clearly both heading for the same place.

'You going in?' He didn't move towards the bistro and for a moment she didn't reply, ambushed as she was by these feelings that suddenly surged inside her as she stood opposite this man who was practically a stranger.

He pushed open the door to let her through and she smiled.

'I'm sorry, you didn't tell me your name . . .' he said and she blushed.

'It's Gabriela.'

The coolness of the restaurant compared to the street was almost chilling and she held her arms across her chest for warmth.

'Table for two?'

A waitress she didn't recognise spoke and then turned, ushering them towards the only free table, near the back of the room, before they could object. Turning briefly to her and pulling a face as if to say *What can you do?* Ivan followed and Gabriela's feet moved after him, as if by their own will.

Lowering herself into the chair and watching Ivan do the same, she felt their legs brush against each other under the table.

'Sorry,' she said, rearranging herself, but he didn't respond.

'So, do you know what you'll have?' the waitress asked, her face moving between them.

'Oh, I'll— you go ahead. I'm going to the loo.'

As she stood, her hands moved quickly through her hair, her legs out of step with the rest of her body. It was as though the internal dial that controlled the senses in her body had been turned up too high. It was a feeling that was hard to pinpoint then, but looking back she would recognise it for what it was: guilt. Guilt for what she had no intention of doing and yet which was also utterly inevitable, even then. Fear, too?

As she moved past Ivan, she became aware of a hint of musky aftershave wafting from his direction. Tom had never worn fragrance. They had laughed at the idea when discussing what they might buy each other as presents on their first Christmas together, over a Chinese takeaway, Tom conceding that he wasn't enough of a proper grown-up to use such things.

'So you're saying you're some sort of man-child,' she had replied. 'Well, that's an attractive prospect.'

'My eternal youth is just one of the reasons why you adore me,' Tom had shrugged in response, and she had rolled her eyes, biting into a prawn cracker, her lip sticking to the surface and leaving a tiny blister.

What had changed, between then and now? The answer was heartbreakingly clear: everything had changed and yet not enough.

'So what brings you here again?' Ivan asked once the food had arrived, two plates of chicken Milanese set between them preventing her from fiddling with her phone by way of distraction.

'I'm working around the corner,' she said, unsure of her tone.

'Oh yes, you work at a charity.'

She made an expression of surprise and he shrugged unapologetically. 'I have a good memory.'

'Clearly.'

'Says the woman who remembered my name.'

She looked down, as if her next question was little more than polite conversation. 'And what about you?'

'Me?' He raised his eyebrows as if her question hadn't been clear enough.

'Are you based around here?'

He nodded, taking a mouthful of food.

'My office is on Pall Mall. Just around the corner.' He stopped and raised a napkin lightly to his mouth, apparently unsure of what he was about to say.

'Listen, I don't suppose . . . Today is my birthday and I was going to go for a drink after lunch, to celebrate. I wonder if you would join me?'

'Oh, happy birthday,' Gabriela said, her voice faltering. 'I'm sorry, I have work—'

It wasn't as though she didn't resist, she would tell herself later. It wasn't like she didn't try to say no.

'So how was the party?' Tom asked above the whistling of the kettle, the following morning.

Gabriela was sitting at the kitchen table, still in her pyjamas, a dressing gown pulled tightly around her body, her hands shielding her face in a futile bid to block the bright sunshine that flooded in through the French doors. When Tom spoke, her mind was somewhere else, picking through the details of the night before, trying to work through the knots gathered in her stomach.

Davy's Wine Bar stood at the bottom of a discreet flight of steps on the corner of Crown Passage. Inside, under the old champagne vaults, a wooden counter ran along the right-hand side, and there were old cask barrels and low wooden tables lit up by candles in bottles. It was like closing the door against the world as they stepped inside, into a space untouched by the rhythms of the streets so that down here it might be any time or season. Her boots pressed tentatively against the stone flooring as if scared of giving her away as they moved towards the back of the bar, where two red leather armchairs were tucked out of sight.

Ivan spoke as though their being here together, in the middle of the afternoon, was the most normal thing in the world.

'You OK with champagne?'

'I'll have a gin and tonic,' she said, and he tipped his head in approval.

It was just a drink with a stranger, she told herself. It was the sort of thing she'd had to do a thousand times before, for work.

'Is it actually your birthday?' she asked over the edge of her drink, which was strong and bitter and sweet at once.

'Of course, why would I lie?'

She raised her eyebrows slightly, her gaze drifting over his left hand as he lifted his champagne flute. There was no ring, though that meant nothing. Glancing down at her own bare fingers, she didn't flinch; the image of Tom retreating as quickly as it had emerged.

There was something so disconnected about this place, about everything in this moment, that she could almost imagine she was someone else.

'Happy birthday,' she said, as their glasses touched. 'So, how old are you?'

His eyes narrowed. 'How old do you think I am?'

Her eyes scanned over him, drinking in the details: the curly hair, still thick but flecked with grey. His skin was lined in that way that made men more distinguished, and women reach for the scalpel.

'Fifty-two?'

He pulled back. 'Whoa, OK, don't hold back.' He took a swig of his drink.

She laughed, 'Oh God, sorry – so how old are you?'

He shrugged. 'Fifty-three.' When he smiled, she felt an ache, as if she were pressing the brakes, too late, just seconds before a crash.

'You're not married?' she asked before she could stop herself.

'If I were married, I probably wouldn't have asked you for a drink.'

Did she blush?

'And you, Gabriela?'

She tilted her head. 'No, I'm not married.'

* * *

It had been his idea to move on, some time later, after enough drinks had been consumed that the stairs on the way out of the bar seemed steeper than when they arrived.

Outside, it was still light, the sky swollen with heat and toxins; when she asked Ivan the time, he told her it was nearly six.

'Shit,' she said and he looked taken aback.

Recovering herself, she added, 'It's just that I left my things at work, and it's too late to get them. I just need to make a call.'

Moving away from him, she let her hand hover for a moment over Tom's number, before opening a new text message instead.

She was drunk. Even if she hadn't intended to continue onwards with Ivan, she would need to stop and eat before she got home. That was how she justified it to herself as she typed, as if it was still not a done deal: *Have to go to a work leaving drinks, won't be too late.*

She was still dithering about whether to send it when she heard Ivan moving behind her and hurriedly added *Gx*. Send. And then it was done.

'So you grew up in London?' he asked as the waiter poured the wine, a pressed white napkin folded over his forearm.

They had moved on by then to a sushi bar overlooking the city skyline, the sort of overly fashionable, eye-wateringly expensive place no one Tom knew would ever choose to come, which was exactly why she had suggested it. Still, if they were spotted there, she could claim to be taking a foreign businessman for a working dinner, in line with her job at the FCO. The job Tom still believed she had.

'Yup,' she took a sip of her wine. 'North London. And how about you, where do you live?'

'Everywhere, nowhere . . .' he smiled. 'My work means I move between London and Moscow, mainly, so I have an apartment there, and here I have a house in Richmond. You know it?'

A sense of relief ran over her; he was wealthy enough that he could easily reside in Hampstead proper, which was just a couple of miles from her house. The distance between their London worlds, her north to his south-west, was so pronounced that regardless of the physical space between them he might as well have said he lived in Tokyo.

'Actually, I don't know it at all, really. I've been once, maybe. But not for a long time.'

Their eyes met and her skin flushed so that she looked down. The effect of the gin and wine she had drunk seemed to have plateaued so that she was in a state of otherness that was beautifully calming.

'You still live in North London?'

She stalled long enough, raising the iced water they had ordered to her lips, that by the time it was necessary to answer, the waiter had appeared again with a tray of sashimi and vegetables carved to look like exotic birds.

'This looks beautiful,' she said and Ivan nodded, ignoring the food and staring across the table at her. It was the first moment she had considered what she must look like to him, in the clothes she picked out every morning to fit the image of the competent mother-of-two, off to King Charles Street to oversee a busy department of civil servants.

How could she have known this morning as she absent-mindedly selected a pale pink shirt and navy ribbed sweater, the black Whistles trousers she had bought herself in the sale on her birthday, where she would end up?

'So, tell me about yourself,' she said once the waiter had disappeared into the darkness of the dining room.

Ivan made a few movements with his mouth, indicating that he was either working out how to explain it, or how most effectively to evade the subject.

'I suppose you would say I'm an entrepreneur, which is a way of saying I do everything and nothing. Mainly I work in sustainable energy. I know it sounds terribly boring but it's interesting – to me, at least – and lucrative. Although I don't think you're supposed to say things like that in England, are you? Too distasteful. I also run charities, as you know . . . and which you definitely *can* say in England . . .'

She smiled.

'And how about you, are you still with Amnesty International?'

She shook her head. 'No, not anymore. The one I'm with now is much smaller. I suppose I'm like you, a bit of this, bit of that.'

Gabriela picked at a piece of sushi with her chopsticks and counted the seconds in her head as the time passed and Ivan said nothing to call her out on her lie.

After a moment he said, 'Shall I ask for a fork?'

She laughed and flashed her middle finger at him before picking up some rice she'd been hopelessly chasing around her plate between her fingers and popping it in her mouth. 'No thanks, I'm fine as I am.'

Ivan nodded, his eyes locking hers. 'Yes, you are.'

Her fingers had fumbled with the keys in the lock as she pushed open the front door to her house later that night, tentatively at first. Stepping inside, she saw that the lights in the living room were off. Closing her eyes for a moment in silent prayer, she walked forward, removing her shoes, holding the bannister to steady herself.

It was nearly midnight according to the clock in the hall. With a shiver of relief, she noticed the absence of light filtering down the stairs from their bedroom. Tom, never one to feel perturbed by her late returns, would sleep through until morning, never stirring to wonder what fate might have befallen her after dark.

Placing her handbag on the hall table, she moved into the kitchen. The room felt like an abandoned stage set, unnaturally still. The light from the streetlights beyond the garden wall illuminated her daughter's colouring pencils, scattered across the Formica dining table. Pouring herself a glass of water, she sat in front of the piece of paper Sadie had left for her, inscribed with the words: FOR MUMMY, LOVE SADIE.

The drawing was of the four of them, Callum substantially smaller than exact ratio would dictate, Tom and Gabriela on either side. There were flowers and hearts etched crudely around them, as if to create a frame, but within its walls none of them was smiling.

There was a sudden sound like a child's bone snapping as the light clicked on in the kitchen. She turned sharply to see Tom in the doorway, blinking in boxer shorts and an old T-shirt.

'Fucking hell, you nearly gave me a heart attack!' She jumped before gathering herself, her heart thumping in her chest as her fingers lifted self-consciously to the skin under her eyes. The thought crossed her mind that she should have taken a moment to look at her face, to see what it betrayed.

He paused for a moment, looking at her, and then frowned, moving over to the sink.

'Sorry, I only turned on the light. I had no idea you'd be back so late.'

Swallowing, she ran a hand through her hair. 'Sorry, I didn't realise either. It was someone's leaving drinks after work, I couldn't get out of it and then I got delayed coming back. I sent you a text.'

'I know . . .' He filled his glass and moved back towards the doorway. 'Are you coming up?'

'In a minute,' she said and his reply was lost as he moved back up the stairs.

She was trembling as she sat at the table, waiting for the sound of Tom's footsteps to fade out on the hallway upstairs. Once the silence took hold again, suddenly the room was cold, the gravity of what was happening consuming her, and she stood, looking about for a shirt or a blanket to wrap around herself, where Ivan's arms had been, but she found nothing.

After a couple of minutes she stood, suddenly unsteady on her feet, and moved towards the stairs, her toes pressing uncertainly on the treads. On the landing there were two doors directly above the kitchen, in the wall adjacent to her and Tom's room. It was her own teenage bedroom split in two with a flimsy wall demarcating Sadie's space and Callum's, the single renovation they had managed since Tom had moved in.

Pushing open the door to Sadie's room, for a moment her eyes struggled to find her daughter in the darkness. And then they did and the stillness of her body, the shard of moonlight slicing across her features – Tom's features – pressed at Gabriela, like the blade of a knife, so that she had to turn away before she felt herself bleed.

'Gabriela? I said how was the leaving party?'

Tom was still standing in front of her with a cup of tea, and she could hear Sadie and Callum squabbling in the hall.

She had been prepared to apologise for her part in the argument the day before, but it seemed to Tom it was long past. How did he do that? How did he so readily move on from those moments, as if nothing had ever happened?

'How much did you drink? You look rough as arses.'

'Thanks so much,' she replied, the normality of his tone helping to smooth the juddering transition from last night to present day.

This role play of theirs was one she knew well and she played her part with ease. 'That was actually the precise look I was going for. With any luck I might also smell as well.'

Making a face of concentration, Tom leaned into her. 'I mean, a bit, yes.'

Pulling back from him slightly, instinctively fearful of what he might sense, she met his eyes and smiled before looking away, feigning a distraction on the other side of the room.

And yet, despite the feeling that followed her around the house, the truth was that she really didn't have much to feel guilty about in relation to her evening with Ivan. She hadn't done anything, had she? Not really. It would have been so easy to say yes when he asked her back to his place. It would have been the easiest thing in the world. But when he leaned in to kiss her good night, once she'd made her excuses about an early meeting the next day, she had turned her face so that his lips pressed against her cheek instead of her mouth, the slight scratch of his stubble brushing against her hair as he pulled away respectfully.

'Well, Gabriela, thank you for the company.'

Was she disappointed that he hadn't pushed harder, that he hadn't expected more from her as he helped her into a taxi, placing a note into the driver's hand, ignoring her insistence that she could take the bus?

'Are you not going to work, then?' Tom asked, before moving into the hallway where Sadie and Callum were waiting in their coats and hats.

'I am, just a bit later than usual today,' she said.

'Good for you.' Tom winked. 'You deserve to take it a bit slow for once. Remember to take a shower though, yeah?' He pulled a face and walked towards the front door, slapping his keys into his pocket. 'Right, kids, say goodbye to your mum, but don't get too close!'

Chapter 29

Isobel

The night air hits my cheeks as I stumble out of the office, my fingers instantly fumbling in my pocket for my phone, punching out Si's number.

Come on, I beg for him to pick up, the memory of the caller's voice ringing in my ears. Instinctively, I feel in my other pocket for the recording device Maureen had bought for my birthday as a thank you for the stories I'd written publicising local fundraising events for the refuge.

'Issy, what do you want? I've got to be in court in the morning.' From the clarity of Si's voice, there is no way he had been asleep and I remember that he is probably still pissed off about what had happened earlier.

'I need you to come over. Please.' My voice sounds rasping. There is a brief pause and then he says, 'Fine. I'll be there in five.'

By the time I get back to the flat he is already waiting at the door.

'Fucking hell, that was quick,' I say. 'I thought you were in bed.'

A self-styled Bolshevik from Tunbridge Wells, Si had launched his own furious protest against rising rents and inflated coffee prices in Kentish Town by moving to a one-bed in Stamford Hill, which is twenty minutes away, minimum, even in a cab.

He looks at the floor. 'I lied, I stayed out.'

'Right. And you just happened to be . . .?'

'Just around the corner from the office? Erm, yes. Jesus, Isobel, do you want me here or not?'

'Sorry,' I say, moving forward and taking his hand. 'Come up.'

The light in the hall still isn't working and as I push open the door to the flat, I briefly imagine it through Si's eyes: the dingy kitchen counter, sparsely decorated with a couple of ashtrays and a jar of instant coffee. The same wall-hanging I'd inherited from the previous tenant when I moved in.

The floors are the original wooden boards, modernised with decades' worth of stains, partially concealed by a battered Persian rug my mother bought years ago at a shop on Highgate Road; it was one of the few things they'd left behind when they moved.

'Listen,' I say, pulling out a bottle of whisky from one of the cupboards, along with two glasses. Pouring a triple measure in each, I pass one to Si, catching him inspecting the rim before he drinks.

'I do actually wash the glasses before I put them away,' I snipe, moving to sit next to him on the tiny sofa. 'Listen, I need your help with something.'

'Oh yeah?' He leans forward and kisses my neck.

'Si, I'm serious, I need you to listen to something.' Pushing him away, I pull the dictaphone from my pocket. 'Just listen to this, OK?'

Si exhales loudly and then I hear the voice again, over the crackling of the recorder. I really should invest in a digital one, though somehow it would feel disloyal to Maureen to get rid of the one she gave me. In the eight months since we've got to know each other properly, she's become as much a mother figure as a friend.

Isobel, I am watching you. No police, or I will kill you too.

'What the hell's that?' Si shifts slightly away from me.

'It's him,' I say. There is a satisfaction in my voice and I stare intensely at him for a moment, challenging him to contradict me this time.

'Who?' He looks concerned.

'It's the man I was telling you about. The one from the Heath,

196

who sent me the shoes! The brick, I . . .' There is more excitement in my voice than fear and Si blinks.

'What the hell? Start at the beginning. He's called you?'

'Yes! I need to ask you something. You studied languages . . .' Si looks up, as if he had misheard the question.

'Listen to this, in the background. If you turn the volume up you can hear talking . . . Is it anything you recognise?'

Noting the desperation in my face, he reluctantly closes his eyes and listens. The recording is grainy but under the fuzz there are clearly men's voices in the background, though the whole thing feels distorted.

'God, I don't know, I can hardly bloody hear them . . .'

Turning up the machine to full volume I press Play again and watch his face intently.

'Yeah I think he's used one of those voice-masking apps. It's all a bit slurry.'

Si shakes his head. 'I don't know what language it is they're speaking but it's nothing I understand.' There's a pause and then he says, 'Is . . .' His voice is cautious. 'I'm really worried about you.'

Without saying another word he leans forward and pulls me gently against his chest. When he releases me a few moments later, he doesn't try to kiss me. Rather, he says, 'I think you should call Oscar.'

Knowing how Si feels about Oscar, I know what it must take for him to mutter these words.

I nod. 'Yeah, I'll call him in the morning,' I say, knowing full well that I won't.

Si is pulling on his trousers the following day, ready to leave for court, when it strikes me.

'Hey, what about that old professor of yours? What's his name . . . something Mansfield?'

'What about him?'

'He worked as a translator . . .' I know this from the only time I ever met him when he spent the duration of our conversation blasting me with the details of his achievements, which include speaking fourteen languages, not least various obscure regional dialects that make him not only an expert in his field but, in his own words, extremely well paid.

Despite being a total arsehole, Professor Mansfield made quite an impression on Si back in his student days, and after several mentions and a single uncomfortable meeting, I had filed his name away for a moment when such a contact might come in handy.

'Isobel, no . . . Just the police, all right? Stop playing detective, for God's sake,' Si replies with a knowing look when I suggest he might give me his number. 'Anyway, I can't just give you his details without asking.'

'Why not?'

'Because I know you, and he's busy and it's rude and—'

I pull back my head. 'Rude? Oh, fuck off, Si. You realise how serious this could be? And anyway, it's not like I couldn't dig out his number myself, it would just save a lot of time if you gave it to me.'

He looks up at me, shaking his head resignedly. 'Fine. At least let me ask him. If he tells me to piss off . . .'

I give him a grin, the first I've mustered in a long time, and immediately Si's face softens. 'But don't harass him, OK? And call Oscar.'

Chapter 30

Gabriela

She was sitting in the gallery at the Sobell Centre watching the tail end of Sadie's gymnastic class the following Saturday when her phone pinged in her pocket.

Callum, who had just returned with Tom from the soft-play area, was sitting on the bench beside her, his cheeks red with heat, his fringe plastered to his head. Reaching into her coat, Gabriela breathed in the signature scent of stale foam and ancient leather on his skin, carried over from the hour he'd just spent happily careering in and out of a pit of plastic balls encrusted with other children's saliva, heaving his tiny body up and down miniature slides, building precarious towers out of brightly coloured geometric shapes.

Tom, who had lost this week's argument as to which one of them would accompany their son while the other parent got to hang out on the seats outside the gymnastics area, keeping a vague eye on Sadie, was queuing for a drink. From this distance, he smiled sardonically at her, miming the process of hanging himself with an imaginary noose as she reached into her pocket, mouthing for him to get her something.

'G and T?' he replied, eyeing up a fridge stocked with Ribena and Capri Sun.

She rolled her eyes amusedly, playing along with this well-worn routine of his, before pulling out her phone and instantly feeling the seat beneath her drop several feet.

The number was unrecognisable but the source of the message was instantly clear:

Gabriela. Sorry I haven't been in touch. How are you?

She must have unconsciously made a sound or a sudden movement because Callum looked up. 'Mama, what's the matter?'

'I'm afraid there was no Bombay Sapphire, so you'll have to make do with lukewarm Diet Coke.'

Tom's voice overlaid Callum's and she jumped, dropping her phone under the seat in front of hers.

'Shit,' she muttered under her breath.

'I'll get it,' Tom said, but before he could lean in Gabriela leapt from her seat, kicking the phone away from his hand.

'Whoa,' he said, pulling himself upright, searching her face.

'Sorry,' she placated him, leaning forward, struggling to play down her jitteriness as she stuffed the phone into her pocket.

Leaning in conspiratorially, she whispered, 'Not that I was looking at presents for your birthday next week and didn't want you to see or anything . . .'

A thought moved across his face as he looked at her, waiting for a moment before passing her drink over.

'Right,' he said with a tone that unnerved her.

She sipped quickly from the can and the force of the bubbles gushed up her nose, causing the liquid to rise in her throat.

'Jesus, are you drunk or something?' he asked as she clapped her hand over her mouth, spilling her drink over her sweatshirt in the process.

'Shit,' she said again, mouthing sorry to Callum when he looked up at her, signalling his disapproval at her use of a prohibited word.

'I'm just going to go to the loo, try and wash this off,' she said, standing unsteadily. She imagined herself under surveillance as she moved through the leisure centre, the echoes of balls slamming in the distance, children screaming in ecstasy and frustration.

There was an overpowering smell of disinfectant as she slid the lock of the cubicle door closed and settled herself on the lid of the toilet seat. Reading the message again, a ripple of apprehension shivered over her. How could she not remember giving him her number? Racking her brain for a memory she knew she would never have misplaced, for a moment she wondered if he could have taken it without her knowing. Had he snatched her phone from the table when she went to the bathroom and dialled his number from it, waiting for her own number to flash on his screen before saving it to his contacts list and returning her handset? He couldn't have, because she had taken it with her, every time. Hadn't she? She wasn't so removed from reality that she would risk Tom calling and Ivan thinking to answer the call.

And then she remembered. As they bustled into the back of the taxi on the way from the bar to the restaurant, the panicked moment when she felt for her phone and found it wasn't in her bag. Convinced that she must have left it at Davy's, she asked Ivan for his phone to call hers, and when it rang it was in her coat pocket, exactly where she had left it. Without even realising it, she had given him her number, stored casually in his recent calls list.

Had he known in that moment that he had it? she wondered, ignoring the thrill that rushed through her. Had he intended all along to make this more than a one-off event? What had he thought when he looked at her?

It was there, in the taxi, that he had wrapped his arm around her for the first and only time that evening, and, for those moments as they swept through London, the rain against the window restricting the outside world to nothing more than murmurs of light against black, she allowed herself to rest against him.

Her fingers hovered between Reply and Delete until she heard Sadie's voice from the other side of the cubicle door. 'Mum?'

She stood and flushed the toilet. 'Hey, Sadie. You all finished?'

'Yeah, Dad told me to tell you to hurry up. We're going to get pizza.'

'OK, darling.' She switched her phone off and stuffed it in her back pocket. 'I'm coming right now.'

* * *

'What were you thinking for dinner?' she asked once they were back at home, following a brief post-lunch trip to the playground on the Heath where they'd watched the kids hurtling across the same obstacles they'd been tackling since they were toddlers.

'I wasn't – I'm not that hungry, we just had lunch.'

She paused, but already Tom's reaction rattled inside her, vibrating so that there was nowhere for it to go except outwards; it was as if they had passed through some invisible door in their relationship so that any respect she might once have held for the notion of treating each conversation with Tom, each interaction, in isolation, had been permanently lost. Now and seemingly for evermore, every exchange between them was a continuation of a previous one; every syllable he uttered that irked her simply the next instalment in an ongoing dialogue designed in a way that seemed it would never end.

She felt herself lurch from zero to ninety in a single sentence, though nothing was any different to how it had always been; Tom ordering twice as much as everyone else, merrily pulling out the joint card only she ever paid into when the waitress arrived.

'Yes, Tom, but the children need to eat three times a day, if you hadn't noticed. Anyway, no one else ate quite as much as you . . .'

'All right, I didn't realise we were on rations . . .'

'There's nothing in the fridge,' she continued, slamming the door shut with unnecessary force.

'All right, Gabriela. Well, one of us can go to the shop.'

'One of us?' she replied. Where was this rage coming from? And yet, she felt justified in her frustration. All week, Tom stayed at home, picking up bits of work here and there as he fancied, the time between dropping the kids off and picking them up completely his own, his mind free from the constant threats that rotated in hers, the tornado of questions Tom never thought to ask let alone answer, and he couldn't even manage to stay on top of the occasional domestic task that would otherwise inevitably fall to her. How could it be she who paid the bills and yet it was still her job to remember to stock up on food as well?

'I'm sorry, Gabriela. Are you insinuating I don't do my fair share?'

'I'm not insinuating anything, Tom. I am simply saying it's nearly four o'clock and in an hour or so the kids will need to eat again, and there is no food in the fridge.'

'And that's my fault, is it? Do you have any idea—'

'You know what? I don't need another argument with you.'

She walked out, ignoring the sound of him calling after her as she moved up the stairs to the bathroom.

But despite what she'd told him, the truth was she did need an argument. Anything to make her feel like it wasn't her fault, all of this; anything to alleviate the sense of shame that was creeping up, pushing through the cracks in the doorframe as she moved into the bedroom and slammed the door, picking up a pillow and screaming into it until her throat burned.

Chapter 31

Gabriela

It was a couple of weeks later when she found herself walking down Pall Mall, precariously close to Crown Passage. Madeleine was still away and the truth, Gabriela realised, was that she was lonely.

I'm in town, I just wondered if you fancied a coffee?

She sent the message only half-expecting him to reply. Besides, what were the chances of him being around and free for a drink at such short notice?

When she saw the moving dots on the screen indicating that he was typing back, her whole chest tightened.

No but I fancy a proper drink. Davy's Wine Bar? In an hour's time?

She stopped in a Starbucks on the way, slipping into the Ladies and checking her reflection. It was just a drink, she told herself as she reapplied her lipstick, adding a touch of mascara to her lashes from the make-up bag she'd slipped into her handbag before leaving the house that morning, as if subconsciously planning it.

He was already there when she arrived and she felt a smile break across her face at the sight of him.

'Good afternoon,' he said as she sat down opposite him.

'Hello.'

'Have you eaten?' he asked and she shook her head.

'OK,' he said, standing. 'Let's go . . .'

* * *

Le Beaujolais was tucked behind Charing Cross Road, the incongruous Parisian font and burgundy signage at odds with the traditional Georgian façade of the London terrace of which it was a part.

'You know this place?' he asked as the taxi pulled up outside.

She shook her head, smiling, as he led her towards the door on the right, away from the main bar and down the stairs into a starkly lit dining room where a series of hatches opened onto the kitchen at the back. The walls on either side of the room were lined with wine racks, mismatched frames and endless shelves of knick-knacks, from old bottles to broken lampshades.

'You said you studied in France, so I thought you might enjoy it . . . They do the best fish soup.'

'So, you live in North London?' he asked later, taking a sip of red wine, and she held his eye.

'It's where I grew up.'

'You have a flat?'

'I rent a room. I travel so much for work it doesn't make sense to have a big place to myself.' She was a natural liar.

'So do you ever come to Richmond?' Ivan asked and she shook her head.

'I don't know it at all. I mean, I think I visited the park as a child, with my parents.'

'They also live in North London?'

She shook her head. 'They're both dead.'

He nodded. 'I'm sorry to hear that.'

'It's OK, we weren't close. Well, my mum and I . . .'

'That's sad.'

She shrugged. 'It is what it is. She wasn't a very good mother.' The words ran off her tongue. 'Anyway, I remember it was beautiful.'

'It is,' he said. 'We should go there sometime.'

She flushed, looking down at her plate.

'What?' she asked a while later, looking up and finding him watching her thoughtfully, and he said, 'You just remind me of someone, that's all.'

'Who?'

'Just someone I knew a long time ago.' Changing the subject, he asked, 'How's your soup?'

'Delicious. Best I've had since Paris, but I haven't been there for so long I'd forgotten how good it was.'

He smiled, his eyes softening. 'We should go.'

'Where?'

'Paris.'

She laughed, 'I thought we were going to Richmond Park? I can't keep up.'

'All in good time,' he said, and she laughed.

He looked at her seriously. 'Why not?'

Feeling the bread harden in her mouth as she chewed, she looked away, replying under her breath. 'Yes. Why not?'

Chapter 32

Gabriela

She had been in the playground, squatting in the damp sandpit with Callum, distracting herself with the memory of that night, the feeling of her head resting on his shoulder in complicit silence in the back of the cab, when her phone pinged a few weeks later.

Gabriela, it's Ivan. I've been in Moscow but I'm back for a few weeks and would love to see you. Let me know.

Her heartbeat quickened as she stared at the screen, stuffing the phone back in her pocket as she heard Tom and Sadie approach.

'There was no toilet roll and Sadie needs a poo so we'd better go,' he said and she nodded, standing and picking up Callum who screamed, arching his back so that she practically had to wrestle him into the buggy.

'We could watch a film later,' Tom said on the way home and she nodded, trying to smile, trying not to think about the message from Ivan warming her pocket, suppressing the butterflies that fluttered in her chest when she pictured his eyes watching her.

'Sure,' she said. 'Why not?'

She didn't reply at first, not for a few days. But then, the following Saturday, after another round of extracurricular activities rounded off with a passive-aggressive stand-off with Tom over whose turn it was to do the dishes, she found her fingers hovering over his message.

She had drunk a glass of wine or two and Tom, who had been out at a gig the previous night, was already asleep upstairs.

Hey. How was Moscow? How long are you back for? she typed, the thrill of it making her squirm.

His reply was almost instantaneous, and it was only once it landed on her screen that she realised that she had crossed another line.

I'm going back on the 23rd.

When she didn't answer, a few seconds later, he sent another:

I was thinking of going away somewhere in the countryside next weekend, will you join me?

I can't.

Why not?

Her fingers hovered above the buttons. Why not? There were so many reasons, every reason, as to why not.

Her hesitation spurred him on.

Come on, Gabriela, please . . . Do I have to beg?

From upstairs, she heard a floorboard creak and her chest tightened.

I can't. I'm sorry, she typed, before turning the phone to airplane mode and switching on the television to distract herself from the sense that a storm was gathering and there was nothing she could do to step out of its path.

'Saoirse and Jim have invited us to stay next weekend,' Tom said the following day.

She couldn't be sure why she was so taken aback.

'Really? Saoirse hasn't mentioned it,' she said, though as the words formed, she realised she couldn't remember the last time they had talked.

'I was speaking to Jim and it came up. They're desperate to see the kids. And anyway, maybe Saoirse thinks you're always busy . . .'

He lifted his paper as he said the final words, as if protecting himself from a potential shower of bullets. But for once she wasn't on the attack.

Saoirse. Gabriela felt a twinge when she thought of her now.

Even before their bust-up on the evening of Sadie's party, their lives had long since started to diverge. It was hard enough keeping up with friends who had children of the same age, who were running the same treadmill within a square mile of where they lived. Saoirse and Jim, on the other hand, were leading a child-free, seemingly untethered existence in rural Devon – and so it was natural that the weekly meet-ups with the woman she once considered her closest friend had slowly given way to monthly phone calls, fading to occasional dinners and then texts berating themselves for leaving it so long and promising to catch up soon. *Just as soon as things settle down a bit.*

And then, things were said that were impossible to come back from.

It made it easier, though, the increased distance between them, given everything that would follow. She could admit that much to herself now. Would the events that had unfolded ever have come to pass if Saoirse hadn't moved away? If anyone could have seen through all of this and made Gabriela hold herself to account, it would have been Saoirse.

'Next weekend?' she said thoughtfully before interrupting herself. 'Oh actually, I can't. It's Madeleine's birthday party, and I can't miss it. You go, take the kids. They'd love it.'

Even as she said it, she felt like a traitor. What kind of person willingly ignored their best friend?

Tom paused as if he wanted to say something more, but then he sighed. 'OK, I'll tell them.'

He was in the bath half an hour later when his phone rang in the pocket of his coat. Ordinarily, Gabriela would have ignored it, but the ringer was so loud that she pulled it out to silence the sound.

When she looked at the name flashing on the screen, something inside her made her answer.

'Hello?'

'Oh, sorry, I—'

'Hi, Harriet,' she said.

There was a pause the other end, then Harriet replied, lightening her voice.

'Hey, Gabriela, good to hear you! Sorry to ring so late, only Millie was asking if Sadie could come over on the weekend and I . . .'

Her words petered out.

'Right,' Gabriela said, as Tom emerged at the top of the stairs in a towel.

'Who is it?'

She looked up at him and spoke pointedly into the phone receiver, without letting go of his gaze. 'Tom's here now, Harriet. I'll just pass you over.'

She slid the phone through the bannisters, placing it on the tread by his feet, hearing him speak unnecessarily brightly into the receiver as she walked into the kitchen.

'You all right?' he asked a couple of minutes later as he followed her into the room. She was standing by the window looking out at the darkness.

Slowly, she turned to him, her face devoid of expression. 'Why? Shouldn't I be?'

'What the hell, Gabriela? If something's the matter, spit it out, please.'

'Nothing is the matter, Tom, I'm just curious as to why Millie's mum is calling you again . . .'

'I'm sorry, what? Gabriela, how else exactly do you imagine I might arrange a date for Sadie, when she doesn't have a phone? Perhaps Millie's mother and I should communicate via pigeon carrier? Or maybe some form of Morse code would suit you?'

'Oh, fuck off, Tom, you know what I'm saying . . .'

'Do I? Do I know? Because, you know, it seems to me like you're always banging on about your mental load, and yet when I make an effort to offload it . . .'

'Oh, what are you even talking about, Tom? Can you hear yourself?'

He continued, unhindered. 'When I go about doing the countless things that I do every day, that go unseen by you, you freak out. It

212

seems to me that I can do no right by you. You know what? It's almost as if you want me to fail.'

His words hung there, and there was nothing she could say to offset them. Because maybe she did want him to fail, maybe it was simply easier that way, to justify the thoughts that wouldn't leave her alone, the things she already knew she was going to do. Maybe she wanted it to be him, not her, who made the first move to leave.

At a loss as to what to say, she marched past him, slamming the door on her way upstairs.

She didn't bother to be discreet as she slumped on the bed, her body vibrating with the thought of Tom and that woman, pulling out her phone and holding it, and feeling – what?

She didn't want to think about it. Instead, she typed.

So, next weekend: where are we going?

Chapter 33

Isobel

In the end, I don't bother waiting for Si to come back with a number. A quick Google search reveals that Professor Austin Mansfield is still a visiting lecturer at UCL, where he was Si's tutor. The email I send him from my work address is not so much misleading as elusive in terms of the nature of my enquiry, whilst massaging his ego in just the right way. His reply is almost instant.

I'm terribly busy, but I could manage twenty minutes tomorrow morning if you could come to me . . .

We arrange to meet at the gates to the university, on Gower Street. At the flat, I pull on jeans and a pale blue shirt. Through the window, there is a blue sky and a light wind brushes the tops of the trees.

It is just past 9.30 a.m. by the time I leave, my hair still damp. Deciding to make my way on foot rather than take the bus, I walk past Mornington Crescent, turning left past Euston, avoiding the more direct route along the endless grey and brown façade of Hampstead Road.

We arrive within a minute of each other, his linen suit weaving precariously across the busy road towards me. He has that unmistakable whiff of academia, old books and stale coffee.

'Shall we go to my office?' he says. Once inside, he directs me towards a studded green-leather chair. Sweeping across to the other side of the desk, he assumes his position with his fingers crossed over each other, his elbows jutting out to the sides.

Following his cue, I reach my hand into my bag and pull out my phone, as well as my laptop and a USB stick. A few minutes later I turn the sound on my computer to full volume. As the fuzzy sound of the recording fills his office, ricocheting off a wall-to-ceiling bookshelf stuffed with thick leather spines, there is the distinct sound of men talking in the background of the recording.

A few seconds later the man's voice kicks in and at this volume his low growl makes my flesh crawl. From the timbre, it is almost certain that he has used some sort of voice-distortion technology.

Professor Mansfield's eyes move in my direction as the recording stops. 'Interesting,' he says after a moment of silence. 'Where did you get this?'

'It's a long story, it's to do with a piece I'm working on,' I lie. 'The thing is, I really need to know what language they're speaking.'

There is no point embroiling him in the truth of it. In my experience, too much truth has a way of making people feel uncomfortable; the trick is to give them just enough.

'May I listen again?'

The enthusiasm in his voice makes me sit straighter, and I nod, smiling, as I drag the cursor back to the beginning of the recording.

Again, there is a low hissing sound and then the men's voices, which seem clearer with every listen.

'Well, I have an idea,' he says eventually, rubbing his chin with his fingers. 'But if you don't mind, I'd like to seek a second opinion.'

'That's wonderful,' I say. 'I can download a recording directly to your computer.'

'Very good. I'll have a word with a colleague and I'll be in touch,' he replies briskly, once it is done, before showing me the door.

I am back in Somers Town, half-heartedly attempting to get residents on Tariq's old estate to talk to me about the problem of knife crime in the area, when I get the call.

'I've conferred with a colleague,' Professor Mansfield says as soon as

I answer. 'It turns out my suspicions were right. Of course, the Balkans aren't strictly my speciality, hence the need for corroboration . . .'

He leaves a dramatic pause. 'The language you heard on the tape, it is Gorani. I'm assuming you won't have heard of it? The speakers are Slavic Muslims, little known to us over here. They come from the Gora region in southern Kosovo between Macedonia and Albania. Over the years the poor fellows have been claimed by Albanians, Bosnians, Bulgarians, Macedonians and Serbs, but the general view is that they should be treated as a distinct minority group, indeed that is how they see it. Rather primitive folk, really, had a tricky time of it during the war, in the Nineties.'

I can picture him expanding, in his element.

'In the main, they sided with the Serbians during the war, then when it officially ended they were left bedded between Albanian territories with much of their culture swallowed up. Most of them fled, all over the place. I believe there is quite a community in London, actually – relatively speaking. Haringey, mostly. Left rather a ghost town back home, I'm afraid to say. Not much there now, though still terribly beautiful, of course . . .'

He clears his throat and when he speaks again his tone is less self-assured. 'As for what they are saying . . . I'm afraid that's rather harder to say. There are very few words we can pick out, it's all very garbled. The recording is terribly unclear.'

There is a moment's disappointment, but then I feel my spirits rise again. I may not know what they are saying, but I am ahead of where I was this morning. I have a language. I know where they are from. Feeling a strain of hope, I speak quickly.

'Thank you,' I say. 'Thank you so much – and if there's anything I can ever do to return the favour . . .'

'Actually, I do have a new book coming out next year. If you fancied giving it a write-up in the paper that would be extremely satisfactory . . .'

Chapter 34

Gabriela

Paddington was heaving, a throng of commuters bustling for space beneath the departures board. Gabriela squinted up at the platform numbers, cradling a cup of coffee in one hand, her overnight bag in the other.

It seemed like another lifetime when she'd stood in this station on her way to clear out her mother's house the summer after her death, once she had seen out her year in Paris – leaving without saying goodbye to Pierre, partly for the thrill she got out of imagining him knocking at her apartment door and finding her gone, and partly because she simply wasn't sure what to say.

Her dad had offered to drive her there, as Tom had tried too, but there was something so intrusive about the idea of him rooting around in her stuff that she ended up making an excuse about needing to do this on her own. In the end, she had agreed to let Saoirse go with her and they had stood smoking roll-ups in silence as they waited for the train to roll into the exact platform she was boarding from now, with the same uncertainty, the strangely familiar feeling that nothing would ever be the same again.

The train was relatively empty. As London gave way to intermittent fields and then rolling hills, she let herself relax back into the seat. Tom had taken the children in the car the day before, piling them in among the sleeping bags, thrown-together clothes and cheap wine and then heading straight to Devon in the Friday night traffic.

She and the kids had spoken on the phone before she left the following morning, Sadie ploughing on at double-speed about Saoirse and Jim's new puppy, Daphne; Saoirse in the background sending her love, too busy cooking pancakes to come to the phone.

She tried to push back the hurt she felt and focus on her own deceit.

'Madeleine's party might go on late, so tell your father I'll give you a call on Sunday,' she said to Sadie, covering her tracks in advance. 'What time will you guys be back?'

'Not until late,' Sadie said, repeating Tom's answer for him, before barely listening to Gabriela's goodbye.

Bath Station echoed with voices as Gabriela stepped out onto the platform two hours later, her feet hesitating before making contact with the ground. Around her, the space seemed to spin with movement and sounds; families reuniting with group hugs, a busker's guitar straining against the screech of brakes.

When her phone rang a minute later, she almost didn't answer. At least it helped her to think of it that way, retrospectively. She liked to think she had drawn back, even briefly, in that moment, hovering on the edge of a line that once crossed could never be stepped back from.

After all, it wasn't too late, not yet. She could have called Tom back then and there and told him she'd had a change of heart. She could have taken the next train down to Devon, which wasn't that far from here, when she came to think of it. The sudden realisation of her proximity to Tom and the children was instantly terrifying and instinctively she glanced over her shoulder as she answered the phone, her tone lightly enquiring, as if the call could be anyone.

'Hello?' Her hand held the phone tightly against her ear, containing the sound of his voice.

'Are you here?'

Did she pause before answering?

'Yes.'

'Come outside, I'm waiting in a car.'

Pressing her overnight bag tightly against her side, she held it both like a shield and an arsenal of weaponry as she moved out through the exit and into the city.

It was immediately obvious even before the headlights blinked surreptitiously: the shine of the buffed bodywork incongruous against the grubby backdrop of buildings immediately opposite the taxi rank. Gabriela could feel eyes on her as the door opened and she ducked inside the car with its impossibly clean seats, devoid of stray crisps and discarded DVDs.

The brief feeling of being watched brought back a sudden memory of Emsworth, of the tail he had put on her. How had she forgotten? The likelihood was that he still had someone watching her now, and yet even that didn't make her think twice before stepping into the car. It was as if in Ivan's presence she felt protected against the world, cushioned against reality. Impenetrable even with her head floating in the firing line.

For a moment he didn't speak, he didn't move forward to greet her in any way. He simply looked, as if memorising everything about her.

'Fancy seeing you here,' she said, and he smiled, his eyes shining.

'It's good to see you.' There was a sincerity in his voice that moved her.

Leaning forward gently, he kissed her on both cheeks and the smell of him was intoxicatingly unfamiliar.

'You said low-key,' he said as the car pulled off. 'And I took you at your word, so I hope you meant it . . .'

'Good,' she said, with a flush of relief, remembering her insistence that they avoid one of the fashionable spa hotels in the area, just in case of bumping into anyone she knew.

'Well, it shouldn't take too long,' he said as the driver let off the handbrake, the sudden movement of the car causing her to shunt forward, and Ivan held out his hand to catch her.

He smiled. 'You should probably put on your belt.'

* * *

The village was the sort of chocolate-box picture-postcard scene she had spent so many years resenting after her mother had left, abandoning them for a similarly provincial existence.

Through Ivan's eyes, she saw it in a more rational light – the beautiful thatched roofs, the walled garden, the church spire piercing the grey sky, as they approached.

He led her through the archway into the inn, watching her to check her reaction.

'Don't look surprised. Even we nouveaux-riche Russians are capable of discretion when the occasion calls for it.'

She tried to laugh as he squeezed her hand, moving purposefully towards the reception desk, but her whole body was trembling. Despite the lightness of the conversation, every part of her throbbed with a wary acceptance of what was happening. She was checking into a hotel with a man she hardly knew, a man who was not the father of her children. With every step, she shifted closer towards a point from which there was no return. Here, in this fragile state of purgatory, hanging precariously between *before* and *after*, the inevitability of what awaited them hovered just in front of her, though still far enough away that she could claim not to see it. There was an irony in that, or perhaps a twisted logic, given what would follow.

And then they were on the stairs, and his hand rested a moment on the door to their room. With a single step, she was inside and the door behind her closed.

They barely left the hotel for the duration of their stay, moving between the bed and the freestanding bath, safe within the confines of those four walls. Briefly they made it to the dining hall, where the sound of other diners vanished so that all she could hear was the tinkle of cutlery and the sound of the blood pounding in her body.

'So what attracted you to Russia?' he asked later that night, stroking her hair, his body cradling hers under the soft cotton sheets.

'I don't know,' she said, her heartbeat quickening at the prospect of another lie. But when she opened her mouth, the truth spilled out. 'When I was growing up, my mother was obsessed with Russian philosophy.'

Noting his expression, she smiled. 'Yes, she was deeply pretentious . . . Like I said, we didn't have a great relationship – I'm not sure she was necessarily the person you'd want to be stuck next to at a dinner party after a few drinks, but she was . . . I don't know, she was a character. I think that's what you call it, someone who is a clever arsehole? She was *impassioned*.'

Ivan laughed.

'Her parents were Jewish and had escaped persecution in Spain under Franco. My grandmother was a Communist, as a direct reaction to Fascism, I suppose. My mother was young when her own mother died and she became obsessed with reading up about Communism, though I don't think she was ever convinced. So I think she transferred that interest to something more palatable; she became obsessed with Russian philosophy and culture instead. She took me to see the Bolshoi at the Royal Festival Hall in London when I was a child, and she sobbed the whole way through. I've never seen her so happy.'

'She sounds impressive,' Ivan said and she felt herself flinch.

'She was,' she said. 'Just not that interested in being a mother.'

Gabriela felt a slight tightening in her chest.

He paused. 'I think we would have had a lot to talk about.'

'You would have,' she said, allowing herself to be distracted from the comparison. 'She would have thought you were wonderful.'

'So she had good taste,' he laughed, rolling her over so that she was facing him. 'And what about your father?'

'He was a maths teacher, a professor at the local college. He and my mother met at a student rally – a veritable cliché – but I'm not sure they were ever suited to one another. My father adored her, and she . . . I suppose she loved to be adored.'

'They didn't stay together?'

She shook her head. 'They were always poles apart. You need something in common, don't you?'

Gabriela felt her voice dry up as she spoke, the realisation taking hold. 'You need more than a child to hold you together, to help you go the distance. Sometimes fondness, even love, isn't enough.'

He watched her then and she spotted his cheekbone clench and she wished she could push the words back into her mouth.

When he spoke he said, 'Life isn't always straightforward.' As he reached his hands towards her face and kissed her gently, any wariness she felt at the strangeness of his expression melted away.

Saying goodbye at the train station on Sunday morning, Ivan respecting her insistence that she take the train home on the basis that she had work to catch up on, she cried, the repercussions of what she had done, what she could never step back from, rattling through her as he held her in his arms. Or maybe she was crying because she had to leave.

'Hey, what's this?' he asked tenderly, touching the tear rolling down her cheek. 'Come home with me.'

She shook her head, urging herself to pull it together. 'I can't.'

'Why not?' There was an urgency to his voice, a hint of frustration.

'It's complicated,' she said and rolled her eyes in ridicule at the cliché. 'No, it really is. I'm . . . I'm not in a position to start a relationship.'

He looked at her, watching the shape of the words tumbling from her lips with an intensity that made her look away, but then his grip tightened and he nodded, considering something she couldn't fathom.

'It's complicated,' she repeated, because there was nothing else to say, and he watched her, a look of acceptance finally spreading across his features.

'OK,' he said at last.

'Thank you for a beautiful weekend,' she replied. 'I'm sorry, I have to go now.'

But even as she pulled away from him, there was a look in his eye that told her he knew she couldn't stay away.

Chapter 35

Isobel

The women's refuge stands on a cobbled side street off Kentish Town High Street. Trying the front door and finding it locked, I move around to the back, stretching up on my tiptoes to peer over the wall.

'Maureen?' I see her head sticking out from behind a shrub, a pair of secateurs in hand. As she stands in response to her name, she puts a hand up to her chest.

'Isobel, bloody hell, are you trying to give me a heart attack?'

I smile back at her. 'Sorry, I just wanted to have a quick word about something. Can I come in?'

'Go around the front, I'll be there in two minutes.'

'Cup of tea?' she asks as we pad through the waiting room, which is stuffed with a couple of desks and filing cabinets; piles of leaflets are stacked on surfaces and there are posters on the wall, advertising helplines and health services. A couple of children play with toys on a small mat in the corner of the room while their mothers talk with one of Maureen's colleagues.

Inside the office is dark and cool. Maureen places an affectionate hand on my wrist.

'How are you, love? It's been a while.'

'I've been trying to call,' I say, taking a sip of my tea.

'Phone's buggered. Sorry, I should have let you know.'

I can't help but think that Maureen sees me as another one

of her cases. The thought of it makes me uneasy, but then if it helps me procure the information I need, perhaps it isn't such a bad thing.

'I need to ask you something,' I say, avoiding eye contact at first, but then settling into it so that by the time half an hour has passed, I've offloaded not just about the incident on the Heath, but about the shoes, the phone calls, about the disbelief of the police. By the time I've finished, I feel a stone lighter.

'Don't get me started on the police,' Maureen shrugs. 'You know what that lot are like. You're guilty until proven innocent – and that's just the victims.'

She pauses to refill my cup.

'You look knackered,' she says as she sits down again, her voice gentle. Reaching for a box of Malboro from my pocket, I sniff. Maureen pushes the ashtray towards me. 'What are you thinking, about the girl? How can I help?'

'I don't know, to be honest, I just . . . I thought maybe you might have heard something or maybe . . .'

My shoulders drop. The truth is, I have no idea what I am hoping for. All I know is that I have nowhere else to turn, and Maureen is one of those people who solves problems. Not least mine.

'You must be petrified,' she says and I look up at her, the words taking me by surprise. I am, and yet it isn't the fear that is driving me; the fear is superseded by the sense that I have to *do* something. Not like last time . . .

Pushing the unwanted thoughts away before they can fully take hold, I turn my attention back to Maureen.

'I just can't stop thinking about her. You get a lot of girls coming through here, I thought it was worth a shot . . . Given the number of women you support, and how small the community we're talking about is; I mean, there just can't be that many people from that part of the world here in North London, and she has to be from around here, right? Otherwise what the fuck would she have been doing on the Heath at 6a.m.? Presumably someone must know her – someone must have noticed that she's gone? It's a tight community. I wonder if any of the girls here have mentioned anything?'

'We've had a few women coming in from the general area you're talking about, over the years,' Maureen says after a while. 'Since the war. Obviously I can't say for sure that this woman, girl, whoever she was, was trafficked here – she could be working in a bank for all I know – but if we're going along with your theory, then . . . well, let's just say in my experience women coming out of the chaos of war are rarely left with their free will. In the Nineties, we saw a lot of girls being brought over from afflicted areas. And once a gang establishes itself, they tend to hold onto that power, even once peace is supposedly flourishing.'

Maureen stops for a minute and lights another cigarette before continuing. 'As for getting someone to talk . . .'

She shakes her head and takes another drag. 'I don't know. I mean, you can try, but this whole industry operates on fear. We're talking billions of pounds, and the men who run the gangs, they're organised. They don't take chances. If you knew the levels they go to in order to ensure these women don't run, and even if they were found they wouldn't talk . . . It's mind games, a lot of it.'

Maureen stops, blowing out a straight line of smoke, before she speaks again. 'Fear, control, power. Most of these girls are groomed for months before they're brought here. Most of them are vulnerable, through poverty or lack of family. They're told all sorts of stories about the lives they'll have in England, and by the time they are faced with the truth, it's too late. They're here, they don't speak English, some of them, they don't know anyone, they've got no papers. They're threatened, and it's not just threats.'

She takes another drag. 'And another thing that might stop someone speaking out even if they are found is that they're embarrassed.'

I make a face. 'Really?'

'It's true,' Maureen says. 'They're not idiots. A lot of these women can't believe they were duped in the first place, they feel stupid. The men who operate these gangs take a lot of time befriending people from situations that leave them exposed. War is ideal because of the chaos, not least the unstable borders. These people thrive on it. And once they have their systems in place, they're not going to give them up without a fight. Plenty of these women in other situations would have been doctors, teachers, whatever. Normal lives. That is often the premise on which they're tricked to come to England in the first place, believing there is a better life awaiting them. A job, money to send back home.'

Maureen sighs, her eyes moving to the clock.

'Listen, I'll have a word with the girls, see if anyone wants to talk. I don't know how much it'll help, but I'll give it a go . . . All right? Now you go home and bloody well rest, will you? I feel knackered just looking at you.'

By the time I leave the refuge the sky is darkening, but I'm in the mood to walk and it takes just half an hour before I find myself inside Tariq's office, almost radiating with expectation.

'OK, I get what you're saying, but I don't understand why you're coming to me with this,' Tariq says, once he's invited me in and patiently listened to what I've just told Maureen.

'I know it's a bit random but, you know, I figured it was worth a shot. You're like my oracle, there's nothing you don't know . . .'

'Don't give me that shit, Isobel.'

'What do you mean?'

'What do I mean? I'm Turkish. I know we might all look the same to you lot, but—'

'Tariq, I know you're Turkish. Chill out, don't be so defensive. That's not what I'm saying. What I mean is you see everything that goes on around here, you said it yourself, and according to my understanding, there's a substantial Gorani community in this area. Haringey, specifically.'

The last bit was a punt, but what Mansfield had said had struck a chord. Given what a small community it was, how many Goranis could there be living in London? If Haringey was known as a stronghold for immigrants from the area, considering its proximity to Hampstead Heath, it was as good a place as any to start.

'The thing is, I know you have . . . connections . . . and this girl, I think she was on the game.'

'How the hell can you know that?'

'I don't. It's just conjecture at this stage. But come on, she was with a man in a bush at 6a.m., a man who physically attacked her . . .'

'What the *fuck*, Isobel, you said she was talking to the man in her own language. That means she probably knew him. For all you know it could have been her brother. I mean, fucking hell, bruv, talk about jumping to conclusions. Besides, what did you actually see?'

'Oh my God, Tariq, I told you, I saw her being attacked. And since then, I'm being *stalked* by the man who did it. Does that sound like nothing?' I tear at my hair with my hands. 'I mean, Jesus Christ, will any of you actually listen to what I'm saying . . .'

'All right!' Tariq holds up his hands at me. 'Fine, I believe you that something happened. Something fucked up. I believe you on that, alright?'

'That's all I'm asking for,' I reply, my voice strained.

We are both quiet for a moment and then I say, 'She was mixed up in something and all I need to know from you is where to look for a Kosovan girl from the Gorani region, who might have been brought here . . .'

Tariq's features tense again, his voice hardening. 'Isobel. Listen, yeah? You are a friend, and as a friend I will give you the benefit of the doubt, but truly I am not pleased by your suggestion. What you are talking about, this people trafficking, prostitution, I . . . Whatever it is you are insinuating . . .' He watches my face for a reaction, 'This is not my territory.'

'Tariq, I know that and I'm not suggesting anything of the sort,' I say, shaking my head calmly, though as I say it I wonder not for the first time how wide Tariq's net is cast. The likelihood that he is involved in nothing more than supplying weed to middle-class fuck-ups is slim, but it suits me better not to think too deeply into what else might be motivating, and funding, the constant change of premises, the henchmen, the endless bolts on the doors.

My poker face is better than his, and I continue steadily, 'I just wondered whether you might know more than most about what happens around here and, well, if you were to help me I might be able to return the favour . . .'

Tariq's expression slips momentarily. It is conversations like this that remind me that he is certainly not the mastermind of this operation. Whatever its extent, he is little more than a frontman; it is his job to know exactly what is going on out there and to report back to whoever is truly in charge.

Fortunately for me, though, he also clearly enjoys the idea that I believe him to be higher up the echelons of power than he really is, and as a consequence has freely given up information over the years, in return for something he can feed back to his paymasters. A heads-up on a planned raid, perhaps, or a police operation that is in the pipeline. Information that is a combination of titbits prised from Oscar – before the recent breakdown of relations – press briefings and the whims of my imagination.

If enough of my information turns out to be correct, even if it is the soft stuff – the stuff that if he'd really thought about it, Tariq would realise was not that much use to him at all in isolation – then it doesn't really matter that the rest of it has been fathomed out of nowhere. It doesn't matter that the raid I'd warned him about had never happened.

Must have been pulled, I'd shrug the next time I saw him. *But wouldn't you rather be safe than sorry?*

'What have you got?' he concedes after a moment.

I shake my head. 'That's not how it works, Tariq, you know that. You tell me what you know then I tell you what I know.'

I watch his hands tense, one of his eyebrows cocked. 'Oh, really?' he says, his eyes narrowing. 'That's strange as it seems to me that you're the one who needs my help.'

There is silence, and then Tariq speaks again, without meeting my eye. 'I'll make a few calls. Anything else I can help you with while you're here?'

'Just a quarter.' I smile at him coolly.

Reaching into the drawer beneath his desk, Tariq pulls out a small block of hash, dismissing the note in my hand.

'Don't worry about it,' he says, turning away from me. 'Next time.'

Chapter 36

Gabriela

She was waiting in the kitchen when Tom arrived back at the house, the sound of the kids bursting out of the car warning her they were home well before she heard the rattle of the key in the lock.

For the umpteenth time over the past hour, ever since Tom had texted to say they were pulling off the M4 into town, she glanced in the mirror hanging at head level on the living room wall.

Her reflection, from here, gave the impression of a decapitated head, and she studied it for any lingering impression of Ivan. A stray hair from where he had pulled her into him, a blotch of red skin where his morning stubble had scraped against her lips.

'Bloody hell, it's clean in here . . .' Tom said as he moved through the hallway.

It was the part of the house she had scrubbed last, carefully polishing the glass frames tacked to the wall, avoiding locking eyes with the faces of her children: a picture of Sadie from a couple of summers ago perched nervously on the lowest branch of the climbing tree in Kenwood, meeting the camera's gaze; Callum, barely toddling, his arms outstretched to the person behind the camera.

When she had placed the frames there, beside the photo of herself and her mother in the same spot, taken by her father, the image of the children had seemed so full of love, yet now as she looked properly at the lines of Callum's features, she saw that he was screaming.

'Hey darling,' she said, turning to Sadie as she approached, a rucksack Gabriela didn't recognise slung over her arm.

'Hello,' her daughter replied, raising her head to receive a kiss. Picking up Callum and holding him tight, following her daughter into the kitchen, she was suddenly desperate to be near them and with her free hand stroked her fingers through Sadie's hair as she settled at the table, slumping her chin between bowed arms on the newly scoured plastic tablecloth.

'You hungry?' Gabriela asked and Sadie shrugged, non-committal.

'Bit.'

'So how was Saoirse?'

'Good.'

'Yeah?'

'Can I watch some TV before dinner?'

Gabriela watched Sadie push back her chair. 'Sure. Hey Sadie, I was thinking you and me should . . .'

But by then Sadie had already left the room.

'Why didn't you come with us?' Callum asked later as she picked him out of the bath, holding him against her wrapped in the Ninja Turtles towel that was suddenly too small.

She twisted him to face her, arranging her features into a picture of brightness. 'I know, it's boring, isn't it? Believe me, I didn't want to leave you either, but I'm going to be around the whole time next weekend. I won't look at my phone once, and you and I are going to go somewhere special.'

'Peppa Pig World?' he asked, his gaze unwavering.

'Not Peppa Pig World,' she said matter-of-factly. 'But . . . there is a new movie I reckon you're going to want to see, and I think there is the possibility of a very large bag of pick 'n' mix to go with it. What do you say?'

As she spoke, she was struck by a flash of memory and she pictured herself at Callum's age, in the foyer of the Holloway Odeon, the stained blood-red carpet beneath her feet as she picked out hardened bananas and sugary shrimps with plastic tongs, her mother's distracted fingers on Gabriela's forearm indicating that she'd had enough.

Callum didn't look away. 'OK.'

There was something about the stoicism in his expression that wrung her heart. She tightened her arms around him.

Chapter 37

Gabriela

'Shouldn't you be at work?'

Ivan ran his fingers gently through her hair and instinctively she flinched, moving away slightly, though they were concealed behind the wall in their usual spot at Davy's, away from prying eyes.

'I've got a few days off,' she lied.

'You have?' A smile stretched across his face. 'Why didn't you say so?'

She shrugged, not understanding the significance of what she had suggested.

'Let's go somewhere,' Ivan said, standing suddenly.

'We are somewhere,' she smiled quizzically. 'We're here, and I'm enjoying this G and T if you don't mind . . .'

He held out his hand. 'Come on, we'll get another drink while we're on our way.'

'On our way where?'

'Do you always ask this many questions?'

'Do you always work so hard to avoid the answer?'

As they walked up the stairs onto the street, she placed the sunglasses on her face, pulling down the wide-brimmed hat on her head. On Pall Mall, Ivan hailed a taxi.

'Where are we going?' she asked, and he remained on the street, leaning into the cab.

'You're going home to get your passport. Meet me at St Pancras in two hours.'

'What—'

He slammed the door and pointed to his watch. 'I need to go and get my things but I'll be there in two hours, waiting. Don't let me down.'

It wasn't like her to relinquish control and yet the excitement fizzled through her as she made her way through the crowds at St Pancras, following the signs to the Eurostar.

Ivan was waiting by the desk and he kissed her gently on the cheek as she reached him. She tried to look formal as they moved together through passport control, in case of being spotted. He was carrying an overnight bag and she imagined him having rushed back to his part of the city from central London, packing his overnight things while the taxi waited outside, the meter running.

She had paused in front of her wardrobe, an exhilarated panic enveloping her as she picked out her underwear, rummaging behind the faded cotton pants and the bras with slightly warped underwiring from years of wear, towards the back of the drawer and the satin matching pairs she'd picked out in the shops a few days earlier, just awaiting the right occasion.

She held the pen firmly in her hand as she deliberated over the note she was leaving for Tom.

I tried to ring but your phone was off. Something has come up and I'm away for the next two days. I'll call if I can. Love, Gx

She paused at the front door, glimpsing the photo of them all one summer in Mallorca, in what felt like another lifetime. But then she stepped outside into the awaiting minicab, and the house receded in memory so that all she could think of was what lay ahead.

Paris was a bustling autumnal scene as they stepped into the private car that met them at Gard du Nord and drove them straight to the Champs-Élysées.

'I thought we could drop off our bags before heading out,' Ivan said as they stepped onto the pavement in front of the Four Seasons.

'I know you like low-key, but this time the choice is mine . . .'

Their suite was a tapestry of plush beige velvet and embossed gold silk curtains leading to a balcony overlooking the Eiffel Tower, the sky darkening around it as evening fell.

'Ivan,' she said, turning to him, and he smiled.

'You like it?'

'I like it a lot.'

'So,' he asked the following morning once they had bathed and were resting on the bed, Tchaikovsky wafting across the room from the stereo. 'What do you want to do?'

She breathed in luxuriously. 'I don't think I'm ever leaving this mattress. It's like lying on a cloud.'

Stretching back into the mound of pillows, she felt the sunlight seeping through the window and warming her skin.

'Sounds good to me,' he said, kissing her shoulder. 'But we have come all the way here, it would be rude not to leave the hotel room at least once.'

'True,' she conceded, her eyes drifting across the rooftops of the city she hadn't returned to since that year of university.

'You're so beautiful,' he said and she squirmed beneath his gaze.

'You are,' he replied, matter-of-factly. 'I just almost can't believe that you're mine.'

There was a flicker in his eye and she drew back in order to see him better, surprised by the intensity of his words.

'I mean, as much as anyone is anyone else's,' he corrected himself. 'Not in the sense that I'm going to lock you in a glass box in my cellar . . .'

'Well, that's an important distinction,' she said, pulling herself out of bed, tightening her dressing gown as she slipped her feet into a pair of hotel slippers, her heart pounding both with joy and a feeling she couldn't quite put a finger on.

* * *

That afternoon, they walked through the city hand in hand, the sense of freedom so strong at knowing how far they were from her other world. She stopped Ivan on the bridge in front of the scarred remains of Notre Dame and kissed him, pressing herself against him until he pulled away, warning her with his eyes of the effect she was having.

'Where next?' he asked, leaning closer. 'Back to the hotel?'

'I just want to walk a little longer first,' she said, the euphoria of the moment too good to cut short.

Stopping to browse the shelves briefly at Shakespeare and Company, they continued along Rue Saint-Julien le Pauvre, along the Rue Saint-Jacques until they reached La Sorbonne. In the square behind the university, she dragged Ivan towards the café where she had first worked when she lived here.

'Let's have a drink,' she said, and they took a seat in the sun and ordered a bottle of champagne, the two of them sitting in blissful silence, their fingers lightly interlaced, as the students milled on either side to and from their lectures.

She had her eyes closed, her face tipped back towards the sun, when she heard a voice she recognised and sat up sharply, causing a sharp pain in her neck.

'Gabriela? It is you!'

His face was older but she knew it at once, the same self-assured smile spreading across his face.

'Pierre?'

'*Oui,*' he shrugged and she stood, hastily breaking contact with Ivan's hand.

'Jesus, how long has it . . . Wow. But what are you . . .?'

He laughed. 'What am I doing here? I work here.' He pointed towards the university.

'You're not serious.'

'I am serious. You can call me *Professor Bernard.*' He shrugged, making a whistling sound as he exhaled through his teeth.

Ivan coughed discreetly beside her and she turned quickly towards him. 'I'm so sorry. Ivan, this is Pierre. He's an old friend . . .'

She felt her cheeks flush as Pierre reached his hand out to Ivan. 'Good to meet you.'

'Likewise,' Ivan nodded.

'But you, what are you doing here? You have some time away from the children . . .?'

'We don't have children,' Gabriela replied too quickly, her head struggling to take in what was happening, to connect the dots.

Pierre looked surprised. 'Oh, sorry, I'm confused. I thought Inès said she had seen pictures of you on Facebook, she thought you had . . .'

'Inès?' For a moment Gabriela struggled to place her and then she remembered Pierre's sister; she had put Saoirse up the week she came to stay while Gabriela was studying in Paris. They must have stayed in touch and become friends on social media – Gabriela always hated how Saoirse had put up photographs of them all without asking her permission, though Tom always convinced her it was harmless.

'I'm not on Facebook,' Gabriela said, as if this settled matters, and they fell into an awkward silence, the three of them standing in front of the table.

'OK,' Pierre said after a moment, giving his best smile. 'Well, Gabriela, it was lovely to see you again.'

His cheeks felt cold against hers as they kissed twice, farewell.

'Ivan—'

She felt him look back at her as the men shook hands and by the time they sat down again their table was cast deep in shadow.

'Who was that?' Ivan asked as the waiter arrived with their drinks.

'Just an old friend,' she said. 'From when I was studying here. We dated for a while.'

He raised his eyebrow.

'It was nothing,' she added, raising her glass to her lips to obscure her face as best she could. 'He was an idiot.'

'Why did he think you had children?'

The bubbles rushed up through her nose and she tried to mask a choking sound. 'I've no idea. His sister made friends with an old friend of mine, and it sounds like she got confused.'

'There's a lot I don't know about you,' Ivan said.

'I could say the same of you,' she replied, turning the tables. 'I don't even know where you grew up. Were you born in Moscow?'

'No,' he said after a moment. 'Kuybyshev.'

'You mean Samara?' she corrected him and he made a noise under his breath.

'I was long gone by the time they changed the name.'

This piqued her interest. How much didn't she know about this man who was here with her, in another country, sharing a bottle of champagne? Up till now, she had chosen not to ask. Leaning forward, she waited for him to carry on.

'So you want to know more about me?' he said, his tone provocative in a way she'd never heard before, and her voice rose accordingly.

'Yes, actually, I do.'

'OK, fine.' He sat up straighter. It was the first time they had locked horns like this and she couldn't tell whether they were fighting or not. 'What do you want to know?'

The question caught her off guard. 'Well, I don't know. Your business, how did it start?'

'I think you probably know the answer to that, Gabriela.' Now he raised his own glass and knocked back half of it in one gulp.

'What's that supposed to mean?'

'Oh, come on, don't play dumb. You read the papers, you've lived in Moscow, for God's sake. How did any Russian oligarchs of my generation manage to build a business?'

He looked at her again, considering something, before carrying on. 'My parents were engineers, making parts for naval ships. They raised me an ardent Communist, an active member of Komsomol, the Communist youth league, failing to mention to me that they were both silent dissidents. I made friends there, and when Gorbachev opened things up I launched a small business, selling shoes. And then it grew, and here we are.'

There was a flicker in his eye, like there was something he wasn't telling her. Something he'd chosen, in that split-second decision, to withhold.

'And you never married?'

'No.' He paused, and for a moment she wondered if there was something he wanted to say, and then there was a clattering of chairs at the table next to them as a group of tourists sat down, and when she looked back at him, the moment had passed.

It was 2a.m. when she woke up in the hotel, not so much to the sound as the feeling of Ivan crying on the other side of the room.

'Hey,' she said, moving towards him, not sure what to do; there was an intimacy to the scene that made her want to wrap her arms around him, and wish she wasn't there, at the same time. 'What's wrong?'

He lifted his head slightly. 'I'm sorry, I didn't mean to wake you.'

'Don't be silly. Are you OK, has something happened?'

'I lied to you,' he said after a moment. 'About being married.'

She felt light-headed, crouching on the floor next to him, preparing herself for what he might say.

'I was married, many years ago. We had a child together, a daughter.' His voice was calm now. 'Masha.' His face creased into a smile at the mention of her name.

'OK,' she said gently.

He glanced briefly at her and then looked away. 'They were killed.'

'Oh God,' she said. 'Oh, Ivan, I'm so—'

'Please don't say you're sorry,' he said, holding up a hand. 'Please.'

'How did they . . .'

'They drowned.' A single tear rolled from his eye.

'How old was she?' she asked quietly, her hand reaching for his.

'Two.'

She closed her eyes, pushing against the compression in her chest. 'Oh God. I can't imagine . . .'

'No,' he said. 'You can't.' He turned to her, then. 'After that, I've never . . . I've never been in love, never allowed myself, I suppose. The day I met you, something about you reminded me of her and. . .'

In the darkness of the room, she felt her throat swell. His eyes glistened with the words she yearned for and yet wanted so badly for him not to say.

'Hey,' she said, hushing him and pulling him towards her.

Neither of them had the presence of mind to hold back, the pull between them too strong, pushing all else from her thoughts.

Chapter 38

Isobel

Tariq calls at eight the following morning, bringing me back from a deep sleep. Twenty minutes later I'm on Royal College Street, ducking into the Renault 5 I bought for almost nothing from a man who had been upgrading to a family estate, the week I passed my test. He'd looked mournfully at my open palm as he handed over the keys and I'd wondered whether it was the old banger he was sad to say goodbye to or whether he was thinking of the passing of his life as he'd known it.

Even at this early hour, the sky outside is a piercing blue, glowing with some sort of promise. Swinging my bag onto the front seat next to a pile of old magazines, empty cigarette packets and discarded cans, I turn on the engine and watch a jet-stream of dust shoot out from the fan.

Tariq's information had been sparse – more of a vague location than an address – yet as I make my way through Kentish Town, along Fortess Road and down Tufnell Park Road, there's a feeling of anticipation.

At Holloway Road, I turn right and then left onto Seven Sisters, past a patchwork of churches and mosques. Going left at Finsbury Park past endless roadworks, I finally pull up outside a cluster of shops lining a quiet curved road. There is the greengrocer's Tariq had described and, next to it, the social club, which he suggested, without using as many words, might be a cover for something more dubious.

With nothing else to do but sit and watch, I pull into the mews opposite, turning off the engine and setting my eyes on the social club, reminding myself, when the doubt threatens to cloud my conviction, that I have broken cases with more tenuous leads than this in the past.

The building in question – indicated by a handwritten sign in childish writing above the door – is an inconspicuous if unconvincing affair, the wide windows in the front concealed by frosted plastic sheets.

I sit and wait, the rush of adrenaline subsiding as the minutes pass, until two hours later I am desperate for caffeine.

Pushing the car door, which resists and then opens too fast, I pat my pocket to check for change before crossing towards the greengrocer's. The bell above the door tinkles as I step inside, and my eyes struggle for a moment to adjust to the relative darkness after the blazing sun in the street outside.

Moving straight for the fridge, I pick up a Red Bull from the shelf before heading to the counter to pay. The woman at the cash desk is deep in conversation with another customer and I stand there for as long as I can bear before clearing my throat.

'Just this,' I say, placing the right change on the counter, cracking open the can as I move back out of the shop.

Stepping off the pavement into the road, I hear the blare of a car horn and a BMW appears out of nowhere, swerving so as not to hit me.

'What the fuck?' I say to myself as much as to the driver and step back onto the pavement as the car pulls into a side street next to the row of shops. Starting to cross again, this time I check for the blind spot, and as I look back I see a young woman, around my age or younger, with thin, bleach-blonde hair pulling herself out from the back seat of the car.

There is something about her pale, Bambi-like legs tottering on shiny black heels, the hollow circles under her eyes visible even from this distance, that catches my attention. Ducking back into the car, where I am protected from view by a smeared windshield, I watch the girl move through the alleyway which runs along the side of the social club before disappearing out of view.

For a moment I sit in the car, drumming a finger uneasily against the steering wheel, taking a moment to gather my thoughts before discreetly pushing open the door and stepping onto the pavement.

Taking a few steps to my right, I can see into the alleyway through the partial screen of a hedge to where the BMW is parked on the cobbles, next to a tree whose roots seem to burst out from the pavement. The car's nose is pointed towards the back door of the building. Without bothering to lock my car, I cross the road, further down this time, and take shelter behind the hedge at the foot of the alleyway where the BMW has been left, at a slight angle.

From here, there is a perfect view through the open back door into the social club. Just as I lift my head above the parapet, I see the driver emerge through the doorway. Behind him are two more girls with the same blackened eyes and vacant expressions as the one who has just gone inside.

Ducking down again, my heartbeat rising in my chest, I hear the man speak and the girls get into the back seat while he lowers himself through the driver's door, with an instinctive glance over his shoulder.

Moving stealthily back across the road as the BMW reverses into the street, my hands shake as I turn the key in the ignition, pulling the wheel all the way to the right just in time to see the BMW shooting up the road.

Gently pressing my foot on the accelerator, the second speaker suddenly comes to life and there is a surge of music as I race up the street after them, turning sharply and feeling my phone drop from my pocket into the footwell.

Chapter 39

Gabriela

Winter emerged like a sheet of ice that year, wrapping itself around the city. The wind that whipped across the Heath battered at the back door of the house, begging to be let in.

Gabriela and Tom were settled in the living room with Callum, having spent the day dressing the Christmas tree all together before Sadie headed out to the cinema with friends.

'Mummy and Daddy bought this decoration in Scotland, the year you were born,' she heard Tom say to Callum as she reached for a third glass of wine, Nat King Cole crackling out from the record player, unwanted thoughts rising up inside her with every note. There was one emerging thought in particular that she was placing firmly out of mind as she picked up the bottle and topped up her glass. Not so much unwanted as unthinkable, for now. A thought that, once named, she knew would overshadow everything else.

She and Ivan had met up at least once a week over the past months, in and around the bars and hotels of St James's Square, creating their own separate world away from the crowds that milled around them. It was astonishing that they were never caught, and yet every moment that their relationship went unchecked acted as quiet confirmation to Gabriela that what they were doing was predestined.

By December, she understood how tightly woven the web of lies had become. Yet for the moments when it was just the two of them, it was so uncomplicated that it was impossible to tally that aspect of her life with the complications that rose up as a consequence of it. That single thread of her existence felt clearer than anything else she had felt in years. He was the only one who asked nothing more of her than she was willing and able to give. There was a transactional clarity to their relationship that she lacked in every other aspect of her life, a straightforwardness to the emotion that ran between them. But the truth was, the complications were impossible to ignore, bleeding as they did into every other aspect of her life.

How long could she keep it up, the charade that had become her daily life? How long could she lie about where she was going each morning, before someone or something caught her out? How long could she distract herself from what she already knew was happening, refusing to acknowledge the sensations that swirled inside her?

Besides, there was the money to consider: how much longer could she pretend to be bringing in a salary each month? On paper, she thought, the options were straightforward: stay or leave. People had affairs all the time, and they either left their partners or stayed. You either did the right thing, or you didn't. And there could hardly be any doubt about what the *right* thing to do would be. If she chose Ivan, she would have to tell him about her children. It would destroy everyone. The possibility made her feel physically sick. No, the only reasonable choice would be to stay with Tom, to save Sadie and Callum from the inevitable fallout if she left.

And yet on the days she spent apart from Ivan, she yearned for him; not just for her proximity to him but also for the escape that his existence – their life together – had come to represent. It was this respite from her other reality that enabled her to miss the children sufficiently in their absence that when she returned to them, she was able to be the mother they needed.

That was how she justified her life with him, when she looked back later, once it was too late: a life separate to, but not necessarily at odds with, her life with Tom. The word *affair* suggested some kind of hierarchy, but she could not think of her relationship with either man as more or less important. Both served a crucial, and complementary, purpose; so much so that it was impossible to think that she could survive one strand of her life without the other.

At home, she and Tom had settled not so much into a loveless arrangement as one devoid of touch. How could she let him close enough that she might give herself away?

'Shit! I didn't realise it was so late . . .' Tom's voice pulled her back into the present: the Christmas tree, the same songs that played year after year.

'What time is it?' she asked, disorientated as if she'd been awoken from a deep sleep.

'Six thirty,' Tom said. 'Sadie will be out of the film in a minute.'

'I'll go,' she replied, too loudly, desperate for an excuse to escape the confines of the house which seemed to grow smaller, more claustrophobic, by the day.

'Really? Should you be driving—'

'I'm fine,' she said, collecting her keys from the table and walking towards the hallway. 'I've only had a couple of glasses. It's Camden Town, it will only take me a few minutes.'

'I don't mind going,' he said, and she snapped at him.

'Tom, I said I'm doing it, she is my daughter as well. I'm not completely incompetent.'

'Fine,' he raised his hands as if she was pointing a gun at him. 'I'll put some food on. Callum, you can help me.'

The night air against her cheeks came as a relief as she walked briskly towards the car, the same practical Estate they'd had since Tom traded in the Renault 5 for something more *reliable*, a few years earlier.

How long had it been since she and Sadie had last spent any time alone together? She longed for her suddenly, a visceral need for her daughter that yanked at her chest as she made her way down Highgate Road, the lamps reflecting against the ice on the road.

It was a Sunday evening and so she pulled up on the corner of Arlington Road, just along from the cinema. From here, she could see them gathered outside the cinema, directly opposite the Jazz Cafe, the very spot where Tom and she had met, in another lifetime, so disconnected from their current reality that the thought barely moved her.

For a moment, she watched them, her daughter and her friends, so far removed from the toddlers she had known vaguely from the local playgroups and parks where other mothers had looked on adoringly at their children while Gabriela distracted herself from the tedium of it all with imaginary emails. And yet now Sadie was seven, and all she wanted was to stop time, to hold her daughter in her arms and feel the need for her exuding from her daughter's tiny body. Though of course by now it was too late.

'Gabriela!'

Harriet's expression was one of surprise as Gabriela moved towards the cinema where a small group of children were gathered outside and squatted in front of Sadie, pulling her into a hug that she quietly resisted, before doing up her coat.

'Am I late?' Gabriela asked in response, trying to put out of mind the suspicions she had had about Harriet and Tom, suspicions she had fabricated, no doubt, to make herself feel less guilty about her feelings for Ivan. Harriet shook her head, pushing her hair self-consciously behind her ears, her smile too bright.

'Not at all. You're perfectly on time. Sadie has been an angel, haven't you, Sadie?'

Sadie nodded shyly, looking away.

'Happy birthday,' Gabriela called out to Millie, who was standing a metre away, whispering with another girl from their school whose name she couldn't remember.

'Well, thanks so much for having her,' Gabriela said, wishing the light emanating from inside the cinema wasn't quite so strong. 'I'm double-parked so we'd better go. Bye, girls.'

'Millie, Sadie's going now – say goodbye,' Harriet called out into the silence.

'Bye, Sadie,' the girls said in unison as they walked away.

'Bye,' Sadie said under her breath, moving slightly ahead of her mother towards the car.

'So how was it?' Gabriela asked, her attempt at sounding cheerful catching in her throat. Was this how it was to be from now on? Having to draw out words from her daughter like a fisherman, her hook repeatedly scratching at the flesh of her catch?

'Good,' Sadie said, looking out of the window from the back seat.

'I missed you,' Gabriela said, her voice barely audible, and Sadie continued to watch the streets of her childhood passing by, as if her mother wasn't there.

Chapter 40

Isobel

After nearly half an hour of following the car from a safe distance, I arrive at a backstreet behind Tottenham Court Road and the driver pulls over abruptly outside a building painted a crumbling, sickly pink.

Driving past the car and pulling up slowly several metres along, I watch in my rear-view mirror. For a moment the BMW is still, and then a side door slowly opens and a pair of pale, bare legs appear from the passenger door, followed by another. A second later the driver emerges too, and the door slams shut.

Again, the man looks around, as if sensing he is being watched. Pushing myself lower in the seat, I follow him in the rear-view mirror, as he beckons the girls with a gesture of his head towards the back door of one of the buildings.

Once the door closes, I find myself staring out onto an empty pavement. Despite being in the middle of central London, the back-street is quiet, lined with terraced houses on one side and a couple of warehouse-type buildings on the other, including the one into which the passengers from the BMW have disappeared.

For a moment, I am stumped. I can hardly go and knock on the door, and yet I can't simply sit here. Just as I am about to open the car door, I see movement once more in the wing mirror: the same man, followed by a different girl this time, emerging from the front of the building.

Ducking down out of sight, I watch the girl follow him,

blank-faced, into the car. Seconds later, the engine starts up and the vehicle screeches down the street straight past me.

For a second I think about heading after them, but something stops me: a familiar figure moves into view – the bright red cap and post-bag flashing in my line of sight as he turns into the building next to the one from which the man and woman recently emerged, pulling his trolley behind him.

Without a moment's thought, I push open the door and walk briskly, trying to look casual, meeting the postman's eye just at the point where he reaches the large black door. Pretending to search in my bag for a pair of keys, I smile.

'Oh, thanks,' I say, glancing gratefully at the letters in his hand.

For a fraction of a second I think he will bypass my extended hand, but then, with a glance, he hands me two envelopes.

My heartbeat starts to quicken as he moves away and I am left standing there holding someone else's post, busying myself with my bag as if rooting around for keys, praying no one opens the door in front of me.

Waiting until he has disappeared from view, I finally dare to look down at the envelopes in my hands.

Pulling my black leather jacket tight around my waist, I stuff the letters into my bag and stare up at the faceless black door, the single bell with an intercom and the tiny camera pointing at the entrance. If the CCTV camera is on, then it's too late to avoid its gaze. And if someone is monitoring it, they've had plenty of time to notice me and come out and ask me what I want.

As far as I can tell, I am alone. Besides, I am too close to turn and leave now.

There is a side gate to the right of the building, partially concealed by black wheelie bins. Walking towards it, I try my hand on the gate, but it doesn't budge. If I can push one of the bins close enough, I think, assessing the tall spiked gates and the wall embedded with cut glass running parallel to the house down a narrow alleyway, I could easily jump straight over.

At that moment, a sound cuts through the air like a grenade and instinctively I fall to my knees, crawling behind the bins as I hear it again.

At first, it is impossible to know from which direction the voices come. There is a man and woman, that much I can tell; the gravelly depth of his voice and the strained plea in hers makes my blood run cold, the memory of the Heath flashing into focus. Just then another man's voice rises above them both and the girl goes quiet. For a few moments more, the men continue with raised voices, and yet it is impossible to understand what they are saying.

In a moment of inspiration, I reach into my pocket for my phone – if I record their words, I can ask Mansfield to translate. But as my hand feels inside my bag, I remember my phone is nestling in the footwell of the car where I felt it drop when I took a sharp turn in pursuit of the BMW.

Feeling a pricking sensation on my skin, I keep my eyes squeezed closed, as if this will somehow allow me to protect myself from whatever situation is about to unfold.

But then the sound changes, morphing into an unmistakable grunting before the girl cries out. A sick feeling settles in my stomach and I feel myself frozen to the spot, the sound getting louder and louder until one of the men makes a long groaning noise followed by a brief silence.

Finally understanding where the noise is coming from, I lift myself up slightly and shuffle along on my knees, peering through a tiny gap between the wall and the back door. Pressing my eyes against the gap, I see an open window at the side of the building. Through it, I can just make out a mattress in the middle of the room, a camera set up at the side. The girl is sprawled across the bed, the men either side.

Before another second passes, I scramble to my feet. Moving as fast as I can back to the car, my fingers fumble with the key in the lock. Placing my foot firmly on the accelerator, I feel my heart beating in my mouth as I race through the traffic lights, towards home.

Chapter 41

Gabriela

Waves of nausea had already begun to pummel at her stomach as she arrived at the kids' school for Sadie's Christmas concert, having been waylaid by a sudden burst of sickness that saw her retching in the toilets of the pub just along from Kentish Town tube station. The following day, Tom would be taking the children to his parents' for the weekend, but she had produced her usual excuse of work to justify staying in London.

The school was an imposing red-brick Victorian building with iron gates. She stood outside, waiting to be buzzed through, protecting her head from the light afternoon shower with her handbag. From the upstairs hall, she could hear the recital in full swing. Perhaps the noise was preventing someone inside from hearing the sound of her repeatedly pressing the buzzer. It was a momentary relief as she peered through the gate to spot Callum kicking a ball against the wall.

'Callum?' He turned and his mouth morphed into a smile at the sight of his mother. Reaching up to press the button to release the gate, he walked towards her and hugged her legs.

'Baby, what are you doing out here? You've got no coat on, you'll freeze. Where's Daddy?'

Callum shrugged. 'Upstairs, talking to someone.'

'Why aren't you up there? You mustn't be out here on your own, anything could—'

She stopped herself, taking his hand and giving it a squeeze. 'Don't worry. Let's go inside, yeah?'

Callum's fingers tightened around hers as they moved into the building. Ruffling his hair with her other hand, she looked up, and instantly felt like she had been kicked in the throat.

Through the glass arch that revealed the staircase to the upstairs hall, she saw them, on the other side of the glass – Tom and Harriet, their faces inches apart. It was as if she was watching the scene from far away, but the detail was clear. Even from here, she could almost feel the urgency that rang between them, their voices evidently strained, her hand on his arm.

It must only have been a few seconds, but it felt so much longer, and when he looked up and saw her, Tom's face fell. Instantly turning away from Harriet, he moved down the stairs, bursting through the doors a moment later and walking towards them.

'For God's sake, Callum. Where the hell were you?'

Instinctively, Gabriela held her arm in front of her son. 'Don't you speak to him like that.' Her voice was trembling.

Over Tom's shoulder, she saw Harriet emerge through the door and her whole body rang with an emotion she couldn't quite fathom.

'Harriet was helping me look for Callum,' Tom said and she said nothing, feeling her son's grasp tighten in hers.

'Well, glad you found him,' Harriet said, her voice brittle. 'Nice to see you again, Gabriela.'

She turned and as the sound of her heels faded, leaving the three of them in the hall, the crescendo of the performance emanating from the hall upstairs gave way to applause.

'We'd better get back up there,' Tom's eyes held Gabriela's as he spoke, with an authority that she hadn't seen for so long that it made her stand straighter and then follow them both towards the staircase.

Not now, his eyes had warned. *Not in front of Callum.*

'Mum!' Sadie ran towards her with a childishness that made her want to cry. For a moment she hugged Gabriela's waist but then she pulled away, neatening her hair with her fingers as her peers filed past.

Looking up, Gabriela saw Harriet moving towards them on her way to the exit, their eyes locking briefly and instantly snapping away again as she moved past.

Harriet and Tom, the words swam in Gabriela's mind. So it was true. She wasn't mad.

When she turned to pick Tom out in the crowd, he was on the other side of the room with Callum, collecting the belongings he had left on his chair.

She struggled with her emotions, overwhelmed, until in the end all that was left was a quiet numbness.

'Darling, you were amazing,' she said to Sadie, leaning in to her, trying to keep the trembling out of her voice.

Leaning in further so that her mouth was pressed against her daughter's ear, she added so quietly that only Sadie could hear, 'Mummy has to go now, I have to be back at work this evening, but you have a wonderful time with Granny and Grandad and I'll see you soon, OK? I love you, so much.'

Not allowing herself to be dissuaded by the expression on Sadie's face as she turned away from her, Gabriela moved back through the crowd of parents, her feet clattering down the stairs until she was outside again. Buzzing herself through the school gates, the first parent to leave after the concert, she ran as if the devil was chasing her, and she was still running when she reached the tube station.

It was only then that she realised she had no idea where she was going. Where did Ivan even live? Richmond, that was as much as she knew. After all these months, she had never been to his house. And he had barely so much as asked where hers was, giving in so easily to her deceit.

Her fingers shaking, she pulled out her phone and dialled his number.

'It's me,' she said when he answered. 'Can I come over?'

Chapter 42

Isobel

The adrenaline is still pumping through my veins when I arrive back at the flat.

Taking a seat at the table, my fingers clutch the two white envelopes, the same name staring back at me from the front of each: 'Goran Petrović'.

My mind scanning the possibilities, I pull open the first letter slowly. It is a generic note from the council, informing the occupier of a rise in business rates, which tells me nothing except that whatever this establishment is, officially and unofficially, it is registered as a business. There had been no company name on the front of the building, which would have enabled me to find a list of accounts and directorships via one of the websites we use at work.

My hands tremble slightly as I slide my fingers under the sealed flap of the second letter, which is stamped, more promisingly, with an EE logo in the corner.

Taking a shallow breath, I pull out a thick, folded wad of pages listing endless numbers. Scanning them, I feel my brain hum with possibility. Closing my eyes for a moment, catching my breath, I go through the pages again, more carefully this time, looking out for anything unusual or telling – a prefix I recognise, perhaps, or a foreign dialling code; anything to give me a clue, no matter how small.

Yet no matter how hard I look, I see nothing that points to an immediate clue. Just mobile number after mobile number, few of the calls lasting more than a minute.

The sense of anticlimax is almost painful.

It had felt like such a clear step forward when I was handed the post and yet now, short of ringing one of the numbers, I am no closer than I had been yesterday.

My brain is cloudy with exhaustion. Sighing, I let my face fall into my palms. The moment I close my eyes I see the girl blinking back at me, a look of terror transferring from her face to mine, and I sit bolt upright again, shaking my head to clear the image.

Pouring another cup of coffee, ignoring the voicemail from Ben flashing on the screen of my phone, which I've set to silent, I sit back in front of my computer and google the name *Goran Petrović* followed by the address of the building I've just visited.

The internet connection in the flat is deathly slow, and by the time I discover the building is registered to a company called PKI Ltd, I have six missed calls from Ben.

My mind fizzing with excitement at this significant progress, I stand and gather my papers, arriving at the office less than ten minutes later. From the moment I step through the door, the plastic champagne flutes on the desks containing the dregs of warm wine and the empty Sainsbury's sandwich wrappers crumpled across desks alert me to my mistake.

'Shit, Si, happy birthday,' I say awkwardly, feeling my colleagues' eyes on us as I move forward to give him a peck on the cheek before deciding that feels wrong and somehow opting instead for a weird jovial arm-slap, the kind American men might give each other at a barbecue.

'Where the fuck have you been?' Ben asks, dropping a load of papers onto his desk.

'Somers Town,' I lie. 'Had a couple of people to interview. Anyway, I'm here now, aren't I?'

Chapter 43

Gabriela

By the time she arrived at Ivan's house, she had four missed calls from Tom.

Drained of all adrenaline, but knowing he would not stop until she gave him some reason for her disappearance after the concert – an answer beyond the one he must have already partially surmised – she texted him back, *I'm working tonight. We'll speak when you're back from Edinburgh,* before turning off her phone.

Ivan was waiting at the front door when she stepped out of the taxi. Dressed as if he had just returned from the office, there was something so incongruous about seeing him there, under the portico at the end of the garden path, lined with perfectly manicured plants and poplar hedges sculpted into a series of shapes, that she was momentarily thrown.

'I'm so happy you came,' he said as he wrapped his arms around her, saying nothing about the absence of any luggage.

Before she could change her mind, she said it: 'I'm pregnant.'

It had been six weeks after her last period when she'd finally acknowledged the familiar sensation in her abdomen, naming it in her own mind. Given how long it had been since Tom and she had last had sex, she knew the baby could only be Ivan's. They had been using contraception, except that one time in Paris. The real shock came when she found a stain of blood in her knickers, and in the twenty-four hours while she waited for a hospital appointment, believing she'd lost the baby before she'd even been able to name its existence, she realised something she could never have believed – she really wanted this child.

It didn't make sense, after everything she had done to avoid spending time with her children, to avoid at any cost the inevitable chaos that parenthood brought. Part of her wondered briefly whether this sudden, visceral longing was on behalf of Ivan, a wish to give him back the baby he had lost. But she was too selfish for that. Perhaps, she reasoned, it was an attempt at redemption, albeit a warped one. She had fucked everything up, and this was her chance to do it again and do it properly. Or maybe, it occurred to her, rather than simply taking over her body, this baby had stolen her mind, too. It wasn't a rational decision, to keep it. It wasn't a decision at all. She just knew she couldn't get rid of it. She hadn't told Ivan her news immediately, hugging the information to herself for a few weeks, adjusting to the momentous reality.

'Say something,' she pleaded once they had settled on the impossibly plush sofa in the living room, out of earshot of Polina, the housemaid he'd hastily introduced as they moved into the hallway.

He exhaled loudly, puffing out his cheeks. 'I'm sorry. I don't know what to say, I'm shocked.'

'Well, you're not the only one,' she replied, folding her legs so that she was positioned away from him, the hurt of his reaction stinging her cheeks.

'Hey,' he leaned over and put his hand on her leg. 'That doesn't mean I'm not happy. I'm just . . . You know. I'm old. I wasn't expecting— After . . .'

'It's OK,' she said, understanding the complicated emotions that must have arisen as a consequence of his past experience. 'I know. I'm old too. Well, older than I was,' she said, flushing at her indiscretion. 'I didn't plan this.'

'But you want it?' he asked gently.

'Yes,' she said, surprised again by the certainty of her response. 'Yes, I do.'

'I don't even know where you live,' he said, with a look of bafflement.

'I told you, it's just a room I rent. I'm away so much for work. I suppose maybe I'm ashamed of it.'

He nodded, smiling finally. 'A baby . . .'

They ate a takeaway for dinner, which Polina laid out on the dining room table alongside silver cutlery.

'You must be tired,' he said once Polina had cleared away their plates, her eyes discreetly watching Gabriela as she stacked the empty containers, barely returning her smile when their eyes met.

'I am actually,' she said, realising suddenly how shattered she was. 'Is it OK if I . . .?'

It was something they had both readily accepted that in all their time together they had never shared each other's beds. Now, she felt self-conscious, an intruder almost, as she pulled back the sheets and curled beneath the duvet.

Ivan's house oozed the established wealth of the cultured classes, his bedroom sparsely decorated with key pieces of art on the walls, and a couple of well-placed books. He leaned down and kissed her on the head, and she found herself wondering about the last time that someone other than him had slept between these sheets.

'I've got a couple of work calls to make and then I'll be up,' he said as he moved out of the room, and she smiled back at him, her hand moving to her abdomen as she lay back on the pillow.

It couldn't have been too much later when she was woken by the sound of barking across the river, which ran along the bottom of the garden. Turning in the bed, she saw that Ivan was still not there. Sitting up, she was suddenly desperate for water. The carpet was soft under her toes as she made her way downstairs, through the dark house. Feeling self-conscious for creeping around, but reluctant to call out for reasons she couldn't explain, she moved through the hallway, which was practically the size of her whole house, until she reached the kitchen.

Going to the tap, she filled a glass from one of the cupboards and was about to move back towards the hallway when she heard a voice from the conservatory. Gravitating towards it, she spotted Ivan, seated with his back to her in an Eames lounge chair.

'I never said anything about a car,' she heard him say, followed by a sharp laugh.

There was a short silence as he rearranged his feet on the footstool, and then she saw him sit up, his voice becoming more forceful. 'Listen, I never promised you anything . . .'

'Gabriela?'

The room was suddenly flooded with light and Gabriela winced, turning to find Polina standing in front of her, her finger still hovering over the switch.

'Hi,' she said, her cheeks burning as Polina stared back at her, her expression unresponsive to her smile. 'I was . . . getting water.'

'OK,' she said.

'Well, I've got it now.' She tried to smile as Ivan moved into the room, his voice uneasy as he looked from one woman to the other.

'Is everything OK?'

'Everything's fine,' Gabriela said. 'I was just thirsty. Sorry, I didn't want to disturb you.'

'That's no problem.' His eyes flicked briefly to Polina. 'Will you lock up down here if we go up?'

Polina nodded as Gabriela moved past, more quickly, towards the stairs, aware of Polina's eyes following her across the house.

Chapter 44

Isobel

I'd intended to use the newspaper's infinitely more efficient Wi-Fi to continue my online search into the owners of the premises off Tottenham Court Road, but with everyone gathering around my desk to toast Si's thirtieth birthday, it is impossible to do so without alerting Ben to the fact that I am up to something.

In the end, I'm obliged to go along when everyone piles out of the office for a drink to celebrate Si's birthday at arguably the shittest pub in Camden.

At around 9p.m., desperate to get back to my research, I spot Si disappear to the bathroom and take it as an opportunity to grab my coat, telling the others I am going for a fag before pulling open the double doors back onto the high street and heading for home.

Autumn is preparing to slink away and it strikes me the months are passing too quickly, the threat of winter starting to creep in, stroking its icy fingertips across the city.

Even as I step out onto the pavement, into the night with its drizzling sky and illuminated grey pavements, I feel a bristling at the back of my neck. By the time I reach my front door, the pane of glass still only covered with cardboard and tape, I know in my bones that something is wrong.

Easing my key into the lock, the sharpness of the feeling lingers, following me into the hallway at the foot of the dark staircase, shadows dancing on the walls, the glow of streetlamps casting a golden haze across the narrow ceiling. Reaching for the light switch, I press it on and off, but once again it isn't working.

Fuck, I curse under my breath.

In the darkness, I hear a sound above the slow creaking of my own footsteps. Near the top of the stairs I stumble back, reaching out an arm just in time to steady myself. When I reach the top and move forward to press a hand against the door, it swings open before I even have time to reach for the lock.

Automatically, my hand plunges along the wall inside the room, searching for the switch. As it comes on, casting the studio flat in a dingy yellow glow, I take a step back.

Across the living area there are papers strewn over the floor, cups, bottles, drawers upturned.

Leaning back against the wall, my heart pounds inside my chest. Suddenly, I hear a noise. Without considering what I am doing, I move slowly towards the bedroom, my whole body on high alert.

For a moment, I am completely still, gathering my wits; even the blood in my veins seems to have stopped pumping. Everything is still, and then I kick the door open, turning on the light and moving into the bedroom, my body now surging with fear and adrenaline as I cast my eyes frantically around the room, and then behind the door. But the room – aside from the unmade bed and the clothes scattered across the floor – is empty.

The next sound comes from beyond the bedroom and I run back into the kitchen, stopping dead as the figure of a man disappears through the front door towards the stairs. Beside me, the bathroom door is slowly moving on its hinges with the reverberations of whoever it was, who must have been hiding in there when I came in.

After a moment's hesitation, I lunge forward, making it to the top of the stairs just as the shadow takes its last step through the front door.

Using the full force of my body, I throw myself from the top of the staircase, taking the steps in twos before landing on my heel, which buckles below the weight. As I fall, the last thing I remember is a bolt of pain slicing up my calf and then my head hitting the skirting board before the world turns black.

Chapter 45

Gabriela

The streets of her childhood felt strange as the taxi moved through Kentish Town, the buildings dirtier, their proportions more cramped after the genteel expanse of Richmond upon Thames.

Keeping her thoughts in the past as the car pulled up outside on the street where she had lived for her entire adult life, she was able to briefly stave off the feeling of pure terror that rose up inside her, irrepressible at last, as the house loomed ahead. Inside, she could see the hallway light was on. Even before she placed her key in the lock, she could picture Tom settled on the sofa in his usual position, not so much watching the television as staring through it, his finger absent-mindedly tracing the rim of his glass of wine.

Did he wonder where she'd been all weekend while he and the children were in Scotland; did he imagine where she might sleep on the sojourns for work that apparently kept her away for days at a time? If the tables had been turned she would never not have asked, she decided – and yet, was that true? How easily had she let this thing with him and Harriet grow; this thing that she could not name?

She had intentionally waited until the children would be in bed to come home, not wanting them to witness the fallout, whatever shape it might take. But now she regretted the decision, longing not only for their bodies to press against hers, but for the distraction they would provide, a foil for the conversation they were about to have, the deep, unavoidable well that was about to open up in the centre of her universe, swallowing them whole.

When she moved through the tiny hallway, rendered even smaller by the contrast to Ivan's wide open entrance, she saw that Tom wasn't on the sofa, or in the kitchen. It was the flash of amber from his cigarette that led her out through the garden door.

The moment she saw him there, the hatred she'd built up towards him fell away. In the darkness, his features were softened so that he was the Tom she had met all those years ago in the club; the Tom who had held her hand through both labours.

Looking up, he attempted a smile, which was instantly obliterated by a wash of sadness. Looking closer, she saw that he had been crying.

'Hey,' he said as she settled on the other chair, the garden light turning off as quickly as it had come on.

'Hey,' she replied. Any wind she'd had left in her as she stepped into the house had been pulled from her sails.

He didn't ask where she had been.

'There's wine in the kitchen if you want it,' he said and she shook her head.

'I'm OK.'

He sighed. 'But we're not, are we?'

His words hung in the air.

'No, we're not.'

'What's going on, Gabriela?'

There was a moment of silence and then she felt her body clench.

'You're asking me?'

His words hardened in response. 'Well, I'm not sure who else I should ask.'

'To be honest, Tom, I would have thought it should be me asking you.'

She wasn't going to be the first to break. She wouldn't let him have this one so easily.

'*You* asking *me* what's going on? That doesn't sound very likely, does it?'

'What the hell is that supposed to mean?' she snapped without raising her voice, aware of the children's rooms above their heads, and the neighbours who could hear their every breath.

'When was the last time you asked what was going on with us, Gabriela? With me and the kids?'

He spread his arms out, gesturing towards the windows where the glow from Callum's nightlight had dissolved into black.

'Oh please, what are you even talking about? Don't make this all about you. That's such a typical male move. You want me to ask you straight, then OK, I will: how long have you and Harriet been sleeping together?'

'I'm sorry?'

'Oh, come on, Tom. I saw you at the concert . . . Remember?'

He cackled then. 'The concert! Of course, the concert you didn't actually see because you were so late. Is that the concert you're referring to? The concert you ran off from, to go back to *work* – to a job that means more to you than your family? That concert?'

'Oh, fuck off, not all of us get to spend our day lording around between drop-off and pick-up, spending someone's else's money . . .'

He stood up then, leaning into her. 'No, fuck *you*, Gabriela.'

He slammed his palm on the table and she saw a curtain twitch in one of the neighbouring houses.

For the first time in her life, she cowered away from him.

'I mean, wow, you really have no idea why we were talking, do you? Not even an inkling?'

Tom's eyes glistened and she felt herself lean backwards in her chair.

'*That woman* is the mother of the girl who has been bullying our daughter so badly that most afternoons after school she shuts herself in her room and cries.'

He was whispering now, but with an intensity that lit his face. 'That *woman* is the person I've been having hour-long conversations with on the phone, when I'm not *pissing about*, trying to work out how to help fix things because you're so busy, so fucking stressed out, that I'm worried if I share this problem with you that you might break. The reason, Gabriela, that we were so involved in conversation is that our daughter is so stressed that I'm worried she is going to be irrevocably damaged at a time when she is also in mourning for her mother, who might as well be dead for the amount of attention she gives this family!'

His voice hummed with quiet rage, his face pulsing with it.

'Why do you think I keep whisking the kids away at any given opportunity, subjecting them to endless bloody car journeys to my parents', to Saoirse and Jim's, to anywhere where we can actually breathe? You think that woman is the threat to our family, Gabriela? You think some mother from school is what is going to be the end of all this? You, Gabriela – your fucking *job*—'

He was laughing, his eyes full of rage. 'You know what, I wish I was so simple! I wish I could go around shagging other women, that it was that easy. But you know the sad truth of all this, Gabriela, is that I could never do that to you. *Never.*'

He shook his finger in her face, as if his words were a point of terrible regret. 'And not just because I love you so fucking much it hurts me to even think of my own life without you, but because I know what that would do to our children. All they want is their mother. But you're too damn selfish to notice, let alone give a shit.'

The night air seemed to crackle with the energy that was rising off him.

'Tom, I . . .' she tried to respond but her words fell away as he stormed into the house, raising his hand against her feeble attempts to defend herself as he walked back through the kitchen and vanished through the hall, leaving a steaming trail of hatred in his wake.

Chapter 46

Isobel

It is still dark when I open my eyes, taking a while to comprehend the throbbing pain in my temples, my head wedged between the bottom stair and the skirting board.

I don't know how long it takes, with the help of the walls, to pull myself to sitting, to acknowledge the metallic tang in my mouth is the taste of my own blood.

When I finally manage to dig my phone from my pocket and call 999, asking for police, an ambulance arrives too.

'I must have hit my head when I fell,' I say.

'Well, it's quite a bump, we should take you to the Royal Free,' the paramedic replies, but I shake my head insistently, triggering another wave of pain.

'I'm fine. If it gets worse I'll come in. My boyfriend will be here in half an hour. Honestly . . .'

When the paramedics finally leave it is just me and two police officers, noting down details of the scene in their notepads, snippets of conversation cutting in and out over their radios.

As I sit watching them, I can't help but imagine the place through their eyes. No fancy TV, no paintings, no expensive jewellery; nothing apart from a laptop, which I'd had with me when I left the house, to tempt even the most desperate burglar. The closest thing to decoration – a precariously stacked pile of books on the table – had been tossed across the floor.

No wonder they didn't take anything, I see them thinking, *if this is all she has.*

I don't tell them the real reason for the break-in. Not after last time, not after Jess. For a moment, I see her, her eyes fixed on the sky, the blue lights flashing above her head.

My only hope is Oscar. OK, so he let me down the last time I saw him, but if I could just persuade him at least to run the finger-prints, which the officers are taking now, once they're logged onto the system and then share the results with me, then I can do my own research.

The chances of him agreeing are admittedly slim, but what other option do I have? And after this, something that even he won't be able to dismiss as a figment of my imagination, he will have to sit up and take note.

Once the police officers leave, placated by my fake phone call to my non-existent boyfriend who confirms he is only a couple of minutes around the corner, I take some painkillers from a drawer and a Xanax and lie on the bed, the blanket mangled around my feet.

My gaze settles on the phone on the side table, and I think for a minute about calling Si. But what message would that send, if I rang him every time I got into trouble? Anyway, it's his birthday, I can't drag him into this now.

With that realisation, I close my eyes. There is no one left to call.

If Maureen is surprised to find me on the doorstep of the centre the following morning, she doesn't show it.

'What happened to your face?' she asks, peering at the cut just above my eye, which is swollen and red, exacerbated by the tears of the previous night.

'Fell down the stairs,' I say before being met by a disbelieving look.

'No, I actually did.'

Leaving me to draw hungrily on a cigarette at the kitchen table, Maureen boils the kettle. When she turns back to me, my eyes move to the small window overlooking the garden, and the ghost of a rose bush.

'I didn't know where else to go,' I say distractedly, pushing the plastic sleeve up and down the cigarette packet.

'That's OK,' Maureen replies. 'Are you all right? Other than the cut . . . You look . . .'

'I can't stop thinking about Jess . . .' I say, suddenly unable to hold it in any longer for fear the force of it growing inside me, festering in every cell of my body, will eventually blow me open. 'I still see her face, you know? All the time. Like she's here. I thought that would stop after a while. Not that I'd forget but maybe I'd think about her less.'

I inhale loudly, using my sleeve to wipe at my nose, waiting for Maureen to interrupt me, but she doesn't. 'The thing is, though, that it just keeps getting worse. Every day, sometimes twice, sometimes more, I'll have a moment when I see her. It could be anywhere. In the street, on a bus. And for that moment, however long it lasts, it's like she's here. It's as if none of it ever happened . . .'

I pause, my face cracking. 'Her face, the way she looks at me, she blames me. Still she blames me.'

Maureen walks slowly towards the table and draws out a chair. I can feel the tears streaming down my cheeks, hot and angry,

When she speaks her voice is gentle. 'What exactly are we talking about, Isobel?'

The question takes me by surprise. This event has defined the past year of my life and, despite having first met Maureen a year or so before it happened, I've never told her. And she has never asked, never pushed me on the time I was away, choosing to accept my streamlined version of events when I said I'd been spending time with my parents in France.

Other than Oscar, I've never told anyone, not even my mum and dad who were happy to write off the weeks I spent with them, largely spent in traumatised silence, as the fallout from the breakdown of my only relationship.

People know – of course they know; everyone seems to *know* some version of what happened to Jess, and has cast their own judgements accordingly. But it hadn't come from me. Ben and Si only heard as much from my own mouth as I needed to tell them in order to explain the need for time off. Presumably the rest had filtered through to them via the rumour mill that no self-respecting reporter could have ignored, but even so they have never mentioned what happened to my face, not directly.

And yet, when I finally start to tell the story now, I find I cannot stop. It's like a purging.

'It was a year ago . . .' I continue, and as I speak, my mind retreats to that summer, London groaning under the relentless heat so that no one knew what to do with themselves. Buses barely moved, consuming the roads like steaming pressure cookers chugging slowly through sluggish streets, the tube system practically melting in on itself.

So much of that time I have since managed to push deep into the recesses of my memory, where it has stagnated, the poison leaking out into my system.

'I was going through a shitty break-up. Something happened and it all got really nasty and I had to move out of his place. It was a weird time, really dark, and I had nowhere else to go. My parents were living in another country and I was making fuck-all money, and Jess had a place in Parliament Hill and she said I could stay there with her for a while. She worked for this awful production company which was full of total cunts. She was too good for it, she was the smartest person I've ever met. Anyway, she was away a lot at the weekends and I was working at the paper in the week and then I guess I was just bored and lonely, and I met this guy . . .' I catch my breath. 'He was awful, I mean I'm not even sure where I found him. Anyway, Jess hated him. She told me she didn't want him staying at the house . . . I hadn't seen him for a while, then one night I went out and he was there and then he came back . . .'

As I think about it now, my fingers pull at my sleeve and I close my eyes against the pain.

I sniff hard, clearing my throat. 'Basically, he had a load of pills, and by the time Jess came back we were both completely wasted. She went skits, properly mental. This guy, she hated him, and she had work the next day and I don't know, I guess the house was in a state, and we had this fight. I don't remember what I was saying. I was just so angry, I don't even know why. I'd just fucked everything up and the last thing I wanted to hear was my best friend telling me I'd fucked everything up.'

When I look up I am almost surprised to find Maureen looking back at me. Her face is blank, giving nothing away, and so I carry on.

'I was horrible to her, nasty. I told her that she didn't really care about me, that she was just trying to make herself feel better by being nice to me; I told her . . . Oh fuck, I don't even want to think what I said. The point is I was a bitch, but I didn't mean it. She was my best friend, I worshipped her. I was just . . .'

Maureen pulls out another cigarette, lights it and hands it to me.

I take a long drag and look out towards the window. By now the light outside has started to fade, the room lit only by the glow of a streetlamp dashed with light rain.

'We had this fight, then I ran off. I was wasted and she was worried what I'd do and so she chased me down the stairs, she was trying to pull me back into the house. We stumbled out onto the street, it was dusk, the sky was this sort of purplish grey, I remember that. It all looked so surreal. She was telling me to come back and she was shouting at this guy to fuck off, and then it got nasty. She wouldn't stop telling me to come in and I tried to push her away but she just wouldn't get off. She wouldn't leave me alone. We kept arguing down the street, and when we got to the corner I ran across the road. I shouted something at her. I don't know what it was I said . . . but it must have stunned her because she stopped. Suddenly, in the middle of the street, she just stopped running as if the thing she'd been chasing had just disappeared.'

Saying the words, I feel that same sense, the dread stretching out in front of me, like a cave.

'Then she looked up, it was like she already knew. As if she'd been given some warning. She turned as if to face it, the car . . .'

Tears run down my cheeks.

'He was driving so fast. She was standing just in the bend of the road . . . I closed my eyes.'

I whisper these final words as if too afraid to say them aloud. 'I didn't see the crash, but I heard it. I heard the screech of brakes, a sort of crunching sound. As I turned, I saw her body, it was up in the air . . .'

'Isobel . . .' Maureen grabs my wrist, her voice shaking with emotion. 'It's not your fault.'

'It is.'

There is a pause and then I say it again, 'It really is. You don't understand. I heard it. I heard her body hit the floor. It was so loud . . . It was almost like . . . I can't describe . . . it was like I felt my own body hit the pavement, and I couldn't move. And then the car, it just drove off. He stopped for a moment, I thought he was going to get out, but he just kept going.'

My voice drops and I look at the floor, my soul drained.

'I panicked. I wanted to go to her but . . . I just couldn't. And then I looked up and I could just see her hand. On the pavement across the street, that's all I could see of her, her fingers pointing out from behind a parked car. It was so still. She wasn't moving. I just . . . I should have gone to her, I should have picked up my phone and called the ambulance, but I couldn't move. I just lay there on the ground and I put my hands over my ears. If I had called for an ambulance, she might have lived. They never caught him, the guy who hit her.'

With those words, it's as if I've been pulled out of a trance. When I look up at Maureen, I wipe at my cheeks with my sleeve. 'Sorry, I'm so sorry, I don't know why I—'

'It's OK.' Her voice is reassuring and I sit up straighter in my chair.

'No, it's not, you really don't need this.'

'I know why,' Maureen says as I push back my chair. 'I understand.' She nods, holding my eyes with hers, gesturing at me to stay seated. 'I understand why it's so important to you, this girl, the one on the Heath.'

There is a pause and then I nod urgently. 'I know it's stupid, I know it's not going to change anything . . .'

Maureen shrugs. 'No, it won't. It won't change what happened to your friend, but if it helps you somehow – if it's something you need to do . . .'

'It is. Something happened, you know? I saw it. I felt it. And maybe this time I can do something to help.'

Finally she pushes back her chair, her knees cracking as she stands. 'We've all got our reasons, love,' she says, moving slowly towards the door, gently ushering me along with her.

'Now, do you need to stay or—'

'No, I'll be fine at home.'

'OK. Now I don't know how much help they'll be, I can't promise anything, but I'll speak to my girls. I'll have a word.'

'Thank you,' I say, my voice weak from the emotional exertion.

Nodding, Maureen smiles. 'Now go and get some sleep. I'll call, soon as I hear anything.'

Chapter 47

Gabriela

Tom had stormed out of the house after their row. When he returned around two in the morning the smell of alcohol slowly enveloped the bedroom. Gabriela lay still, careful not to alert him to the fact that she was awake, and yet part of her, however wary, was desperate to reach out and touch him.

Something about the intensity of his outburst had moved her in a way she hadn't felt for so long that she had almost forgotten the feelings she once had for him. Now she realised: she needed him to make her feel like she wasn't already dead. That night, as he faced her, the rage pouring from him like venom, she had felt more alive in Tom's presence than she had in years.

He barely met her eye over breakfast the following morning and when she leaned in to kiss him goodbye, he flinched.

'About last night,' she said, as she stood by the doorway looking back at him, but he shook his head dismissively.

'Let's just forget about last night.'

For the first couple of hours after he left the house, she managed to keep the inevitable thoughts at bay, but by the time she had finished scrubbing the bathroom and the kitchen until her fingers were raw, she had no choice but to face it: Tom was not having an affair.

The next morning she left early and headed for the tube, exiting at Charing Cross – not sure where she was heading but desperate to immerse herself in the crowds.

Drawing out her phone, she saw two missed calls from Ivan. Pushing through a knot of tourists gathered on the Strand, she stood with her back against a wall, the guilt swelling in her throat as she listened to his voicemail.

'Gabriela, please call. We need to talk.'

There was a pause, as if he was going to say something else, but then he hung up.

She had needed the shield of the crowds, the anonymity they afforded her, the protection of countless strangers moving at a thousand different paces and directions, none of them asking anything of her. But now the pollution was like a fog, the sound of the traffic and the dustcart obliterating her thoughts so that no matter how fast she moved she couldn't escape the feeling that the world was closing in on her. She was trapped.

'Gabriela?'

When she turned, she saw Johnny standing in front of her, an apparition from a previous life. For a moment, out of context, she struggled to place him. It was only then that she realised, consciously, where she was. Looking up over his head, she saw the steps leading up to King Charles Street.

His expression changed when he saw her face.

'I thought it was you. Are you OK?'

'I'm fine,' Gabriela said too quickly, her voice breathy as if she'd been running.

Closing her eyes, she tried to clear her head. She needed to recall what he might know of her situation, what lies he had been party to, the version of her that she needed to embody in this moment. But, of course, he knew nothing about her and probably cared even less. They had worked together for a while, that was all.

'What are you doing around here?' he asked.

'I'm—' she paused. 'I'm just going for a walk.'

'OK, well, good to see you,' he said, and she could see from his face that he was pleased to find a natural break in the conversation, an excuse to walk away. She could imagine him cursing himself for having called out to her. She could almost hear him returning to the office and pulling out a chair beside Serena. *You won't believe who I just saw*, he'd say. *Acting really strange.*

Turning, she walked as fast as she could away from the direction of KCS until she reached Buckingham Palace, allowing her knees to buckle as she sat at a bench overlooking the hordes of tourists peering through the gates, like hecklers rattling the bars of a prison.

When she heard her phone ringing in her bag, she pulled it out and saw Ivan's number flashing on the screen.

'Hello?'

'You didn't call back,' Ivan said. He sounded hurt.

She ran a hand through her hair. 'I'm sorry, I've had a lot on.'

'I've been thinking,' he said, straight away, as if he had been sitting with whatever he was about to say for a long time and needed to get it off his chest.

'If we're going to do this, we need to do it properly.'

'What does that mean?' She knew exactly what it meant; what she had always known, on some level, that he'd ask.

'I want you to move in with me.'

The silence that followed was filled with so many emotions that she couldn't pinpoint a single one. In the end, the only answer she could find was the truth.

'It's not that simple.'

'Why not?'

'It's just not. I have other commitments. My job . . .'

'What has moving in with me got to do with your work?'

'It's all-consuming, Ivan. I'm away so much and— I want my independence.'

'Your independence?' His voice was disbelieving.

She had nothing left to say. She felt empty, used up. So she said, 'Can I think about it?'

This time it was he who went quiet. 'Right,' he said at last. 'Well, it doesn't sound like I have much of a choice.'

* * *

For the rest of the day, she kept walking, stopping only to buy a new SIM card and phone, with the number she would give to Ivan to stem the constant fear that he would call while she was with Tom, or vice versa.

Once she had set up the new device, she texted him to say she'd had to give back her work phone and this was her new number, not elaborating in her message but already forming the back story in her mind: due to government cuts, the charity was clamping down on non-work-related calls and as a result she'd bought herself a new phone. There was no reason for him to question that the number he'd been dialling wasn't her work phone, or that she didn't already have a personal device. It wasn't as though he'd seen evidence of a glut of family or friends who'd need to contact her.

He didn't reply to the text, and she took it as a sign that he was still reeling from her refusal to immediately commit to moving in with him.

'How was your day?' Tom asked when she got home. He was sitting on the sofa watching the news, his voice still wary, unsure of where they were in relation to one another. It was like a dance, these interactions, no one sure who was to take the next step, or where it would lead.

'Tiring,' she said, placing her bag on the table.

'There's pizza,' Tom said.

'Thanks.'

She took out a plate from the cupboard.

'Where are the kids?'

'Upstairs,' he said. 'Hold on . . .' He stopped talking to turn up the volume on the TV.

'Gabriela?' he called over to the kitchen area. 'Isn't that your boss?'

As she turned she saw a photo of Guy Emsworth, his porcine features filling the television screen as she moved across the room, the sight of him making her skin bristle.

'An employee of Mr Emsworth's department told the tribunal that Mr Emsworth, who until today was a leading director at the Foreign and Commonwealth Office, discriminated against her after she refused sexual advances . . . Serena Ghosh—'

'You didn't tell me about this,' Tom said, turning to look at her where she stood behind the sofa, her whole body pinned to the spot.

'I didn't know,' she said, her eyes fixed on the screen though the words no longer reached her.

In that moment, the ground fell away.

As she moved into the next room, she pulled her phone out of her pocket and dialled Madeleine's number. The dialling tone told her she was back in England.

'Are you watching the news?' Madeleine said when she picked up.

'Yes,' Gabriela said. 'Are you back? Can we meet?'

Chapter 48

Gabriela

She was on her way to meet Madeleine the following day, having told Tom and the kids she was taking a lieu day after her working weekend, when the bank rang. The news of Emsworth's dismissal was still swimming in her head as she answered the phone. Amidst everything that was happening with Ivan, with so much else to keep her awake at night, Gabriela had almost forgotten he existed.

'Ms Shaw, I'm calling about your mortgage. I just wanted to check everything was OK as we seem to be missing a repayment,' the voice at the end of the phone said.

Gabriela's mind had been firmly elsewhere, trying to compute the scant details from the previous evening's news report, so that she had to make the woman at the end of the line repeat herself, stopping briefly to shelter from the wind in South End Green.

'That can't be right,' she countered. There was no way she could have missed something as big as this, and yet how long had it been since she went through her accounts?

'I'll call you back,' she said, picking up speed as she moved towards the cash machine attached to the old cinema in South End Green where she'd watched her first ever film with her dad. The cinema had long been closed, the building gutted, the contents and all those memories scooped out and dumped in a landfill somewhere before the shell of the building was converted into an M&S food hall.

Mentally, she tried to draw out the details from the past few weeks, finding her thoughts moving just out of reach whenever she tried to focus on one, shifting so that she couldn't quite pin it down. She had never felt sick with Sadie or Callum, but she seemed to have an almost constant feeling of nausea this time around. Keeping on top of her finances while juggling the complexity of her various lies, meant her brain was constantly being pulled in six directions at once. It was as though her own body and mind were now working against her, pulling tricks so that whatever she did, she was doomed to fail.

There was a wind whipping through the trees. As she stood in the queue for the cash machine, she glanced back over her shoulder to check she was alone. It was new, this most recent feeling of being watched. She felt it in waves, the sensation that some creature was crawling through the crevices in her body, worming its way inside the knotted jumble of thoughts in her head, threatening to expose her.

The sound of the buttons as she entered her pin number focused her attention on the screen in front of her. Her fingers, she saw now, were shaking; the skin in the grooves of flesh between her forefinger and thumb was pink and chapped. Her bank balance emerged, and she paused to think about the implications of the numbers in front of her, the minus symbol confirming what she had just been told. And then she remembered: the new boiler at her mum's house, which would have eaten up the money that came in from that month's rent. How could she not have foreseen this? Yet with all that was going on, was it any surprise that she couldn't hold together situations that she would never previously have let go unchecked?

The overarching implication was less straightforward to dismiss. The fact was that while until now she had just about made ends meet, suddenly things didn't seem quite so certain. She needed money.

In another moment, she might have rung Tom. She might have asked him if he could access any of the cash due from the job he had been working on; but right now, riddled with uncertainty as she was, could she really risk rocking the boat? Could she trust that she was robust enough to withstand the questioning that might have followed?

She couldn't be sure, afterwards, that she even made the decision consciously. Pulling out her other phone, she dialled his number, her fingers moving as if of their own accord.

Her face moved into a smile at the sound of his voice.

'Gabriela!' Despite his huffiness the day before, he sounded pleased to hear from her.

'Ivan,' she said, hesitating only for a second. 'Listen. I need to ask a favour. I'm so sorry and I wouldn't usually ask – I really wouldn't – but . . .'

'Gabriela,' he stopped her. 'You know you don't have to do that, just tell me what you need.'

She closed her eyes and took a deep breath. 'I need to borrow some money.'

By the time Gabriela reached the Freemasons Arms, she was feeling calmer, Ivan having promised to transfer the cash to her so that it would arrive by the end of the day. Despite the weather, Madeleine was seated outside, under a heater, a pashmina wrapped around her.

'Jesus, it's been so long,' Madeleine said, hugging her tightly.

'Well, in my defence, you do now spend half your life flying around, saving the world . . . But we can talk about that later.' Gabriela paused a moment before carrying on, 'What the actual fuck?'

Madeleine nodded. 'Assume you're talking about our old friend Emsworth. Yeah, well, it looks like the discrimination case was an easy way out for him.'

'What do you mean?' Gabriela said, inching forward in her seat.

'I mean, perhaps it was a convenient distraction.'

'A distraction from what?'

Madeleine shrugged, her expression clouding with frustration. 'I don't know, exactly. As you say, I've been busy, and with you now a full-time Stepford Wife – I assume that's what you meant by "new job" – my insider knowledge is somewhat diminished.'

Gabriela pulled a face, looking away as she said, 'It won't be for ever.'

'You don't have to defend yourself to me. You've got to do what you've got to do. . . I think it's great! Anyway, from what I've heard, the FCO decided to roll with this version of events to avoid a larger embarrassment. We both know we weren't the only ones who were onto him, and it seems this option was deemed preferable to having the reputation of the organisation placed in jeopardy if the whole truth came out.'

'What whole truth?'

'Oh, come on, Gabs – if I knew that . . .'

Gabriela didn't know what to say. The fizzing in her stomach was part satisfaction at knowing he'd been caught out, if only for a diversionary reason. His reputation was still in tatters, and that was something. Yet she couldn't help but wonder who he might try to bring down with him. Although, from what Madeleine was implying, he was not being encouraged to speak out, rather to disappear quietly.

'Anyway,' Madeleine said, changing the subject. 'What's making you look so worried?'

For a moment, Gabriela considered drilling her for more information, but she knew Madeleine, and there was no point in probing further if she was not in the mood to share, assuming she knew any more than that, which there was no reason to believe she did. Besides, it wasn't in Gabriela's interest to encourage Madeleine to keep digging. Not now.

'It's Sadie,' Gabriela said. 'She's been really anxious. I don't know, I just feel like I've fucked everything up.'

Madeleine stretched her hand across the table and squeezed her arm. 'You have not fucked everything up. Don't say such ridiculous things.'

'No, Mads, I really have.'

'How? You've done what you thought was best for your family, I'm in awe of you.'

It was out of character for Madeleine to say something so heartfelt. Looking away, Gabriela was briefly bitten with shame and she thought how easy it would be to tell her, how easily she could let it all spill out: about Emsworth, about her affair with Ivan, her pregnancy, the lies she had told Tom about her job . . . The fuck-ups that were so huge, so sprawling that she could barely think about them as anything other than a sequence of individual facts for fear that they would otherwise steamroll her.

What shall I do? Part of her wanted to scream, to fold herself into her friend's arms and feel herself disappear, even if just for a minute.

But whatever it was that was holding her together at this point was precariously fragile; all it would take would be for one part to be stripped back and the whole thing might collapse. Pulling away at one of the panel of lies could be the thing that ended up dismantling everything.

She might have considered leaving Tom, but his outburst had stalled her. Tom loved her, and more importantly he loved their children with a ferocity that she could never manage. Perhaps, too, the thought of him with Harriet had stung her so deeply that she knew she could not let anyone else have him.

But she loved Ivan, that was also a fact. He was the antidote to everything she resented about her life with Tom, and so, as unlikely as it might seem to some, she reasoned that moving between these two worlds was the perfect solution. As long as no one found out, and maybe they didn't have to. She was hardly the first person in history to have maintained two families simultaneously. Admittedly she couldn't think of another woman who had done so, but maybe women were just better at not getting caught.

So far, the evidence would suggest she could keep this double life going. How long had she convincingly kept up her pretence to Tom; how long had she been lying to him without him ever suspecting a thing? And Ivan had no reason to doubt her. It was risky, it would be hard work, but what wasn't that was worth having in life?

Pulling herself together, she smiled at Madeleine.

'You know what, I really don't want to talk about it. Tell me about you. What's been happening at work?'

Much as she knew Madeleine would have been willing to go there with her, had she chosen to have an intense heart-to-heart, Gabriela could almost feel her friend's relief as she steered the conversation back to safer ground. Madeleine relished nothing more than talking about whatever investigation she had been working on.

'Well, I'm off to Hanoi again next week to interview some under-cover workers we've placed as part of our plan to track the various stages in the chain. It's all very well targeting the smugglers in Vietnam and the UK, at the front end of the operation, but the next step is to weed out the facilitators. There is a whole chain that we're piecing together. You know how it is, these things take time, but we're getting there. And then there's another angle we're looking at too – women and girls being trafficked in from parts of Eastern Europe to work in the porn industry. I tell you, the fun never stops . . .'

She lit another cigarette and regarded Gabriela for a moment in a way that made her shift in her seat. Did she imagine her friend's eyes flicking towards her belly, which had begun to swell, her body understanding too well, even at this early stage of pregnancy, what it had to do next?

'Gabriela,' she said gently, her face soft with worry. 'Are you sure there's nothing you want to tell me?'

Pouring herself a glass of water to avoid Madeleine's intense gaze, she nodded.

'I'm sure. Like I said, I'm just tired. Being a full-time mum is relentless.'

'Perhaps you should go away for a while,' Madeleine suggested softly as they parted. 'Take a break. Have some time on your own, away from the family and everything else . . . I'm sure Tom would understand.'

There were many things Madeleine might have been trying to tell her, but all Gabriela was aware of was the plan forming in her own mind.

Chapter 49

Isobel

I am in no mood to go home after I leave the refuge, and so I keep walking, turning right onto Delancey Street and through the doors of the nearest pub. Ordering a double whisky, I seat myself at the furthest table, positioned so that it is impossible to catch anyone's eye.

Soon, I feel a numbness like an anaesthetic taking hold, less to do with the whisky than the relief of finally talking. Now that I have spoken at last, my words breaking the walls I had built around me, I feel strangely calm. There is no sudden surge of guilt or trauma or anxiety. I am not cleansed exactly, but for the first time in as long as I can remember I realise I am no longer clenching my stomach.

Knocking back the last drop of whisky, I stand to leave, the breeze on my cheeks reinvigorating me as I head back to the flat.

Once I am ensconced in front of my laptop, a cup of coffee by my side, I pull out the envelope and once again type *Goran Petrović* into Google, along with the company name PKI Ltd, to which the address near Tottenham Court Road is registered.

When nothing comes up, I click on the website of Companies House and press on the link to 'Get information about a company', ordering the registration details and accounts.

These won't arrive in my inbox until the following day, but when they do they will provide me with the names of the nominated directors, and that expectation bolsters me.

I have barely pressed Send on my request when the phone rings on the table next to me. I recognise the number at once.

The voice at the other end of the line is laced with a sense of urgency. 'I have someone here who might be able to help you . . . could you come now?'

Chapter 50

Gabriela

'I think you should stop working for the time being. You can go back, but you've been looking so exhausted and I just think it's not worth it. I'm sure they will welcome you back with open arms once you're ready . . . I intend to give you an allowance each month so you won't need to worry about money anymore . . .'

Ivan's words spun around her head as she made her way home from the pub. There was something about his voice when they had spoken on her way to meet Madeleine that she was still struggling to put her finger on.

The smell of cooking hit Gabriela as she put her key in the door, not long after six. What struck her next was the absence of noise, except for the hissing of oil on the hob over the sound of the radio.

Tom looked up as she walked in, a smile spreading across his face.

'What's going on?' she asked, moving warily into the room, where the table was laid for two with a bunch of daffodils set between the serving spoons.

'What do you mean?' he asked, frowning.

'Why is it so quiet?'

'Oh, you mean the kids?' he said. 'I sold them.'

Moving back to the cooker and flipping the chicken breasts sizzling in the pan so that they spat out oil, he spoke more loudly.

'Sadie and Callum are watching endless episodes of some brain-rot or other on Netflix on the laptop in our room, so you and I are having a grown-up supper for two. At 6p.m. because that's how I roll.'

Gabriela accepted a plate and sat down, eyeing him suspiciously. And yet there was no reason why she should be suspicious of this Happy Families routine of his. It was how it went, with Tom: the more significant their arguments, the more likely they were to be followed up by a display of domestic bliss. She wondered how his own self-deceit tasted as he swallowed it.

'I hope you're hungry, because I made way too much,' he said, heaping sautéed potatoes onto her plate.

'Starving,' she said.

'How was your day?'

She held up her hand to show she didn't want more wine. 'It was good. I just caught up with some things I needed to do, you know, life admin stuff. Work's been so full on, we're starting to pull together links in the chain, and—'

She could already tell Tom was building up to something, though it wasn't clear yet what it was until he interrupted her.

'I've been thinking . . . With the new year coming up, I started thinking about resolutions and what I want from life and . . .' He paused briefly. 'I think we should move.'

She stopped chewing, waiting for him to carry on, but he just looked up at her, as if trying to gauge her reaction.

'Sorry?' she said, after a moment. 'I thought you loved this house—'

'I don't mean I want another house . . . What I mean is that I think we should move somewhere totally different. The coast, near Saoirse and Jim, maybe? Or, I don't know, anywhere: southern Spain? We talked about that, didn't we, years ago, how one day we'd travel, buy an old finca and—'

She tuned out his voice, unsure whether this was his idea of a joke.

For a moment she was silent, struggling to find a reasonable answer as to why they shouldn't go. It was true, when she was pregnant with Sadie they had fantasised about downsizing one day, relocating to somewhere hot and rural, living off the fat of the land – and the proceeds of the house.

But that was a lifetime ago, before any of this. Before she realised that the idea of living in a remote house anywhere with only Tom and the children for company made her want to crawl under a rock and die. Before she had placed the detonator under the foundation of their lives and waited for them all to be destroyed.

'Why are you looking at me like that?' Tom said. 'I know it sounds a bit reckless, but I mean, Jesus Christ, you only live once, don't you? And your job . . . Come on, you can't tell me it's making you happy? You're miserable, and Callum has only just started big school, it's the perfect time to do it. Besides, the house must be worth a fortune by now.'

'It's *my* house,' she said, before she could stop herself.

Seeing the hurt in his expression, she softened her tone. 'Tom, I'm sorry, I didn't mean that – but I can't. I'm not miserable, I'm just busy – I'm at the critical part of an operation and . . . I've got to go away.'

The final words came out before she had time to properly form them.

'What?'

She breathed in. 'I have to go back to Moscow for a while.'

Tom's voice was faint, 'What's a while?'

Gabriela had already made the mental calculations. If she left in a month's time, she would be four months pregnant – any longer than that and she couldn't guarantee she would not be showing more than she could possibly explain away, not the third time around. Even if it had been so long that she couldn't remember the last time Tom had seen her naked.

'I don't know exactly – seven, maybe eight months?'

'Eight months?' he echoed, disbelieving. He seemed to be beyond words. The following silence was crippling. There was nothing she could do but fill it.

'I know it seems like a long time, but maybe it will be good for us . . . to have a break from each other. Things haven't been . . . Please, Tom, don't make me feel guilty about this.'

Still he didn't speak, his fork hanging above his plate as if his body had forgotten how to move.

'What about the kids?' They were the words she had been dreading. 'We could come with you. It could be an adventure. You always said you wanted one of those.'

'*No!*' she snapped. She paused, collecting herself, then went on more calmly, 'We've done it before, and you knew, Tom, that this is part of my job. You've always known.' The only way forward was over and through, wading past the obstacles she couldn't bear to acknowledge.

Tom inhaled, cupping his chin with his hands. Sitting back in his chair, as if seeing her in a way that required inspection from a greater distance, he nodded slowly, and for a hideous moment she wondered if he suspected. He didn't though, and she was almost angry at him that he could look at her and not see what was happening in front of his eyes, the changes that you couldn't ignore. But then how could he ever have guessed?

'I'll be back,' she said, her voice cracking. 'I'll make it up to Sadie and Callum. To you.'

He didn't move his eyes from her face.

'Whatever you need to do.'

There was something so discomforting about the acceptance in his words, so heartbreaking, that she closed her eyes.

'Hey, Gabriela, no . . .'

As he walked around to her, pressing her body into his, she heard the bed above their heads creak and then the sound of her children's feet on the stairs.

Chapter 51

Gabriela

'Hey, we said no tears. Remember?' She brushed Callum's fingers away from his eyes, the morning she left.

'Mummy will be home before you know it! And we can talk all the time – any time you're missing me, you just ask Daddy to call me on WhatsApp, OK? That way the call will be free.'

Or, rather, this way no one would notice the absence of a foreign ringtone.

Her daughter gave her a broken smile.

'I'm sorry,' Gabriela told her, though she hadn't intended to use those words, dangerously interlaced as they were with so many things she couldn't say. 'I'm going to call you every day, OK?'

'I want you to take Otto.' Callum shifted forward, proffering his stuffed rabbit, the one he had slept with in his bed pretty much every night since he was born.

She felt a fist in her stomach. 'I can't take Otto, he's your—'

'I want you to take him, to keep you warm. Joseph says it's so cold in Russia that they have polar bears.'

She laughed, her voice cracking in her throat. 'Well, you can tell Joseph there are no polar bears in Moscow – certainly not in April – but if you can spare him, I would adore to take Otto with me.'

'It'll be a brilliant adventure for him,' Tom said, ruffling their son's head. It was the first time he had spoken for a while and when she looked at him, she pretended not to detect the strain in his features.

Tom had been hurt when she refused his offer for the three of them to see her off at the airport. It would be too hard, she told him; too emotional, for everyone. And he had nodded along, as if he had believed it was that simple.

She didn't look back after she closed the front door. Even when she felt her children's eyes following her down the street through the slatted blinds in the living room, their stares urging her to turn, to give them a final wave; to give them the reassurance they so badly needed.

Instead, she kept her attention fixed on the pavement in front of her as she moved towards the cab, the wheels of her suitcase catching against chinks in the concrete, busying herself with the mechanism of the passenger door, and finally her seat belt. The clicking sound was the doors of a prison cell locking behind her.

It was only once the car had turned the corner that she let her head fall back, and the tears burn down her cheeks, saliva catching in her throat.

Chapter 52

Isobel

By the time I reach the refuge, I am out of breath.

'That was quick,' Maureen says, pulling open the door.

'Is she here?' I ask, already knowing the answer.

Maureen nods towards the open doorway, where a young woman about my own age sits at the table, beside another slightly older woman, with glossy skin and an expensive coat.

'This is Dana,' Maureen says and when the young woman nods in acknowledgement, her lips crack under the weight of frosty-pink gloss, turning up slightly at the corners in an attempt at a smile.

'And this is Madeleine. Madeleine works at the National Crime Agency,' Maureen adds and Madeleine nods, her eyes sharp and unreadable as they meet mine.

'Dana has been working with the organisation to help report suspected instances of trafficking. She has been hugely brave in working with Madeleine, and she thinks she might be able to help you.'

'I'm not here in an official capacity,' Madeleine says. 'Maureen mentioned your enquiries, and I thought of Dana. Maureen tells me you're a brilliant journalist, and very trustworthy.'

There is a flicker in her expression that tells me she thinks this is an unlikely notion, but she is clearly as in awe of Maureen as I am.

'Thank you,' I say and Madeleine shakes her head.

'I thought it would be good to meet you, put a face to a name. I was in the area anyway.'

Why do I suddenly feel like I am the one who is being investigated? Yet I would have done the same thing in her position. It's always helpful to try to connect the dots as and when they arise, even if you don't know yet which ones connect, or how.

My eyes move back to the girl, who drags self-consciously on a cigarette. Finally, Dana clears her throat and looks cautiously towards Maureen before starting to speak.

'You know, I wonder why you want to do this,' she says quickly, her eyes locking onto mine. 'This world that you are prodding at, it is no joke.'

Maureen looks encouragingly at Dana. 'Isobel just wants to help . . .'

Sniffing again, Dana flicks her ash into a glass bowl and my eyes catch her tiny wrists; there is a trail of scars along her arm, red and scabbed over. When she catches me looking, she quickly pulls her sleeve back down and I wonder what Madeleine offers her in return for help.

'There is a woman who meets girls like us in London. She *looks after* us.' Dana spits out the final words. 'Gordana, that's her name, I don't know who she is. All I know is that she lives in a flat in Elephant and Castle. They send the girls to her on the promise of work – as a nanny or a cleaner, or maybe in the hope of studying at college.'

Dana's gaze moves to her hands, her expression unreadable behind thick layers of mascara. 'But for girls like us there is not such a job. The day I landed in England, he said I'm going to work as a nanny with children . . .'

'Who is *he*?' I ask.

'A man,' she says, holding my look. 'I met him in Tirana while I was waitressing at a restaurant. He came in every day for two months and we became friends.'

Dana's voice grows quieter as she speaks. 'I was hoping to study and he told me he could help me. He said he had friends in England who ran an agency for nannies and that he could help me get a job.'

When she pauses, Maureen leans across and puts a reassuring hand on Dana's arm. 'That was a long time ago now.' Her voice fades out and she picks up the packet of cigarettes and taps it absent-mindedly against the table.

'After the day I left Albania I never saw him again.'

I leave what I hope is a respectful amount of silence before I speak again. 'And when you got here, you were met by this Gordana woman?'

Dana pauses before looking down. 'They gave me a drink with something in it, it knocks you out and then when you wake up it's hard to focus. There were three men who escorted me onto the boat, they said they had my papers, and then at some point they dropped me off with Gordana.

'There was another girl there.' Her eyes move up to mine, slowly. 'Her name was Eva. She was a Gorani but she spoke a little English, we talked a bit. She was nice. She said she was going to stay with her sister. Then we fell asleep and when I woke up, she was gone.'

Her words hold me in my seat.

After a moment there is a beep and I see Madeleine make a face as she looks down at her phone.

'I'm so sorry,' she says, standing. 'That's the person I'm due to meet. I have to go. Isobel, a pleasure to meet you. Maureen assures me that this is all off the record.'

I nod, resenting her attempt at control, but say nothing, and Madeleine smiles, turning to Dana. 'We'll speak soon, OK? Thank you, Maureen. No, no, you stay there, I'll let myself out.'

Once the sound of the clacking of heels followed by the front door closing fades, I hesitate for a moment before speaking again, not daring to meet Maureen's eye, grateful that the NCA woman has already left. 'OK. This Gordana woman, do you have an address?'

Chapter 53

Gabriela

The day Sadie was born, Gabriela had felt like she had been catapulted down a long, twisted, sealed slide and spat out into a world that was bright and dazzling and fraught with danger. It was like being led by the hand into a magical garden, and then struck over the back of the head with a lead pipe.

She had been so prepared for the birth. The antenatal ward at the Whittington Hospital, the air thick with disinfectant, the same corridors of the same hospital she had walked down when Valentina first got sick, turning right towards the oncology unit where the doctors talked about 'streamlined integrated pathways' and 'patient empowerment' before pausing for breath long enough to hear her mother ask, 'How long until I die?'

Not long after she told Tom she was pregnant, he had returned home one evening with a book the size of a bible, which promised to tell them everything they needed to know in preparation for the birth of their baby. And it did, right up until the point when the child arrived, a tiny screaming human dependent on them and them only: the moment at which any plans Gabriela might have had fell apart.

For all Gabriela's panic, though, for all the sense that she simply wasn't ready, Sadie seemed to know what to do. From the moment she lay in her mother's arms, conscientiously showing up on her due date, it was as though it was Sadie who was leading the charge. It was as if, Gabriela had thought briefly, her daughter didn't need her at all.

'So this is your first pregnancy?' the consultant asked as she and Ivan settled in her office in the private clinic he had insisted on. Gabriela held the doctor's eye, not knowing then how much a scan could reveal, but understanding it would break patient confidentiality for the doctor to contradict anything she said, or reveal her in another way to Ivan who, though responsible for the fees, was not, after all, the patient.

Gabriela was still for a moment and then she nodded.

Turning suddenly to Ivan, she said, 'I'm sorry, I'm really thirsty. Is there any chance you could grab me a bottle of water from the machine?'

He paused for a moment and she sensed a flicker of resentment at being given a chore – or perhaps he was wondering why she hadn't accepted his offer of a drink five minutes earlier. But then, feeling the eyes of the doctor on him, he smiled stiffly. 'Of course.'

As he left the room she leaned forward and said, as quietly as she could, 'It's not my first baby.'

The doctor didn't flinch. 'OK. Perhaps you and I should arrange an appointment for just the two of us? Next week?'

Gabriela nodded, taking the business card from the woman's outstretched hand, just as the door handle rotated and Ivan walked back into the room.

'The machine is broken. We'll have to get some in a moment.'

'There's a fountain in the reception area,' the doctor said, berating herself. 'Sorry, I should have said.'

'Is there something you're not telling me?' Ivan asked as she scrambled in her handbag in the doorway of the Portland, on their way out.

'I can't find my sunglasses,' she said, panic rising in her voice as she searched for the oversized tortoiseshell frames she'd bought a couple of weeks earlier with money from her allowance.

'You must have left them at home,' he said and instinctively she pulled at her coat and wide-brimmed hat, feeling exposed in this central part of town.

'I had them!' she snapped, and the couple passing into the revolving doors started slightly at the sound of a raised voice.

'Oh, they're here.' The relief jolted her back into the present, away from the possibility of her children, heading into town on a school trip, turning a corner and finding the mother who was supposed to be in Moscow standing just miles from their home, with a strange man.

When she turned to Ivan, her sunglasses now shielding her eyes, he was looking at her with a pained expression.

'Gabriela, I'm worried about you.'

'Oh, come on, I panicked because I'd lost my new glasses, it's hardly something to—'

'I'm not talking about your glasses,' he said, pulling her arm gently so that they were facing one another in the street, people all around them.

'Do you want this baby?'

'What?' Her voice was clipped. She moved closer to him. 'What's that supposed to mean?'

'It's a simple question.'

It was, and it stopped her dead. *Do I want this baby?*

'Yes,' she said, her head moving up and down of its own accord. 'I do.'

'Why?'

His voice was completely even as though it was the most natural question in the world.

'Why what? For God's sake, Ivan, you're—'

He didn't rise to her bait. 'Why do you want this baby, Gabriela?'

She shrugged. 'Because I want the chance to be a mother.'

Chapter 54

Gabriela

Six Months Later

'It's a beautiful day, let's go for a drive,' Ivan suggested one morning when Layla was barely a month old, walking into the bedroom with a tray and pulling open the curtains. The coffee and the biscuits he had bought back from a recent trip to Vienna were laid out with Polina's signature precision.

Polina was a person whose age it was almost impossible to guess. Perhaps so many years of servitude had stripped her of any personal defining characteristics; above all else, she was Ivan's housekeeper. And yet, Gabriela felt, it was hard to look at her without trying to catch a glimpse of the person she managed so successfully to mask.

If she had to guess, Gabriela would have placed her somewhere between her mid-thirties and late forties, though it was difficult to see her as a contemporary, able as she was to do things that, no matter what age Gabriela reached, she was doubtful she could ever master. The sort of things that women were supposed to know, not least when it came to children.

Sometimes she wondered if Polina had ever had a son or a daughter of her own. Somehow, it felt wrong to ask. Or perhaps it was the answer that she feared, the uncomfortable possibility that she'd had to abandon her own child in order to look after theirs. Whatever the truth, Gabriela was sure she could never have done this without her.

'Go where?' she asked Ivan, stifling a yawn.

It had been a night of a thousand feeds, all of which Ivan had been immune to as he slept through with ear plugs in the spare room, and Layla was snoozing in the bed next to Gabriela now.

He leaned down to kiss their daughter tenderly on her forehead, and Gabriela whispered, 'Don't, you'll wake her.'

'Don't ask so many questions,' he said. 'Just pop on some clothes, something comfortable, and I'll gather Layla's things.'

'Fine, but let me drink this first,' she said, imagining the massage he would have booked her in for or the country walk and pub lunch he might have planned.

'No problem, but have a shower straight after, we need to leave within the hour.'

Ivan was out in the driveway, fiddling with the car, as she stepped into the bathroom upstairs. The marble floor was warm underfoot and she caught a glimpse of her own reflection as she let the dressing gown fall to the floor.

Though Layla was still sleeping in a crib by their bed at night – a notion Ivan had initially resisted before accepting the quiet comfort of the spare room, with its king-size bed for one and plush curtains blocking out the light that would otherwise spill through the floor-to-ceiling windows overlooking the green – her nursery was already fully prepared.

Gabriela's stomach had turned the first time she saw it, coming home to find the cloud-themed wallpaper and matching prints above an elaborate white cot. Holding onto the doorframe for strength, she had a flash of the wooden cradle Jim and Saoirse had picked out years earlier, when Sadie was born.

'It's all pink.'

Ivan had studied her face for a reaction.

'The 4D scan was pretty unequivocal. Don't tell me, you've always wanted a son . . .'

She breathed in. 'It's not that.'

'You hate it.'

'I don't hate it.'

'You do. Look, we can change it . . .'

'It's beautiful,' she said, kissing him gently on the mouth, pushing down the sickness that was rising inside her.

Layla screamed as Ivan strapped her into the car seat, but soon the cries settled as the engine started and they pulled out of the drive.

'OK?' he asked from the driver's seat and Gabriela smiled wanly, looking out of the window at the parade of shops that were still alien and yet slowly becoming familiar to her. She was barely bold enough to walk further than the high street for fear of being spotted by some friend of Tom's who might happen to be passing through the opposite end of London.

'Mmm, just sleepy,' she answered and he touched the radio, which was set to Radio 3, the sounds of Chopin enveloping her.

'Close your eyes,' Ivan said as they reached the traffic lights, and she let them drift shut.

Briefly, she lifted her lids again a while later, and saw fields fluttering in and out of focus as sleep overtook her once more.

'Gabriela?' Ivan nudged her gently and she started. Sometimes in sleep, she would forget where she was so that she would wake up expecting to see Tom's face lying in the bed next to her.

When she half-opened her eyes, she was not in bed but pressed uncomfortably against the door of the car. As she came to she felt that they were still. Stretching, she caught a glimpse of the mobile hanging from Layla's seat in the back.

'We're here,' Ivan said.

Gabriela rubbed her eyes, only remembering she had applied mascara when she pulled her fingers away and saw a line of black.

'Where?' She sat straighter in her seat, recognising the low grey building even before she saw the word 'Departures' come into focus.

'Jesus, what are we doing here?'

'We're going on a little trip.'

'What? What are you . . .'

315

Ivan cocked his head. 'Don't look so worried,' he laughed.

'But I don't—'

'Hey, shush . . .' Layla had started to cry, the fractured build-up warning of proper tears.

Ivan opened the door and unbuckled their daughter. 'Not you, too,' he said, lifting her out and holding her against his chest. Moving around to the front of the car, he handed her to Gabriela.

'I think she's hungry.'

She was too stunned as Ivan passed their daughter into her arms to say a word. Instead, she sat back in the passenger seat, lifting her top and placing her nipple in her daughter's mouth, which she latched onto with such force it was as though she feared it would soon be gone for ever.

'I thought you were moving over purely to the bottle,' Ivan said, but Gabriela was still too shocked to reply.

Once the frenzied sucking had settled into a rhythmic pull, she spoke again.

'Ivan, I don't understand.'

He looked up at her and smiled. 'We're going to Moscow.'

Chapter 55

Isobel

The journey to Elephant and Castle is just six stops on the train from Kentish Town, past Farringdon and Blackfriars. The London landscape, something I rarely have a chance to relish, stretches out before me like a jigsaw in which some of the parts have been switched around so that I no longer recognise the picture.

Stepping out from the station onto the street, the smell of petrol hovers in the air. Everything is cranked up to the highest notch, the sound of cars swooping around the roundabout, the odour of burnt sugary meat.

Following the map on my phone through the clothes rails and stalls in the market that circle the shopping centre at ground level, past a group of elderly Jamaican men in smart clothes and brimmed hats immersed in a game of dominoes, at Walworth Road I pass the spectre of the old Heygate Estate, now gone.

Gordana's house is several streets away – a purpose-built, one-up, one-down with yellow bricks and a nondescript front garden. On either side the houses are immaculate, the gardens planted with carnations and roses in bright pinks and reds; to the left an old lady scrapes a broom up and down a pristine path. I feel the old woman's eyes follow me through the gate towards a dark brown door. If it wasn't for her burning stare, I might have lost my nerve, but under her scrutiny, I find myself pressing the doorbell. When there is no answer, I look up and catch a curtain flickering in the upstairs room.

Invigorated by the sighting, I take up the knocker, this time banging hard, causing the old lady to start.

When there are no footsteps on the stairs I reach for the letterbox and push my mouth against the lightweight tin flap.

'Hello?' I clear my throat and then call out again. 'Gordana?'

A moment later there is a shuffling in the hallway and the door pulls open a crack.

'Who are you?'

'I'm a journalist. Can I come in?' I ask, though it is more of a statement than a question. 'Or we could talk here.'

The woman's eyes are like shards of glass. I feel the door press back against my toes as I try to work my way inside, but then Gordana spots the neighbour whose broom has slowed to a hovering position over a spotless front step.

'Through here,' she says, ushering me into the kitchen, which is sparsely furnished with a small table and three chairs, a blue highchair pushed into one corner.

Without taking her eyes off me, Gordana backs herself against the counter, pulling at the scarf framing her face.

'Who are you?' she says, her voice hard and wary.

When I don't answer, she repeats herself. 'I asked you a question. Who are you and what are you doing in my home?'

There is more than a hint of threat in her voice now, and I feel my hands clench. Gordana spots it, and glances warily at the clock above the sink.

'Expecting someone?' I ask.

Her eyes flash with a hint of amusement. 'I'm curious. You are very brave coming to my house. Walking into the home of a perfect stranger. Whoever you are, you are very brave. Or very stupid.'

'But that's it, you see; you're not a stranger to me, Gordana. There's a lot I know about you. We have a mutual friend. A Gorani girl. Eva is her . . . sorry, *was* her name. You remember her, don't you? I see from your face that you do. It's admirable really,' I say, raising my eyebrows. 'Considering how many girls you've helped traffic into this country.'

Gordana hisses, 'I would choose your words very carefully if I was you . . .'

There is a stinging silence and then I say, 'All I want is to know where she went. Eva. I want to know where they sent her. I have no interest in you. Your name doesn't even need to come up. Unless . . .'

Through the quiet, there is a baby's cry from the next room.

I look at her and cock my head. 'Oh dear,' I say. 'Is that your baby? Oh dear, I wonder what will happen to it when the police . . .'

'You have no idea what you're getting involved in,' Gordana says, shaking her head at me. 'No idea.'

'So tell me,' I shrug. 'Eva, where did they take her?'

'There was a girl,' she says at last, the baby's wailing getting louder from the next room, though she makes no attempt to go to it. 'Gorani, like you say.'

I wait, my breath tight.

'She was going to live with her sister. That's all I know.' Her voice is quieter now, defeated. 'Please, I need you to promise me my name won't come up. They can't know I told you.' Gordana's face is desperate. 'Please. My son.'

I lean forward in my chair. 'This sister. Where does she live?'

Chapter 56

Gabriela

Heathrow's Business Class lounge was hot. Her head throbbed as she took a glass of champagne from the attendant's perfectly manicured fingers, trying to steady the trembling in her hands. What the fuck was going on? How could he think it was OK to do this, without running it past her first – and yet, she reasoned, was it that different to Paris? Wasn't it those unexpected acts that were in part what had attracted her to him in the first place? Why did she feel like the ground had torn open beneath her?

'Will your husband have one?'

'He's not my husband,' she said, wishing she could suck the words back in as soon as she'd said them.

Only hesitating for a second, the waitress laid down the second flute and walked away. Trying to push down the feeling that something wasn't right, Gabriela let her mind circle the particulars of how he had done it without her noticing. The arrangements made behind her back, the conspiring with Polina, the silent accessing of her passport. She felt a chill as she pictured him rifling through her things; the bags she had already stripped of any remnant of her other life.

But still, he shouldn't have done it. It was not his place to rifle through her life like that. She felt herself bubbling with rage at the thought of it.

Pulling Layla closer towards her, she closed her eyes and the

321

image of Sadie and Callum appeared, their faces slightly out of focus. How could she leave them here, without them knowing she had gone? And yet, it was the least rational of thoughts. Moscow was exactly where they already believed her to be. Instantly, her mind turned to Tom. How could he have let her go away like that, how could he sanction it, her spending seven months in another country with thousands of miles between her and her babies? Everything about this was wrong. The thought of leaving them here in England made her physically retch. What if there was an accident, what if the plane . . .

'Are you OK?' Ivan's footsteps sped up behind her, and he laid a hand on her arm. 'Are you sick?'

She flinched. 'I don't feel well. I'm not sure this is a good idea,' she said, meaning every word.

'Ssshh, you're just anxious. It's going to be wonderful. I have everything arranged. My mother is desperate to meet you, and sweet Layla . . .'

He ran a finger over their daughter's hair and she shivered. Ivan's mother. How had she never accounted for this moment?

'I don't have anything with me. My clothes, make-up . . .' She fumbled for words. The fact was, she had hardly brought anything from home at all when she took up residence in Ivan's house. She was used to travelling so much for her work, she told him, that she had got into the habit of not having many things; it was simpler that way.

'Anything you need, we can buy when we get there. Believe me, you won't want for anything, I'm going to look after you.'

He leaned in and kissed her forehead and she breathed deeply, absorbing the scent of him, reminding herself that this was Ivan. This was the man she loved. It was natural to be fearful, but everything would be fine. Letting her face press against his chest, the sound of his blood pounding against her ear, she said it again and again, imagining that if she said it enough, eventually she would believe her own words.

* * *

The flight took 270 minutes. She experienced every second like a countdown to her own execution.

By the time they landed, it was as though she had crossed into a parallel world, her mind numb, as if the shock had shut down certain parts of her brain.

The car that met them at Sheremetyevo airport was almost a carbon copy of the Range Rover 4x4 they had left back in London; blacked-out windows and smooth leather seats. Ivan, who mostly used a driver when travelling on business, barely used the car and it had become yet another thing of his that had become Gabriela's by proxy, without him ever asking for anything in return. At least not verbally.

The endless pine forests on the outskirts of the city which had been white with snow the last time she was here were now green, the July sun streaming in across the wide cloudless sky.

The apartment was on the top floor of a blue terrace on Krivoarbatsky Lane, a narrow street set back from one of the wider boulevards, lined with trees. It was a part of town Gabriela knew reasonably well, a short walk from the British Embassy, and the proximity to this aspect of her history both thrilled and unnerved her as they stepped out of the lift and into the flat.

'Wow.' Her eyes took in the floor-to-ceiling windows flooding the space with light, the portraits hanging on the wall reminding her of those which adorned the grand staircase at KCS.

'You like it?'

'It's stunning.' Her voice trailed off as her attention was caught by a nude painting above the fireplace. 'Ivan . . .?'

'You like Modigliani?'

She turned to look up at him. 'You can't be serious.'

'Why not?'

Layla pulled at Gabriela's hair in a way that signalled it was time to feed, and grateful for the interruption, she practically fell into the sofa, this time having the presence of mind to take out one of the bottles she had prepared in London from her bag.

It suited her not to ask how much money he had, to put the thought out of her mind despite the considerable allowance that poured into her bank account every month. As far as she was concerned, there was no shame in it, it was a more than reasonable recompense for her loss of earnings. She didn't factor in that she hadn't earned a wage for months before they had met. She also didn't stop to give much thought to how she might justify the portion she syphoned off each month, secreting it quietly into her and Tom's joint account.

Tom. The moment she thought of him, she felt a jolt. She could go for so long without thinking of him, without thinking of their children, and then – bang – there they were, and for a moment everything else fell away and every part of her stung with the pain of it.

Chapter 57

Gabriela

'What if she hates me?'

The car was pulling up outside the Ritz-Carlton hotel the following day. Gabriela pulled at the lining of the dress Ivan had bought her on their shopping spree the previous afternoon, at the GUM shopping arcade.

'She'll love you.'

'How do you know? Mothers always hate their son's partners, it's the law . . . Are you allowed babies in here?'

She eyed the opulent displays of champagne as they walked through the lobby with its black marble colonnades, her fingers sweating lightly against the handle of the buggy.

'Will you please stop worrying?' Ivan squeezed her arm reassuringly. 'She will love you, because I love you, and because you're impossible not to love. As for the baby, this is Russia. Anything goes, if you have enough money.'

'Mama.' Ivan rose to greet his mother when she arrived in the dining hall, almost half an hour later. She was as short as he was tall, and she seemed to shrink further in his arms.

'I told you I would send a car.'

'I like to walk, you know that.'

She went for Layla first. '*Kotik!*'

She held a hand to her chest as she leaned in to kiss her grand-daughter, her eyes sparkling.

'*Rad poznakomitsya s vami.*'

His mother smiled and turned to Ivan. 'And she speaks Russian. Where did you find her?'

He was about to answer when the phone rang in his pocket, and as he pulled it out, his expression turned cold. Looking up quickly he said, 'I'm sorry, I have to take this.'

Briefly, Gabriela heard a woman's voice at the end of the line as he moved into the next room.

'Who was that?' she asked lightly when he came back a few minutes later, his forehead creased.

'Nothing, just work,' he said, and she watched him ease back into the role of the prodigal son. When his phone beeped again a while later, he pulled it out, his eyes flashing over the message before he pressed two buttons and she heard the sound of the message being deleted.

'But won't you come inside?' Olga asked, when their car pulled up outside her flat a couple of hours later, the evening sun casting long shadows across the courtyard in front of her apartment block beyond a locked gate.

'We should be getting back,' Ivan replied, but Gabriela interrupted. 'Of course we will.'

Whatever reservations she'd had about meeting Ivan's mother had been immediately allayed as she cooed over Layla, stopping to look up at them as if they were remarkable for having given her life.

He hesitated. 'Fine, but we mustn't be long. We have a booking this evening . . .'

She was already halfway out of the car, unclipping Layla from her seat.

'Meet us here in an hour,' Ivan instructed their driver as he stepped onto the pavement and followed Olga and Gabriela through the gateway.

'We've lived here ever since we moved to Moscow. How many years is that?' She half-turned to her son as she opened the front door, without waiting for an answer.

Inside, the apartment was modestly furnished: rows of books and a couple of animal skins lined the wall. Through the window in the living room, there was a school building, children of primary age running back and forth in the playground. Momentarily, Gabriela had a flash of memory of Sadie and Callum and her chest tightened.

'Ivan is always trying to get me to move, but this is my home,' Olga continued as Gabriela's eyes ran over the framed photographs lining the bookshelf. In one of them, she saw a younger Ivan next to a woman with dark curls, between them a baby.

'Wasn't he handsome?' Olga said, moving closer behind Gabriela.

'He still is,' she replied. 'Is this . . . ?'

She heard the old woman exhale quietly. 'That was Masha.'

There was a flushing sound from the bathroom and then Ivan walked into the room. He stopped when he saw them by the photographs. 'Shall I make tea, Mama? Please sit, you'll be exhausted by the time we leave.'

Once Ivan had moved out of the room, Olga spoke again, conspiratorially. 'It nearly broke him. If it wasn't for his work . . . And now you, and dear Layla . . .'

There was a rattling of crockery against wood as Ivan returned into the room carrying a tray, and Gabriela turned away from the photographs, a wave of guilt kicking her in the back.

When Ivan woke Gabriela the following morning with a cup of coffee and a fresh croissant that had been delivered to the door while she slept, she took a moment to understand where she was.

'I have to go out for a couple of hours, to meet a client for breakfast,' he said. 'You don't mind, do you? I'll leave money – and you have Victor's number in case you need to be driven anywhere.'

'It's fine. I'm tired, I might just chill out here for a bit. Won't we, hmm?' She directed her final words at Layla, who was kicking her legs in the bed next to her mother.

'Great. Well, I'll come and pick you up at 1p.m. Be good.'

She watched Ivan disappear down the street, on foot, his phone clamped to his ear. It was another beautiful day and at the end of the street the spire on the Ministry glistened in the sunlight.

Once he was out of sight, she moved to the front door and applied the chain before moving quickly back through the apartment, into the bedroom where her handbag lay on the dressing table.

Calling out reassurances to Layla, whom she could hear fussing in the other room in a way that suggested she wouldn't go straight back to sleep, she slipped her fingers inside the bag and pulled out the SIM card from within the tiny tear in the lining that you wouldn't know was there unless you were looking for it.

It was too risky to hold onto two phone handsets now that she was permanently at Ivan's, where her belongings were relegated to a single chest of drawers, constantly exposed to Polina's attentive gaze. So she had started to make do with rotating two SIM cards with one handset, switching between the two numbers, telling Tom she was caught up and unable to have her phone switched on, on the occasions when he rang and it reached her voicemail. Not that he had ever questioned it.

She hadn't spoken to Callum and Sadie in days and her nerves twitched with excitement as she drew the phone from her pocket and removed the back of it. Taking out the original SIM card and slipping it into the pocket of her dressing gown, she inserted the other, waiting for the screen to light up.

It took a few seconds for the voicemail sign to flash, followed by two texts.

'Hi love, the kids are desperate to talk to you. Give us a call when you have a second.'

And then, *'Me again. Everything OK?'*

It took half an hour to feed Layla to sleep, her resistance in the face of such pressing time limitations making Gabriela tense with frustration.

When she finally drifted off, Gabriela laid her on the bed and closed the door before pulling out her mobile.

Tom answered after two rings. 'Hey, bloody hell, we'd begun to think you'd been abducted by aliens.'

'Is that Mum?' It was Sadie's voice in the background and the tears stung at Gabriela's eyes but she forced them back.

'Hi darling!' she called out as if it was the most natural conversation in the world, and Sadie took the receiver.

'Mum, where were you? We were trying to call.'

Pressing her eyes shut, she replied, 'God, I'm sorry, baby, it's been so busy here. I've missed you so much, but I'm going to be home in a few weeks.' The thought was so sweet and so terrifying. 'Is Callum getting excited about his birthday?'

'Yes,' Sadie replied, and Gabriela could tell from her tone that she was trying to protect her from something.

In the background, she could hear crying and Tom's hushed voice.

'Is that him? Why is he crying?'

Panic rose in her chest, her breasts tingling with pain.

'He just misses you,' Sadie said quietly.

'Oh, baby,' she said, pressing her hands against the window. 'Can I talk to him?'

There was a brief rustling at the end of the phone and then a sniffing sound.

'Callum?'

He didn't answer at first.

'Callum, it's Mummy. Hello, baby, I miss you too. I was just saying to Sadie, you're going to be five soon – can you believe it? Such a big boy.'

His voice broke into tears again. 'I want you, Mummy.'

'I know, darling.'

'Why can't I see you?'

'Oh, Callum.' For a moment it was as though her heart might rupture.

'Hey, tell you what, ask Daddy to switch the call to video . . .' Any doubt in her mind was cast aside by the sound of her son's heartache. Besides, what would be the harm? Ivan wouldn't be coming back for ages.

A couple of moments passed before she saw her son's image emerge on the screen. A second later, she saw her own face appear in the corner, and an involuntary smile appeared on Callum's face.

'Hey, I want to see.'

It was Sadie's voice and after a brief wobbling motion, her eyes appeared next to Callum's.

Gabriela's heart swelled. 'Hello.'

'There you are,' Tom's voice said and she felt a stab of pain.

'Hey you.'

'Mummy, you look tired,' Sadie said and Gabriela realised she was still in her pyjamas.

'Hey, let me see where you are . . .' Callum said and at the sound of his voice she faltered, though only for a moment. On the brief occasions she had agreed to video-call from the house in London, she'd had to bunker up in one of the bedrooms and pretend to be in a meeting room or the bathroom, without any immediate access to the outside world to share with them.

Now was her chance to prove to them where she was – to show them that she hadn't lied.

'Look,' she said, moving towards the window and unlocking it. Pushing it open, she held the handset out onto the street and let it linger for a moment on the view of the government building that could not be mistaken for anywhere but here.

'You see that? That's Moscow.'

As the words came out of her mouth, she felt a wave of self-satisfaction and relief for the evidence she had finally been able to provide them with. When she looked out of the window and saw Ivan's face looking back at her, she felt such an intense stab of horror that for a second she thought it might have been her mind playing tricks.

Chapter 58

Isobel

It is dark as I stand on the platform at Elephant and Castle, waiting for the train to take me back north, my body pulsing with nervous energy.

Part of me wants to take the next train to Kentish Town and then run the mile or two straight from there to the address Gordana has scrawled on the back of a scrap of paper. But a rational voice in my head tells me to slow down. *Not tonight*, the voice says. *For God's sake don't rush this.*

Instead, I step out of the train station onto the high street at Kentish Town. Rather than catching the connecting tube to Camden Town, I stop at the newsagent's, picking up a half-bottle of whisky to calm my nerves and a box of cigarettes. Making the twenty-minute journey back to the flat by foot, the cold snaps at my heels.

It is not until I am outside the door that I remember the state in which I've left the flat. With everything that has happened since the break-in, I'd almost forgotten. Now, the memory of it makes me shiver.

As I place my hand on the front door, I see that in my absence the landlord has heeded my request and had the pane of glass replaced.

There is a sense of relief but still I am cautious as I fiddle with the key before walking upstairs in the dark, my fingers tracing the line of the wall.

Half-expecting to see a window flapping open or some other

trace of a second intrusion, I see the room is just as I left it: papers strewn across the floor, my laptop open in the middle of my bed. Pouring a large glass of whisky, I reach for the freezer door, realising I am famished.

Inside there is little more than a half-empty tray of ice cubes, a packet of congealed peas and a loaf of bread.

From the back of one of the cupboards I pull out a tin of beans and heat those along with two slices of bread. All the while, I manage to keep my mind on the task at hand, not allowing it to wander to what I have to do next.

It is what I've been waiting for: a real lead, something that might actually tell me what I've been so desperate to know – and yet now I feel a hesitation deep within myself.

Once I've eaten, I wash my face in the bathroom; the packet of fluoxetine stares back at me from the counter. How long has it been since I last took one? Popping out two, and then a third, to be safe, I swallow them down with a mouthful of water straight from the tap.

Back in the bedroom I top up my glass and retrieve the new packet of cigarettes from my bag.

Reaching for an ashtray, I pull out my phone for the first time since I left Elephant and Castle, and see the answerphone symbol flashing on the screen.

The voice informs me I have two new messages.

'Hey, it's Si. I was just wondering how you were doing.. . .'

Si sounds drunk; something about his voice makes me cringe and smile at the same time.

'So, anyway, maybe see you at work or . . . Yeah, OK then, see you, bye.'

I listen to him fumble with the phone, cursing under his breath before the line falls dead.

The second message is from Oscar: 'Isobel, it's me, I need you to call me as soon as you get this.'

The sound of his voice sobers me instantly. Moving to the sofa to stretch out my legs which are suddenly so tired, I call back, but his phone goes straight to voicemail.

Soon, I can no longer resist the woozy sensation enveloping my brain. Dropping my glass gently to the floor I lean back on the sofa and close my eyes.

I wake to the sound of my phone. My eyes flying open, I pull myself sharply out of my stupor.

'Hello?'

'Hi, it's me,' Oscar says.

I sit up, rubbing my temples with my thumb and fingers. 'Hi, what time is it?'

He clears his throat. 'Half seven.'

'In the morning? Jesus.' I sit bolt upright, my vision barely keeping up.

Oscar's voice is cool. 'We've had a call from Missing Persons. Apparently one of our officers put in a call requesting information. Which is strange as I've spoken to her and she has no recollection of ever making that call. And funnily enough, the call was made not long after her ID badge went missing, on Sunday.'

I swallow.

'Oscar, I . . .'

'Anyway,' he says, his voice steady, 'I think you'll want to see this.'

As I sit in Reception at Kentish Town police station, waiting for Oscar to escort me upstairs, I am conscious of the penetrating gaze of the officer behind the glass.

When Oscar finally arrives, something in my chest lifts. Closer up, I notice his hair is devoid of the usual gelled coif, his shirt ruffled.

'Through here,' he holds open the door. As I pass through, I can't help but breathe in his familiar smell.

Casting my eye around the open-plan office, I see we are the only ones here.

'Crime doesn't start till 9a.m. these days, then?' I say, and instantly regret it.

'Aren't you usually complaining that we're all locked in offices rather than out on the streets?'

He tries to look blasé, ruffling through a neat pile of papers.

'Sit,' he says, pointing towards a chair. I know it is his from the familiar scent of the jacket hanging over the back.

Clearing his throat, he pulls out a photo. 'Her name's Eva Krasniqi. She's been missing a week. Landlady logged it a few days ago in Brighton . . . It might be nothing, you know how unreliable this kind of information can be, but well, thought you might want to have a look . . .'

He keeps his gaze fixed to the picture.

I take a moment to adjust to what Oscar has said; blinking, I allow my eyes to settle on the image of the girl. In this picture her hair is a faded red, clearly dyed, chopped shorter than I remember, just above her shoulders, but they are the same large brown eyes and teeth that overlap slightly at the front. In this photo, she is wearing a hospital robe; in her arms lies a newborn baby.

Looking at the woman's face, I feel the colour drain from my cheeks.

With a start, I feel Oscar's hand on my arm. 'Are you all right?'

The finality of the image hits me like a giant wave. Suddenly, all the adrenaline, the need to convince Oscar – and myself – of what I'd seen that night on the Heath drains away, and what is left is a feeling of total deflation.

There is something about the tenderness of the image, this intensely personal moment, that makes me feel like an intruder. Looking away, I clear my throat.

'So it is the woman you saw?' Oscar asks.

'It's her.' I stare for one more moment and then I blink hard. This should have been my moment of glory, the moment I was proved right, and yet rather than feeling victorious I just feel horribly sad.

Oscar nods. 'There's something else. We got the results through from the fingerprints at your flat. The person who attacked you, he was already on the system for dealing. Looks like you wrote about the gang he was working for last year. Just some kid, took advantage of the broken front-door pane. Who knows who was paying him. You might want to keep your head down for a while.'

I stand, breathing deeply. My voice sounds far away when I speak. 'Right.'

'We've got an address for her sister,' Oscar adds as I move to the door. 'We'll get someone from family liaison down there to speak to her. So you don't need to worry about this anymore. Go home and rest, yeah? I'll call you when we know more.'

Chapter 59

Gabriela

She hadn't said goodbye. So instinctive was her reaction to the eyes staring back at her from the street that she immediately pressed the cancel button, her children's faces instantly vanishing. Running to the bathroom, she pushed the door closed and fumbled, her fingers like sticks of jelly, as she attempted to remove one SIM card and replace it with the other from her pocket.

The moment she managed to wedge the new SIM in position, she heard banging at the front door. Opening the bathroom and moving back into the hall, she could hear Ivan's voice saying her name. By the time she reached the front door and unhooked the latch, Layla's cry was calling out from the bedroom.

'What's going on?' he said as she opened the door, her cheeks hot, the sound of Layla's screams rising from inside the apartment.

'Sorry about the latch.' She moved quickly to the bedroom. 'Habit, I suppose. You're back early?'

He placed his keys and gloves on the table in the hall.

'Things didn't take as long as I had expected them to. Who were you talking to?'

Her face was focused on Layla as she lifted her out of the cot.

Pretending to be distracted by the crying, she barely turned. 'Hmm?'

'Just now, at the window. You were on the phone.'

She tried to laugh. 'That. Oh, I was making a movie. Don't laugh, it's ridiculous.'

'A movie?'

'Like a home movie.' She couldn't find the words quickly enough. 'You know what I mean, I was filming the view and then saying where we were. Oh God, I feel so stupid. It's just a little thing for Layla, I thought it might be nice when she gets older to have a memory of our first trip here together.'

Finally allowing herself to look up, she caught Ivan's eye and his mouth twitched before forming a hesitant smile. 'You sentimentalist.'

Kissing her on the forehead, his lips lingering on her skin a moment too long, he took Layla from her arms and she quietened almost instantly.

'Let's have a look, then.'

'Sorry?'

'The film. Let's see what you got.'

She paused, her smile threatening to crack. 'OK,' she said, pulling the phone from her pocket, the sweat seeping through her palms.

'Give it to me, then,' Ivan said, though he was limited from reaching out by the way he was holding Layla.

She took a step back, keeping her eye on the phone, too nervous to make eye contact.

'Shit.' She looked at the screen before moving away from him towards the door. 'It didn't record. I'm such a Luddite, I must have not pressed the button properly. I'll go and make us some tea.'

Chapter 60

Gabriela

'Where did you say we were going for dinner?' she asked later that afternoon, walking into the dressing room where Ivan was picking a watch from the drawer.

The room was perfectly illuminated by a series of lights impressed like jewels into the lush Italian wallpaper. On one side, it was lined with perfectly pressed shirts mirroring the ones that hung in the dressing room in London. Silk lavender bags hung from the rails.

Ivan had laughed the first time she saw the dressing room in London, watching how Gabriela's eyes widened at the rows of almost identical suits and leather shoes buffed to a shine on a plinth that ran along the bottom of the exposed wardrobe.

'I know, it's a bit Patrick Bateman,' he winced. 'But Polina likes to keep it in order, and who am I to complain?'

She made herself smile now as she moved forward to help him fasten the top button of his shirt, breathing in the same heavy fragrance she'd noticed the day they met. He seemed to have forgotten about the film she'd claimed to have made and Gabriela was keen to keep his mind on the present.

'Tonight, there are a couple of friends I want you to meet.'

'Oh,' she said, taken aback. Why was she so surprised? As far as Ivan was concerned, they were a regular couple – why would he not seek to introduce her to his nearest and dearest, in his homeland? Yet she felt a shiver as she pictured it; or, she would wonder later, had she drawn that detail in, with the benefit of hindsight, knowing what was to come?

'Sounds lovely,' she said, forcing a smile. 'But what will we do with Layla?'

'My mother will have her. She wants to spend as much time as possible with her while we're here.'

'Really? Do you think she'll be OK?'

Ivan laughed as if her insinuation that his elderly mother might not be capable was so preposterous that it didn't warrant acknowledgement.

'She's had a child herself, don't forget, Gabriela. She's perfectly capable.'

Was there a flicker in his eye?

She swallowed. 'Of course. Well, I'll just have a quick shower.'

'No hurry,' he said. 'The car will be here in an hour.'

Café Pushkin was exactly the kind of place where the high-ups at the FCO would take foreign visitors when they came to stay: a lavish pastiche of Russian life, heavy on wood panelling and caviar, light on subtlety.

'It's Irena's choice,' Ivan said as they pulled up outside the peachy baroque façade, the car depositing them directly in front of the doors that opened for them as they approached.

'As you'll see, she's not one who believes that less is more. But she's an impressive woman. You'll like her, I think.'

Andrei and Irena were already waiting when they arrived. Irena stood first, dressed in an almost spray-on blue dress with one shoulder strap, draped in a fur stole which brushed against Gabriela's arm as they air-kissed hello. There was a spark of recognition, and yet Gabriela blinked it away. After all, Ivan had already told her that Irena never came to London.

'This is my husband,' she said.

Andrei had put down the phone he had been fixated on and stood to greet them.

'Irena,' Ivan kissed her on both cheeks before holding out a hand to Andrei. He was shorter than his wife, with dark hair slicked away from his face.

Turning his attention to Gabriela, Andrei said, 'It's a great pleasure to meet you. It's not often we get a peek into Ivan's private life.'

Ivan shot him a look which Andrei ignored. 'He's a dark horse, this one. But I can see why he'd want to show you off.'

'Will you have a gin and tonic?' Ivan asked, leaning in protectively towards Gabriela as she took her seat, pouring herself a glass of sparkling water from the bottle on the table.

'Please,' she said before returning her attention to Andrei.

'It's good to see you, too. So you and Ivan work together?'

There was a moment's hesitation, and then, with a tone that suggested he was keen to slide the conversation in a different direction, Ivan said, 'Andrei and I have known each other for years. Since we were children.'

'And you?' Irena turned her attention from Ivan to Gabriela. 'How did you two meet?'

'In London, in a restaurant,' she replied vaguely, taking a sip of her drink.

'A restaurant? How old-fashioned,' Irena laughed.

'Gabriela chatted me up while we were both on our lunch breaks,' Ivan said, and she nudged him playfully with her elbow. 'She bowled me over with her command of my mother tongue, among other things.'

'You speak Russian?' Irena looked intrigued. 'Why?'

Gabriela started momentarily at the directness of Irena's question, though why should she not be direct? 'I worked here for a while, for a charity.'

'A charity?' Irena repeated. 'Which one?'

'Well, originally I was with Amnesty International, but now I'm working for a very small outfit, I'm sure you wouldn't have heard of it. We're involved with refugees. Because of the delicacy of the situation for some of the people we work with, I can't say too much. But it's a brilliant job, I love it.'

'Sounds exciting,' Irena said, and when Gabriela looked away she felt Irena still looking.

'If you don't mind, I'm just going to visit the Gents,' Ivan said a while later. Her fingers brushed over his thigh as he made to stand.

'Are you ready to order?' the waiter asked Andrei in Russian, interrupting a brief silence after Ivan left.

Irena leaned in to her husband. 'I think I'll just go to the bathroom while you do that. You know what I like.'

Looking up from the menu, Andrei turned his attention to Gabriela. 'Do you have any preference?'

She hadn't yet looked at the options and spent a minute scanning through the main courses before picking out the sea bass. When she looked up again, Irena was returning to the table, Ivan a few steps behind her.

As he took his seat, Ivan reached for her hand under the table; his fingers were bone-dry.

'But you've had a baby!' Irena said, as if the thought had just occurred to her, reaching down to a bag by her ankle.

Not quite knowing what to say, Gabriela smiled in response and took the bag Irena extended to her above the glasses.

'I'm afraid it's only a small gift, but I couldn't resist it.'

The present was wrapped in gold paper and a huge pink bow. As she opened it, all of the eyes at the table on her, she pulled out a stuffed rabbit, as soft as a real bunny, its ears long and tapered.

Holding it up, Gabriela suppressed a shiver, picturing Callum's face as he accepted the gift from Saoirse, grabbing it from her with tiny fists.

It was almost identical, aside from the wear and tear Callum's version had acquired over the years. Otto – the toy Callum had sent her away with to defend her against the polar bears.

'Do you not like it?' Irena asked, a note of hurt in her voice.

Gabriela cleared her throat, coughing away the choking sensation.

'Oh, it's so lovely. It's beautiful, thank you – I'm just a bit . . . emotional,' she said and everyone at the table laughed indulgently.

'Huge congratulations to you both.' Andrei held up his glass and the rest followed.

'It's perfect, Irena,' Ivan said, finishing a mouthful of crabmeat. 'Hopefully we can now prise her away from that tatty old toy she is so attached to.'

'Hey,' Gabriela said defensively, feeling her gut tighten.

She had never meant for Ivan to see Otto. She had been unpacking her suitcase the day after they arrived, while Ivan popped to the store. He had returned earlier than expected and seen the stuffed toy on the floor beside her clothes.

'It's my old bunny,' she'd told him, an instinctive response to explain away its presence in her bag. 'I thought Layla might like it.'

He had half-smiled. 'Sweet. You could have washed it, though,' he joked, picking it up and giving it a sniff; it was still smeared with jam from Callum's breakfast the day Gabriela left.

Could it be a coincidence? It wasn't possible and yet, what else could it be? It was a ubiquitous toy; half the children of North London had one. It was probably the same in Moscow.

The room suddenly felt stiflingly hot.

'*Za lyubov*,' Andrei said, holding up his glass.

Ivan turned to Gabriela, clinking his champagne flute against hers. 'To love.'

As he spoke she felt a tunnel opening up in front of her, a train roaring towards her so fast that she was powerless to step out of its path.

Chapter 61

Isobel

Heading out onto the street, I feel I have reached the end of a journey. The sky outside looks different as I step onto the pavement. Deaf to the horns and the sounds of another day about to start, I turn left onto the high street where I hail a black cab, resistant as I still am to Uber, along with any other app that tracks your movements, digital or physical.

The world passes by in a blur as the car makes its way through Tufnell Park, turning left by the Odeon onto Holloway Road, and then right again towards Hornsey, the driver occasionally glancing back at me through the rear-view mirror as the car glides over speed bumps.

Finally, we pull to a halt on a stretch of road lined with a cluster of shops.

I don't bother waiting for change. Looking at the piece of paper in my hand, I take a few steps towards a blue door to the left of the grocery shop and, before I can change my mind, I knock twice.

It will be hours if not days before Family Liaison turn up, and this is something I have to do alone. I owe her that much, at least.

A few moments later, I hear footsteps on the stairs.

'Hello, can I help you?' The woman at the door is pale and wan, dark circles etched around her eye sockets.

I take a deep breath, hoping she won't question the absence of uniform, and pull out the badge I swiped from the inside pocket of Oscar's coat, where it hung over his chair, before I left. 'I'm sorry to bother you. I'm Sergeant Morley, I'm with Kentish Town police. Would you mind if I came in for a minute?'

There is a hesitation, but then the woman moves aside and lets me into a narrow hall lined with a coat rack holding a single denim jacket.

Upstairs, I am met by the smell of coffee. The flat is small but homely and I try to keep my eyes from creeping all over the woman's personal possessions.

Wrapping her turquoise hooded top tightly around her waist, the woman says, 'How can I help you?'

'I'm sorry to intrude, I—' As I open my mouth to speak, I hear the jangle of keys at the front door, followed by movement in the hall.

When footsteps press against the treads of the stairs a few moments later, the woman in front of me looks up, and then backs towards the doorway just in time for me to spot another, slightly younger woman stepping through the door, a baby held against her chest.

The copper hair-dye from the photo has faded to the chestnut-brown I remember from my blurred memory of that night and at the sight of each other, we both step back, the mutual recognition instant.

Eva looks as if she has been shot, holding the child against her body like a shield. Just as I open my mouth to speak, to say the words I have not yet fashioned, we all hear it, the sound of fists hammering on the door, followed by Morley's voice calling through the letterbox. 'Open up! Police!'

Chapter 62

Gabriela

The following morning Ivan pulled open the curtain and revealed a clear blue sky.

'I thought you might be interested in seeing some of the projects we're working on,' he said later that day as the car swept around Patriarshiye Ponds, pulling over in front of the apartments opposite the one Gabriela had stayed in when she had just arrived in Moscow. She had a flash of memory of those first few days, staying at Emsworth's flat. She hadn't questioned at the time how he had afforded such a place; it wasn't an official FCO residence, she knew that much.

'I've just got to drop something off to Andrei,' he said, before stepping out of the car, then walking across to the lobby and disappearing inside.

'Andrei lives here?' she asked when he got back into the car a few minutes later.

'Not really. He owns a couple of the apartments,' he said, turning to stroke Layla's head as she snoozed in the car seat.

Gabriela felt a note of alarm ringing in her ears but she pushed it away. Was it so strange that they owned apartments in the complex that was occupied by her former boss? After all, it was one of the most coveted blocks in Moscow, an obvious draw, surely, for both monied oligarchs and senior FCO figures who fancied a bit of cultural heritage while they swaggered around the city? She felt a stinging on her thigh and when she looked down saw she was pinching herself so tightly with her fingernails that she could see the indentation in the flesh beneath her tights.

Looking away, Gabriela focused on Layla's face, the soft lines of her eyelids, the skin so delicate and new. She was still at that age when she seemed to spend more time asleep than awake. Briefly, she imagined what Layla might be like in a few years. Would she be anything like Sadie? The thought made her stomach flip.

'Is everything OK? You've been quiet ever since dinner last night,' Ivan said. When she looked up at him, his face seemed less familiar.

'I'm just tired. Maybe it's jet lag.'

'Right,' he replied, reaching for her hand and squeezing it. 'Andrei and Irena seemed to take to you.'

'Really?' she said, trying to push away the thought of the bunny, the exact replica of Callum's rabbit. *Stop it*, she told herself. She was being paranoid. After Emsworth's threats, and the ordeal with Sadie on the Heath, it was understandable. But there was no way Irena could have known about Otto.

Yet there was something about Irena, the way her eyes followed Gabriela at dinner, that she couldn't stop remembering. Perhaps she was just interested, she told herself. She and Ivan were clearly close, and why wouldn't she be intrigued to meet the mother of his child? Gabriela shivered as she thought of his dead wife, trying to blot out the photo she had seen of Masha, her eyes too evocative of Layla.

'You were right, Irena is very impressive. What exactly does she do? I never got to ask.'

Ivan looked out of the window as the car began to slow. 'I'm never quite sure. Look, we're nearly here.'

The house stood at the edge of the Presnensky District, an area better known for the zoo and the State Museum of Oriental Art. The building itself was akin to the sort of upscale boarding school you might see in a Hollywood interpretation of aristocratic English life.

'We don't call it an orphanage, it's a home for children,' he said as they moved through the hallway, lined with floor-to-ceiling chests filled with books.

'Ivan, this is extraordinary,' she said.

'We have around thirty children living here, full-time,' he said as a group moved through one of the doorways, accompanied by a woman who seemed to recognise Ivan.

'Some of them require specialist support and so we have teachers and therapists who work with them on site.'

'I can't believe you haven't told me about this before,' she said as they reached the upper floor, stopping briefly to peer into one of the bedrooms where there were four neatly made beds. The walls were hung with framed paintings of flowers.

'You never asked,' he said, and she felt a pang of relief followed by a niggle of guilt. Why had she not asked him more about his work? Was it because she was scared of what he would say?

'Maybe we'll spend more time here. There are other places I'd like to show you, but they can wait until next time. There are still so many things we have to learn about each other,' he added.

She smiled, trying to suppress a feeling of unease, then she took Ivan's hand, lifting the other to the sling in which Layla was pinned against her chest.

'There's no reason why we shouldn't spend more time here, right?' he said, as if in passing, strapping Layla back into the car seat twenty minutes later.

Gabriela paused, trying to keep her voice level. 'I mean maybe, down the line. But don't forget I'm going back to work in a few weeks.'

She couldn't understand why he was forcing the issue.

He didn't answer until they were both seated and the car was rolling back down the driveway, the perfectly tended grass glistening on either side, and through the gates.

'So you're still planning on going back?' His voice was harder.

She didn't reply straight away. 'Of course I'm going back, Ivan. I've always been open about that.'

He kept his gaze pinned on the traffic outside the car. Did she imagine the tears glistening in the corners of his eyes?

'I suppose I imagined once Layla was here, you might feel more committed to her than your job.'

'Committed?' Her voice rose again. 'I'm fully *committed*, Ivan.'

He turned sharply to her. 'Don't raise your voice to me in front of our daughter.'

Turning his attention to the driver, he said in English, 'Straight home. I've lost my appetite.'

Chapter 63

Gabriela

The day she left Layla, tears streamed down her face.

When she pictured home she imagined a ravine, two bodies of rock once whole, torn in half with a gaping wound.

'She'll be fine, she knows me so well. Don't you, baby?' Polina assured her, taking Gabriela's sleeping daughter from her arms and holding her to her own chest as the surrogate parent she was, intermittently, to become.

'I know, but she's only six weeks old.' Gabriela was unable to stop her body from shaking.

'You'll be back soon,' Polina added, her voice more tender than usual. 'Besides, sounds like you don't have a choice.'

Remembering the lie she had fed Ivan about the foreign conference she had to lead, Gabriela swallowed. 'You know I wouldn't be going, if it wasn't so important.'

Polina ignored her words. 'I'll look after her, you know that, and Ivan will be back in a couple of days, too.'

Gabriela thought of him heading off on another one of his business trips, the argument from last night still percolating in her mind. He had been so bemused by her suggestion that there was little difference between him going off and leaving their daughter and her doing the same thing that it felt like another chasm had opened up that she could see no possible way to get back from.

'But you're her mother,' he said, this alone was a rational argument.

It was baffling, she thought, this change of heart. He had been so understanding when she was pregnant, so on board when she repeatedly explained to him that she would still have to do stints abroad, even when the baby was young; drilling it into him so that there could be no mistaking her intentions down the line.

Yet the look on his face when she'd told him she was going away for a week, to work on the case she'd left early during her maternity leave, made her feel as if she had never prepared him for it at all.

'Like I said in Moscow, I suppose I just assumed that once you had the baby you'd feel differently,' he said again when she asked him what was wrong, refusing to meet her eye.

She had studied him long and hard last night, waiting for him to tell her it was OK, but he simply leaned down and kissed their daughter on the head, and walked out. By the time she woke up, he'd already gone.

It was only once she was in the cab home that she realised her mistake. She had been reaching in her bag for her phone – anything to distract herself from the baby screaming for her on the other side of the city – when she felt her fingers land on the bunny's fur. As she pulled the toy from the bag, instantly she knew what she'd done.

She had almost forgotten Otto entirely, but when she moved past Layla's room the previous evening as she prepared to leave, escaping to the relative serenity of the top of the house after her fight with Ivan, she spotted the bunny abandoned on the shelf, slumped over in the half-light. Creeping into the room, careful not to wake her daughter, she'd lifted it up and placed it discreetly under her arm.

In the hall, she'd heard Ivan's footsteps following her up the stairs and she'd moved quickly back into their bedroom, stuffing the toy in the bottom of her bag and placing her make-up and book on top to obscure it, should Ivan for any reason glance inside at the contents.

But as soon as she drew it out now, she knew what had happened.

Briefly, she remembered the *That's Not My . . .* touch-and-feel books which she'd read repeatedly to Callum when he was little, borrowed from the same library in which she had spent hours when she was young. Closing her eyes, she imagined him on her knee as she regaled him with the details revealing how this particular item wasn't the narrator's lion or pirate or train.

With a rising sense of panic, she pictured her son. There was no way he would see this toy and not know immediately that it was not his Otto.

Her voice breaking, she called out to the driver as the car idled along Kentish Town High Street. 'Can you stop, please? I need to run into McDonald's quickly.'

Inside, she moved towards the counter. 'Do you have any jam?'

Noting the attendant's expression, she continued, 'OK, I'll have a Big Mac, with ketchup, please.'

Clutching the food, her bag over her shoulder, she made her way towards the bathroom. Inside, she dumped the burger in the nappy waste bin and crouched down, tearing at the foil lid of the plastic ketchup container. As the foil tore open, she ingested a mouthful of the sweet-sharp-tasting liquid and when she looked up she caught her own reflection, red goop smeared down her chin.

Lifting the rabbit to her mouth, she dabbed it on the stain, being careful to replicate the placing of the jam Callum had left on Otto the day before she left.

But when she pulled the toy back and looked at it, the colour was all wrong. Wiping her mouth with a tissue and throwing it in the bin along with the sauce packet, she looked down at the rabbit that wasn't Otto and, without warning, her vision flooded with tears.

Feeling her knees buckle, she collapsed into the space between the toilet and the door and ignoring the meter on the cab ticking outside, she sat there, her whole body heaving with tears until she could cry no more.

Chapter 64

Isobel

At the sound of the door being broken down, each of us pauses. For what feels like a lifetime, we stand there, afraid to move, afraid to shatter the moment – terrified of what comes next. But then Eva's sister calls out and Eva runs towards the landing, away from the stairs.

Seconds later, the sound of the front door being kicked open is followed by the slamming of feet on the treads.

'Get down,' the first officer says as two others run in the direction of the landing where he pins Eva against the wall, her face pressed against the plaster.

'You're under arrest,' I hear him say, and I feel the world tip once more.

'I'm a journalist,' I shout, raising my hands above my head, feeling I might fall as another officer runs at me, a third emerging up the stairs and holding Eva's sister against the kitchen counter.

'Leave her!' I hear Oscar's voice shouting at the officer who has lunged at me, and when I look up I see him standing in front of me, Eva behind him being led out in handcuffs.

'No,' I say. 'You've got it wrong.'

Oscar shakes his head without a hint of satisfaction.

'I'm afraid we haven't.'

Chapter 65

Gabriela

She could never have imagined she would feel shy around her children, but the day of her return, she felt more than nervous, she felt exposed. It wasn't just the prospect of watching what she said, of only recalling those months away within the permissible limits of what her family was allowed to know, checking herself on every detail, every consonant and vowel – a habit to which she had become accustomed and yet which became no less cumbersome as time passed. It was the fear that they would look at her and see what had changed.

'Mum? She's here!'

She could hear her children's voices at the top of the staircase as she turned the key in the lock, muscle memory reminding her to push a little further to the left than common sense would suggest.

As she stepped through the door, she looked up, and when they saw her, Sadie paused, as if with one look at her face she sensed her mother's apprehension.

The familiarity of the hallway felt like a blow to her solar plexus.

'Darlings,' she said as Callum ran towards her, hurling himself at her with a ferocity that made her wince.

'Careful!' Her voice was sharper than she had intended it to be and he took a step back, wounded, but then she bent her knees and scooped him into her chest.

Looking over his shoulder, she reached for Sadie with her other hand, the tears filling in her eyes as she joined them, the three of them contained like that until Tom moved into the hall behind them.

It was the sight of Tom that floored her. The way he hovered, the slight movement in his face as he looked at her, so familiar it was like curling up in front of a fire.

'There she is,' he said, the smile she knew so well creeping over his face, the lines deepening on his forehead. He was wearing an oven glove on one hand and as he stood there watching them. Slowly, Gabriela extricated herself from her children's embrace, placing a hand against the wall and pulling herself straight.

She hadn't expected the strength of emotion as he wrapped his arms around her, and she found herself instantly soothed by his touch.

'Hey, it's not that bad to be back, surely?' he laughed, pulling away to wipe the tears streaming down her cheeks with the side of his finger.

'I've missed you, so much,' she said, her throat swelling, wanting to stop time; to pause the four of them, the smell of shop-bought lasagne drifting in from the kitchen. And yet, how could she think that? Instinctively, her breasts pricked as if scolding her, and she pictured Layla. How could she overlook her baby so easily? And then, before she could stop herself, she thought of Ivan, picturing him as a manifold: one body but two men. The Ivan she had met that day on Crown Passage, the bereaved father, the autonomous, decisive businessman, the person who had rushed her off her feet. And then who? What did she see next? Pushing the second image away before it could come fully into focus, she heard Tom speak again.

'I've missed you too.' There was almost a ferocity to his voice and she let herself fall into him again, her fingers clinging to his back, realising how tired she was. How utterly out of her depth.

'I bought presents,' she said in a bid to distract herself from the memory of what she'd left behind.

Hauling the suitcase into the kitchen, she felt winded as she reached into the side pocket of her suitcase.

'Wine?' Tom asked, and she nodded, grateful for anything to take the edge off. Anything to soften the claws tearing at her throat.

'OK, so this is for you,' she said, once she was settled on the sofa, the smell of it both familiar and unsettling; the same hot-rock burns – scars from the nights when Tom and she would lie here for hours in stoned silence in the early days.

This room had become an almost constant backdrop: her past and her present – and yet what of the future?

Sadie smiled politely as she lifted up the sticker book and the collectable plastic toy. Gabriela instantly regretted them as she saw her daughter's face drop; it was the sort of present she would have loved once, but now the inappropriateness of the selection made her cheeks flare with embarrassment.

'I'm sorry, there wasn't much in Moscow. If I'm honest, I bought them at the airport on the way back. I didn't think you'd fancy a matryoshka doll.'

As she said it, she realised Sadie probably would have.

Quickly, she added, 'We'll go shopping, an early birthday present, OK?'

Reaching back into her bag for the bars of chocolate and the bottle of whisky she had bought for Tom, she heard Callum, who was clutching the blue train she'd bought him, utter the words she had been dreading.

'Where's Otto?'

Without flinching she reached further into her bag. 'Here he is.'

She pulled out the small, floppy-haired rabbit, the same baby blue fur, the same velveteen ears as the stuffed toy Saoirse and Jim had bought for him when he was a baby, and which had barely left Callum's side before he gave it to her, to keep her warm on her trip.

Before he had even taken the toy in his hands, he said, 'That's not Otto.'

Blanching slightly, she laughed. 'What are you on about, you funny thing? Of course it's Otto, who else would it be?'

There was a note in her voice and she felt Sadie turn to look, interested now.

'His hair is too blue and his eyes aren't the same.'

She turned to Sadie, rolling her eyes affectionately, before turning back to Callum.

'Oh, darling, you just don't recognise him because it's been so long . . . His fur just looks a little different because I gave him a wash. You should have seen him, after all our adventures . . . He was filthy!'

Gathering up the chocolate and the booze, she stood and held out her hands. 'Now, I think Dad's making dinner – are you going to help me give him these pressies, hmm?'

Letting Otto hang by his arm, Callum followed her to the counter.

It was only once the children had gone to bed that she realised how much she was dreading being left alone with Tom. Callum's eyes had been drooping as bedtime approached, his head lolling against her arm as they watched the familiar Friday night TV, the canned laughter of the audience adding a hint of menace. She longed to hold him there, to keep this barrier between herself and Tom, and the inevitable questions, the closeness that she could not give him, not yet.

Sadie had curled her feet under her legs on the far side of the sofa, and whenever Gabriela tried to catch her eye, she felt Sadie's gaze fix more firmly on the television set.

'Well, I think it's time you kids headed up,' Tom said when the credits began to roll on a repeat of *The Simpsons*, signalling it was eight o'clock.

'I don't want to,' Callum said, as Sadie picked herself up from the sofa, without a word.

'Come on, son. Mummy's knackered. We all need to go to sleep now, it's late,' Tom cajoled him.

'I want a story,' Callum persevered.

'Not tonight, you've already stayed up past your bedtime . . .'

'It's fine,' Gabriela interrupted, grateful for the extra time with the children, for the intimacy of those precious moments she'd wished away when they were tiny, curled up on the bed reading *Goodnight Moon*.

It was once she was back downstairs, the sound of the water she'd just turned on crashing against the bathtub above the living room, that she felt the sense of dread closing in.

'So, are you going to tell me what it was like?' he asked, once she emerged from the bathroom, the bedrooms upstairs having fallen silent.

What would the time be in Moscow? she wondered, looking up at the clock, which read 21.33. It would be past midnight. For a moment, she shuddered, stifling a yawn, and Tom lifted his head slightly to look at her.

'It's OK, we don't need to talk now . . . you need to sleep. I've changed the sheets so it should be nice and cosy. Why don't you head on up and I'll turn off the lights down here?'

She nodded, smiling gratefully, and walked towards the door, turning briefly to watch him going through the usual evening routine, admitting to herself for the first time they were living on borrowed time.

The next morning was a Saturday. At some time around nine, Callum idled at the doorway to the bedroom before slipping in and climbing under the covers, as he had used to when he was tiny. Tom had already gone downstairs, believing Gabriela to still be asleep. When Sadie appeared in the doorway a while later, she beckoned her inside.

'I missed you,' Sadie said after a few moments, her voice so quiet Gabriela wasn't sure whether she wanted her to hear it. Pressing her eyes together tightly, she ran her fingers gently over Sadie's hair.

By the time they emerged in the kitchen, it was nearly ten. The back door was open, presumably to purge the smell of burnt toast.

She hadn't slept so long or so deeply since before she'd left the children, despite all that should be keeping her awake, and there was something both disorientating and guilt-inducing about the experience.

'I've made poached eggs,' Tom announced, turning to her and smiling.

'Sounds perfect,' she replied, taking a seat at the table next to Sadie who immediately set to work, writing neatly in her school-book.

'What topic are you doing this term?' she asked, leaning in and inhaling deeply to soak up the smell of her, admiring the pale pink roses on her pyjamas. 'Are those new?' she continued before Sadie could answer her initial question, and Sadie nodded.

'Dad bought them.'

For a moment she felt irrationally wounded. There was so much she didn't know about the past few months, so many questions she had been unable – or unwilling – to ask, during their snatched phone calls.

'One egg or two?'

She cleared a space on the table as Tom placed the plate in front of her, on which he had already served toast and two eggs.

'This looks great, thank you.'

She thought of her breakfast the previous weekend. The typical Russian fare that was more about show than tradition: caviar, borscht, the champagne which had gone straight to her head, giving her the sort of frontal lobe headache she hadn't experienced since Callum was a baby and she found herself temporarily struck by migraines, which the doctors dismissed as the result of dehydration (*'Very common in breastfeeding mothers'* – as if that fact alone should soothe the blinding pain).

Tom was working hard to keep everything as normal as possible as they pulled on their shoes and headed out for the family stroll across the Heath, which he'd suggested as he tidied away the plates after breakfast, indicating for her to stay seated as he did so.

That day, she was precious cargo, long-awaited and newly received from faraway lands; exotic and highly breakable.

There was a hint of summer in the air as they made their way towards the entrance by the tennis courts. It was a clear day and sprigs of colour lined the verge as the path led up and away from the tribes of dog-walkers and hungover parents wrestling with screaming toddlers gathered around the café, guiding them towards Kenwood.

'Why don't you run ahead and climb on the trees over there?' she said to Callum, pointing towards the fallen trunks he had shuffled along as a toddler, bundled in a padded bodysuit, a look of terrified confusion gripping his features.

Callum tugged on her arm, gripping her hand more tightly with his own and shaking his head.

He did this when he was hurt or felt abandoned. She had forgotten it about him, the same behaviour he had displayed when she went away on shorter work trips when he was younger. His way of showing her he hadn't forgiven her for leaving him was to hold on as tightly as he could.

Would Tom have received the same reaction had it been him who had gone away? Would friends and strangers have recoiled to hear that he was leaving his child for months on end, she wondered, if the tables were turned? It was a pointless question, of course: Tom was not going anywhere.

'That's OK, you don't have to go, I just thought you might want to,' she said to Callum, lightly squeezing his hand. 'Once we get to Kenwood, we can have a hot chocolate.' It was all she had in this moment. Simple offerings: food, drinks, nothing too cerebral.

And so it continued for the following week. Her adjusting back into family life, Tom accepting her self-imposed distance in a way that made her want to shake him.

And then finally, the following Saturday night, as they settled down with a bottle of wine on opposite sides of the sofa, he snapped.

'Is this how it is now?'

She looked up, surprised by the timing of his offensive but also relieved.

'I'm sorry?'

'You and me. We're just going to cruise along like estranged housemates for the rest of eternity?'

She shifted in her seat.

'I'm sorry, I know I've been . . .' She let the words drift off, hoping he would step in to fill the silence. When he didn't she continued hesitantly, 'I just . . . It's weird, being back. I'm sorry, I know I shouldn't say that, but – well, that's just how I feel.'

He nodded, grateful for her honesty.

'I get that.'

'Thank you.'

'But, Gabriela, it's just me. It's just Tom, you know you can talk to me . . .'

She shook her head. 'I know. I know I can.' She reached her hand to him. 'I want to, it's just there are so many things that I can't . . .'

'I don't give a shit about that stuff, Gabriela.' His voice suddenly rose. 'I'm not interested in your work stuff. Whatever is going on with that, I don't need to know. I just . . . I mean where did you stay? What did you eat?' He was fumbling around for words. 'Bloody hell, I don't know. We don't even have to talk about Moscow, I just want words, Gabriela. Anything.' His voice fell quieter. 'I just want you.'

Chapter 66

Isobel

Silence has descended by the time we arrive on the Heath, Oscar having driven me to the police station first, leaving me nursing a cup of strong sweet tea while he filled in the necessary paperwork. While he'd had his back turned, I'd returned the badge he must have already noticed was missing, though he hadn't mentioned it, slipping it under a pile of papers so that it wouldn't be immediately obvious.

Dusk is settling as we pass the duck ponds on Millfield Lane where huddles of fishermen in camo-trousers and fleece sweaters are lined up like oversized gnomes at the edge of the water, their rods stretched out in front of them.

Walking in silence a metre apart from one another, we follow the path round towards Kenwood House, turning right as the ground becomes hard and cracked, broken with thick roots which twist under our feet.

From here I can already see the forensics with their white boiler suits and their tents pitched against the light wind which whistles across folds of green and brown.

'She buried him there,' Oscar says, filling the silence as we approach, pointing to the shaded patch of land a couple of metres from the thicket where I saw the attack take place.

'She did a good job of it. She must have had someone to help her. The theory we're working with is that she initially hid the body and then came back with her sister and the tools needed to dig a shallow grave. Not even the foxes had found it by the time we got there. That might have been when she found your shoes and your purse, and decided to use them to scare you off . . .'

I frown before speaking for the first time in at least an hour. 'But even I noticed the ground had been disturbed – surely when you followed up on that . . .'

Oscar looks away.

'You didn't even look, did you?'

He sniffs, refusing to meet my eye, 'I should have done. I'm sorry.'

There is so much I could say but what good will it do now? Instead, I fix my gaze away from him in combative silence.

'Issy, come on, you can hardly blame me. Do you know how many insane phone calls I've had from you in the past year? How many madcap theories you've tried to embroil me in, one way or another? Even after what you did to me? Besides, there was nothing to go on. But you wouldn't hear it. What the hell was I supposed to do?'

'Nothing to go on? You didn't fucking look!'

This time it is his voice that grows louder. 'Seriously, I'm sorry if I sound like a prick, but it's been really tiring tiptoeing around you all the time . . . I know you've been through a lot and I'm sorry, I'm so sorry about Jess – but you can't behave the way you've been behaving and expect to be treated . . . Anyway, you fucked me over, Is! Do you have any idea how much you hurt me? Do you have any idea how hard it was to lose you like that, and then, just as I was starting to move on with my life, to have to watch that happen to you, and not be able to be there?'

He stops, breathing in hard. Both of us are silent for at least a minute before he speaks again. And when he does, the strength of my enduring love for him, even after all these years, nearly topples me.

'I'm sorry, Is. I wish I had listened to you earlier.'

'Yeah, well, it probably would have been better if you hadn't at all.'

'You did the right thing,' he says, and I laugh bitterly.

'Getting a girl arrested for murder because she defended herself against a man who had trafficked her? That's what you think happened, right? I don't call that the right thing.'

'Her situation will be taken into account. Her baby . . .'

The tears sting at the corners of my eyes. 'Why didn't she just stay in Brighton, once she'd escaped? It sounds like she had built a life there for herself. Why did she come back?'

Oscar pauses. 'You really want to know?'

'Of course.'

He inhales. 'The father of Eva's child was also her pimp – he was an old family friend from her village who persuaded her to come to London. He was a friend of her sister's and they had trusted him. He joined a gang involved in trafficking women and he targeted Eva and her sister, promising them a good life in London. When Eva got here, he blackmailed her into prostitution. Eventually, he got her pregnant – she knew he was the father because he was the only one she slept with without contraception. When she discovered she was pregnant, she ran away to Brighton to start a new life.'

'Fuck. She told you this? But it doesn't explain why the hell she came back.'

Oscar nodded. 'The baby was ill. Eva wanted to be near her sister, and so she came back to London and the baby went into hospital, in the Royal Free. She was sleeping at the hospital to be with the baby and one day, in the early hours of the morning, this prick shows up. She was terrified that he would hurt the baby, and so she went with him. When they were outside the hospital, he told her he was taking her with him, that she couldn't take the baby with them and she tried to run. Apparently he caught up with her somewhere here, near where you saw them. They started to fight, he was saying she had to get back to work, that she had a debt to pay off. He threatened her and the child. She says she can't remember what happened after that but the next thing she knew, she had hit him with a rock. Then she looked up and saw you. . .'

We stand in silence for a minute, watching the men in paper suits ducking in and out of the police line.

Finally, I say, 'And the baby?'

'The baby's fine. It had pneumonia but it seems OK. That was the child at the house – and he's stayed with her sister.' He clears his throat. 'For now at least. Social Services have been informed.'

Isobel shakes her head. 'All this time I just thought that if I could just do this one thing, if I could just atone for Jess in some way . . . I'm a fucking idiot.'

I raise my eyes up to the sky, hating myself for not being able to keep it together, on top of everything else.

'You know, the thing that happened with us. . . I'm not sorry,' I say, before I can think better of it. 'It was my body, my choice . . .'

'It was *my baby*,' he snaps, his voice breaking, and I shake my head.

'You don't get to choose.'

He takes a step forward. 'I didn't want to *choose.*' There are tears shining in his eyes. 'I wanted to know, I wanted to support you in your choice . . . I wanted—'

The sound of his phone makes us both jump and when he pulls it out, I see his girlfriend's name flashing on the screen.

'Just give me one second, OK? Don't move, wait there,' he says, motioning to me with one hand before turning to take the call.

'Hi, babe . . .'

As he walks away, just far enough that his voice is out of reach, I move my gaze back to the London skyscape and take a deep breath.

Reaching into my pocket, I pull a cigarette from the packet. With one final glance across the horizon I turn and walk down the hill, away from the policemen with their dogs, and away from Morley, without looking back.

Chapter 67

Gabriela

After that first night at home, the week of her return, she struggled to sleep. While Tom lay beside her, dead to the world, she stared at the ceiling, clinging to the duvet, imagining Layla on the other side of London, without her. Less than two months ago she was still inside her body; how would she cope now? Where would she think her mother had gone?

There were things she had prepared for, knowing as she had that she would not always be able to be there. She had mixed breast and bottle-feeding from the start for fear she would be unable to wean her baby off in time for her to leave, though it pulled against her every instinct to lure her away from her body, to stop her latching on when she went for the nipple. She had been ready for that, along with the tales she had been prepared to tell to explain away the abdominal scar if for any reason the birth had ended up needing a C-section. Though in the end she hadn't.

The birth itself had passed with relative ease, in the corporate environs of the private hospital Ivan had paid for, but there were things she hadn't anticipated, things so fundamental that she had not let herself so much as imagine them. At the forefront of it all was the sense of all-consuming loss: the intangible but unavoidable fact that everything about this was completely wrong.

There were smaller things, too, that caught her off-guard. Her inability to remember any of the milestones of early motherhood meant that though she had already done it twice before, Gabriela seemed to have no recollection of the stages at which anything was supposed to happen. The unknowing of it, the constant cycle of surprises, amazed and terrified her.

In the immediate days after she arrived back in Dartmouth Park, she feigned a list of errands that would allow her to get out, to breathe, to scream into her own hands.

The GP's waiting room seemed smaller than she remembered and she struggled to focus on the out-of-date magazines, finding herself standing and pacing the room while she waited for her name to be called.

'It says here you have struggled with insomnia before,' the locum GP said as she scanned through her medical history.

'Yes, but I've never taken medication. Usually I've tried other things and they've eventually helped.'

'What sort of things?'

She thought of the late-night glasses of wine, the over-the-counter antihistamines that had in the short term done a job of sorts in numbing her mind.

'You know, cutting down on screen-time in the evenings, less coffee . . .' she said, her voice fading out.

'OK. What do you think is different now from last time?'

Briefly she pictured her previous trip to this same surgery, the conversation with yet another locum doctor who didn't know her from Adam, in the weeks after she'd walked out of the FCO, when the churning of her own thoughts had first started to keep her awake at night. In another snapshot, she saw her baby, screaming for her mother on the other side of the city.

'I don't know, really. I suppose things got better. But recently things have become . . . stressful again.'

'Stressful how?'

'Family things. I've done everything I can. I just really think I would benefit from a few good nights' sleep. I don't want to take medicine long-term, really . . . I understand the dangers. But if I could just have something to help me get over this phase, then once I'm back into the rhythm I can continue the lifestyle adjustments you recommended . . .'

The doctor held her eye for a moment before conceding. 'You're not pregnant, are you?'

Her belly, which had been so protruded for the first three weeks after Layla was born that she worried it would never return to normal, had flattened so that she was not much bigger than she had been when she left. Still, as a defensive move, she wore loose-fitting shirt-dresses and made passing comments about the immense portion sizes in Russia, and the lack of exercise. If Tom noticed the extra flesh, he thought better than to mention it.

Gabriela felt her cheeks burn, though she knew the question was nothing more than protocol. This was not a test. Even if the doctor had noticed her recent pregnancy with Layla registered on her notes, there was no reason for her to believe anything was out of the ordinary. There was no way of her knowing who the father was, and she had no reason to ask, or to care.

Gabriela had to restrain herself from biting the doctor's hand off as she handed her the prescription for a batch of eszopiclone, reeling out the suggested dosage with the final warning, 'Pills are only a short-term solution. Behavioural therapy is the best approach, in the long term.'

'I'm sure,' she said, smiling gratefully, slipping the prescription into her pocket.

As she crossed the road towards home, she felt herself looking over her shoulder, unable to shake the sense that she was not alone. By the time she reached Chester Road, her feet were moving so fast that she felt she would trip. As she made her way up the path towards her front door, she thought of Emsworth before shaking the image away. Whatever it was he had been embroiled in, he'd been caught out. No one was watching her anymore. She was paranoid, justifiably perhaps, but the fear she was experiencing now was misplaced. The thought of Emsworth, the man responsible for sending her entire life into disarray, being caught out should have filled her with some sense of satisfaction and renewed purpose, even if he hadn't been hung out to dry in quite the way she might have hoped.

It might even have been possible to get her job back, to contact the FCO and explain what had happened, at least to get a reference. But the thought brought not even the slightest sliver of pleasure. When she looked back on those days, it was like looking at a different person, a hologram that might or might not have ever existed at all.

That night she took one of the pills she'd procured from the GP and sat on the sofa. With Tom out playing a gig at a local pub and the children already asleep, the house felt too quiet. Flicking on the television, she sat on the sofa and felt suddenly aware of the pitch-black sky through the terraced doors. It had never occurred to her before that they needed curtains, but suddenly she felt so exposed it was though she was on stage.

Standing, running to the doorway, imagining a cross marked on her forehead as she made her way across the room, a gun pointed at her head from the shadows of their tiny garden, she switched off the light. In the darkness, her heartbeat slowed, and instinctively she knew she had to talk. The voices that rang in her head would not be silenced. Tell Madeleine. There was no reason not to; she was no longer in a state of denial about how deep in she was. Madeleine would know what to do, or at least she would know what to say.

Pulling her phone out of her bag, she dialled the number and cursed as the voicemail kicked in. Retrieving her laptop from her bag, she composed an email, headed *Lunch?*, keeping the tone light in the text.

The bounce-back was immediate: *I'm out of the country on business* . . .

'Fuck!' The sound of her own voice made her jump and for a moment she imagined herself running out of the front door. Instead, she walked upstairs, the house in darkness, and lay on the bed waiting for the sleeping pills to pull her under.

Around 3 a.m., unconsciousness finally enveloped and held her there, deep in its embrace until just past 9 when, stirring in bed, she heard the key in the lock telling her Tom was home after dropping the kids at school.

He didn't come upstairs and when she heard the door clicking closed again ten minutes later, she ventured down and found the kitchen immaculate, only then recalling Tom saying something about having a job to quote on this morning. She looked around the room; the house felt strangely like a stage set, all the correct props in their rightful place but something about them artificial. Sitting at the kitchen table, she felt as though her limbs had been severed and her body was floating along on a stream, unable to pull herself back as the sea opened up ahead.

Chapter 68

Gabriela

She claimed she was taking the first ten days after Sadie's school broke up as holiday leave from the job Tom still believed she had, and the four of them went on day trips to Margate and Brighton, courtesy of the generous allowance Ivan placed into her account each month.

'I just travel so much for work, it would feel like a busman's holiday to go abroad,' she'd reasoned, when Tom broached the possibility of heading somewhere more exotic, knowing that she couldn't leave England with Layla as young as she was.

'That was nice,' Tom said as they settled on the train back from Brighton to Victoria, laying out an M&S picnic on the table in front of them, Callum already asleep.

Sadie's hairline was smudged with sun-cream, and she absent-mindedly swung her feet as she tucked into an egg and cress sandwich.

'She seems happy,' Gabriela said, only then realising how long it was since she'd seen her daughter so content. She reached across the table and squeezed her.

'She likes us spending time together,' Tom replied and Gabriela felt his words bristle against her.

On the way home from Victoria station, taking the tube straight through to Highbury before jumping in a cab, she felt a prickling sensation at the nape of her neck. Every so often she felt herself turn, her eyes scouring the crowds for something she felt but could not see.

* * *

For the unimaginably elongated stretch of Sadie and Callum's school holidays, she had to revive the charade that she had a working life, leaving the house early in the morning and killing time wandering the more obscure streets of London, terrified she would bump into her children.

While she'd fleetingly wondered whether now was the time to tell Tom she had packed it in, she instantly remembered the cover the job gave her for the stints she spent with Ivan. She managed weeks here and there, telling Tom that she had work trips abroad. Did he wonder where she was, those nights holed up in another city or country? Did he try to picture the bed in which she slept?

She tried to push this thought out of mind as she took the bus to Aldgate and walked along Commercial Road, turning off onto the canal somewhere near Limehouse. Making her way along the path, the Thames stretching out on her right, the towers of Canary Wharf looming over the water in the distance, she felt the same fluttering sensation she'd experienced on the way back from that day trip to Brighton brush over her skin, and when she turned, she imagined a figure pulling back into the shadows.

Moving forward more quickly, listening out for footsteps, she took a deep breath and turned suddenly, ready to confront whoever was following her. But as she turned, there was just a single jogger making his way along the path behind her. The pounding of his trainers, the unexpectedness of his pace caused her to take a step back and hold onto the railing, the only thing standing between her and the river below.

Catching her breath, she watched the man disappear around the corner before closing her eyes and leaning down. When her phone rang a moment later, it was Polina, calling to update her on Layla while Ivan was away on another one of his increasingly frequent work trips; trips that suited Gabriela because the less he was around the less likely he was to question her own periods of absence.

'I'm putting the phone to her ear so she can hear you speak,' Polina said and Gabriela felt a pulling in her chest.

'Layla? It's Mummy. Can you hear me? Hello, darling . . .'

As a cyclist spun past, she felt herself withdraw slightly. Though she couldn't pinpoint how and why, she understood on some level that the unravelling had already begun.

'Can't you come out with us today, Mummy?' Callum asked the following morning as she ran fingers through her uncombed hair in the kitchen, her bag already on her arm.

'You know, why not?' she said, overcome by a sudden sense of duty to her second-born.

'You'll come?' he said, his face joyful and disbelieving in equal measure.

'Really?' Tom queried. 'But I thought you had that big meeting to prepare for, I thought you couldn't—'

'That's not until next week,' Gabriela interrupted him, sensing a thought she didn't like taking shape in his mind.

'But I'm sure you said—'

'Oh look, forget it, if you don't want me to come . . .'

'Gabriela . . .' Tom followed her through the house. She moved away from him quickly, fearful of the prospect of a conversation.

'Don't be like that, of course I want you to come,' Tom said, attempting to overtake her in the narrow hallway, past the disorderly row of shoes stretching from the front door to the kitchen. 'I'm just saying I thought you had to . . .'

She didn't answer, moving more briskly towards the door. As he stepped in front of her, he kicked several pairs of shoes out of his path and held out his arms to prevent her from leaving. 'You can't do this, not again. Talk to me! Why are you always walking out on us?'

'Get out of my way!' she shouted back at him, her voice echoing through the house as she wrenched open the door, slamming it behind her. She could hear Tom's voice yelling back at her from inside, and she clamped her hands over her ears, running as fast as she could until her feet could run no more.

* * *

Ivan was away again. As the demands of his work became greater, it became so rare that their diaries overlapped that on the occasions when they were together, it was an ongoing process of re-assimilation.

For the most part in those moments of familial adjustment, they talked about Layla, and Polina – Ivan reassuring her that she had no reason to worry on the occasions when she confided – in order to explain away the sudden rush of emotion that would consume her at times – her fears that Polina was a better mother-figure than she was.

Though Gabriela knew it frustrated him, she was too shattered and scared of being spotted to visit the high-end restaurants or cultural events he booked them into. Mainly, they would eat at home and watch films; she was too tired even to read the books Ivan bought her in airport bookshops when he was on his way back from wherever it was he had been, foreign texts mimicking the type of highbrow reading she'd impressed him with in the early days of their relationship.

When the conversation ran out, they sat on the sofa in silence, watching the mouths of the characters on the enormous state-of-the-art television move as she wondered what it was that they had ever talked about.

As autumn took hold, and with it the imminent prospect of days spent walking the streets in the cold, Gabriela was so tired from nights flitting in and out of consciousness, plunging in and out of dreams in which her two worlds would finally collide, that she longed to curl up in a state of hibernation and never get up. She could almost picture the various strings of her life coming loose, tying themselves around her neck in endless knots.

She couldn't even remember the last time she had seen Madeleine. Their lunches had become fewer and farther between with Madeleine so often working abroad, and then they'd stopped. Sometimes when she looked back on that part of her life, it was as if she had dreamt it.

At home she had stopped talking to Tom altogether about her work, besides the brief, passing details of the destinations he believed she was moving between, sometimes for just a few days at a time, sometimes more, as part of her role working government-to-government – and he had stopped asking. With every unasked question, Gabriela felt another of the sparks that had once flickered between them die out.

She told Tom she was off to Amsterdam for a few days, though it could have been the Congo or Bermuda for all that he seemed to notice. She was bored and frustrated to the extent that she had to resist the urge to make her stories more and more outlandish, just to see if there was ever a point at which he would start to question anything.

Ivan had arrived home that afternoon, heading straight upstairs after the briefest of hellos. Gabriela waited for him in the living room, nervous of what had triggered his obvious mood.

The older Layla got, the harder the separation became, with Gabriela's anxiety so strong that she could still hear her child screaming by the time she was halfway down the street. Layla had started waking in the night again after a period of sleeping through and had just drifted off on her mother's lap when Ivan breezed into the room.

'I'm taking Layla to Moscow,' he announced, presenting this fact as a *fait accompli*.

'I beg your pardon?'

'On Monday, we'll be gone for a week.'

'What are you talking about? You can't—'

He looked at her from where he was standing by the fireplace, slipping off the cufflinks from his shirt and placing them on the coffee table.

Feeling her heart beat faster in her chest, Gabriela lifted Layla from her lap, careful not to wake her, and settled her sleeping body on the sofa beside her, before standing.

'You can't do that.'

'I can't do what? Take our daughter to see her grandmother?' He sounded genuinely bemused. 'Why would you care where she is if you're not going to be here anyway? If you're so much more committed to your . . . What would you call them, these "causes" of yours?'

'Ivan, that is not fair, and you know it.'

He looked at her, tilting his head as if working hard to recognise her.

Avoiding his gaze, she continued, 'What if something happened, if there was an accident?'

'Oh, come on, accidents can happen anywhere, and it's hardly as if you haven't spent a week away from your daughter before. Besides, Polina will be with us, she is more than capable.'

More capable than you are, he didn't have to say.

Ignoring the implication, she shook her head. 'I don't like it.'

But Ivan simply stood, laughing dismissively. 'Well, I'm afraid it's not up to you, Gabriela. You can't have it both ways. Either you're here or you're not.'

She watched him as he moved out of the room, trying to discern the real meaning rattling through his words.

Chapter 69

Isobel

I stop at the office on my way home and write up the story of the discovery of the body on the Heath, today, leaving out any of the details of my own involvement, mentioning only the victim and the twenty-four-year-old woman taken into custody while a murder investigation is underway. I write with detachment, trying not to picture Eva in her prison cell, the mother I put behind bars for a crime I couldn't condemn, the baby destined to a life in care.

Ben thanks me with a raised arm above his computer screen before I walk out of the door and towards the flat, the darkness no longer threatening as I make my way through the entrance and up the stairs.

Whoever it was who had been watching me has now been caught, thanks to DNA, and besides, he was never the figure I'd thought him to be. The person I'd imagined had had his own life snuffed out with a single blow from a rock – an act of self-defence by a young woman who had trusted him, and whose life he had ruined.

I had been wrong. Time and again, I had made myself believe something that simply wasn't true. Oscar was right, they were all right: I was a mess. I *am* a mess. But there was one thing he would always be wrong about – it was *my* choice, and I made the right one. In that instance, at least.

Before I have time to change my mind, I move to the cupboard in the kitchen and pull out any booze I can find – whisky, the dregs of an old bottle of vodka, the limoncello Si had brought back, ill-advisedly, from a trip to Sorrento, that had barely been touched. Ceremoniously gathering the bottles on the kitchen table, together with my cigarettes and the bag of Xanax from the drawer in my bedroom, I pause for a moment before reaching for the packet of cigarettes and returning them to my pocket.

Pulling my hair back into a bun before removing the lids from each bottle, I pour the pills into the sink and wash them away with the remainder of the alcohol.

When I've finished, I stack the bottles by the front door and reach into the cupboard under the counter, pulling out a cloth and a bottle of antibacterial spray.

The next morning it is like waking up in a different flat, every surface clear and scrubbed within an inch of its life. Once I've brushed my teeth, I ring Ben. Though he does not explicitly say so, I infer from his unnaturally convivial tone when I ask for some time off that he is relieved. I am a live wire and he is glad to be rid of me for a few days.

'Si will keep an eye on any developments on the Heath murder, you have a rest.'

Si. I feel a pang of guilt when I think of him. I will call him, once I've figured out what I have to do. Once I've given myself a chance to breathe in a way that I haven't been able to, not since Jess died.

In any other circumstances, it would irk me, having to hand over a story like this to another reporter. But I want nothing to do with it. I want to forget it ever happened. Briefly, I wonder if Si will connect the body with the attack I'd told him about, but why would he? They were two totally different events – one real, one imagined – my fictional version bearing no resemblance to the facts.

'Going anywhere nice?' Ben asks.

'I don't know,' I say truthfully.

'Well, whatever you do, enjoy it. You deserve a break. Don't forget to put on your out-of-office that if it's urgent they should contact one of us.'

Lifting open the lid of my laptop, I log onto my work emails. As I move the cursor towards the out-of-office button, I see an unread message, the title of the sender standing out amongst the PR spam. *Companies House.*

I click open the message.

With all that has been happening, I've forgotten that I even requested it. I should delete it. After all, what use is it now? I want nothing to do with any of this, I've done enough damage.

And yet, as my fingers hover for a moment above the keyboard, I feel them move from the 'Delete' symbol to 'Open documents'.

Just one last look, I tell myself. Just one look, and then I'll leave it.

Chapter 70

Gabriela

It was a perfect winter's day, frost settled across the immaculately pruned hedge as they reversed out of the driveway.

'Have you got the nappy bag?' Ivan asked as they moved along the crescent, their daughter already asleep in the car seat.

'Of course I have the nappy bag,' she replied, snorting in a way that was intended to make a statement. Briefly, she turned to offer some sort of riposte, but what would be the point?

It was true that she had become forgetful over the past months; focusing so intently on the crucial elements meant that everything else fell through the cracks. But she wasn't the only one whose mood had shifted. Since his return from his trip to Moscow with Layla, Ivan had been so distracted that she had barely seen him at all.

At first she had enjoyed them, these newly expressed mood swings of his: both as a precursor to exhilarating sex, and a demonstration of an emotional range that Tom had always lacked. But recently the outbursts had been replaced by a quiet broodiness.

'I hope you like it. The spa is new and they have wonderful masseuses,' Ivan said as they picked up speed a few minutes later, his tone changing completely. 'I've booked you in for ninety minutes tomorrow. Once you've had a good night's sleep. The beds are world-class, not to mention the in-house babysitting and crèche.'

She could tell he was trying to atone for his snappiness and she reached out her hand to touch his, as it moved the gearstick into fourth.

Without turning to her, he said, 'You know, I haven't been entirely honest with you.'

'OK,' she said.

'Part of the reason I wanted to take Layla home was that my mother is ill. She's not dying, not yet, but she is frail and the doctors . . . Well, they want her to go into a home, but she refuses and . . .'

There was a moment as he prepared himself to finish his sentence. 'And I was thinking, with everything that is happening with my business here, it might make sense for us to move there, at least for a few months, or years, while she is getting better, or . . .'

Gabriela's hand instinctively pulled away from his and he turned briefly to her in the passenger seat, assessing her reaction.

'What? I thought you would at least think about it. It makes sense, Gabriela . . . I mean, what's holding us here? You have no family here anymore, and my mother is desperate to spend time with her only granddaughter. And I want Layla to know her roots. Besides, I know how much you love Russia . . .'

'What is holding us?' It was the best she could manage to say. 'What about my work, for a start? For God's sake, Ivan, you're not the only one who has a job. What about my *life*? I mean, Jesus, you can't just spring something like this on me and expect me to—'

It was then that Gabriela saw her.

Just as the car pulled up to the traffic lights, there was Sadie. So close, Gabriela could have wound down her window and called out to her.

Her beautiful daughter, with two other girls – girls she vaguely recognised from school events – and a woman she hadn't seen before. One of her friends' mother? Her eyes moved between Sadie and the girls, both looking so much older than her daughter, so much more self-assured, their long hair swishing as they moved across the pedestrian crossing, leaning in to each other, laughing at a private joke.

From this distance, unable to call out, watching her through the blacked-out glass, Gabriela could see Sadie's unease, how she stood slightly away from her friends, not quite in with the joke.

Gabriela was oblivious now to the sound of Ivan's voice in the seat next to her. Ivan, who had watched her first-born moving across the road in front of him and not known a thing.

Sitting up straight, craning towards the vision of her daughter disappearing on the other side of the road, being absorbed into the crowds, her nails dug into the seat so that when she pulled them away a minute later, they had left scratch-marks in the leather.

'Gabriela, are you OK?'

When his voice came into focus, she realised she was leaning on the dashboard, her eyes unblinking. When she looked up and spotted her reflection in the mirror, her skin looked grey, her mouth contorted in a way that Ivan could not have ignored.

'What's going on, are you sick?'

'Yes,' she gasped.

'Do you want me to pull over?'

'No,' she shouted, imagining her daughter, just feet away from them. Her voice was suddenly high-pitched and urgent. From the back seat she heard Layla, waking suddenly, breaking into a cry.

'Keep going, Ivan, please, let's just get there. Please don't stop!'

'Gabriela?'

Ivan's voice was soft and muted on the other side of the door.

In the darkness of the hotel bathroom, the terrazzo tiles were cool against her back as she leaned against the wall of the walk-in shower.

Before she could push the thought away, Gabriela saw Sadie, the same age that Layla is now, in the bath at home, splashing her palms flat against the water and screaming with laughter. In the memory, she watched from the doorway, having just come in from work, Sadie and Tom oblivious to her presence.

She stood there watching for a moment and then she, too, laughed, at the sheer joyfulness of her daughter's expression. Yet when Sadie looked up and saw her there, her face fell apart. Pushing herself to

387

standing, sending water cascading over the side of the bath, she started to whimper for her mother, calling for her to pick her up. But there was no towel and so Gabriela moved out of the room to get one, and by the time she came back Sadie wouldn't look Gabriela in the eye, let alone let her hold her.

Closing her eyes, Gabriela drew in the silence on the other side of the door before Ivan spoke again. It was then that she realised she was shaking with cold. Standing, she took a towel from the heated rail on the wall and wrapped it around herself.

'Gabriela, I'm worried, are you OK?'

'I'm fine,' she managed, her voice disconnected from her body. 'I feel feverish, I think it's just a cold. I'm going to get dressed and have a lie-down.'

There was a hesitation and then he said, 'All right, well, I'm going to take Layla down to the crèche. You don't want lunch?'

'You go. I'll have something later.'

She imagined him straightening himself and winking a reassurance to their daughter.

'No problem. Sleep well.'

When she woke later, Ivan still wasn't back. Sliding open the windows, she looked out over Harvey Nichols and the Lamborghinis and Brazilian blow-dries that typified this corner of Knightsbridge: just a couple of miles from the part of the city in which she had grown up, but another world entirely.

Feeling in need of a change of scene, she walked down to the spa, moving gingerly at first, checking that there was no one there who might recognise her, however unlikely it seemed in a place that cost this much per night.

Leaving her clothes in the locker room and moving through to the spa area, she peeled off her robe and opened the door to one of the steam rooms where she was hit by the smell of eucalyptus, so strong it filled her throat, seizing her chest so that her breath became slow and heavy.

Leaning back against the tiles, the heat making her flinch, she closed her eyes. When the door sprang open a moment later, she felt herself gasp.

'Sorry,' a woman's voice said and she smiled as she settled herself on the other side of the room.

Finally, Gabriela allowed her eyes to close again and saw Tom's face drift in front of her, her fingers tensing against the ledge she was sitting on, the sweat streaming from her forehead mingling with the tears that shook her body.

How much longer could she go on like this, the lies following night and day so that there was no rest, even in sleep? And yet, how could she escape? Unless she told Tom. When the thought occurred to her now it seemed the most lucid she'd had in a long time.

Leaving Tom, she was under no illusion, would mean exposing herself not just to him but also to Sadie and Callum – but what choice did she have left? Leaving Layla was not an option, not when she was so young, so in need of her mother in every way.

And yet, in order to come clean to Tom, to be able to live a life with Ivan and Layla, and still share access to Sadie and Callum, she would have to tell Ivan about them too. When she thought of him, a chill rolled over her skin, despite the intense heat clinging to every wall. But this wasn't about him, this was about the baby. She would do the right thing. Wouldn't she?

Once, she almost laughed to herself, all of this had seemed possible, right even. Yet however she looked at it now, she could see she was doomed. The only way forward was self-annihilation.

Unable to stop the thoughts from flooding through her mind, she went back to their suite and took one of her sleeping pills, falling, at least temporarily, into sweet oblivion. She was still dozing when Ivan returned, the light from the crack in the curtain illuminating his silhouette as he moved through the bedroom, a shopping bag held behind his back.

She watched him through half-closed eyes from the bed.

When she heard the sound of him talking from the walk-in

wardrobe, a while later, she sat up and stretched, her bones cracking. Wondering whether it was time yet to collect Layla from the crèche, she stepped into the slippers by the bed and walked towards the other side of the suite, following the hushed tones of Ivan's voice.

Moving slowly behind him, trying to stay quiet so as not to disturb his call, she stood there for a moment until he turned, the phone to his ear, his face falling when he saw her.

'Jesus, Gabriela,' he said, once he'd gathered himself, holding his hand over the microphone.

'Sorry,' she replied, hurt by the aggression in his voice.

'I'll call you back,' he spoke into the speaker and then, giving her his full attention, 'Don't sneak up on me like that.'

'I wasn't sneaking, I just didn't want to disturb you. Where have you been?'

'I went for a walk. I thought you could do with the time to yourself. We should go and get Layla. Did you go to the spa?'

'Yes,' she said, following him back into the bedroom.

'Right. Well, you're not dressed so I'd better go down. Have a look at the dinner menu. We'll order room service tonight.'

'Sure. Ivan, is everything OK?'

'Everything's fine,' he said. 'Why shouldn't it be?'

Waiting until she'd heard his footsteps disappear down the hallway, she stood and moved back towards the walk-in wardrobe. There was something about the way he had looked at her before he left the room that made her self-conscious of her appearance. Since Layla, her skin had been prone to break-outs, and the sleepless nights were taking their toll on other parts of her body too.

She slipped the nightgown over her head and pulled a dress from the hangers, hearing something drop at the back of the wardrobe.

There was nothing obvious that had fallen to the floor. Pausing, she pushed her fingers into the clothes hanging from the rail and felt along the back until she touched a bag, partly suspended against the back of the wardrobe, pinned in place by a couple of wooden hangers. It must have fallen from the open shelf above and become lodged there.

Pulling it out, she saw it was the same bag Ivan had been holding behind his back when he came in earlier. It was made of thick card, with ribbons for handles, and when she peered inside, without giving herself pause to think, she saw two boxes.

Her heartbeat quickening, she was aware of the front door unlocked in the other room, just paces from here, with Ivan likely to return soon with Layla from the crèche. Her fingers fumbling with the catch, she cracked open one of the boxes and found a woman's watch encrusted in diamonds.

'Gabriela?'

Ivan's voice was suddenly there in the next room, followed by Layla's cry.

'Coming!' she shouted, stuffing the box back into the bag and pushing it back on the shelf above the wardrobe, hoping that's where it had been stashed before it fell, turning just in time to see them both in the doorway watching her.

'You got dressed?'

'I felt like a mess. Do you like it?' She took a step towards him, distracting him with the soft red silk she'd bought with his allowance a week earlier.

'It's beautiful,' he said, handing her Layla, and as she held her daughter against her chest, she felt ripples of unease, like cuts, up her arms.

Chapter 71

Isobel

Lighting a cigarette, tickling the tip of it with the flame of a match and enjoying how it suddenly burns orange, I watch the company records open up in front of me on the computer screen.

My eyes move over the company name: *PKI Ltd*, and halt at the name of the Directors: *Unlisted*.

Ignoring the voice in my head telling me to stop, telling me all of this is over, that I've already fucked it up, I keep scanning through the pages as it becomes clear the company is not owned by a person, but by another company, The Stan Group, whose details are in turn registered to the British Virgin Islands.

'Of course it is,' I say aloud, spurred on by the discovery. Where else would a crooked company be based than behind the protection of the world's biggest tax haven?

It is at moments like this that I wish I'd had the kind of formal journalism training that might give me the next steer forward. The office already knows I won't be back for a few days. I imagine them nodding approvingly at the benefits that will surely come from some time off, relaxing and gathering my thoughts. Space to process things, as everyone has been so keen to advise.

Picking up my phone, I dial Si's number, half-expecting him not to answer, given he is supposed to be in court.

When he picks up, he sounds even more eager to speak to me than I am to him.

'Si, listen . . . Just a quick one. I'm going through some papers – I'm helping Jess's mum with something.' I know any mention of Jess will curtail any potential further questioning. 'You know when you're going through the details of records from Companies House. Doesn't there always have to be a name attached to it?'

'Not necessarily. But there'll have to be a signatory. Not necessarily the person who owns the company, mind . . .'

'Thanks, Si,' I say, hanging up before he can ask anything further.

Scrolling down, I find it: signatory: *James McCann, associate at McCann Legal and Partners, Queen Square, London.*

Chapter 72

Isobel

Ordinarily, I would have used LexisNexis to do a background check on a company, after my usual trawl of Companies House. Usually, the website would help throw up information on a company's directors, their dates of birth and sometimes even their home addresses. Except in this instance, as is often the case with companies who have something to hide, I can't, as they are registered in the British Virgin Islands.

Again, I might otherwise have made use of the electoral roll search, which had been known to provide invaluable data when people had forgotten to tick the 'no third-party disclosure' box when buying a new fridge or something equally seemingly innocuous. But in this instance, without a director's name to go on . . .

I am beginning to wonder if this is the universe's way of telling me to give up when I remember a trick Si showed me in my early days with the newspaper, as we researched a shady local business together. If you had a mobile phone number, you could do a reverse search on the electoral roll and see if the number matched a person who was registered.

Jumping up, I pull the wad of the phone bill from the drawer where I have left it, and start to scan through the numbers.

I had pored over the list when I first opened the letter without noticing anything useful, but this time, something jumps out at me:

there are two numbers that come up again and again. My whole body humming with anticipation, I type the first one into the search. But the result is unequivocal: *Unknown number*.

I try again, but no matter how many times I repeat the search, the result is the same. Whomever the number belongs to is not registered to the electoral roll.

Taking a swig of water, I try the second number, typing more slowly this time. My finger hovers above the enter button for a second, and when I press it I close my eyes, bracing myself for further disappointment.

When I open my eyes again, I blink. There on the screen is a name: James McCann. The signatory from the company's records.

Without pausing, I type into Google. It takes several clicks to find the correct James McCann, Partner at McCann Legal and Partners, a law firm just off Queen Square in London.

Excitement rippling over me, I keep going, copying and pasting the name of the business, and trawling through endless web pages.

For a legal firm, there is very little on file about what it does. Finally, though, a picture catches my eye. Unlike the other stock headshots, this one is of McCann in a party setting, in the archive section of a newspaper. The image is of three people standing side by side, each holding a glass of champagne.

The caption under the faces reads: *Philanthropists Irena Vasiliev and Clive Witherall with lawyer James McCann.*

Typing the words Irena Vasiliev into Google, the list of articles is endless. *Irena Vasiliev wanted by Interpol for a number of crimes related to money laundering and financial terrorism, and for assisting a dictator.*

The next, extracted from a piece entitled *London: The Money-Laundering Capital of the World*, read:

Vasiliev, a 46-year-old Russian who enjoys the protection of her government and is also wanted for supporting violent regimes in Africa, specialises in helping extraction and energy industries, oil and gas industries launder their money. One inside source said,

'British banks are so full of corrupt money that to take it out could cause another financial crash.'

Lighting another cigarette, I flick back to my emails. Hovering for a moment over the out-of-office button, instead I pressed the hide button and continue to scroll through the results, unaware of the day outside fading to night.

Chapter 73

Gabriela

Tom was not expecting her back until the Monday afternoon. This freed her up to have lunch with Madeleine, at last, before returning to the house. She was as excited and brimming with nerves as if it was a first date, also humming with anticipation for what she was about to do.

As she said goodbye to Ivan and Layla at the doorway to the hotel that morning, her heart beat so fast that she felt her chest might explode. At almost six months old, it was almost impossible to leave her daughter, her resistance to her going getting stronger each time she left. Gabriela's arms tensed around her daughter and she drank in her smell before handing her back to her father with reluctant hands.

'So we'll talk when I'm back,' he said and Gabriela nodded, focusing on her daughter, telling herself to let her go.

'Gabriela, is something wrong?' he asked and she shook her head, forcing herself to look at him, unprising her fingers. 'No. Nothing's wrong. I'll call you . . .'

She got off the train at Great Portland Street, walking through Regent's Park, the light reflecting off the top of the pale stone of the Nash buildings. Despite the bright sunshine, a shiver ran through her as she exited onto the Outer Circle and walked along Parkway. The feeling that followed her was fear tinged with an emboldening, a sense that at last she was going to do the right thing.

When she tried to transpose her memories of the people she had known and loved over the years as she walked back through the streets of her childhood, she found she could no longer imagine it as it was, but as she crossed onto Pratt Street, the familiarity of the signage soothed her. Inside Daphne's, the white tablecloths and dark wood furnishings were of some small comfort.

Though she was early, Madeleine was already waiting, not in their usual table in the window but in one of the booths on the right. The sight of her risked triggering the emotions that were brimming near the surface.

Kissing Madeleine on each cheek before taking her seat, it took all Gabriela's self-control not to lean in and break down on her shoulder. In all the years she'd known Madeleine, the lines in her skin deepening and taking new form, her friend had never fundamentally changed. And yet today, there was something different about her, something dancing just out of view.

Even as Gabriela had walked there, the thoughts of the weekend circling in her mind like sharks in an ever-shrinking tank, she hadn't been sure whether she would tell her. But finally, as she sat in front of her now, she knew what she was going to do. There was no longer room for the lies that had permeated her life for so long that she no longer knew what the truth was; the lies had swollen so grotesquely that they were crushing her.

It wasn't just Madeleine she was going to reveal herself to. She was going to tell Tom, as well. He would hate her for it, but he could hardly deny that their life together had fallen apart a long time ago – and he would never stop her seeing the children, that much she could count on. Sadie and Callum would be hurt, of course they would. But she was their mother and she loved them, and they would understand, eventually, that this was never about them.

Madeleine cut her off, mid-thought.

'What will you drink? Wine?'

When she looked up, the waitress was standing next to them.

'Actually, I think I'd like something stronger. A brandy?'

'Two of those, please,' Madeleine said before turning back to Gabriela, eyeing her in a manner that felt unsettling. Was she reading something in this already?

After a moment, her voice adopting a tone Gabriela didn't recognise, Madeleine said, 'Talking of something stronger, I've just been in your old neck of the woods. I drank so much vodka, I think I can still feel it in my liver.'

'Moscow?'

Instinctively, Gabriela bristled, but then she realised that Madeleine was referring to her stint in Russia in the early days at the FCO, and she exhaled, enjoying the relief of this momentary distraction from the chaos in her brain as she spread the napkin over her lap, smoothing out the creases with her palms.

'What were you doing in Russia?' she asked and Madeleine raised her eyebrows.

'What am I always doing? Work. Is there anything else in my life apart from work? God, sometimes I wonder if I'm getting this living thing all wrong. But no, I shouldn't say that, not now when things are finally coming together.'

'That's good to hear.'

It was less than a minute since Gabriela had had her whole story on the tip of her tongue ready to fall into her friend's lap, but the shift in tone meant the conversation was going somewhere else and she couldn't say why, but she felt wrong-footed, like suddenly she didn't know where to start.

'Anyway, we always end up talking about my work. I'm such a narcissist. Tell me about you, what's going on?'

'Here we are, ladies.' The waitress arrived and settled their drinks and their usual selection of starters on the table in front of them.

Taking a long sip of her brandy, Gabriela tried to gather her thoughts, but even thinking of an alternative narrative to explain away the past months – it had been months since they had last met, and yet, she thought, it could have been years, a lifetime – made the pain in her head worse.

'No, tell me about Moscow. I'm interested, it's been so long since I was there,' she said, instinctively deflecting attention away from herself but also aware that this conversation was heading in a direction over which she had no control; she could feel the lies spilling out already.

'Is it?' Madeleine asked, and Gabriela paused, their eyes locking before she looked away.

'Well, I shouldn't tell you this, but we always share things with each other, don't we? Besides, who are you going to tell, right? So you know how I told you we were closing in on some of the peripheral figures? Well, one of those is a Russian-owned company . . .' Madeleine paused. 'But there are a few things we need to tie up first.'

Gabriela felt the ice cube she had been swallowing stick in her throat. When she spoke, her voice was small.

'Right.'

Madeleine looked up for a fraction of a second before returning to her mouthful of broad beans.

'Aren't you going to ask which company?' She didn't wait for a reply. 'Oh, it's one of those intentionally oblique ones – offers a breadth of legitimate services, specialising in energy supply. But like so many of these companies, they dabble in sidelines. After all, that's where the money's at, right? As well as bursts of philanthropy. In this case, a children's orphanage no less.'

The fork dropped from Gabriela's fingers, clattering against her plate, and Madeleine watched her, silence crackling dangerously between them, before she asked, 'Gaby, is something wrong?'

Chapter 74

Gabriela

The pavement seemed to rise up in front of her as Gabriela moved through Camden Town, back towards the house, Madeleine's words still spinning in her mind.

'It only came up because I was talking to colleagues here who are investigating a businesswoman called Irena Vasiliev on grounds of corporate tax evasion, on a huge scale, along with a number of other substantial crimes.'

Madeleine had barely looked at her as she spoke, her voice so quiet she could hardly hear it. *Irena Vasiliev.* The name echoed through her head as she moved, instinctively, her body taking over from her addled mind.

'They brought the case to me in private as they wondered if I knew anything. Because the thing is—' She looked at Gabriela then, catching her eye and holding it. 'Whilst going through the documents, the secret recordings and the evidence brought by insiders who have been working on the case, evidence has been amassed that one of Vasiliev's associates was having a relationship with a woman who used to work for the FCO.'

Gabriela's blood ran cold as she recalled Madeleine's face, watching her as she slipped a pile of papers across the table, the details jumping out like bullets.

Mr Ivan Popov is director of a number of global companies. One

*of them is GEF Energy Ltd, a business engaged in the provision of
renewable energy and solar power. The ownership of GEF is divided
between an investment company and another company, the Stan
Group, registered to the British Virgin Islands.*

Following Gabriela's eyes across the page, Madeleine tore off a
piece of bread, speaking between mouthfuls, in an effort at noncha-
lance. 'Unofficially, the Stan Group, which shields itself behind the
anonymity of one of the world's biggest tax havens, is known to be
run by Irena Vasiliev, a prolific Russian criminal. You might have
heard of her?' She paused for effect, but she didn't look at Gabriela.
'This associate of hers, Ivan Popov, is implicated in bribery related
to his efforts in running GEF outside of Russia. Vasiliev herself is
unable to leave her mother country for fear of prosecution. The UK
is not the only jurisdiction she's wanted by, not by a long shot, and
the powers that be seem keen to give her protection in Moscow.'

Unable to speak, Gabriela simply stared at Madeleine as she
continued.

'During the course of ongoing NCA investigations, recordings
have been made of Popov telling Vasiliev about bribes he was facilitating to get the company contracts in certain Caribbean countries.
One of the ministers involved, apparently, was making more and
more outlandish requests, and more frequent too: expensive jewellery
and watches for the minister's mother . . . He even requested a
£500,000 car at one stage.'

Her mind flipped to the bag stashed behind the wardrobe in the
hotel suite. Ivan's face when he walked in and found her there – to
think, in that moment, the worst possible conclusion she could think
of was that he might be having an affair.

Leaning forward, Madeleine placed a hand on the papers and slid
them back towards her. 'It goes on.'

Gabriela felt herself nodding, but still no words would come. How
long had she known?

'But the bottom line is, Popov, one way or another, is going to jail. The other reason I'm now involved is because it turns out Mr Popov is quite a busy bee. And while he has been working hard to cover his tracks in this case, he has taken his eye off the ball elsewhere. Namely another sideline he runs supplying false student visas to traffickers, to help them move people from Russia to France and the UK, via Poland, usually. When all this comes out, well, you can imagine the papers are going to have a field day.'

Madeleine had watched her as she stood up, pushing herself out of the booth, the acid rising in her gut.

'I'm going to go to the bathroom.'

Gabriela moved across the restaurant, keeping her eyes on her feet as if to make sure the ground was real and strong enough to hold her.

Behind the bathroom door, she put her hand to her mouth and drew the breath in and out of her lungs in sharp bursts to stop herself hyperventilating, the image of Ivan and then Irena flashing in front of her. It couldn't be true. There must have been a mistake. Shaking her head, she struggled to clear her mind of the image: Emsworth, Nguema and Vasiliev, in that meeting in Moscow. How had she not recognised her at the restaurant? And yet, she'd never seen her face. No, there was no way of her knowing they were the same person. Though could she really claim not to have known something was wrong?

'Gabriela?' Madeleine was knocking on the toilet door.

She stood with her back against the wall, as far away from the cubicle door as possible.

Madeleine's voice continued calmly, 'Even if he makes it back to Russia, we are working on ways to bring him back here to stand trial. You know as well as I do the sentences for people involved in facilitating people trafficking. That's an offence subject to life imprisonment, in some cases. There are potential fraud charges, too: we're going to strip him bare. Not to mention how the press will spin the story, when they get hold of it.'

The press. The words hit her so hard she could almost feel her teeth fall out.

Her next thought was Layla. If Ivan was going to jail, what would become of them? If there was fraud involved, the chances were that they would seize his assets, take his money – and hers? Any money she had now was his, except for the house in Dartmouth Park and her mother's place in Wiltshire . . . Another bullet struck her chest. Might the authorities not feasibly try to retrospectively claim cash from her, and then where would she be? Where would Callum and Sadie live if she was forced to sell their home?

She closed her eyes, blocking out the headlines she could already see forming in her mind: *Former FCO employee leads double life with Russian oligarch involved in human trafficking.* The words Sadie was now old enough to read, at least in part.

Her fingers fumbling on the handle of the door, she paused for a split second before pushing open the door and facing Madeleine.

'Tell me what I need to do.'

Her fingers were no longer her own as she typed the message to Ivan, the sound of car horns blaring as she pulled her house keys from her bag, knowing that Tom would not yet be home, that she still had time to think: time to process the thoughts clawing at one another in her head.

Just checking you got home OK. Gx

The sound of his reply a moment later made her jump.

All fine, just packing. Excited to catch up on your news.

What had she been thinking, contemplating telling him that she was going to quit her job? Had she really been planning to break up with Tom, to expose him to the truth, to expose Sadie and Callum? Had she really imagined they would play happy families on alternate weekends, she and Ivan and their three children on day trips to Legoland? For a moment she wondered if she had lost her mind.

The moment she pushed open the door, she heard the familiar strains of Shirley Scott from the kitchen and instantly she knew Tom was home.

'Hey,' he said, sticking his neck around the doorway from the kitchen, a smile stretched across his face.

She must have looked taken aback to see him there as his face fell. 'You've forgotten, haven't you?'

'Forgotten what?' she said, collecting herself as she moved into the hall.

'Sadie's parents' evening. We talked about it on Friday before you left.'

Vaguely, she remembered the conversation. She put down her bags. 'Of course not, I just thought we were meeting there. I'm glad you're home.'

The words rushed out of her and she moved towards Tom and pulled him so close to her that he laughed with surprise.

'I love you,' she said, her whole body shaking with the realisation. 'Oh God, I love you so much.'

Chapter 75

Gabriela

Now

Outside, the morning sun filters through the cloud as the sound of Callum and Tom pulling on their shoes in the hallway behind her gradually fades. It is only once she is halfway down the street that she lets herself start to engage with what she has to do now. Looking into her bag, she pulls out her phone, half-expecting to find a text message from Madeleine. They have not spoken since lunch yesterday, but there is no message and she doesn't know whether she is relieved or dismayed. No message telling her that this was all a joke, that she had got it wrong, after all.

Briefly, Gabriela recalls Madeleine's words not long after she side-shuffled from the Foreign and Commonwealth Office to the National Crime Agency – which already feels like a lifetime ago – crossing the river to continue the fight against organised crime in the stale headquarters in Vauxhall.

'They pride themselves on being the UK's answer to the FBI, but that's obviously a joke. There is a complete lack of proper cops. It's all people like us, civil servants. Impotent pen-pushers. Though we're operationally independent – notionally, at least.'

Except they aren't impotent at all. They are coming for her, and there is only one way to escape.

Madeleine's words circle relentlessly in her mind as she steps onto the train, and off again at Kew Gardens.

They had taken a seat back at the booth, a table of food untouched in front of them, while Madeleine finished what she had come to say. 'Emsworth was on the payroll of Vasiliev's operation. The Nguema character you mentioned to me a while ago, the one Emsworth was having the meeting with, he and Vasiliev were business partners, together with a third man, one Clive Witherall. Witherall and Nguema are also under investigation for a number of dealings, including suspected arms trading. You heard about the chemical spillage in Equatorial Guinea. Well, it seems Witherall's company, TradeSmart, was working with Nguema to cover their arms dealing business by using units containing chemical waste to import their product, the idea being that anyone working at the port who saw the chemical waste symbol would do little more than a nominal check, for fear of getting too close to the hazardous material that was concealing the weapons.

'Anyway, they fucked up. One of the local companies they hired in Bata to dispose of the chemical waste dumped it next to a village. It was a disaster, as you can imagine. Various agencies, in the UK and elsewhere, have been looking into the spillage, trying to connect Witherall and Nguema to the operation. Vasiliev's involved, too. One of her many projects: she has a number of side-hustles, very millennial.'

For a moment, Madeleine had clearly forgotten the basis on which they were having this conversation. This wasn't a catch-up between two old colleagues. When she remembered, her face darkened again. 'Emsworth was one of their inside men. It was his job to keep abreast of what was happening, in terms of how much the FCO knew and any future deals that would affect their operations. That's why he wanted to get rid of us. We were uncovering too much. Me, in terms of the human trafficking work I was doing in Hanoi, which connects back to Vasiliev, and to Nguema, whose company ran a lot of the boats that were used for the human freightage. And you: well, you were simply in the wrong place at the right time. Presumably after you saw Emsworth in Moscow, Vasiliev and Nguema were spooked. He must have tried to test you, with the various activities he asked you to do; and perhaps for a while you were deemed reliable . . . And then you weren't. Once he got rid of me – I was considered far too active, I imagine – he kept you on as someone he could keep an eye on: keep your friends close and all that . . .'

Gabriela took a long gulp of her drink and set down the glass, nodding to the waitress for another. Without sedation, she wasn't sure how she could stay sitting there with everything she was hearing.

'Every piece of information we uncovered during that operation he was handing straight back into the hands of his paymasters: traffickers, arms dealers. That is why the FCO needed to get rid of him. But obviously it would be too embarrassing to expose how much they had let slide. And so it was easier to see him off on a more palatable charge.'

'Serena,' Gabriela said, swallowing.

Madeleine nodded. 'I mean, it was kind of genius. To push him out on the grounds of sexual discrimination . . . no one who had worked under or around Emsworth would ever be suspicious that it was anything but a legitimate case.'

'How do you know all this?'

Madeleine looked away.

'OK, then, why didn't you tell me at the time?' Gabriela's voice was little more than a whisper.

Madeleine laughed. 'Why didn't I tell you? You think I should have trusted you?'

Gabriela looked down in shame, wondering how much Madeleine knew.

'And what's changed?'

Madeleine regarded her, her eyes narrowing.

'What's changed is that now I know you weren't aware of what your boyfriend was up to – and now that you do know, I need to find out if you have anything useful on Popov and Vasiliev. I need to know if you can help us bring them down. Because if you do that, you won't get dragged through the mud when this all comes out in court. There is still a chance for you to salvage what is left of your life.'

'Polina?' She is struck by the silence resonating through the house as she walks through the front door, pushing it closed behind her with a wariness she cannot name.

'Layla?'

How long has it been since she phoned from the supermarket? It can't have been more than half an hour, and yet the house is still, her daughter's changing bag absent from its usual hook in the hallway.

Moving more swiftly now, her heartbeat quickens as she places her keys on the counter in the kitchen and looks out over the garden. The quiet beauty of it never fails to touch her, and yet the sudden lack of leaves and flowers has transformed it into a space she almost doesn't recognise.

Perhaps her daughter is asleep in the bedroom and Polina is in the bathroom, she tells herself as she moves back towards the stairs, padding up the striped red runners. She is moving from Layla's bedroom, which is empty, into the master bedroom, the blinds having been pulled back so that the room is flooded with light, making her squint as she looks around the his and hers bedside tables, the recently acquired Matisse hanging above the headboard.

Moving faster still, she lets her eyes roam the room and in the silence she must reconcile herself to the fact that she doesn't truly know him at all. She doesn't know anything about his life, not really, just as he knows nothing about hers. Much as she wants to believe he is unaware of the purpose of the visas his company doles out, she cannot think that he is so naive, so detached from the work to which he dedicates so much of his life. Either he knows, or he chose not to ask.

But what does that matter now? Either way, she understands what she has to do.

Pulling out her phone, she dials Polina's number but it goes straight to voicemail.

Banging doors as she moves from room to room, she calls out her name. 'Layla?' But she is not here.

A sick feeling rises up inside her as she reaches the top of the stairs. Just as she takes her first step, she sees Polina's silhouette at the door. In her arms is Layla, her face breaking into a smile as she sees her mother.

Gabriela runs down the stairs to her, her whole being shaking with relief as she envelops her daughter in her arms.

Polina laughs, taken aback.

'Where were you?' Gabriela says forcefully, looking over her daughter's shoulder at her.

'By the river,' Polina says, her voice more wary now. 'Layla was restless so I took her for a walk. Is everything all right?'

Closing her eyes, she relaxes her grip on Layla slightly.

'Sorry. Everything is fine. There was just a change of plan, that's all. I panicked . . .'

She gives Polina a reassuring smile and says, 'If it's OK with you, I thought I might take Layla out for the day. What do you think, Layla? You and me, shall we go out somewhere nice?'

When Layla smiles, there is a familiar expression, the way her mouth curls up at one side, and she realises it is herself who she is seeing. Layla has always looked so much like her father, the same tight dark curls, the same dark eyes, the prominent brows. If she hadn't come out of her, Gabriela might have questioned her provenance before this moment, before this flash of her own face in her daughter's.

'You want to come with Mummy? OK, let's do it!' She turns to Polina, giving her brightest smile. 'Is there a change of clothes in her bag?'

'Of course. And a couple of nappies, and her dummy. I know you're keen for her to give it up, but it offers her comfort when you're gone, and I really don't want to take another thing away from her right now.'

She means nothing by it, but this comment makes Gabriela flush. The smile falters on her lips.

And yet, Polina is right, because she knows Layla better than anyone. She has spent more time with Layla in her short time on earth than anyone else. It was Gabriela's lap she chose for cuddles when all was well, but it was Polina to whom she instinctively turned when the tears rose in her eyes.

'I'll go and get packed then,' she says, moving towards the hall, regretting not having gathered all that she needed before Polina returned.

And then she hears the door click open and a voice calling her daughter's name, and when she turns she sees him standing in the doorway, blocking their escape.

Chapter 76

Gabriela

It takes a moment for Gabriela to compose herself, and when she does, she sees that Ivan is looking at her in a way that makes her rearrange herself on the spot.

'But what are you doing here?' she asks, recovering herself just enough for the sentence to form.

'I was about to ask you the same thing . . .' He lingers for a moment as if awaiting a reply, and then he says, 'My flight was cancelled. I'm leaving tomorrow instead.'

'OK,' she says, after a moment. 'My course was postponed. I didn't see any reason to tell you, as you were supposed to be away.'

'I see. Well, that's worked out well then, hasn't it?'

'Hasn't it?' she says, as he leans in to kiss her, the bristle of his beard scratching her cheek.

'I'll cook for all of us. Polina, too,' she says as evening folds in, having spent the afternoon resisting the urge to stare at him, to scour his face for evidence of what he does and does not know.

She moves into the kitchen and puts on the apron hanging on the back of the door – the one she had made, with a print of Layla and Ivan with Ivan's mother from their trip to Moscow, the three of them on the sofa in her apartment.

'Polina,' Gabriela calls out. 'You'll eat with us, won't you? I need a drink,' she says, turning to Ivan. 'Do we have gin?'

'We seem to have run out,' he says. 'What about something else? We have wine or—'

'I really fancy gin. Do you think you could run out and grab some, while I prepare this?'

He pauses. 'OK. If you're sure you can't have something else.'

'I'm sorry,' she says. 'You don't mind, do you?'

Polina walks into the hall and out of nowhere she has a flicker of memory of Madeleine talking. *Information from insider informants.*

Pushing the voice away, she looks back at Ivan and he shrugs, then pulls on his coat. 'Anything else?'

'I don't think so,' she says.

Moving back into the kitchen, she waits until she hears the door slam shut and then she pulls out her phone, her fingers struggling to keep up with her mind. Googling *Heathrow flights Moscow delays*, she closes her eyes briefly, silently praying she has got it wrong, that he hasn't lied about his flight being cancelled. Because why would he come back and lie about it, unless he knows something?

Following the links to a page entitled *Live flight information*, she types in *Moscow* and waits as the results emerge on her screen.

She spots Ivan's flight within seconds, and next to it, the departure information. *GATE CLOSED.*

And in that moment, her stomach drops as if a boulder has been stuffed down her throat.

Chapter 77

Isobel

It's nearly three in the morning before I finally sleep, my head spinning with information overload.

When I wake the next day, around midday, unusually rested but somehow drowsy from the excess of unmedicated sleep, I force myself to brush my teeth and shower, pointedly ignoring the computer that sits drained of life on the kitchen table.

Forcing myself to put on my shoes, I pick up my keys and move down the stairs towards the street and head across the road to the café. Once I have my coffee in hand, I stand in the doorway and look out at the cars, wondering where the hell to go.

Turning left, I ignore the usual path towards the office to my right where the road splits at Camden Town tube station, veering towards the Stables market, weaving through the crappy jewellery and incense stalls, stopping briefly for a crêpe when my stomach tells me it's time to eat.

It must be around two when I make my way past the Hawley Arms, resisting with every inch of my body the desire to step into the pub. Instead, I sit by the canal and smoke until the packet is empty, watching the ducks pick at the contents of an old plastic bag. After a while I turn back and exit onto the street at the bottom of Kentish Town High Street.

Turning left, I stop at the Owl bookshop and browse the titles before carrying on, passing the refuge, walking without stopping until I reach the Heath.

Jess's memorial bench stands at the top of Kite Hill. It is less than two weeks since I sat here on the way back from the squat party, and yet already it feels like a lifetime ago.

The trees have begun to shed their leaves and I wish I'd worn a scarf. The light is fading from the sky. I should head home and make food, but I want to stay here a while longer. Drawing my feet up onto the bench, I look to my left and notice a man walking up the hill towards me from the direction of South End Green. For a moment, I shiver. As he moves closer, I notice he is smoking a cigarette and it is almost as though he senses I am going to ask him for one even before I call out. Without saying a word, he walks towards me and offers me the packet. I take one and nod my thanks, reaching into my pocket for a lighter as he moves away again.

Closing my eyes, I inhale, imagining the sun caressing my cheeks, Jess's laughter as we ran through the grass towards the bandstand, the promise of another long summer.

When I open my eyes sometime later, the sky is dark. In the distance, stationary blue lights throb on one of the streets just off the Heath. From here I can see an ambulance and several police cars. Whatever has happened, it's not an old lady who has slipped in the bathroom.

For a minute I picture myself following the path from here down to the street I know well, with the tall, wisteria-clad houses. I imagine myself standing at the foot of the front steps with their expensive tiles, and calling out to one of the police officers for information on what has happened.

And then I breathe in; I turn and walk in the other direction.

At home, the tidiness of the flat momentarily confounds me. Moving across to the kitchen counter, I deposit a bag of supplies on it, pulling out a loaf of bread and some cheese and then turning on the kettle.

Watching the flow of pedestrians on the street through the window, I wait for it to boil before moving to the sofa, sitting cross-legged, eating a sandwich, flinching as the mug of tea burns my lips.

For a minute, I flick through the channels on the TV, but there is nothing on and so, moving back to the table, I pick up my computer and lift the lid, wondering what sort of film I will choose to watch. The laptop is still dead and so I plug it in to charge, trying to ignore the voice in my head telling me it's long past time for a drink.

Seizing the distraction of the computer when the screen lights up, I lift the lid and the photograph from my previous search stares back from the page.

Not now, I tell myself. Watch a film, for God's sake. Just for one night, chill the fuck out.

But there is something about the image of the three people in the photograph that will not let me go and as I read the caption again, I move back towards the sofa, dragging the laptop charger with me, the sound of the television disappearing into the background as I begin to type notes.

James McCann is an associate at McCann Legal and Partner, off Queen Square in London. McCann trained as a solicitor before joining the firm in 2004.

In the official headshot accompanying his biography on the law firm's website, it is hard to determine the colour of his eyes, which meet the camera's lens with a self-assurance that is less debatable.

As I trawl through the pages on Google, as well as the usual social media sites, trying to throw up any more information about this man, the only trace I find of him is on LinkedIn, which simply states a repetition of the brief line on his firm's website, as his job description. No background on his education. No former employers.

The frustration throbs at the front of my head. I could kill for a drink. Pinching the top of my nose between my thumb and forefinger, I close my eyes. How could it be that a lawyer at an apparently top-class firm, judging from its presentation, could be so invisible?

Or rather, why? Most lawyers were like peacocks, desperate to be looked at. It wasn't like he was a prosecution barrister, who might fear retribution from aggrieved clients.

From the little I have gauged about McCann, he is the signatory for PKI Ltd. From the lack of visible presence online, and the fact that, according to its listing on Companies House, it is owned by another company, there is every reason to believe this is little more than a shell. Flicking back to the only other image of McCann I can find, at the party, as if something in his face might give him away, my attention turns to the other man in the photo.

When I copy and paste his name into Google, the information is more forthcoming. Clicking on a newspaper obituary from the previous month, I read:

The late David Witherall, who died this week after being hit by a car in his home city of London, was the heir to the FTSE 100 company TradeSmart, owned by his father, Clive Witherall. He leaves behind a wife and two children.

There is a photo accompanying the article. A young family, on a beach somewhere, their faces turned to the sun. They are crouched down, each of the parents with an arm over one of the girls.

Something about the picture has an almost hypnotic effect, and as I stare at it, my headache eases. After a moment I look away and highlight the second name from the caption: Irena Vasiliev.

Running my eyes briefly again over the article I've previously read, denouncing Vasiliev as a money launderer and supporter of violent regimes in Africa, a thought strikes me and I move the cursor back up to my search history.

Highlighting the name of the company TradeSmart, I open a new window and search for Companies House.

And there it is. As the page opens up before me, I sit forward, adrenaline pumping.

'*Shit.*'

My fingers are shaking as I pick up the phone and dial the office.

'Ben,' I say, as soon as he answers. 'I've got a story. It's to do with the murder on the Heath . . .'

Chapter 78

Gabriela

'Are you OK?' Ivan asks when he arrives back at the house a few minutes later, with a bottle of gin. 'You look nervous.'

'Me? I'm fine,' she says, working hard to still her trembling fingers, spotting the pestle and mortar still in view on the counter.

'Probably just need a drink.'

She lets him pour, while she stirs the beef bourguignon she has defrosted, a hunk of icy flesh thawing in the pan. While he does so, she watches him, imagining, and then trying to block out, the thoughts that must be scurrying around his head. Why didn't he go to Moscow? Does he know what she is planning?

No, she tells herself, not letting her mind go there. There is no way he could know. Besides, he is not a threat, not directly. There is no evidence to suggest that he is violent, or anything other than the middleman: morally reprehensible, perhaps, but not necessarily dangerous. Not to her, not to their daughter. She has a mental flash of Masha's face in the photo on Ivan's mother's wall and closes her eyes.

'Can I help?' Ivan asks, and she jumps.

'God, you gave me a shock! No, it's all under control. How about another G and T?'

'You drank the last one quickly. Good job I'm not counting,' he replies as he takes the glass she has discreetly emptied into the sink and pours out another double measure for each of them.

'Drink up,' she says, watching him down another glass before encouraging him to refill. 'Otherwise I'll be drunk on my own.'

He raises his eyebrows and moves into the other room to answer a phone call as she serves up the food, glancing behind her as she reaches into her pocket for the powder she crushed from the sleeping pills in her pocket while Ivan was at the shop buying gin, pouring half into Ivan's bowl and the other half into Polina's before stirring quickly with a spoon and carrying them through to the living room.

It had been a last-minute decision, made in panic, to take the remainder of the pills from her washbag. She has no idea if the dosage she has left will be enough, or too much. She is not thinking straight enough to weigh up the risk. All she knows is that she has to get Layla out.

Fleetingly, she thinks of Madeleine's final instructions: 'In order to get witness protection, we'll need you to testify against Emsworth. Your eyewitness testimony of the meeting in Moscow, and the photo of the papers he was copying. And anything else you have on him.'

'Where's Layla now?' Madeleine had added, businesslike, and Gabriela had barely registered the fact that she already knew about her daughter's existence; there was no time to question how long she'd been aware of this double life of hers, nodding along with her lies, her jaw tensed.

'She's with her nanny,' Gabriela said and Madeleine nodded.

'OK. Well, I assume you'll want to take your daughter with you.'

'Of course.'

'Very well. You have twenty-four hours to get her and gather Tom and the kids somewhere safe. I'll be waiting for your call.'

Neither of them had reckoned on Ivan being home. Because why would he be?

'Another glass of wine?' she asks as they settle in front of the television after dinner.

'No,' Ivan says firmly, holding up a hand. 'I feel—'

He cuts himself off, and in the hallway she hears Polina moving back towards the living room. Slipping her head around the doorway, she looks pale. 'Thank you for supper. I have loaded the dishwasher. If you don't mind, I'll check on Layla then I'll head to bed. I'm feeling tired.'

'You and me both,' Ivan says, stifling a yawn.

'I know. Me too. Actually, why don't we go up?'

It takes less than ten minutes before Ivan is fast asleep. Resisting the urge to feel his pulse to check he is alive, she gets out of bed and heads into the hallway. Through the crack in Polina's bedroom door, Gabriela sees that she is also asleep.

Making her footsteps as light as she can, she moves into Layla's room and lifts her daughter slowly from the cot, willing her not to cry out. When she starts to stir, Gabriela buries her face in her baby's head and whispers hushing noises before pressing her daughter to her chest and feeling her breath level out again.

The buggy is already assembled in the hall and she tiptoes down the stairs, holding her breath so tightly that she fears she might pass out.

As she reaches the bottom of the stairs, she hears a light switch on above her and she stops, her whole body frozen to the spot. Clutching Layla to her, she listens to the footsteps crossing the landing towards the top of the stairs.

She steps back so that she is pressed against the wall, in shadow, but then the bathroom door closes and she hears Polina cough lightly as she uses the toilet.

Waiting there, she listens to her run the tap and then step back out of the bathroom. There is a moment's hesitation at the top of the stairs and Gabriela waits, in horror, for her to come down in search of a glass of water, the effect of the tablets crushed into her food making her mouth dry. She shouldn't have woken up at all, given how comatose Ivan was, but she hardly ate any of the dinner Gabriela produced, unlike Ivan, who had settled in for two helpings while she watched on, silently urging him to keep going. Gabriela had been relieved when Polina had headed upstairs so early, clearly worn out.

For a fleeting moment, she wonders if it was something else that had been bothering her, making her look so wan, but then she hears her move back towards her room, pausing only briefly in front of the door to Layla's room, where she has bundled the covers so as to mimic her shape in the dark.

Once Polina's door has been pulled to, though still slightly ajar as she always leaves it in order to listen out for Layla, she moves quickly, opening the front door, careful not to make a sound, and lifts the buggy outside into the night, with her daughter still asleep in her other arm.

She has just a small bag, which she hooks over the handlebars of the pushchair, only strapping Layla into the seat once they are safely down the road, out of earshot in case she might call out at the disturbance. But she doesn't. She barely stirs as Gabriela pulls the blanket over her.

Walking quickly away from the house, she gives a discreet look over her shoulder as they turn the corner towards the high street and the cashpoint where she withdraws £300 and slides it carefully into her bag.

Waiting until they are out of sight of the CCTV cameras that line the main street, dark as it is this late in the evening, she stands back slightly so that she is concealed by a doorway, before pulling out her phone and ringing one of the smaller cab firms.

'Hello, I'd like a car for a long-haul journey, as soon as possible, please,' she says, reeling off the address of the house they are in front of. 'I'll need a car seat. As soon as you can. My name's Jill.'

'You off on your holidays then?' the cabbie asks as the car sweeps onto the M4, half an hour later.

'Something like that,' she says. 'If you don't mind, I'm just going to make a phone call. Is it possible to put on the radio?'

Waiting until the music plays, she pulls her phone from her bag and stares at the screen for a moment before searching for Saoirse's number and pressing call.

She answers after three rings and the sound of her voice strikes Gabriela in the solar plexus. 'Gabriela?'

'Hi,' she says, the emotions rising up in her chest. 'I'm sorry, did I wake you?'

'No.' There is a pause. 'Are you OK?'

'I'm so sorry to do this, but something has happened and I need your help.'

'OK,' Saoirse replies immediately.

'Can I come and stay for a night? Tom and the kids will come separately.'

Gabriela keeps her voice low so that the driver does not hear, should any questions be raised further down the line. Because she is not foolish enough to think that Ivan won't come looking, even if he is behind bars.

'No problem,' Saoirse says, without warmth. She knows, in a way that she can no longer deny, that her absence over the years has cut deep. But nothing she can do will ever stop Saoirse being there for her when she needs her. To her, the sort of friendship they have is a life-long contract, unbreakable no matter what.

'You know I wouldn't ask, if it wasn't . . .'

'I know,' she says. 'What time will you be here?'

'I don't know, I've just left London.'

'Fine,' she says. 'I'll text you the address. I'll wait up.'

'Thank you, Saoirse.'

But by the time Gabriela has finished saying her name, she has already hung up.

She calls twice before Tom answers, his voice thick with sleep.

'Tom, listen to me – what I'm about to say makes no sense but I need you to do exactly what I tell you to, OK? I need you to get up immediately and go and get the kids. Pack a bag, just a few bits; I have our passports . . .'

Instinctively, she places her hand over her bag, in which she has placed Layla's passport alongside those of her family.

'Our passports? What the hell, Gabriela—'

'Tom,' she interrupts him, flicking a look at the driver who is too busy humming along to the radio to be distracted by the tone in her voice. 'Just do as I say, OK? I wouldn't be saying it unless it was very important. You need to grab a change of clothes for the kids and come straight to Saoirse and Jim's. I'm on my way there now.'

She can tell he wants to ask something else but he restrains himself, saying instead, 'Right. Can you at least tell me why?'

'I'm sorry,' she says. 'I'll tell you more when you get here.'

Chapter 79

Gabriela

Saoirse's house is a white cottage at the end of a winding path, set back on the edge of a cliff which tumbles down towards the sea. By the time she and Layla arrive, dawn is breaking and a sliver of pink sky cracks through the dusty grey.

Gabriela cannot remember the last time she was here, but she remembers being terrified by the sheer drop. Looking at it now, the volume of the sky above and beyond them, she feels for a moment like she can truly breathe.

As the taxi pulls away, ready to make the long journey back to the city, she turns to the house again and spots Saoirse in the doorway. She is leaning against the doorframe, her arms crossed as if inspecting her oldest friend and not quite understanding what she is seeing.

Once they make eye contact Saoirse stands straighter and moves towards Gabriela, her eyes clocking Layla and the buggy and the absence of bags.

A moment later, her arms are wrapped around her and Layla, the strength of their embrace making Gabriela feel safe in a way she hasn't for so long.

Looking down at Layla, Saoirse lets her face soften into a smile, lifting her hand playfully to Layla's fingers and saying, without looking at her, 'And who's this?'

Layla gazes back at her, her eyes hooded with sleep, and she recoils slightly, her mouth moving into a frown.

'Don't be shy,' Gabriela says, holding her tightly. 'This is Layla. Layla, this is Saoirse. She's an old friend, and do you know what? Saoirse has a puppy . . .'

It is ridiculous. She is just a baby, but Gabriela doesn't know how else to fill the silence without screaming, and without missing a beat, Saoirse plays along. 'Oh my goodness, do you like puppies, little one? Do you . . .?'

Drawn in by their role play, Layla lets herself be lifted from Gabriela's arms and taken inside by Saoirse, while Gabriela follows, her whole body shaking.

Chapter 80

Isobel

'I thought you were supposed to be taking a break?' Ben asks when I reach the office, pulling the chair from behind my desk and moving it next to his. Si is out and no one else is around, but still I keep my voice lowered.

'I am,' I say, leaning forward and placing a piece of paper scrawled with names between us. 'OK, so the murder on the Heath, the body they found . . . I've been looking into it and the woman they've charged with the murder is a prostitute, right? She was trafficked here from Kosovo. The men she works for, who brought her here, are operating under a shell company called PKI Ltd, which is based in London, next to Tottenham Court Road, but according to Companies House is actually owned by a company called the Stan Group. The Stan Group, about which there is fuck all useful information online, is registered to the British Virgin Islands. OK? Now bear with me. . . The Stan Group has connections with a Russian criminal organisation run by a woman called Irena Vasiliev, who operates seemingly with impunity behind the shield of Moscow.'

She ignores Ben's confounded expression, holding up a finger to silence him as she continues, barely stopping for breath.

'The Stan Group, it turns out, also owns a number of companies – most of them shell companies – including a renewable energy company also based in London and a couple of dubious sounding charities. . . And – here's the interesting part – they are part-owned by a British company called TradeSmart, who you might have heard about recently.'

Ben opens his mouth as if to speak as I answer my own question. 'The founder and CEO, Clive Witherall, has lived in South End Green for years, one of those massive houses just beyond the tennis courts. He passed down the house – and the day-to-day running of his business – to his son David, who died recently after being hit by a car. We covered the story. It was a hit and run in Swiss Cottage, no one was ever caught . . .'

'Isobel, what the fuck . . . Will you stop for a moment,' Ben says.

'Just hear me out,' I reply, sharply. 'TradeSmart has been implicated in a massive toxic waste spillage in Central Africa. You know the case I'm talking about, right? No charges were ever brought but there were rumours.'

'OK, stop,' Ben says and I stop, reluctantly, the facts still moving around in my head. 'I mean, Jesus. What is all this?'

'I don't know yet.'

'You don't know?'

'Not yet! But what I'm saying is that this is a massive fucking story. I don't know what the story is yet, not exactly, but I can feel it. You need to let me look into it, and I promise you—'

'Isobel, you're supposed to be on leave for stress!'

'Excuse me? I never said that.'

Ben shifts in his chair. 'Some things don't need saying.'

I ignore this. 'There's another thing. The name of the signatory, for all these companies – including PKI Ltd, the one responsible for the trafficked girls – is a fancy-pants lawyer. James McCann. He's the fucking connection.'

'Isobel, this is a local paper, for God's sake, not the . . .'

'Not the *New York* fucking *Times*! I know, Ben! I know. But this murder, committed by a trafficked prostitute happened in the Borough of Camden. The owner of the company connected to the people who run girls, including the young woman who is being held for a murder that took place in Camden, lives in fucking Camden. The lawyer, who is a director for both companies, operates from a firm less than a mile away from where we are now.' My voice is suddenly on the edge of screaming. 'And what, you're telling me you don't want this story? Because it's too good?'

'No, Isobel, I'm telling you I don't know if I want you to pursue it because for one thing, you seem pretty fucking wired right now. And for another: do you even know what this story is?'

I slap my hands against my face in frustration. 'Not yet, because I've only just started looking into it! I can't guess the story, can I? I have to uncover it, which takes time. . .'

Ben narrows his eyes in an expression that sits somewhere between surrender and awe. He breathes in and then exhales, throwing his hands in the air.

'And can you prove any of this shit?'

I shake my head again, unable to prevent the smile forming on my lips. 'Not yet. But I will.'

Chapter 81

Gabriela

'Gabriela?' Saoirse raises her eyes in an expression that is both pleading and concerned as Layla rests on Gabriela's lap, her eyes flitting, drifting shut.

Mouthing the words, she asks, *What is going on?*

Gabriela shakes her head. 'Later, please?'

Moving up to the spare room, she settles her daughter in the cot Saoirse has set up for her – the same one Callum slept in on visits when he was tiny, the familiar pale blue ducks lining the bumper causing a flash of memory to his little body, the crown of straw-blond hair at the back of his head.

When she hears wheels heading down the driveway a while later, Gabriela looks out from the bedroom window and sees that Saoirse's car has gone. In its place is their family estate, the headlights hovering for a moment as she looks down, and she can just about make out Tom looking up at her from behind the steering wheel.

'Mum!' Callum runs towards her as they meet in the kitchen, Sadie standing back slightly and then coming in to hug her as well.

'Hi, darlings. Oh God, it's so good to see you. Come to bed . . .'

'But it's morning, I'm not tired,' says Callum, his face breaking into a yawn.

She looks up at Tom and his face looks old. He doesn't say anything and she returns her attention to their children. 'Come on,' she says. 'It's still so early. You two are sleeping up here. You can play if you like, but don't be too loud, there's a little person asleep in the room next to you.'

'What little person?' Callum asks at the same time as Sadie says, 'Mum, what's going on?' and she squeezes her arm.

'I'll explain soon; it's a long story and I need to talk to your dad.'

When she walks back into the kitchen, Tom has poured himself a drink from a bottle on the side. He makes no attempt to offer her one.

'I spoke to Saoirse, she rang as she was leaving. Whose kid is it, Gabriela?'

Moving to the cupboard and fetching another glass, she pours herself a brandy and sits at the kitchen table.

'Her name is Layla. She's the daughter of one of the women who was trafficked to the UK, who was working for us.' She pauses, gathering herself. 'The case imploded. One of our moles leaked information back to the traffickers and—'

She waits, allowing Tom's imagination to fill in the gaps.

Closing her eyes, she takes a moment to hold herself within the narrative she has been building in her mind over the past day.

He takes a swig of his drink. 'Shit.'

'Yes,' she says. 'It's really shit. This child's mother is dead, and it's my fault.'

'Gabriela,' Tom reaches his hand across the table. 'I'm sure it's not. Where are you taking her now?'

There is a challenge in his voice that belies the pragmatism of his words.

She pauses. 'I'm going to look after her. We are. Because if we don't they'll find her and they'll kill her too.'

Tom is silent for a moment, and when he speaks again, his face moves into an expression that is almost a smile. 'Sorry?'

She holds his eye, her jaw tensed. 'I have to, Tom.'

Any trace of a smile disappears then. 'No, you bloody don't. What about us, for God's sake? Your family? I mean Jesus, Gabriela, if they're after the baby that means you're putting *our* kids in jeopardy!'

She has prepared herself for this reaction, but she knows Tom, she knows that he cannot keep it up, this level of resistance to her. She knows that she has no other option than to push through, to make him understand that this is what is happening.

'There is no way they can connect the baby to me.'

'Well then, give her back!' Tom's expression has settled into horrified indignation. 'I mean, what the fuck, you're not making any sense! How are we even having this conversation?'

'If I give her back, she'll go into care.'

'That's not our problem.'

'Yes, it is.'

'No, it's not.'

'It is, Tom! Her mother, she made me swear if anything happened to her, that I would make sure Layla was OK. I can't let her down. I won't.'

Gabriela's voice is desperate now; the tears fall thick and fast so that no matter how quickly she pushes them away, more fall in their place.

'I'm sorry,' she says. 'I'm sorry.'

Tom sighs heavily on the other side of the table, and when she looks at him she sees there are tears in his eyes, too.

Chapter 82

Gabriela

Once she has had a shower, desperate to clear her mind, she heads back downstairs, leaving Layla sleeping in the cot at the end of her bed. On her way down, she puts her head around the door of Saoirse and Jim's room and sees her older children side by side in the bed. Sadie's arm is resting protectively over her brother's body. For the first time it strikes her that there is no trace of Jim in the house.

In the kitchen, the kettle is warm to the touch and as she refills it at the sink, she spots Tom at the cliff edge at the end of the garden where the land gives way to the sea. Gabriela stands and watches for a while, through the small square frame of the window. His hair, mostly grey now, moves with the breeze and she has an overwhelming urge to reach out to him.

He must sense her approaching as she walks down the hill towards him, a pot of coffee and a mug in her hands, for as she takes a seat on the bench next to where he is standing, he doesn't flinch.

'Do you remember the first time we came here?' he asks as she takes his cup from him and refills it, handing it to him before pouring one for herself.

'Callum was a baby. It was just before you went back to work after your maternity leave; Sadie must have been nearly three. I remember thinking how lucky we were. Jim and Saoirse, they had this house, this freedom, but we had each other, the kids. A family. You know how much I wanted to move to the country, even then, but I remember

439

looking out from the house and seeing you and the kids lying out on a rug down here and thinking *fuck it, it doesn't matter*. I thought no matter what happened, so long as I had you, my family, I was the luckiest man in the world.'

She sighs, struggling to remember the holiday. There is a flash of recollection, but when she tries to hold it there in front of her the image moves away. There is so much from that time that she cannot remember.

He turns to look at her and she says, 'But you've changed your mind?'

'I just need you to tell me the truth,' he says, and she tries to hold his eyes.

'I don't know what you mean.'

Tom continues to stare at her for a moment and then looks back towards the water.

'Whose child is it, Gabriela?'

There is a note in his voice that stops her answering straight away.

'I told you,' she says, lifting the coffee cup to her lips.

Tom snorts quietly, 'Of course you did.'

'I don't understand. What exactly do you want me to say?'

'I don't know. I don't know what I want anymore.'

'Look, I can see you're upset. I get it, obviously I get it, this whole thing is insane, but I've been doing a lot of thinking, and you're right, things haven't been OK for a long time. Us, the kids . . . I want a fresh start. My job isn't working, Sadie hates her school; Callum, well, Callum needs more time with his mother, you said it yourself. I think we should sell the house and move somewhere completely new. Start again. Like you said.'

There is silence as my words drift out to sea. Tom appears to have barely registered what I've said. But then he speaks. 'You're serious, aren't you?'

'Yes.'

'Us, and that child.'

'Yes.'

'That baby that the authorities have so readily let you take, without ever meeting me or our children?'

'These are exceptional circumstances, Tom. The government agencies are involved, they—'

'Exceptional circumstances? Jesus, Gabriela, this isn't a case of you getting a note for PE – we're talking about you, about *us*, taking possession of another woman's child!'

He turns and looks at her. 'I mean, holy crap, give me some credit. Give me an ounce of fucking credit for once in my life, would you? Can you do that? You're honestly telling me that I should risk putting our kids' lives in danger for the child of a complete stranger based on absolutely no information about how it came to be in your possession?'

He is gathering speed now.

'I mean, surely there is protocol, Gabriela? Basic checks, a safe house, for God's sake? They can't honestly think that—'

'Jesus, Tom, what are you saying? Are you saying I'm making it up? That I'm lying? I mean, what the hell do you think – do you think I've kidnapped her? Do you think that I've stolen someone's baby and I've—'

The sound of crying cuts across the garden suddenly and when she looks up, Sadie is standing in the doorway of the house, holding Layla in her arms. Gabriela runs to them, afraid Sadie might drop her.

'She's really sad, I think she wants her mum,' Sadie says as Gabriela takes Layla in her arms and instantly her cries quieten. When she turns back Tom is watching them with a look that she knows she will never forget as long as she lives.

Telling Sadie to go inside, that they will be in in a minute, she turns back down the hill towards Tom, and she knows that it is over and wonders how she ever believed she would get away with it.

'She's your child,' he says, and she holds his look, clutching Layla to her.

He takes a step back towards the cliff edge and she says, 'I'm sorry.'

'What . . .?' His face is ashen, the cup gripped tightly between his fingers.

'Tom, I'm so sorry, I can—'

'She isn't mine,' he says, as if working through the facts in his own mind.

She shakes her head, knowing she should take Layla back in, knowing she shouldn't be witnessing this. But she can't leave.

'Whose is she? I mean, what the fuck?'

'It doesn't matter.'

'*It doesn't matter?*'

'I didn't mean that, I mean . . . Fuck, Tom, I can't explain this now. In Moscow . . .'

Tom's face falls a bit further and it's as if the pieces of a jigsaw are slotting slowly into place.

'Oh my God,' he says, his words breathless.

'Tom, we need to get away. I know this is insane – it is insane – but we have to leave. It's not safe.'

'You're mad,' Tom says, looking at her in a way that reminds her there is no route back from this. 'You're out of your fucking mind.'

She takes a step towards him and he throws his hand up, and Layla lets out a sharp cry.

'It's OK,' she says, her mouth against her hair. 'It's OK, baby.'

'You need to go,' Tom says, pacing back and forth suddenly, as if the ground is threatening to fall away from him at any moment. His voice is trembling and she doesn't know whether to reach out and touch him.

'Tom,' she says. 'This doesn't have to mean the end of us. You said it yourself, the kids need us together. They need stability.'

'Stability?' Tom stops now and looks up at her as if she has made a brilliant joke.

She moves Layla to her other hip, trying to keep her calm, bouncing her with such intensity that she starts to grizzle again.

When Tom talks again, it's like he's working through a thought process aloud. There is an edge of triumph in his voice, as though he's made a brilliant discovery. 'You know, actually I don't think you are mad. I don't. I think, in fact I would say I'm a 100 per cent certain, that it's so much simpler than that. You're completely selfish. That's it. And actually, I can't really blame you because the truth is you've always been like that. Ever since I've known you it's just been about you. About what you want, what you need. At every single step, even after the kids . . . And I, I went along with it. I mean, did you even ask Saoirse about what happened with Jim?'

He reads her face like a book.

'Course you didn't. He's left her. It happened months ago but, well, you've had other things on your mind. Obviously . . .'

She feels the sea air slapping her face and for a moment she fears she will drop Layla, that all the strength in her body has vanished. But then, presumably feeling herself slip, Layla pulls at her shoulder and she feels her body righting itself.

'Now,' he says, clarity coming to him in stages. 'You and that baby need to go. You can write, when you work out where you'll be. With the father, I presume? Are you in touch? Actually, spare me the details.'

For once in his life attempting to take charge. For a moment she nearly claps. How long has it taken to get to the point where he is actually attempting to assert some control? And then his words sink in.

'Me?' she says. 'You're asking me to go? Tom, come now, it's my house.'

He looks at her with such astonishment that she looks away. 'You're telling me you want to leave *and* you want to turf your children out of their home? Classy, Gabriela.'

'That's not what I'm saying, Tom. We can all go, together . . . You're the one saying it's over. Besides, you can't go back there – it's not safe.'

For a moment he is frozen in disbelief, speechless, and then his face collapses.

'Not safe? What the fuck are you even talking about? You're a piece of work, you know that? Do you know how much I loved you?' Hot tears are falling from his eyes now, his nostrils flared with a rage she has never seen him express before.

'They're my children, Tom. You can't really think I would walk away from them?'

He looks up to the sky and howls with laughter, as she says, 'I'm their mother!'

'Oh,' he sniffs. '*Now* you're their mother?'

'Yes,' she says. 'And it's my house and my money, and do you think the courts would side with you: barely employed, no savings, nowhere to live?'

Layla cries out and Gabriela realises her fingers are crushing her. The sound of her daughter's discomfort snaps her out of her own head.

'You shouldn't be listening to this . . .' she says, turning to take her back to the house, and then she sees Sadie, standing a metre behind her, her face streaming with silent tears.

Moving backwards, as if her mother's gaze burns her, she says, 'I hate you. I *hate* you.'

Chapter 83

Isobel

I work through the night, reading through page after page of files relating to anyone connected with the businesses and people I have highlighted in the case so far, only stopping to make myself a cup of coffee once daylight strains through the blinds.

As I reach my arm into the fridge to pull out the milk, my phone rings. It is an unknown number and I pause for a moment before pressing answer.

'Isobel Mason?'

The voice at the end of the line doesn't wait for a response. 'This is Robert Phelps.'

Of course it is. I have been wondering how long it will be before one of the nationals gets in touch, looking to tap me up for information on the Somers Town stabbings, now that they've finally caught wind of what's going on.

'Hi,' I say, stifling a yawn, wondering what pitiful payoff they will be offering this time.

'I suppose you know why I'm calling,' Phelps says. I know his byline from occasional comment pieces, but I'd thought he was an editor on the main paper, not a reporter.

'I can imagine,' I say, preparing to tell him to stuff his demeaning offer, though I'm so tired I can barely pull together a basic sentence.

He pauses. 'Oh, really? Well, I suppose it was just a matter of time. My new deputy editor here was in touch with you a while

445

back, when he was with the *Guardian*. You might remember him. Vihaan Khatri?'

'Vihaan?'

'He tells me he offered you a job, but in the end you didn't take it. Why was that?'

I stumble. What the hell? 'I . . .'

'Don't answer that, actually,' Phelps continues. 'It doesn't matter. Whatever they were offering, I reckon we can do better.'

'I'm sorry?' I say. 'I don't understand what you're—'

'Don't be self-effacing. We're impressed with you, Isobel. Your work at *Camden News* is . . . Well, it's too good for a local rag. I think you should come and join us.'

The alarm on the fridge screams at me to close the door.

'So, what do you say about coming in for a meeting? Next week suit you?'

Chapter 84

Gabriela

The sound of the windscreen wipers scraping against the glass punctuates the silence as Gabriela watches the fields morphing into a scenery she cannot yet fully imagine.

Her eyes move between the wing mirror, checking for signs that they are being followed, and Tom, who sitting beside her in the driving seat, focused on the road, his face completely unreadable to her now.

The drive to Plymouth will take less than an hour at this time of day.

Behind them are their children – her children – the three of them side by side in the back seat, Sadie's face red and swollen, fixed away from her mother's. Callum is looking at Layla, whose eyes are closed in sleep, as if regarding a strange animal, trying to work out whether it poses a threat.

As the car moves along the motorway, their broken but irrevocably fused together family locked within its doors, she pulls out her phone and dials Madeleine's number. As she does so, she hears her words again, yesterday, in the restaurant.

'Irena knows who you are. We have a phone recording from the day Ivan told her about you. It was not long after you became pregnant. Of course she had you investigated, someone was following you for weeks. When she found out you had another family, she told Ivan.'

Her heart had stopped briefly at that, recalling that feeling she couldn't shake, the sense of constant surveillance that she had put down to a guilty conscience.

Madeleine continued. 'He didn't believe her, and then even once she'd provided him with incontrovertible evidence – photos, I think, of you and the kids, of Tom – he still chose to believe that you would leave them eventually. He told her he'd always known it was complicated, that you'd never lied about that fact.'

For a moment, as Madeleine had spoken, she'd felt sorry for him. All along, he was waiting for her to tell him she'd chosen him. Despite all the evidence telling him she would never leave her family, he had still chosen to believe she would.

She swallowed, remembering the shift in Ivan's way with her, how tetchy he'd been for a while not long after she told him about the baby, and then the outburst when she told him she was going back to work, how out of character it had seemed. By then he had known she had another family, he had known about Tom and Sadie and Callum. He had seen pictures.

The thought makes her feel physically sick. Not just sick for him, but for herself, too. How is it possible that she can feel betrayed at this revelation? And yet she does.

Turning her thoughts back to what she has to do next, she presses the call button and the phone rings just once before Madeleine answers. 'Gabriela?'

'Yes,' she says. 'I have them. We're all here, we're driving, as you said.'

'Wait there, I'll call you straight back,' she says.

A moment later, her phone rings and when she answers Madeleine says, 'This is a better line . . . You remember where you're going?'

She recalls the address Madeleine had scrawled on a piece of paper before pushing it towards her in the restaurant. She can still see her perfect looped scrawl making out the name of the final destination, reached by passenger ferry once they have handed over their car to be disposed of accordingly. The address Madeleine had held in front of her before picking up the piece of paper and tearing it into pieces.

When Madeleine speaks again now, without waiting for an answer, her voice is businesslike. 'Do you have a pen? I'm going to give you the number of the man who will meet you. Gabriela?'

'Yes,' she says. 'I'm listening.'

'You have already destroyed the SIM card you used to communicate with Ivan?'

Gabriela swallows. 'Yes.'

'Because if he ever traces it . . . If Irena traces it and finds out where you are . . .'

'I know,' she says, her voice snapping.

Madeleine pauses. 'Write this down. Call the number straight away. It's for the man who will meet you at the house, he will tell you what you need to do next.'

'I have a pen,' she says, bracing herself for the next stage.

'Right,' Madeleine says. 'His name is Harry. Harry Dwyer.'

Chapter 85

Isobel

I have barely hung up from the call with Robert Phelps when my phone rings again. This time, as I look down, I see Ben's name flashing on the screen.

The previous conversation has caught me off-guard, and the sight of my boss's name floods me with guilt. I hadn't said no to Phelps' offer, not outright, though I also hadn't said yes. I would come in and have a chat, that's all I had agreed to.

Before I can stop myself, I shake my head to clear my thoughts and press 'Answer'.

Before I can say a word, he speaks. 'You're not going to believe this.'

'OK,' I say slowly, pouring a dash of milk into my coffee.

'There's been a suicide.'

He pauses for effect and I roll my eyes, kicking the door closed with my foot. 'Ben—'

'It was in one of the big houses in South End Green. Yesterday evening . . .'

I stand straighter, noting the excitement in his tone and my mind flips back to the ambulance I'd seen by the edge of the Heath.

'It was the wife,' he says, his voice light with amazement. 'Anna Witherall. The wife of the TradeSmart bloke you mentioned, David Witherall. The one who died last month. She hanged herself.'

I step backwards and lean against the fridge door, his words ringing in my head.

'Isobel, are you there?'

'Yes,' I say, catching my breath, moving to the kitchen table and gathering the papers strewn across the surface. 'I'm here.'

Acknowledgements

Part of this book is a substantial reworking of an idea I had a decade ago whilst part of a writers group led by the poet Martina Evans. I am indebted to Martina for her encouragement and for pointing out the disconnect between writing news, which encourages us to work within strict constraints, and writing fiction which is about tossing prescriptive methods aside. Many thanks also to Vanessa Beaumont and Kate Prentice, who were early champions of Isobel.

I'm ever amazed by the time and insights people are prepared to offer, and for that I would like to thank Jimmy L, Richard H and Simon C, for their help as well as Shaun Walker for his remarkably inexpensive translation services.

Endless thanks to my agent and personal therapist Julia Silk, to my editor Ann Bissell for always knowing what is needed – be it a new scene or a glass of champagne – and to my dream publicist Felicity Denham, who together with Ann has made the process a hell of a lot of fun.

Last but never least, to my husband, Barney, and my children, for putting up with me and being so proud. Special shout out to the not-yet-literate Jesse, to whom this book is dedicated, for his honest appraisal: 'But if I can't read, how do I know it's good?'

And to my amazing mum for plugging the gaps, of which there are many, always.

Read on for an excerpt from
Charlotte Philby's new novel

THE
SECOND
WOMAN

8th July 2021

Prologue

London, the day Anna dies

It is dusk. The road is not yet dark but the early evening glow of the streetlamps casts pools of light, like fingerprints, along the pavement. The figure moves quickly, heartbeat rising as the house comes into view. The wisteria that had burst with new life just a few months earlier now clings to the brick like sinew, exposed beneath the skin of a corpse.

From this vantage point at the bottom of the tiled front steps, it is possible to see through the panes of glass in the front door that the hallway is dark. At the back of the house a wall of glass overlooks the perfectly manicured lawn rolling down towards the Heath, the moonlight blotted out by the shadows of the trees.

The children are not home yet, but they will be soon. There isn't much time.

Hearing the faint sound of the car doors closing in the street, the figure takes a step up towards the front door, flinching at the brushing of rope against skin as the men from the car pass by and disappear up into the shadows beside the entrance, just out of sight.

When they have taken their positions there is a sharp intake of breath, and then a single knock.

The voice, as it calls through the letterbox, is firm.

'Anna, it's me. Open the door.'

When she does, her expression transforms. 'What are you doing here?'

Harry

The journalists gathered inside the Coroner's Court are growing restless. Through the arched window of the courtroom the leaves of the oak trees in the Vestry of St Pancras sway against a clear blue sky. But in here, there is no fresh air.

The jury benches are empty, giving a ghostly quality to the room. There have been no jurors present since the inquest started. There seems to be no need in a case such as this, the inquest serving as little more than a rubber stamp to officiate an inevitable conclusion.

Beneath dark beams that line a gabled roof, with blood-red ceilings and matching carpets, the twelve or more reporters squashed together along the mahogany pews at the back of the room are agitated from the heat. The coroner, seemingly unfazed at the front of the room, continues to consult her notes. On the table in front of her, which is reserved for family and friends, two women sit: the older one perfectly still – the dead woman's mother, her body closed in on itself as if in retreat from the world. The younger woman sits beside her but set slightly apart, her spine poker straight, making no effort to push back the red curls that fall around her face. Behind them the father-in-law, who wears a fedora hat, even in this heat, coughs into his sleeve. The woman next to him pulls a tissue from the pocket of her immaculate trouser suit, handing it to him and giving his elbow a comforting squeeze.

'I'll now call my final witness.' The sound of the coroner's voice silences the ripple of impatience moving along the press benches. A young woman stills the pencil she had been absent-mindedly drumming against her notepad. Harry, a few seats along, bites his lower lip, eyes fixed ahead. His fingers touch the outline of the old NUJ card hanging from a lanyard around his neck.

The summoned witness is small and sharp. He wears glasses, his nose like an upright skimming stone. The eyes of everyone in the room follow him intently as he moves towards the microphone, his manner suggesting he is savouring every moment with his captive audience.

When he reaches the stand, he pauses, adjusting his microphone before repeating the oath.

'I solemnly and sincerely declare and affirm that the evidence I shall give will be the truth, the whole truth and nothing but the truth.'

'Thank you, Dr Blackman,' the coroner says. 'And will you please explain to the court your relationship to Marianne Witherall?'

'Of course. I am a psychiatrist. I am – I *was* – Ms Witherall's doctor in the final two years of her life.'

The energy in the room changes. Beneath the silence of the crowd, there is a fizz of excitement.

'When you say you were her doctor . . .'

'I was employed by the family. There was an intervention, if you will, not long after the birth of her twin daughters. David, her husband, was worried. So was her father-in-law, Clive Witherall.'

The doctor glances briefly at the older man in the hat, seated in the benches.

'Anna – sorry, *Marianne* – had been suffering from postnatal depression.'

'And you treated her for her depression, Dr Blackman?'

'That's right.'

'And what did that treatment involve?'

'It was a combination of talking therapies and medication.'

'What sort of medication?'

'She took an SSRI, sertraline specifically, owing to the fact that Ms Witherall was still breastfeeding at the point of commencement.'

'It was you who prescribed the drugs?'

He pauses. 'Not at first. It was the hospital who suggested them initially. I oversaw the increase in dosage. She'd started with 50mg per day. When that failed to have the desired effect, the daily intake was gradually increased to 200mg.'

'Why was that?'

'Ms Witherall wasn't coping. She was detached. She was struggling to bond with her children. My suggestion at this time was that she ought to seek in-house treatment, but she refused. And David, her husband, was keen to support that decision.'

'How long did you treat Ms Witherall for her depression?'

'Just over three years, until she . . . Until she died.'

'And did you prescribe any other medication during that time?' the coroner asks.

Dr Blackman pauses, running his tongue over his top lip.

'No.'

'And in your professional opinion, do you believe that Ms Witherall was of a mental state that she might have taken her own life?'

Dr Blackman sighs regretfully. 'I do.'

There is a scuffle on the press benches, the excitement too much to contain. Although whichever way, this is a story that will continue to elicit plenty of hand-rubbing on Fleet Street. Either she took her own life or she was murdered. However you look at it, the story of the beautiful fallen heiress is gold dust, and this lot will continue to pick at the remains until there is nothing left, or until they are distracted by the smell of fresh blood. Whichever comes first.

'Thank you, Dr Blackman,' the coroner says, crisply. 'Please return to your seat. The court will now adjourn for a short while so I can prepare my conclusion. If the family would leave first, and wait in the family room. Members of the press, owing to your volume, please wait outside the court until you are called back.'

The journalists have barely finished their second cigarettes when the coroner's officer calls them into the courtroom for her conclusion. Harry doesn't join them, slipping quietly away to the corner of the adjoining gardens until he hears the crowd being summoned back in.

The coroner sits still at the front of the room, studying her hands while she waits for the final reporters to shuffle back into their seats. The woman with the red hair has her arms held protectively in front of herself. Even now, he won't let himself say her name. Anna's mother looks as though she has not moved since the onlookers cleared out, before piling back in again.

'I would like to start by thanking the witnesses for their time. I am satisfied that I have reached my conclusion in reference to the circumstances of the death of Marianne Witherall. In a case of suicide, there needs to be clear evidence so that the coroner is sure beyond all reasonable doubt that the deceased intended to take their own life. This is different from other conclusions, where we just have to be sure on the balance of probabilities. Based on the presence of the note, which as we have heard was confirmed to be in Ms Witherall's handwriting by Consultant Graphologist Hannah Birch, along with the testimony of the police officers who first attended the scene, Sarah Marshall, who found the body, the forensic officer who studied the body, and Ms Witherall's psychiatrist, Dr Blackman, I confirm that I am fully satisfied with the conclusion that on the date in question, Ms Marianne Witherall died by suicide.'

The woman with the red hair slumps slightly, her posture softening at the news. The older woman barely flinches.

Focusing her attention on the table in front of her, the coroner continues, 'I would like to offer, on behalf of the court, my sincerest condolences to Ms Witherall's family, not least her mother and her daughters, Stella and Rose. The inquest is now closed.'

Artemis

Greece, the Eighties

The sun was already stretching over the port when Artemis came to, perhaps awoken by the sound of her own moaning. Or maybe it was the cloying damp of the sweat on her forehead that caused her to shiver and stir, her heart tapping out a rhythm against her ribcage.

She had been deep in dreams of the earthquake – the same dream, mutated over time: the earth cracking so that the ground opened up beneath her, preparing to draw her in. Screams quickening into a shrill vibrato.

Artemis sat upright and gave herself a minute, taking in the scene, as if half-expecting to find herself in the old cot-bed she had slept in as a child, in the village at the top of the mountain rather than where she had passed out the previous evening, safely tucked up down by the water in the same house she and her family had lived for the past twenty years. Ever since—

She paused her thoughts there.

Reaching for the Walkman on the side table, she pulled the headphones over her head and pressed play, hearing the click before the music seeped in, Simple Minds' 'Don't You (Forget About Me)' instantly blotting out the world around her.

Sinking back into her pillow, she closed her eyes and drank in the sounds, dozing for a few minutes before standing to face the day, dressing quickly and heading out into the sun-bleached morning.

It was a Saturday, mid-July. On the street she turned right, away from the corner window of the bakery where her mother would have long been at work, away from the fishing boats bobbing at the edge of the water. She stretched her hands above her head, then reached into her bag for her Walkman. Pressing rewind, she yawned as she moved up the mountain path, towards the old village and the freshly emerging tremor lines that she could not yet see.

The old village, which stood at the top of the mountain, rang with the intermittent sounds of new life that summer. Twenty years after the earthquake that had taken their home and what lay inside, her father, Markos, behaved as though this act of nature had been a cruel and cunning ploy orchestrated by foreign developers seeking to take hold of the island on which his family had lived for generations. Even now, he refused to come up here, too scared of the ghosts that lingered among the olive trees, repelled by the steady churn of diggers as Europeans – from across Germany and France predominantly – snapped up property that had lain abandoned for two decades.

Artemis despaired of and loved her father in equal measure for his unshakeable loyalty to a past life. In the two decades since the house had fallen, taking with it his youngest child, the carcass of the building now symbolised for Markos a physical and spiritual sacrifice. Unable to focus on the true horror of his loss, the earthquake represented not just the event that had taken away his three-year-old daughter, but had become an emblem of a world – *his* world – that was now under threat from the emergence of a frivolous new Greece. To his broken mind, the earthquake was no longer an act of God but a threat to the foundations of the land he loved.

It wasn't rational, of course, but then what would be an acceptably rational response to the death of a child? This wasn't a question his fellow villagers were willing to take time to consider. So many people had lost so much that night, and in refusing to come together with his neighbours in his suffering, unwilling to conform to their collective grief, Markos had outcast himself and – by association – he had cast out his family, too.

The last time Markos ventured to the old village, he had returned with a look of dread. Rena had held out a hand to comfort him but he pushed her away.

'Perhaps regeneration is exactly what this island needs,' his wife had tried softly. 'A bit of fresh life – for all our sakes.'

'What are you saying, Rena? You think we need to *move on*?'

She barked back at him and Artemis had snuck away, leaving them to scrap like dogs over the bones that lay buried in the rubble.

Artemis walked with no particular direction in mind this morning, running her fingers along the mottled stone of the narrow alleyways, past flashes of the original Venetian walls and an old Byzantine church, her head bobbing occasionally to the beat of her mixtape. The morning sun brushed lightly against her skin, warming her.

Athena would be working all day. They had agreed to meet that evening at the opening of Nico's, a new restaurant that was launching in the village's central square. Now that foreigners had started to trickle in for the summer, Athena was keen to hang out in the places where she imagined some loaded, far-flung visitor might step in and whisk her off her feet. This was despite her on-off relationship with Panos, the boyfriend Athena was head-over-heels in love with one minute, and in total denial about the next. Absent-mindedly, Artemis scuffed the dusty path with the toe of her shoe as she walked her usual route to Carolina's shop. Athena had no idea what she had; more to the point, she had no idea what it was like to be Artemis and to be considered an untouchable, even among boys like Panos; nice boys. And God knows those were few and far enough between.

It wasn't that Artemis needed, or really actively wanted, a boyfriend. But there was something about the idea of someone wanting *her*. Objectively speaking, she was attractive. On the island, though, she was branded for life – partly due to her father's idiosyncrasies, and partly due to manifestations of her own trauma, which ranged from the nightmares to, when she was younger, wetting herself in class; both irresistible fodder for the bullies who smelt her weakness, along with the urine that had sometimes streaked down her legs suddenly in the middle of a lesson, causing her to freeze.

And then there was Jorgos.

Artemis shuddered. Pulling out a cigarette and lighting it, she stopped and inhaled sharply, perching on the edge of a low wall where the side of the mountain tumbled down to the sea, grateful for a sudden gust of light wind.

It was early still and the few tourists who might follow the sign guiding them from the street at the top of the village, through Carolina's grocery store and out towards the makeshift gallery in the back-room where Artemis' paintings hung against stone walls, would likely still be asleep. She could afford to take a moment. Reaching into her bag, she pressed stop on her Walkman and closed her eyes, breathing in deeply as the ghosts rose up around her.

There was something soothing about sitting here, letting that night play out on loop in her head. In wakefulness, she could control the way her mind worked through the memory in a way that she couldn't in sleep, though she never found the answer to the same question that came up again and again. Up here, in the middle of the day, the heat prickling against her skin, Artemis could try to make sense of what had happened – why she had survived while her sister, Helena, who had been sleeping just a few feet away, had not. It was the same question she would sometimes see flash behind her parents' eyes when they looked at their remaining child. The question that vibrated silently between them when they fought.

It was a morbid pleasure, returning to this spot, one that offered the same eerie solace now as it had then, when the bullying was at its worst. Back then, Artemis would sneak out through the back door of the school at the end of the day, running all the way up the path to the ruins of her old family home. It was here that she would sit and wait until she knew the boys who would otherwise have taunted her all the way back to the bakery would have grown bored and headed home to their mothers. No one, not even Athena, knew that she came up here, back then or now. There weren't many things she had to herself on an island as small and as incestuous as this one, but this spot was her own private world.

Reaching into her bag, she pressed play and turned the volume up to full before pulling out a sketchbook and pencil. As the tip of the lead touched the paper, she felt a hand on her shoulder. The unexpected contact caught her off-guard and she lurched away from it; feeling herself about to fall, her hands gripping the inside of the wall.

The man touched her shoulder again, this time to steady her. 'Whoa. Are you OK? I didn't mean to scare you . . .'

He spoke in English.

'I'm fine.' She shook her head. Something about the look of concentration on his face made her expression soften into a reluctant half-smile. 'Oh, it's you.' She paused. 'Honestly, I'm fine . . .'

'Bloody hell, you speak English?' he said.

'Better than your Greek,' she replied, rubbing her arm where he had grabbed it.

'Well, it's all Greek to me.' He laughed, without blushing, and she remembered the self-belief on this man's face as he'd asked her about one of her paintings in the gallery, the previous Saturday. He was a few years older than she was, maybe twenty-eight or twenty-nine, and a commanding presence in every respect. Twice he had been into the gallery in the past couple of weeks, poring over the strokes of her brush on the canvas. It wasn't unusual to see the same faces again and again at the height of summer, given the scale of the island, but something about this particular face had caught her attention.

'I was actually going to ask you directions,' he ploughed on. 'I came for a walk and I appear to have got a bit lost.'

'Really? Where are you staying?' she asked.

'I'm not quite sure. That's the thing about being lost, you see,' he replied, rubbing his chin. 'I've bought a house here. I say *house* – it's more of a shack, really. Just over . . .' He looked at her and shrugged, as if where it might be was no longer of relevance. 'Somewhere over there.'

She laughed, despite herself. There was something vaguely ridiculous about the prospect of this man ever being lost.

'What's your name?' he asked.

She paused. 'Artemis.'

'Artemis.' He repeated it, enunciating each syllable, and she felt a chill brush over the backs of her knees.

'Clive, Clive Witherall,' he replied, reaching out a hand and holding her with his eyes until she had to blink.